**Jane O'Reilly** would like to say that she's the secret love child of Wonder Woman and grew up on a tropical island in the Pacific, but in reality she grew up in the north of England where it was quite cold and if anyone had any super powers, they kept them well hidden. After university and a brief and very misguided spell as a teacher, she decided it would be better for everyone if she stayed at home and looked after her children. She wrote her first novel when her youngest was a baby, and has published numerous contemporary and erotic romances with Harlequin Escape and Carina UK. But what she really wanted to write was a book about a space pirate in which she could blow things up . . .

# BLUE SHIFT

## BOOK ONE
## THE SECOND SPECIES TRILOGY

*Jane O'Reilly*

piatkus

PIATKUS

First published in Great Britain in 2017 by Piatkus
This paperback edition published in 2017 by Piatkus

3 5 7 9 10 8 6 4

A CIP catalogue record for this book
is available from the British Library.

ISBN 978-0-349-41658-8

Typeset in Baskerville by M Rules
Printed and bound in Great Britain by
Clays Ltd, St Ives plc

Papers used by Piatkus are from well-managed forests
and other responsible sources.

MIX
Paper from
responsible sources
FSC® C104740

Piatkus
An imprint of
Little, Brown Book Group
Carmelite House
50 Victoria Embankment
London EC4Y 0DZ

An Hachette UK Company
www.hachette.co.uk

www.littlebrown.co.uk

*For Caroline and Matthew,*
*who wanted to see their names in a book*

# CHAPTER

# 1

## 24th June 2187

Vessel: The *Finex*. Class 2 long-haul freighter
Destination: Earth
Cargo: Platinum ore
Crew: Eleven
Droids: Two

In the semi-darkness of the control room, Jinnifer Blue slouched back in her seat, put her boots up on the controls, and slurped down the last few mouthfuls of lukewarm Soylate from her white Plastex cup.

The air around her hummed with the vibration of the three phase drives that powered the freighter, and smelled like it had been through the recycler several times too many. It was hot and her underarms were damp, her hair greasy. At least she only had her own stink to put up with. The rest of the crew were asleep on the bunks in their cramped quarters, wired up to the onboard system that would feed measured amounts of Easydoze into their systems and wake them up when it was time to run maintenance checks.

She'd volunteered to take this shift. No-one had argued,

1

because no-one else had wanted it. Jinn didn't mind. She liked the quiet, liked having the deck to herself. It wasn't that her crewmates were openly hostile, as such, but they weren't exactly friendly either, and there was only so much negative tension one person could take.

They were flying through straight space on autopilot, on a routine voyage transporting platinum ore from Colony Three back to Earth where it would be used to repair the huge filtration units that supplied the Domes with warm, breathable air. The trip was a long one, seventeen jumps, taking almost a month. Three weeks had already passed and Jinn knew the remaining seven days would drift by even more slowly, especially given that their only cleaning droid was on the blink. Swinging her chair back round, she stared at the screens hovering in front of her and assessed their progress. She had three jumps left to make, but the next one wasn't for another twelve hours.

She liked working as a pilot for the Galactinex Corporation and she was good at it, which had been a major relief after she'd gone through the nightmare of the genetic modification and prosthetic surgery needed to fly a ship like this. All professional pilots had to have it – first of all changes to their DNA which increased their healing rate and then the injection of tiny Tellurium nanobots into the bloodstream. The initial procedure wasn't so bad, but then the bots started to replicate and that meant pain. She'd spent three days in a medically induced coma. Then monitoring bands had been fitted to her wrists and she had also been given a retinal implant, fused to the bone by her right temple. Two weeks of intensive training later, she was a fully qualified space pilot, and Galactinex had put her to work.

Jinn didn't particularly like having to spend two days a month on Earth, but it was better than living there permanently. Earth was cold and dirty.

Dropping her feet to the floor, Jinn got up, stretched out the knots in her back and decided that she could do with a walk. She always felt like this when they got within a few days of their home planet. Tight, edgy, her stomach sore and her skin uncomfortable. It would pass once they'd dropped off their load and were headed in the opposite direction.

She turned away from the control panel, decided that maybe she'd spend some time in the chemicleanse. There were only a couple of hours of the shift left, and so far it had been utterly uneventful. No-one would notice if she took a break. She decided that she'd eat something, too, and thought about where she might spend the four days of downtime she would get when they returned to Colony Three. Becoming a pilot and leaving Earth had been the best decision she'd ever made, even if she was limited to only two minutes in the chemicleanse and had to eat silver rice. It had been a good decision. The right decision. The only decision. There was nowhere else she'd rather be than in the pilot's chair. Not back on Earth, even though she'd been raised in a Dome, with warmth and real food. Not on one of the Colonies, either, even though living there she'd have privacy and a cleanse tub and space sickness would be a distant memory.

Being the only Dome brat on board didn't make things easy, though. The rest of the crew had been raised in Underworld cities. Pretty much everyone who signed up for prosthetics and a corporation job had been. People who had grown up in the Domes didn't usually go down that route and Jinn wouldn't have either, if she'd had any choice. But she could win the others round, she was sure of it. Eventually she'd make them see her as a useful part of the crew, and in the meantime, it was better than being back home.

The Domes were huge man-made structures dotted across the remaining landmasses on Earth. Each one had been built on the remains of a capital city – Washington, Sydney, Delhi, Tokyo, and her birth city, London. The original architects had promised space, clean air, protection from the freezing cold that had spread across the planet after scientists had been a little too successful in their attempts to reverse global warming. But somehow, the Domes had been built too small.

The refugees who had come to the Domes expecting to find a safe haven couldn't get in, because all the space had already been taken up by the wealthy from the capital cities on which the Domes had been built. Eventually, the refugees had taken matters into their own hands. They couldn't get into the Domes, so they had gone under them, digging their way down past the old transport tunnels and sewer pipes. The government did what it could – there was food in the form of silver rice imported from Colony Four, and contraceptive shots, and basic building materials. It wasn't like people in the Underworld cities had nothing. And Jinn hadn't exactly had a dream childhood, despite growing up with money. She got why Underworlders didn't like people from the Domes, but she really felt her crewmates should give her a break.

As far as she was concerned, she had plenty in common with the rest of the crew. They all had prosthetics. They were all tied to the corporation for the next five years, or until they'd paid off the loans they'd been given to pay for the treatment. The seven Earth-controlled colonies, located on various asteroids between Mars and Jupiter, supplied the human population with the food and fuel Earth could no longer provide for them, given how little plant life remained.

They were all facing the same future. Fifty percent of workers didn't make it to the end of the five years. Half of those didn't survive the first twelve months. Still, the Underworld cities provided a seemingly endless stream of new recruits willing to deform themselves with the prosthetics needed to work on the colonies, and the government was willing to keep paying the corporations that ran the colonies for their goods. But Jinn wasn't planning on giving the government or the corporations a day more than she had to. She was going to start saving her credits. She'd be out of here before the five years was up. And then she'd get her own ship, and she would be able to go where she wanted. Screw Earth, and screw the corporations.

She'd have control. She'd have freedom. She'd have . . .

Something was wrong.

The phase drive had stopped.

The freighter jerked to a standstill, as if a giant hand had reached out and grabbed it. It shouldn't have been physically possible for a vessel the size of the *Finex* to stop like that. But it did. Jinn was flung backwards, falling hard, the base of her spine taking the brunt of the impact. The lights went out as she hit the floor, sinking her into darkness so complete that she wondered for a moment if she'd gone blind. Everything hurt. Everything. All she could do was lie there and think about pain.

Then the emergency lighting switched on. The alarms started screaming, an electronic shriek that threatened to break her skull and made it impossible to hear her own thoughts as she staggered to her feet and turned to look at the control panel. She grabbed the back of the pilot's chair, hanging on to it as the freighter tilted left. Empty Soylate cups went flying, as did discarded pieces of uniform and a couple of personal comm. units.

Pulling herself round, Jinn pushed her backside into the chair and gripped the edge of the control panel, forcing herself to stay seated. The data screens flashed. She stared at them, trying to make sense of the streaming feed, but none of it meant anything. They had been cruising along Space Lane Seven. It wasn't the busiest of routes, but it wasn't the quietest, either. Now with a dead phase drive, they weren't so much cruising as floating, and the last thing she wanted was to get in the way of another freighter. They weren't exactly designed to stop in a hurry.

'Viewscreen on!' she yelled.

Everything around her seemed to freeze. She couldn't breathe. She wasn't even sure her heart was still beating. There, floating alongside the *Finex*, was a ship. Not a freighter, or one of the smaller transporters used by the traffic police, but something else. It was long, fat and bulbous at one end, narrowing to a slender point at the other. It reminded her of the giant squid trapped in the frozen seas back on Earth, with its strange curving shape and the eerie way it was just … there.

It drifted closer, sinking lower. A vast glowing orb moved across her line of sight like a curious eye. Jinn jumped in her seat, her heart pounding up into her throat. She swallowed, fingers shaking on the control panel. She pressed her feet hard into the floor and tensed the muscles in her legs. 'Just a search light,' she told herself firmly, as the eye moved. 'Just a light. Not a cannon.' That didn't stop her from feeling like a specimen under a scope. The ship appeared to have been made from multiple vessels, taken apart and then stitched together with rivets and filth. She had never seen anything like it. It wasn't a government ship, nor did it belong to one of the corporations. That left only one possibility.

Pirates.

Why? Jinn silently screamed, terror stealing her words as the other members of the crew came staggering onto the control deck, all in various states of undress, smelling of chemical sleep and confusion.

'What in the void is going on?' asked Zane. He was the longest-serving and therefore the most senior employee on board, something he liked to remind everyone of. Frequently.

'Pirates,' Jinn replied, her tongue thick and heavy. 'It's pirates.'

'Are you sure?'

'See for yourself.'

Someone swore, a short, sharp word.

'Don't just sit there!' Zane yelled at her. 'Get us out of here!'

Shamed by her own stupidity, Jinn pressed her palms against the small, circular ports that would link her to the onboard system. Within seconds, the tiny Tellurium nanobots that inhabited the flesh of her forearms had formed into long, thin wires and pushed their way out of her hands and into the port. Wetware connected to hardware, and she was in.

It took her precious seconds to navigate her way through the onboard system, which seemed to be in the middle of a full-scale meltdown. Jinn overrode it and switched to emergency protocol, which would enable her to fly. But the freighter was big, and it was heavy and fully loaded. It wouldn't move in a hurry. 'Shit,' she muttered, when she realised that it wouldn't move at all.

'What?'

'I can't power up the phase drives.'

And so the scramble for the emergency escape pods began. Zane moved first. Heavy boots thudded on metal as the crew sprinted to the little transports, located down in the belly of the freighter. Why hadn't she thought of that? There was a way out of this and she was sat in the pilot's chair like an idiot as the *Finex* drifted closer to the pirate ship, close enough for her to see the individual metal plates that formed the hull. From the way the freighter was moving, she knew the pirates had them in a tractor beam. There was a chance that the emergency pods would be able to avoid the pull if they used the freighter as a shield. That chance was a lot bigger if she was piloting one of them. She had to get to one of the pods, and fast.

Pulling in air, Jinn focussed on the tiny nanobots, willing them to disconnect and move back inside her body. The view screen was still active. As she watched, a small docking portal in the side of the pirate ship spiralled open and a spacewalk emerged, unfolding its way through space. They were going to be boarded.

Jinn had spent enough time watching the streaming news-feeds to know what that meant. She closed her eyes, and with one massive push of concentration, dragged the Tellurium back inside her body and disconnected from the computer. Her hands burned but she ignored it as she sprinted down into the belly of the ship, chasing her way down endless sharply angled staircases. Her boots clattered on the metal, her palms slipping as she tried to grip on to the safety rails.

She was almost at the hatch that led to the escape pods when she heard the spacewalk connect. Every second was precious now. She had to keep moving, and that seemed to switch off her fear. She felt nothing, thought about nothing, simply moved to the first hatch and pressed her thumb against the lock pad. It didn't open, the light flashing red to indicate that the pod had already jettisoned. Jinn rushed to the second hatch, repeated the process. They couldn't all have gone. They couldn't. A shiver dropped down her spine as she stood staring at the hatch door, the slow flicker of the emergency lighting showing her the world in brief flashes of sickly yellow light.

'Hull breach detected,' came the voice over the internal loudspeaker. 'Immediate evacuation recommended.'

'Thanks for the advice,' Jinn muttered. A hull breach meant that the pirates had cut their way in. They would find her in a matter of minutes. Or, worse, they wouldn't, and she'd still be on board the *Finex* when they set it adrift, when it was left to float out into space with a rapidly diminishing oxygen supply and malfunctioning onboard computer.

'Shit.' She tried the lock one last, desperate time. She was aware of something crowding the edges of her consciousness, an instinctive sense that danger was closing in, moving closer with every second wasted. Abandoning the second hatch, Jinn moved to the third and final one. She jammed her thumb against the lock, staring intently at the control panel. The light stayed red, stayed red.

Then it changed to green. The hatch door spiralled open, and Jinn found herself staring into the belly of the little escape pod. Three of her crewmates were inside. Their heads jerked round and they stared at her. 'There's no room,' Zane said.

'They've already boarded.' Jinn moved closer to the hatch, wrapped her hands around the opening and set a foot to the edge, ready to get in with them. 'If I pilot us out of here, we can use the ship as a shield. Avoid the tractor beam.'

'This is a three-person pod,' Rula said. 'It doesn't have enough oxygen to support four.'

'We're on Space Lane Seven,' Jinn pointed out. The pirates were close. She could almost taste their sweat in the air. 'We'll get picked up long before we run out.'

'I'm not taking that chance,' Zane replied. His hand flicked up, and in it Jinn saw a blaster. 'Get away from the hatch. Or I'll spill your guts all over the floor, Dome bitch.'

'Don't do this,' Jinn pleaded. Deep down, she had known they disliked her, but this was more than that. She looked at Zane. 'Let me pilot. It's our only chance.'

His response was to power up the blaster. 'Get the fuck away from the hatch. I won't tell you again.'

The blaster whined. Jinn closed her eyes.

Then two strong hands closed around her upper arms and jerked her away from the hatch opening. 'What have we here?' said a voice, deep and rough and unfamiliar.

Those hands turned her around, and Jinn found herself looking up, up, and into the face of a man she didn't know. Thick eyebrows framed hard green eyes separated by a nose that was slightly out of kilter. If the dark hair hadn't already told her he was an Underworlder, that nose would have. All his features were like that, slightly too big, not quite in line, like he'd been put together in a hurry. It was hard to guess his age. His skin said early twenties. His eyes said something else entirely. She saw no obvious signs of prosthetics, but his size screamed genetic modification.

And her body screamed out in fear.

'Take her!' Zane yelled from somewhere behind her. 'She's Dome-raised. You'll get decent credits for her!'

The pirate kept his gaze fixed on Jinn. 'I've already got more credits than I can spend.' He lifted a hand, wrapped a lock of her hair around his finger, the white contrasting sharply with his skin. 'Now what is a Dome brat doing on a Galactinex freighter?'

'I'm the pilot,' Jinn managed.

'I see.' He poked the retinal implant at her temple. Then he grabbed her hand and examined the implant that banded her wrist, the lights glowing amber to indicate that it was functioning. She knew if he increased the pressure, her bones would give. She could sense that in him, that impossible strength. It was why she didn't try to fight him off.

There were others with him, too. They were in the shadows, and Jinn could barely make them out, but they were there, a menacing backdrop to the scene. She ignored them. They didn't matter. This one did. She'd imagined pirates to be half starved and dirty and desperate, but this man wasn't desperate at all. His clothes were expensive, he didn't smell, and he didn't seem in any particular hurry to get on with the business of stealing everything on board the ship.

'Please . . . ' she whispered.

'Please . . . what?' he asked.

'Please don't hurt me.'

'Now why would I do that?'

'Because . . . ' she began, but the sentence remained unfinished, as the sound of the hatch door closing behind her cut through her words.

The pirate released his grip, and Jinn almost fell. It was only through sheer force of will that she stayed anything close to upright, and when she regained her balance she realised that he was no longer in front of her.

He stood at the hatch, and the hatch was open. One big hand wrapped around the edge of the opening, and one big black boot rested casually on the base. She saw him lift that hand, saw him beckon her crewmates out of the pod. Heard the whine of the blaster and the call of *pirate scum* a second before it was fired. Instinctively, she held her breath, her entire body shaking. It better have been a clean shot, because she didn't even want to imagine what this man would do if it hadn't.

A half-breath later, she found out. It all happened so fast that she barely had time to comprehend it. All she could think later was that maybe her mind had replaced reality with the memory that she would recall time and time again, of the pirate moving at a speed no human possessed. Of her crewmates flying out of the escape pod, their bodies shooting across the narrow deck before they hit the wall and dropped to the floor. She could taste shock in the back of her throat, the slimy bitterness of it, coated with a thick overlay of fear. Were they dead? Her mind told her to move closer, but her body refused to obey. All she could do was stand there, an open target, and wait her turn.

The pirate climbed out of the pod, the blaster in his hand. There was blood on his shirt and plenty of it, a bloom of red against the white, but he didn't move like a man in pain. He strode straight past her towards the rear of the bay where the rest of his crew waited. Jinn could see movement in the shadows, then more as they stepped forward. Lean bodies, gleaming, hungry eyes. All of them were dark-haired, with the expected prosthetics. She saw miners, farmers, engineers, though these were undoubtedly Bugs, people who had skipped out of their colony jobs before they'd paid off the cost of their modifications.

'Strip it down,' the pirate said to them. 'Take the ore and the droids, and whatever else you can find.'

'Aye, captain,' one of them said. Silver streaked the sides of his dark hair, and his left hand had been replaced by a prosthetic, the kind that spun and flicked out an assortment of intricate tools. A biomechanical engineer, which meant he was intelligent and highly skilled, not some low-rent thug. He wasn't what she'd expected. None of this was what she'd expected.

The engineer gestured to the others, and they got to work. Some of them moved further into the ship, some of them detached laser-cutters from their belts and began to strip out the walls of the bay. Like a group of starving scavengers, they picked it clean, but they did it carefully. Nothing was trashed, nothing was broken. Obviously they weren't just going to take the ore from the hold, they were going to take everything. By the time they'd finished there might not even be a ship for them to leave her on.

The opportunity was there, again, and this time Jinn took it. But she stumbled as she made her way towards the now-empty escape pod, her feet sliding in the blood that patterned the steel plate beneath her feet. If she hadn't, she might not have heard the voice that came from behind her.

'Help me.' It was little more than a whisper, that desperate plea. 'Please.'

Jinn glanced back. It was Zane. She risked a glance at the

pirates on the other side of the bay. They were rapidly dismantling the cooling system, stripping out the pipes and wiring that allowed the vessel to stay at a temperature that the human body could tolerate. Without it, the freighter would rapidly start to overheat. Blood would warm, enzymes would denature, and the biological systems that kept the body functioning would stop. Anyone left on board would, quite literally, start to cook.

'Bloody supernova.' Jinn turned, started towards Zane. She couldn't leave him to die like that. She barely made it two paces before the pirate captain was in front of her.

He stared down at her with those odd green eyes. 'Don't be foolish,' he said. Then he turned, strode over to her crewmate, and planted one big boot firmly on Zane's chest. 'They made their choice. I offered them work on my ship. They didn't want it.'

Zane struggled against the weight of that boot, but it was futile. Jinn flexed her fingers and wished desperately for a weapon. A blaster, a knife, a personal comm. unit she could fling at the pirate's head. Anything.

'Now make your choice,' the pirate said. He gestured to the pod. 'Leave.' He gestured to the rest of the bay. 'Or stay and die with the rest of your crew. It's up to you.'

'Why?' she asked, unable to help herself, knowing the choice she had to make, yet wanting to delay it. Not wanting to face that inevitable moment when she would leave her crew behind, leave them to die. 'Why let me go?'

'You're Dome-raised. No-one cares what happens to a few Underworld workers. But you . . . I don't need that sort of trouble.'

From the other side of the bay, a shout pushed through the hot, sticky air. 'We're done here, captain. Two-minute countdown.'

'Get back to the *Mutant*,' the pirate replied. He barely raised his voice, yet it had the power to carry across the space. Then he looked at her, straight at her. 'You heard,' he said. 'Get in the pod.'

But she couldn't. She couldn't willingly leave the others here to die. Not while there was still a chance. 'Let me take them with me.'

'Why?'

'Because . . . .' she began, but the words were cut off when she saw Zane push himself up on one elbow. In one unsteady hand, he held a pocket grenade. If he threw it, it would kill all of them. 'No!' she screamed.

But the pirate had already seen. He broke Zane's arm with a swift kick, which sent the grenade flying up. The pirate caught it, balancing it on the palm of his hand for a moment, then deftly deactivated it and slid it into his pocket. Zane lay sprawled on the floor, his arm bent at a peculiar angle, his eyes dull. A thin trickle of blood ran out of the corner of his mouth as his throat worked for air.

Jinn turned, flung herself towards the escape pod. Feet slipping, hands struggling for grip, she made her way inside, scrambled into a seat. As the restraints automatically wrapped themselves around her torso, she punched the bright red touchpad that would trigger the emergency launch. The hatch spiralled shut and then she was blasted out into space. The pod spun as it rushed away from the freighter, turning her world upside down, and doing the same to her stomach. By the time the boosters kicked in, slowing the pod to a speed that didn't make her want to puke, the *Finex* was little more than a fragment in the distance.

There was no sign of the pirate ship, only the skeleton of her ship floating alongside Space Lane Seven. She watched it in agony, the only sound that of her own laboured breathing. She watched as it drifted, watched as it burned, watched until there was nothing left.

Then she lowered her hands to the ports on the control deck and plugged in. 'Sir,' she said, when her superior appeared on the vid screen. 'I need help.'

# CHAPTER

# 2

> Vessel: The *Santina Hawk*. Class 2 transporter
> Destination: Ataxis System
> Cargo: None
> Crew: Two
> Droids: Two

Twenty years after her encounter with Caspian Dax, Jinn was no longer reminded of him on a daily basis. She'd paid off her debts, and traded the slow bulk of a haulage freighter and the company of an Underworld crew who never let her forget that Dax had let her live for something better. She'd kept busy and kept out of trouble. She'd made the most of what life he had left her with.

The *Santina Hawk* was a Class 2 transporter, smaller and less luxurious than a Class 1, but wickedly fast, modified to make multiple jumps with minimal downtime. It was plain and anonymous, the perfect vessel for slipping unnoticed into ports and space stations. Bounty-hunters favoured them. So did the Security Service, and for the past sixteen years she had been working for them, chasing down criminals and taking them to the *Alcatraz 2*, the vast prison ship orbiting Earth's moon. It seemed ironic that she had fled Earth and the restrictions of life as a politician's daughter only to end up working for the government, but these were the cards that fate had dealt her. Plus, she needed the credits. She really, really needed the credits. Otherwise she'd have found a way to get out of this particular pick-up.

She'd always known there was a possibility that one day she'd get a warrant with Caspian Dax's name on it. But with literally thousands of agents picking up thousands of warrants, it had seemed so unlikely that she hadn't thought it would actually happen. She had stared down at the screen, watching as the black letters of his name blurred against the white before coming sharply back into focus. She'd told herself that her reaction was ridiculous. It hadn't helped. She'd reminded herself of the other changes she'd made, let the hot weight of the additional Tellurium she'd had injected warm her hands and shore up her courage. That had helped.

The ship currently orbiting the fifth moon of Ataxis had also changed since the last time she'd seen it. It was bigger now, less angular, more aggressive. Partial identity markings were burned into the plates that formed the hull, and Jinn knew that if she checked them, she'd find they belonged to vessels that had long since been declared lost. Possibly even a freighter she'd once piloted.

She liked to think she didn't scare easily, but this ship terrified her. The huge twin drives mounted on the rear suggested that it was capable of a high straight speed, and the sleek shape indicated that it could jump. She might have admired it, might have felt the desire to sit in the pilot's chair and see what it could do, if she hadn't been so bloody afraid.

'Maintain speed,' said the man belted into the seat next to hers. Bryant was tall, blond, and marked by a degree of physical perfection typical of a Dome brat. In theory, as two Dome-raised Security Service employees, they should have got along. They had more than enough in common. And he didn't hog the sole chemicleanse unit or empty out his Autochef on the first day and then try to use hers. Plus he kept his hands to himself.

But they might as well have been from different planets, so huge was the difference between them. Jinn had Tellurium and Bryant used Smartware, a far more advanced technology. Bryant took his Smartware off at the end of the day. For him it was little more than another layer of clothes. Fine mesh gloves allowed him to connect to the onboard computer. Lenses replaced the retinal implant. There were even full suits that could be used for repair work, though they didn't have one of those on board. As far as Bryant was concerned, she was inferior and he never let her forget it. To be fair, she suspected Bryant felt that way about everyone, but as there were only the two of them on board she bore the full weight of his ego.

'I know what I'm doing,' she said, her palms pressed firmly against the control panel.

'Alter trajectory twelve degrees port,' Bryant continued, as if he hadn't heard.

'I said, I know what I'm doing.' She had flown some of the most challenging vessels on some of the most difficult routes, with and without a wetware interface. 'It's hardly a grade ten manoeuvre!'

'Your pulse is one eight two,' Bryant said calmly.

'So?'

'You have a resting pulse of fifty-eight. It would appear that you are finding this a little stressful.'

'Then maybe you should shut up and let me do my job!'

Bryant turned back to the screen in front of him. 'Do not blame me for your inability to perform under pressure.'

'I'm perfectly capable of performing under pressure,' she replied. 'I'm the pilot here, Bryant. I have the Tellurium, not you.' And more than he knew. So he should just back off.

His mouth hardened. 'I don't know how you can live with that junk polluting your body.'

'It's easier than living with you,' she muttered.

'What?'

'Nothing.'

The ship ahead of them remained locked on the same trajectory, shrouded in darkness as she flew them closer to it. The *Hawk*'s onboard computer reported no sign of activity, no heat signature from the phase drive, no sign that the ship was functioning. 'Are you sure he's on board?' she asked Bryant. 'I'm not picking up any sign of life. Maybe it's been abandoned.'

'He's on board,' Bryant said.

'How do you know? We've spent the past six months picking up warrants all over the place. Everyone knows that the government is cleaning house, Bryant, and everyone knows why. If I thought agents were looking for me, I wouldn't stay on my ship. I'd get a galaxy away from it.'

'My intelligence reports indicate Caspian Dax is on board that ship,' Bryant said, his tone cold, flat. 'Maintain speed. Fly straight towards the stern.'

Heading straight for it would surely bring them in line for a head-on collision. 'You can't seriously . . .'

'Do it,' Bryant said. 'Unless, of course, you'd rather go back to piloting freighters.'

He knew her history, or at least he thought he did. He didn't know the real reason why she'd left Galactinex, or that she had enough Tellurium in her system to form a blade. If he did, he might treat her with a little more respect. Then again, he might have her kicked out of her job. That much Tellurium wasn't exactly legal.

It took every bit of nerve Jinn possessed to alter the flight path of the *Hawk*, putting them in line with the sharply pointed stern of the ship ahead. 'This is suicide,' she muttered.

Bryant said nothing.

Then the stern of the huge ship began to change, splitting open like the petals of a flower, a huge black flower, spreading wider, wider, revealing more darkness within. This didn't just look like suicide, this *was* suicide. Instinct had her wanting to change course, to nosedive away from it, to put the transporter anywhere but here. She fought it.

Within seconds, she felt the jolt that signalled the ship had caught the *Hawk* in a tractor beam. They had no chance of escaping the strong magnetic pull. Forcing herself to breathe, Jinn retracted her nanotech, willing the tiny robots back inside her body, disconnecting herself from the computer. The *Hawk* was no longer under her control and she had no choice but to accept it. She folded her arms and sat back in the pilot's chair as they were slowly, inevitably swallowed up into the dark belly of the much larger ship.

'You knew it could do that,' she said to Bryant. But she hadn't. Last time she'd encountered the *Mutant*, it hadn't possessed this sort of technology. But then a lot could change in twenty years. She certainly had.

'Yes,' he responded, his fingers flying over the control panel of his comm. station.

'And you didn't think to share that information with me?'

'You didn't need to know,' he replied.

Jinn shook her head and clamped down on the urge to put a blade to his throat. She was here to work, not to start a fight with Bryant. A few more runs and she'd have enough credits saved to retire, to buy herself a little one-person condo on Colony Seven. To finally have the Tellurium removed.

She turned her attention back to the view screen. They were only a couple of hundred metres away from the *Mutant* now, and she couldn't help but admire the pirate ship that was responsible for the theft of thousands of tons of platinum ore, carbon plate, food, droids and anything else Caspian Dax could get his hands on. The tractor beam pulled them deeper and deeper into the darkness, the phase drive of the *Hawk* quietly humming as the onboard computer flashed.

Then the phase drive stopped. The lights on the control deck went off, and a cold wash of déjà vu struck her. Dax hadn't upgraded everything. He was still using the short-range electrical pulse that temporarily scrambled the systems of targeted vessels. Within seconds, the emergency lighting flicked on. She glanced across at Bryant, who was bathed in the sickly yellow light. He was on his feet, his expression cool as he checked the charge on a stunner. He gave her a nod. 'Be ready to leave as soon as the prisoner is on board,' he said. And with that, he turned and walked briskly off the control deck.

Jinn stayed where she was, strapped into the pilot's chair. Usually they picked up warrants from space stations, from ports, from colonies, places that were easy to find and easy to leave. She'd never had to escape from the belly of a pirate ship before. Was it even possible to escape? It must be. Bryant wouldn't have done this if he didn't have an exit strategy.

She wished he'd told her what it was.

'Cameras on,' she ordered the onboard computer.

'Specify,' the system replied.

'External view,' she instructed it. 'Let's get a look at where we are. And patch into Bryant's personal feed.'

Two small screens flickered on in front of her. On the higher one she could see the outside of the transporter, and her surroundings. They seemed to be in some sort of holding bay. The outside of the *Mutant* might be astonishing, but this part of it was pretty pedestrian. Riveted aluminium walls. A couple of loaders, the kind that could be run automatically or driven manually. To one side was a long row of storage compartments, each one easily the height of the *Hawk*. There was no sign of life. Everything was eerily still and silent.

Switching her attention to the other screen, Jinn saw what Bryant saw through his Smartware lenses. He was walking along a corridor, high ceilinged, dimly lit. The walls and floor were both some sort of bare metal, the walls decorated with beautiful angular patterns, though she couldn't see if they were painted or simply carved into the surface. Circular doorways cut in on either side, every one identical. Bryant ignored all of them. It was clear from the way he moved that he knew exactly where he was going, and something about that gave Jinn pause, though she didn't know why. Bryant was never unprepared.

He took a left, moving steadily along another corridor. Emergency power only allowed for a black-and-white feed, limiting Jinn's view, but she watched regardless. This corridor had one doorway. Bryant headed straight for it. She gripped the edge of her seat as he dealt with the electronic lock, disabling it with an explosive entry charge. Smoke blurred the image for a moment, then it cleared and she saw the iris door contract open. The quarters on the other side were empty – where was everyone, anyway? – but Bryant didn't stop to search them. He strode straight past the wide bunk without pausing, heading straight for the chemicleanse unit at the rear. Even in black and white, Jinn could see the glow of the entry pad, indicating that it was in use.

She held her breath.

Bryant opened the door to the chemicleanse a fraction. Jinn saw a strip of flesh. She sucked in air as Bryant fired his drug gun and whoever was in the chemicleanse stiffened and sank to the floor. Then he pushed the door to the unit fully open and looked down at his prisoner. It was definitely Dax. Even if he hadn't been lying with his head to the side, his face clearly visible, she would have known from the sheer size of him.

Bryant flicked out portable restraints. The straps wrapped themselves around the prone figure, binding his arms, his legs. Bryant glanced down at the controller he held in his hand, thumbed the touch screen, and turned.

Jinn kept watching as he made his way back to the transporter, the restrained figure of Caspian Dax rolling along in front of him. She watched until Bryant appeared on the upper screen. He stared straight at the camera and gave her the signal that indicated she should plug in, though the phase drive was still out.

She hated taking orders from Bryant. 'Screens off,' Jinn said. She placed her hands over the narrow ports in front of her and gritted her teeth, though the flinch as the Tellurium connected her nervous system to the wires and circuits of the onboard computer was mostly habitual. She was used to the sting she felt every time the microscopic machines linked together, forming the slender wires that pushed their way out of her flesh.

Connecting wetware to hardware allowed a pilot to fly at speeds that would be unthinkable with hand-held controls, to make moves that would be impossible if reaction time had to be allowed for. A pilot had to be outstanding to even be considered for Tellurium. With it, they were incredible. Jinn had long suspected that the reason Dome brats hated prosthetics was because they feared they made the Underworlders better than them. And they were right. A pilot with Tellurium was superior to one using Smartware. They would also die sooner, but that was beside the point.

A couple of minutes later, Bryant strode onto the control deck. He took up his position in the seat next to hers, as calm and unaffected as if he'd just spent the past sixty minutes napping in his quarters. 'Cargo's locked down,' he said. 'Let's go.'

He had barely said the words when the emergency lighting flicked off and the main power system kicked on. The phase drive roared into life, vibrating the floor beneath their feet. Through her connection to the onboard computer, Jinn could see that all systems were fully functional, and they had full power. She could not only fly, she could jump.

Carefully, she floated the *Hawk* up. The view screen flickered to life. The mouth of the *Mutant* was still open, those steel petals still unfolded, the vast, star-dotted expanse of space stretching out, beckoning her.

She didn't hesitate to answer the call. 'Buckle up,' she said to Bryant, as the *Hawk* started to move. 'We're getting out of here.'

# CHAPTER

# 3

**20th August 2207**

> Vessel: The *Santina Hawk*. Class 2 transporter
> Destination: The *Alcatraz 2*
> Cargo: Prisoner X427M. Identity: Classified
> Crew: Two
> Droids: Two

Fifty hours later, they were heading for the A2. Their prisoner was secure in the cargo hold and Bryant had disappeared into his quarters, leaving Jinn alone with her thoughts and her fear.

She couldn't stand it.

Jinn hadn't always wanted to be a pilot. Truth be told, she hadn't known what she wanted to be. She knew what she'd been told to be, but that hadn't quite worked out, and by eighteen she'd wanted to leave home desperately enough to take any way out she could find.

She hadn't had the credits to set up on her own, to apply to one of the Dome academies for a course of her own choosing. So she'd done something that Dome brats never did. She'd applied for a job on one of the colonies. The aptitude tests had suggested that she was best suited to pilot nanotech, so that was what she'd been given after she'd gone to a Medipro centre to get the genetic modifications needed. Everybody used Medipro. Not because they were the best, necessarily, but because they offered finance to anyone with a basic ID.

Learning to fly had been her way to escape, and it had been both a blessing and a curse. Pilots didn't have to cope with the dangerous conditions on the colonies, and were almost guaranteed to survive the five-year contract. But the Tellurium that circulated in her bloodstream was toxic. The average pilot was lucky to see seventy. With the extra Tellurium that Jinn had in her system now, she knew seeing in her fiftieth birthday would be a miracle.

Standing in the recreation bay of the *Hawk*, wearing the same ugly uniform she wore every day, she wished she could resign right now. But she couldn't. For one thing, the *Hawk* was currently travelling at a phenomenal speed. She could hardly say *stop, I want to get off*. And in a few more hours she'd be needed back on the control deck. Until then, she had time to kill.

She could sleep, she supposed, if she were able to sleep right now. She could eat but she wasn't hungry and anyway, the only food left on board was the nutritionally balanced but disgusting silver rice in the supply cupboard back in her quarters, and she didn't think her stomach could handle any of the bland, gritty paste right now. Grown on Colony Four, the farming colony, it was shipped back to Earth in vast quantities. Most of it was rationed out to the Underworld cities, the rest used as an emergency food supply on ships like hers. It didn't take up much space, it didn't go off, and it provided everything the body needed. Sadly, it also wasn't very nice.

Jinn didn't normally eat it, but they'd bounced straight from their last warrant to this one, and there hadn't been time to properly restock the *Hawk*. Maybe that accounted for some of her black mood. She didn't do well without half-decent food.

Fortunately, the webTV provided a welcome break from reality. She could revel in the often bizarre lives of the celebrities who filled the entertainment channels and could always be relied on to take too many mood enhancers and be caught in the seediest of pleasure parlours.

Jinn flung herself onto the padded V-shaped seating that ran along the edge of the recreation bay. She put her feet up on the seat, knowing Bryant would hate it. 'Computer, webTV on.'

'Which channel do you require?'

She considered this for a second. 'Entertainment Universe.'

She sat through a story about a well-known Flyball player who was trying to dissolve his relationships with three of his seven wives, the shameful return of a screen goddess to rehab, and a conveniently timed ten-minute advertisement for the rehab centre she was using. By the time it had finished, Jinn had the irritating jingle stuck firmly in her head. At least she'd know where to go if she ever developed a Euphoria addiction.

'Lights down,' she ordered, slumping further down on the couch. She'd give her right arm for a cup of warm, sweet Soylate right now, but all the Autochef had to offer was a bag of vitamin water. The sooner this contract was over, the better.

Advertisements promoting the latest in cosmetic enhancements danced across the screen, promising full-body rejuvenation, including organ repair. Fantastic stuff, if you could afford it. The advert ended and a newsbreak was announced seconds before a glossy, beaming news reader filled her vision. 'Our representatives returned from their most recent visit to the Intergalactic Senate today,' said the woman, the background filling with a perfectly captured panorama of the senate facility, which was housed on a planet in the Kepler system. Lying four jumps beyond the furthest of the colonies, Colony Seven, it was somewhere that Jinn had never been, and never expected to go. She was happy sticking to Earth-controlled space. She had no desire to get involved with their alien neighbours or politics.

The senators sat on floating platforms arranged in a sweeping circle. The camera zoomed across them, drifting past the various alien species before lingering on the platform assigned to the representatives from Earth.

Jinn sat upright. Her mother, Ferona, stood with six others, all dressed in matching white robes, still and silent behind the senator. A note at the bottom of the screen said that it was archive footage. Knowing it was old didn't make her feel any better.

Dammit, she wanted to see misbehaving actors, not this.

'Screen off.'

The system obeyed her instantly.

Jinn wondered if Ferona ever thought about her. Probably not. She had been a mistake that needed to be fixed, preferably by other people, not a child to be loved and cared for. Her mother had barely given her a moment's thought when they'd been sharing an apartment. It was even less likely that Ferona would think about her now, when they hadn't seen each other in over twenty years and she had a senator to manipulate.

Annoyed with herself for even thinking about it, Jinn folded her arms and glared at the screen. First Caspian Dax, and now her mother. What hideous nightmare from the past was going to pop up next?

Then light swept away the darkness.

Jinn blinked, her eyes stinging. Blood roared in her ears as she scrambled to her feet. 'Give me a full systems report,' she ordered. 'What on Earth was that? Why did the lights come on?'

'I turned them on.' The voice came from behind her.

Jinn pulled in a breath. She flexed her fingers, willing her blades to stay hidden. 'Bryant.' She slowly turned around, keeping her hands at her sides. 'What is it?' she asked, outwardly calm, though inwardly she was struggling to contain her fury. Damn Bryant. Why couldn't he have given her some warning? Why did he have to be such a dick?

Bryant picked a bit of invisible dirt off his uniform. 'You didn't programme the autopilot for docking.'

*What?* 'I never programme the autopilot for docking,' Jinn pointed out. 'Surely you've figured that out, after nearly six hundred drop-offs.' Her heart rate had slowed a little. She forced herself to focus on the hum of the phase drive, the taste of the recycled air, and reminded herself that assaulting Bryant was not a good idea.

'You're supposed to programme the autopilot for docking,' Bryant pointed out. 'It's mandatory in case of pilot injury.'

'We're on a government transporter,' Jinn replied. 'This is as safe as it gets. Unless you're planning on injuring me yourself, which I wouldn't recommend, it's virtually impossible for me to hurt myself.' Shaking her head, she strode over to the console mounted in the wall next to where Bryant stood. Numbers flashed on the screen, showing their speed and location. 'We're exactly where we should be,' she said. 'We'll dock with the A2 on time. Everything is going according to plan.' The hair on the back of her neck prickled, and she knew Bryant had moved closer.

'There's no need to be so defensive,' Bryant replied, staring her down. 'I am simply requesting that we follow procedure.'

Anger swamped her, and she didn't care if he knew it. Bryant didn't outrank her. 'You're the agent,' she pointed out. 'I'm the pilot. You're here to deal with the cargo, not to tell me how to fly.'

'It's because of our cargo that I'm suggesting you use the autopilot,' he said, his gaze fixed steadily on her. 'If I said that there was no need to use auto-restraints because I could handle him if he tried to escape, you'd be the first to complain, and you would be right. I suggest you show me the same courtesy.'

Jinn could feel the tingling in her hands, in her wrists, a sure sign that her emotions were getting the better of her. But the last thing she wanted to do was show Bryant her blades. If he knew she had enough Tellurium in her system to not only connect with the onboard computer but to form a lethal weapon, he'd report her to her superiors before she could blink. 'Why?'

'You haven't slept in seventy-two hours,' Bryant said. 'Security Service rules state that a pilot must spend at least five out of every forty-eight hours asleep in order to fly.'

'How do you know I haven't slept?' Jinn threw back at him, refusing to admit that there was any truth in what he said.

'Are you denying it?'

Jinn said nothing, simply scowled at Bryant as he put himself in front of the console and brought up her activity log for the past three days. She'd been careful. She'd made sure she spent enough time in her cramped personal quarters, and she'd altered the information in her personal data log so that it looked as if she'd slept, even though she hadn't. She couldn't, not until they were safely away from the A2 and the hold was empty. Maybe she could have taken a measure of Easydoze. There were several capsules in the medical kit. But she'd been afraid that something would happen while she was unconscious.

'You look like shit,' Bryant said. 'You can fool the computer system, Blue, but you can't fool me. You are not fit to dock this ship and you know it. Programme the autopilot.'

'Or what?'

'Or I will be forced to place you in temporary custody and dock the ship myself.'

Jinn didn't need years of working with the man to know that he would do exactly that. The cold gleam in his dark eyes told her, as did the hand that gripped her upper arm. 'You can't dock this ship.' She tugged her arm free. 'You're not a pilot, Bryant.'

'I have basic pilot training. Believe me, I am more than capable.'

'But you're not a pilot,' she said again. 'Do you have any idea what the clearance is on the entrance to the docking bay? Even I find it difficult.'

'Then you had better programme the autopilot.' With that, Bryant marched out of the rec bay, heading along the narrow corridor that led to the flight deck.

Jinn closed her eyes and swore quietly to herself. It didn't matter that Bryant had threatened to lock her up until the mission was over. It didn't matter that he'd threatened to dock the ship himself. What mattered was that he was right. She wasn't in any fit state to dock the transporter. And it had been more like eighty hours since she'd slept, and she knew exactly why.

Caspian Dax. They had transported others equally as dangerous, psychopaths and sadistic murderers and vicious rapists, leaving them on the A2 to endure their punishment for as long as they could survive it, and it hadn't bothered her at all. But Dax was different.

He had a reputation for taking what he wanted and asking questions later, if he asked them at all. Barely a week went by without the streaming newsfeeds reporting that he'd taken another ship, another consignment, another life. After he'd let her escape from the *Finex*, her new crewmates had made it their priority to make sure she knew about every single incident. They had never let her forget that Dax had spared her. They thought she'd traded something for her life – sexual favours, credits, her crewmates – and nothing she could say could persuade them otherwise.

When she'd left Galactinex and gone to work for the Security Service, she'd promised herself it would stop, and it had. Until now.

Jinn wanted to dock the ship herself because she wanted to know that Caspian Dax was on board the A2. She needed to land the transporter inside the cargo bay of the prison ship, hear the exit ramp lower, and see him walk out into the bay. She didn't want to spend another second of her life paying for something that had happened twenty years ago.

She kicked the wall. And then she gritted her teeth and followed Bryant along the narrow corridor that led to the control deck. His broad shoulders were relaxed inside his perfectly fitting uniform, and if he could feel the negative vibes she was directing at the back of his head, it didn't show.

'Are you sure about this?'

Bryant swung his chair slowly around to face her and sighed. 'This isn't up for discussion,' he said. 'Don't make me ask you again, Blue.'

There was just enough menace in his tone to make her pause.

'Fine.' Jinn set her hands to the control deck, steeling herself for the sting as the nanobots in her bloodstream rushed to her hands, forming the thin, sharp wires that pushed their way through her fingertips and fused with the circuits of the ship. She felt the jolt as the connection was made, then the familiar warmth that came with being plugged in. In front of her, the screen flashed to life. 'Welcome, Jinnifer Blue. Do you wish to suspend the current autopilot programme?'

It was so tempting to take control and show Bryant exactly what she could do, even when she was so tired that it was all she could do to stay upright. But if she screwed up this contract, she wouldn't get paid, and she needed those credits.

'No,' she said. 'Extend current programme.' The system linked her in to the current flight path, taking her through a fast-moving version of it, the remaining three-hour journey condensed into a couple of short minutes. It didn't take her much longer than that to set the autopilot for the final approach to the A2 and the subsequent docking, her neural pathways linking with the onboard computer, creating the perfect mesh of memory and stored data that would allow the ship to fly as if she was controlling it. No computer could surpass the human brain when it came to this apart from AI droids, and they weren't allowed to fly. 'Do you want me to programme our take-off too, or are you going to let me fly us out of there?'

'I'm sure I can handle take-off,' Bryant said.

It was then that Jinn realised he was no longer in his seat at the comm. station. She'd been so engrossed in programming the autopilot, her attention focussed so completely on the screens in front of her, that she hadn't noticed him move.

Nor had she noticed the stunner in his hand.

The explosion of cold under her skin told her he'd shot her with it. The rapid descent of darkness told her he'd shot her close, with the maximum power the weapon allowed. 'Bastard,' she heard herself say, as the darkness overtook her senses, leaving nothing behind.

# CHAPTER
# 4

**20th August 2207**
**Paris Dome, Earth**

As the skimmer circled the Dome, waiting for a landing slot, Ferona Blue closed down her screen, tucked the work cube into her pocket, and looked out of the window at the landscape below. White stretched as far as the eye could see, land blending into sky. It would snow before night fell.

It always snowed before night fell.

Jagged remnants of the city that had once been Paris stuck up through the crusting of ice, stubbornly refusing to remain buried. There was no movement on the surface. Occasionally some of the feral dogs that roamed the wastes could be seen hunting for what remained – thin, half-starved rabbit, or one of the vicious two-tailed cats that seemed somehow able to survive despite the hideous polluted conditions. But not today. Her wrist comm. indicated that the external temperature was −17. Inside the skimmer, and inside the Dome, it was a comfortable twenty-one degrees. The Underworld city, dug deep under the Dome itself, would be a sweaty thirty-two.

Ferona had visited the Underworld city built underneath the Dome in London back when she'd been the minister for

Underworld Communities. It had been a stinking, filthy place. She hadn't stayed long. After that visit, she had returned to her apartment and washed every centimetre of her body several times. Her clothes had gone into the recycling unit, and her report had gone to the president on time. She had recommended either increasing the supply of silver rice from Colony Four, or stricter reproductive controls. The president had made noises about personal rights, saying that the single child limit already imposed on the Underworld cities was strict enough. But he hadn't increased the welfare budget.

As the skimmer angled in towards the landing port, Ferona removed her attention from the view outside. Her two assistants sat opposite her, both of them still feverishly working on their cubes.

Swain had been at her side for the past five years. He was both loyal and deeply intelligent, his understanding of the law matched by his knowledge of economics. Next to him sat Lucinda, an insightful PR specialist who also had a PhD in behavioural psychology. Both Dome-raised and educated, they had been handpicked straight from the academy by Ferona herself. She knew what needed to be done. They knew how to make it happen. Her current position as Minister for off world affairs could be a complicated, difficult job. She was responsible for space stations, repair stations, the colonies, the humans occupying them, and the aliens those humans offended. There were no holidays. There was only sleep because her assistants made it possible.

The skimmer bumped slightly as they set down on the port.

Lucinda lifted her head. 'We aren't using the internal gate?'

Ferona rose from her seat as her restraints automatically rolled back. 'Clearly not,' she said. It could mean only one thing. 'The president must have called a full meeting.'

'This may work in our favour,' Swain pointed out, as he too rose from his seat. He smoothed his jacket and tucked his work cube into the small case he always carried.

'It may,' Ferona acknowledged, as the exit door of the skimmer hissed open and lowered to the ground. The cold bit instantly. She had dressed carefully, in a heavily embroidered coat that concealed her body from neck to knee, but it was designed for Dome conditions, not for this. Tucking her hands inside the wide sleeves, she made her way down the ramp and out into the bitter wind.

She walked quickly and not just because of the cold. Other skimmers were landing at the edge of the port, the sound of their engines a low rumble against the fierce push of the wind. There would be time to talk to the other ministers once she was inside. She could see from the insignia on several of the vessels that representatives from the major corporations had also been invited, though she didn't understand why. Any discussions involving them should take place in small, private meetings with good food and good wine, not here.

Holding back her annoyance, Ferona headed for the already crowded train platform positioned in the centre of the landing port. Security agents lined the walkway, their dark grey uniforms a stark contrast to the bright white of their surroundings. All of them had their faces shielded against the cold and the glare and all of them were armed, their weapons held firm and ready.

She didn't acknowledge them, and they didn't acknowledge her as she strode past them and onto the waiting train. She took a seat. 'Busy,' murmured Lucinda as she folded herself neatly into an empty space.

The carriage filled quickly, the doors closed, and then they were off, speeding towards the towering Dome. Where some cities had opted to build multiple low buildings, here there were only three, huddled together, spiking high. And so the Underworld city that had grown underneath it had spread far beyond the perimeter of the Dome. Black metal discs the size of skimmers ringed the landscape five kilometres out from the edge of the Dome, letting the city below pull in much-needed air. As they moved closer, Ferona could see movement around them as

32

workers in heavy, dirty clothing hacked at the ice that formed on the vents. Small fires burned orange in rusted braziers in a pathetic attempt to keep the workers warm.

Work stopped as the train flew past, the turbulence blowing out the fires, then its speed began to drop as it entered the Dome and eased to a halt inside the brightly lit station. The doors slid open. Ferona walked out. She inhaled deeply, pulling in clean air that smelt faintly of tobacco mingled with the scent of the baking pastries sold by the food carts. The station itself was stylish and pleasant, decorated with antique tiles and ornate brass that gave her a sense of having been transported several hundred years back in time. Even the droids had been designed to fit in with their surroundings. Dressed in chic navy blue uniforms, they swished around the platforms, sweeping up, checking tickets, hauling luggage. Only the streamlined carriages that hovered just above the rails destroyed the illusion that she was in 1920s Paris.

They joined the stream of bodies moving along the platform, and stepped onto the moving walkway that would take them directly to the government offices. Glancing around, Ferona acknowledged the other ministers with a sharp nod of her head, even the ones she disliked.

As the walkway reached its destination, all of them were funnelled into the vast meeting hall, moving past portraits of every president dating back to the inception of the Global State, and there were plenty of them. Gold frames bordered the faces that every Dome child was expected to know. The walls were a lush, velvety red, the ceiling high and decorated with exquisite gilded plasterwork.

It wasn't real. The view screens were only turned on when the hall was in use. The rest of the time, this was just a blank, empty corridor. Still, it was very convincing, and Ferona enjoyed the spectacle. Perhaps one day she would see her own picture up there. It was a pleasing thought, though it wasn't what drove her. She had bigger plans for the future.

Inside the meeting hall, the seats were arranged in a series of long, curving rows that faced a raised podium. Ferona headed down to the front, found her assigned seat, and carefully arranged herself in it. President Vexler acknowledged her with a nod. He was charismatic, charming, a figurehead. But the real power belonged to the man standing next to him. Mikhal Dubnik, the vice-president.

The hall filled quickly, and Vexler took to the podium and churned his way through the niceties before matters of health and welfare were quickly dealt with. The Underworld population continued to grow, despite the vigorous enforcement of reproductive control. The colonies continued to produce food and fuel, and the prices continued to rise. There had been an outbreak of a new strain of viral flu in New York, though fortunately it had been contained within the Underworld city and had not reached the Dome.

Ferona saw the vice president lean in and whisper something to Vexler, who sat up straighter in his chair. 'Have additional medical supplies been dispatched?' he asked. His voice carried around the hall. But Ferona knew the question had not come from him.

The health minister, floating large above them all on a projected hologram, coloured slightly. 'Protocol has been followed,' he said.

'What is the survival rate?'

'At the moment, seventy-five percent.'

Ferona watched as the vice president leaned in once more.

'That seems a little low,' Vexler said.

'With additional resources, we estimate that a survival rate of ninety percent is entirely possible.'

Those words hung in the air as a moment of silence followed.

'What would be the optimal survival rate?' Ferona whispered to Lucinda.

Her head lowered as she activated her work cube and her fingers flew over the surface. 'Taking into account cost of medical care, welfare cost of the surviving population, projected replacement costs for resources used against potential future workforce contribution, thirty-eight percent.'

Negotiations began. No-one wanted to argue with the president. Or, more correctly, they did not want to argue with Dubnik. By the time they had finished, enough resources had been offered to guarantee a survival rate of eighty-five percent. What a waste. The hologram of the health minister disappeared, and Ferona tapped her fingers on the arm of her chair, impatiently waiting for the meeting to move along.

The president turned his attention to Ana Rizzola, Earth's representative in the Intergalactic Senate. 'Senator Rizzola,' he said. 'Would you care to give us your report?'

Ferona already knew what the report would contain, as she had accompanied Rizzola to the last meeting of the Intergalactic Senate, and the two of them were often required to work together. When humans made an off world mess, Ferona dealt with them, and Rizzola smoothed things over with whichever alien senator had decided to take offence.

Rizzola rose to her feet, as was the custom in the senate, though not here. The hologram stretched to accommodate her image. 'As you are all aware, the most recent scientific reports have indicated that the core temperature of the Earth is continuing to fall. It is believed that this will eventually reach a critical point at which it will no longer be able to sustain human life. As you are also aware, in 2175 the space outreach programme identified a planet in the Cygnus arm of the galaxy which is capable of supporting human life without the need for mass terraforming. We would be able to live there normally. To breathe the air. To build. To not only survive, but to thrive.' Rizzola took a moment to let this sink in. There had been strong arguments for terraforming a planet closer to home. Mars had long been touted as a possibility, and if they had two hundred years to spare, it might be an option. But they didn't. 'Spes is our future,' she said. 'That's why we named it after the goddess of hope. If we stay here, we will die. Humankind will be relegated to history. Lost. Forgotten about.

'We can reach this planet,' Rizzola continued. On the hologram, Ferona could see the straight line of her back, the confidence in her posture as she said it. 'But in order to do so, we will have to pass through several sectors of space controlled by some of our alien neighbours.'

They were all aware of this. Rizzola wasn't telling them anything new. But she was a skilled orator. She knew how to hold a room, which was why she'd been elected as their representative in the senate. And she held this one. Ferona could feel the tension. Everyone was holding their breath, waiting to hear if Rizzola had been able to negotiate terms with any of the other races.

'At the moment, whether or not we will be able to pass through that space still remains uncertain. As you know, the Security Service has been working hard over the past few months to capture and incarcerate all criminals with outstanding warrants. Because of this the senate has agreed to debate the issue of our relocation to Spes. I hope to be able to persuade them to put the matter to a vote, with a majority being sufficient to allow safe passage for Earth ships through all the necessary sectors of space. I would like to personally thank each and every one of you for the work that has been done to bring us to this point. Unfortunately, there is still much to be done, but together, I am sure that we can achieve it.'

There was a moment of stillness while that sank in. And then the hall erupted as a thousand ministers and councillors and corporate leaders got to their feet and started to shout. It was more than they'd had a month ago, but it still wasn't enough for them. What had they expected? Did they really think that having the Security Service throw a few extra criminals in prison would be enough to persuade all the other members of the senate to let thousands of human ships dirty up their space?

Ferona relaxed back in her seat and watched as tempers flared and frustration boiled over. If you wanted something to happen, she thought to herself, you had to do more than stand in a meeting hall and shout.

'Call to order!'

The vice president's voice boomed around the space, a crack of power. The noise dropped to a simmering murmur.

'We have the support of the Lodons,' Rizzola said. 'They have already promised me that we have their vote.'

'And the others?' Dubnik asked.

'Some are on our side. But the Sittan and the Shi-Fai dislike us,' Rizzola admitted. 'And they will vote against us.'

But Ferona had plans to change that.

# CHAPTER
# 5

**21st August 2207**

Vessel: The *Santina Hawk*. Class 2 transporter
Destination: The *Alcatraz 2*
Cargo: Prisoners X427M and 1238B. Identity: Classified.
Crew: One
Droids: Two

The darkness didn't last forever, though it felt like it had when Jinn started the slow crawl towards consciousness. Her heartbeat came back to her first, weak and unsure, followed by her limbs and then her skin. It felt like she was burning from the inside out, muscles stiff and painful. How long had she been out?

Longer than a few seconds, she knew that much. The electrical blast that Bryant had hit her with had been vicious, far more powerful than the light shocks she'd experienced during training. They hadn't caused this level of disorientation, of confusion, though admittedly it had been a long time since she'd last been shot with a stunner and her memory might have smoothed the edges off the experience.

But that didn't answer the most puzzling question of all. *Why had Bryant stunned her?* She'd programmed the autopilot as he'd requested. She might not have been happy about it, but she'd done it. Her mind raced back to the conversation they'd had in the rec bay, when he'd threatened to take her into temporary custody if she didn't sleep. Is that what this was? Some sort of health intervention? If he had been that desperate to get her locked in her quarters, all he had to do was ask. No, she thought to herself, as her fingernails scratched the strangely cold, strangely hard surface beneath her, he'd have had to do a little more than ask. But not this.

Jinn pushed herself up onto her elbows. She needed to get upright, get moving. Walking off the after-effects of a stun shot hurt like mad, but it was the best way to help the body recover. Her quarters were too small to get any decent movement going, however. The corridor would be a better option. She staggered forwards, fumbling blindly in the dark for the exit. As soon as she had enough credits put away, she was going to take that stunner and shove it up Bryant's arse and fire it. That thought kept her going as she took a couple more steps forward. No sign of the door. That wasn't right. Her tiny cabin was no more than four paces across, not including the skinny bunk that automatically folded away when she wasn't using it. 'Lights!'

The system obeyed her immediately.

She wasn't in her quarters. She was in absolutely the last place she wanted to be. The dark walls of the cargo bay stretched out in front of her. The space was long and narrow and unpleasantly claustrophobic, the walls too close, the roof too high. Pipes ran horizontally up to the higher levels of the ship, the gravity generators at the far end of the bay humming as they pumped out heat.

Jinn staggered to the solitary elevator car that ran between the cargo bay and the upper levels. The doors were supposed to open automatically. They didn't. 'Let me in!' she shouted. 'Open the bloody door!'

'The elevator cannot be used at this time,' the system replied in its emotionless monotone.

'What do you mean it cannot be used? Get it down here! Now!'

The system responded with silence.

'Open a comm. link to the control deck!'

More silence. She would kill Bryant for this. 'What are you doing?' she screamed. 'Let me out of here!'

Nothing responded. The elevator didn't hum with movement, and the comm. screen on the wall next to it remained blank. Until she came up with something more effective than shouting, she was trapped. Jinn pressed her back against the wall, chest heaving, bile rising in the back of her throat as she got her first real look at their cargo.

Caspian Dax lay face down on a medibed that would have been more than adequate for a normal-sized human male. But he was not normal-sized. His feet hung over the edge, his arms over the sides. He was powerfully built, heavy through the shoulders and thick through the thighs. Possibly even bigger than he had been the first time she'd encountered him. A network of tubes ran from one solid forearm to the floor, feeding him the drugs and fluids needed to keep him both asleep and alive.

The fact that he was unconscious did nothing to assuage the consuming fire of panic that surged through her body. She could not be down here with him, especially not when they were minutes away from docking with the A2. She could not be down here when the system woke him up, when the ramp lowered and she had to either head out onto the A2 or stay in the hold and die from Diborane poisoning.

There had to be a way out. Jinn took in her surroundings in a quick, sweeping glance, all senses on full alert now. White lights glowed at the edge of the floor, lighting the whole space with a strange, eerie glow. Rough, heavy-duty aluminium plates were bolted together to form the roof, the walls, the floor. Even if she could break through them, there was nothing on the other side but space. At one end of the hold was the ramp that would lower as soon as they were inside the docking bay of the A2, and at the other was the useless elevator.

She closed her eyes and slowly lowered her hands to her sides.

She was trapped. She was trapped, and she was going to die down here. This couldn't be happening. She was so close to being out of this, to her retirement on Colony Seven.

Why? Why would Bryant put her down here? Had he been ordered to leave her in the hold? Was that it? Had he somehow found out about the illegal Tellurium she was carrying inside her body and reported it to her superiors? She'd always known the risk she was taking, but the risk of not having a way to defend herself had been greater.

A massively amplified version of a familiar noise echoed through the hold. They were docking with the A2. The autopilot she'd programmed was taking them inside the vast prison ship. There was no escaping this, not now. She'd sealed her own fate by being too damn good at her job.

Jinn stared up at the ceiling, saw small dark openings appear before being filled with the white Plastex spikes that would spray out the toxic gas designed to drive them onto the A2. Diborane didn't just stop the heart and poison the lungs. It ate its way through flesh, reducing an adult human to a liquid mess in under five minutes. It was, by all accounts, a hideous way to die. Assuming, of course, that Caspian Dax didn't kill her first. He'd let her go once. She wasn't stupid enough to think that he'd let her go again, especially not when she was partly responsible for his capture. Unable to breathe, she turned around, forcing herself to look again at the medibed and the man strapped to it.

The bed was empty.

Air got stuck in her throat as she stared at it, at the slack bundle of dripping tubes slung across it, at the dark spots of what could only be blood trailing across the white sheet. Then the full weight of Caspian Dax slammed her back against the wall. The force of the contact made her teeth knock together and she could have sworn she heard her skull crack. Strikingly familiar green eyes locked on to hers, burning with anger. His huge body was vibrating with more of it as he held her there, pinned against the wall. 'Where am I?' He put just enough pressure against her neck to let her know that he meant it. 'I asked you a question,' he said. 'Where in the *void* am I?'

'This is a Security Service transporter,' she told him, her voice shaking. 'We've just docked with the A2. And if you don't let me go, I swear I'll . . .'

'You'll what?' he asked, glancing around them as he spoke. 'That uniform doesn't hold any weight with me. And from the looks of it, it doesn't hold any weight with your crewmates either, given that you're down here.' He looked up. Jinn followed his gaze. The gas jets were fully engaged.

'Let go of me.' It was suicide to negotiate with him, surely, but Jinn couldn't think straight, not with his thumbs resting on her windpipe. He'd cut his hair, she thought to herself, though it seemed a stupid thing to notice in the circumstances. He didn't look older, though she could see the years on him somehow, and those strange green eyes were just as hard. He didn't release her. She could feel the Tellurium heating in her hands. She flexed her fingers as it broke the surface of her skin. She was ready. Whatever happened, whatever he did, she was ready. There was no point trying to hide the Tellurium now. If she couldn't get out of the cargo bay before they docked with the A2, she was dead anyway.

'I know you,' he said. His gaze tracked over her face, over the implant that curved around her right eye.

'No you don't.' The lie snapped out of her, short, hard, afraid. Her knees shook as he leaned in closer.

'Yes I do. Twenty years ago I kicked you off a freighter. As I recall, your crewmates tried to sell you to me, and when that failed, they tried to kill both of us.'

'You're mistaken,' she told him. Over their heads, the spikes had lengthened. Any moment now, the gas would start. She struggled against his hold. 'Just let me go before they start the damn gas and we both die!'

'How did you find me?'

'I don't know!'

One dark brow slanted upwards. He squeezed harder.

'I'm the pilot!' She tried to swallow. 'My partner, Bryant, he found you, not me. My job is to fly the transporter. That's it.'

'So why aren't you flying it? Why are you in the hold? What did you do to make your crewmate hate you this time?'

'I don't know!'

Above them, she heard a faint hiss and her stomach turned over. The Diborane molecules were light, so they would sink slowly, giving prisoners time to escape if they wanted to. But if they waited in the hold for too long . . .

She'd had enough. In one swift movement, she brought a knee up against his groin. But he was too fast for her, or he'd anticipated the move. He blocked it. And that was when she got to work with her blades. The right went up into his gut. The left slashed across his shoulder. He roared with pain and loosened his grip on her. It was all she needed. Slippery as a fish, Jinn dropped to the floor, rolled away from him, then scrambled to her feet and started to run. At the end of the hold, the ramp was already down, giving her a first glimpse of the inside of the A2.

'Wait!' he yelled, but she was in no mood to listen, or to obey. She wasn't stupid. Caspian Dax was a product of a harsh Underworld upbringing. He'd signed up for mods at the age of eighteen and had made it halfway through treatment before stealing a ship and disappearing. He'd killed twelve men on his way off the planet. Killed them in cold blood.

Five years later he'd amassed a fleet of a dozen stolen ships and was regularly intercepting vessels moving between the colonies and Jump Gates 16 and 17. The *Finex* had been just one of hundreds. Jinn had seen pictures of ships that had received the same treatment, broken, burnt-out fragments floating dead in space, their cargo destroyed, their crews slaughtered. Pirate was too romantic a term for this man. He was a thief, a vicious murderer, and she'd just stabbed him.

By the time she reached the bottom of the ramp, Jinn's muscles were burning and her lungs were screaming. She'd been too afraid to breathe, not wanting to get a single molecule of the Diborane into her system, too afraid of what lay ahead to do anything other than force her legs to work. At the bottom of the ramp, she made a rapid spin to the left, moving into the shadows at the side of the A2's docking bay. She crouched there for precious moments, fighting for air.

Overhead, the ceiling soared high, the full height of the A2, a stark reminder that the prison had once been a freighter, before it became a prison ship housing those men considered too dangerous to be held on planet. Almost all of them were Bugs. Women had their own prison, the A3, located on the Moon itself, which made Bryant's decision to leave her here all the more confusing.

She crept forwards almost to the edge of the shadows, far enough to see the swivel of the transporter's hull cameras as they tracked her movement.

Bryant was watching her. 'Why?' Jinn whispered, though she knew he couldn't hear her. He probably wouldn't tell her even if he could. She asked the question anyway, wanting to know, needing to know. But given the situation she was in, it seemed like the least of her worries.

She got to her feet and started to run.


For a long moment, Dax remained where he was, alone in the cargo bay of the little transporter, wondering what in the galaxy had just happened. If he wasn't bleeding all over the floor, he'd think it was the anaesthetic playing tricks on him. But it had been real. A woman had been left in the cargo hold with him. He had no idea why. Given that she'd knifed him, he wasn't sure he cared.

The wounds were already healing, but the memory of that flash of agony would take a little longer to subside. Grabbing the basic prison kit that sat at the side of the medibed, Dax pulled on trousers, shirt, boots. He left the rest. The hiss from the jets was louder now. He didn't have much time. Sprinting to the edge of the ramp, he made his way down it and out onto the A2.

He had to find some way to transmit a message to the *Mutant* and get away from this place. Then he was going to find out exactly which member of his crew had sold him out to the Security Service, and he was going to make them wish they had never been born. His thoughts strayed to the woman, alone on an all-male prison ship, but he jerked them back under control. He didn't know why she'd been left here, and he wasn't sure he wanted to know. She'd just have to take care of herself. Judging by those blades, she was more than capable.

Dax pulled in air, let it out again, rolled out the ache in his shoulders. Thanks to his genetic modifications, his eyesight was better than that of the average human, his healing rate faster, his reflexes razor sharp, but the effects of the anaesthetic the agent had used to knock him out lingered. His head felt like it was being punched from the inside, nausea roiled through him and he had a strange, bitter taste in his mouth, a sure sign that he'd been pumped full of K.

He forced himself to ignore it.

At the other end of the docking bay he could see the entrance to a tunnel, presumably leading deeper into the ship. Looking around, his options were pretty limited. He could either stay where he was, exposed and vulnerable, or he could see what delights were waiting for him at the end of the tunnel. He listened hard, trying to track the sound of footsteps. The last thing he wanted was to get caught unaware. The prisoners on the A2 were half starved and desperate, and that made for a dangerous combination. Even a genetically modified pirate could find himself in trouble in a place like this.

There was still no sign of the woman, and he found himself again wondering where she was. Surely she couldn't have got that far, unless some of the prisoners had already found her and she'd been dragged off somewhere. Dax scanned the floor, saw no sign of blood. There would definitely be blood if she'd been attacked. Moving silently, he moved to the edge of the docking bay and pressed his bulk flat against the wall. He was too big to have any hope of hiding, but he wasn't about to make himself an open target.

It didn't take him long to reach the tunnel. It was dark and silent, the walls crusted with some unidentifiable substance, but he decided to risk it. There was an unexpected chemical smell in the air, a potent bite that he associated with medical clinics, and it made him pause, made him press himself even more tightly against the wall, halt his breathing, every sense on high alert. Something wasn't right here. He should have seen signs of the other prisoners by now. The air should smell of disease and filth. He should be able to hear . . . *something.*

And then he did. A fierce, terrified, all-too-female scream that made the blood run cold inside his veins. He didn't consider whether or not he should respond. He didn't wait to see if that scream came again or try to convince himself that it was nothing more than the remnants of K polluting his system and playing with his mind. He simply marched to the end of the tunnel, fists up, ready to tell the woman that he'd help her out this time, but the next time she fucked up she was on her own.

# CHAPTER

# 6

## 21st August 2207

Vessel: The *Alcatraz 2*. Prison ship
Destination: N/A
Cargo: N/A
Crew: N/A
Droids: Unknown

The tunnel twisted and narrowed, forcing him onwards into the darkness, and Dax had the strangest feeling that he was being driven forward, herded like an animal into a trap. He saw exits that went left, right, but all of them had been closed off, leaving him only one possible route. He kept going. He moved quickly, all senses on full alert. She couldn't be far now.

He was almost at the end of the tunnel when he saw her.

She lay on the floor, limbs stiff, back arched, caught inside a laser cage. A little silver dart protruded from the side of her neck. Her gaze latched on to him, pleading with him to help her.

His first priority had to be finding the source of the dart. He scanned the walls, the ceiling, and finally the floor. There was nothing obvious. But the damn thing had to have come from somewhere.

There was a small control panel mounted in the wall. Colour-matched to everything else, he hadn't spotted it at first glance. He contemplated trying to use it, and then put a fist through it instead. It sparked and smoked, the broken panel tumbling down in pieces that clung to the ends of curling, coloured wires.

The laser cage switched off, and Dax saw what lay beyond the tunnel. The restrictive darkness gave way to the pale light of a vast medical bay. Row after row of medibeds were lined up with perfect precision. The walls were white Plastex, the floor an expanse of more of the same. Tubes looped from portable drug stations to the bodies that occupied the beds as monitors silently recorded every heartbeat, every breath. This wasn't a prison ship. This was something else.

A dart whizzed towards him, missing by millimetres as he leaped over the woman and dropped into a crouch, one knee to the ground, shoulder to the wall. The first medidroid came at him from the side, moving fast but not fast enough. Dax jumped it, and took it down with a rapid swing of his right fist that severed its head from its body. It dropped to the ground in a twitching, sparking heap, clear liquid oozing from its broken neck. He kicked it away. It slammed against the wall, the impact denting a crater in the Plastex. He took out a second in the same way, not even waiting for the body to stop twitching before he sent it skidding across the floor.

Four more moved in. Dax charged at the droids, dealing with them in the same way that he'd dealt with the others. Swiftly. Thoroughly.

Then he turned his attention to the woman. He could tell from the way those dark eyes followed him that she was conscious, trapped inside her immobile, drugged body. 'Stay calm,' he told her as he set one hand to her neck, found her pulse, a slow, sluggish beat. He pulled out the dart and tossed it away. 'It's probably Pentamol. It'll wear off in a minute.'

Dax swept his gaze across the room. So many medibeds. He stopped counting when he got to triple figures. The occupants were pale, unconscious, only the lower halves of their prone forms covered. All the ones he could see were male. Tubes trailed from their arms into the walls. All of them were restrained, strapped to the beds by thick black webbing that crisscrossed their bodies. It seemed like overkill given their comatose states.

He didn't know what in the void this place was, or what was going on here, but he didn't like it. All his instincts told him to get out, to do it alone and do it now. But something kept him where he was. He took a brief moment to study her, this woman he'd let go once before. The white-blonde hair and dark eyes were the typical Dome colouring. Her features were even, perfect, her skin smooth and unblemished. He'd expect nothing less from a Dome brat. When he'd been younger, Dome girls had fascinated him, but he'd soon learned what those girls thought of scruffy Underworld kids.

He monitored her pulse for a few more seconds before he felt the increase that signalled the Pentamol starting to wear off. She jolted upright, heaving in air with a gasp that was almost a scream. 'Just breathe,' he said. 'The dizziness is the drug wearing off. Don't try to move.' But she didn't listen. Within seconds she was kicking out at him, trying to get up.

He pinned her down. 'What happened?' he asked.

'Get off me!' she shrieked.

'Answer the damn question.'

'There must be a pressure pad in the floor.' The words came out half mangled, as if she didn't quite have control over her tongue. 'I stepped on it and the cage switched on, then I was on the floor. That's all I remember.'

'There's a medical bay at the end of this tunnel,' he said. 'Know anything about that?'

Her eyes went huge. 'What?'

'I'll take that as a no.' He grabbed her arms, hauled her to her feet. 'Let's get one thing straight. If you so much as think about stabbing me again, you're on your own. Is that clear?'

She nodded. The fighting stopped, though he could still see

the fire of it in her eyes. He could hardly blame her. He was feeling pretty damn full of fight himself. 'I don't know what is going on here,' he said. 'I am sure that I don't want to know. My crew can get us out of here, but I need to bounce a message to them first.' Slowly, cautiously, Dax released his grip and stepped back.

She fell straight to the floor. Dax reached down, hooked a hand under her arm and hauled her upright. 'Focus,' he said, pushing her back against the wall. 'Some of the Pentamol is still in your system. I need you to act like it's not. I don't know how long it will be before more droids get here, but you can bet your last credit they're on their way.'

'Are you going to kill me?'

'That depends.'

'On what?'

'On you.'

She blinked, her brow creased. She was breathing fast. 'What about them?' She pointed to the prone figures stretched out on the beds. Her eyes were wild.

Dax looked at the others. 'I don't know,' he said. 'And we don't have time to figure it out.' Twin sets of elevator doors at the other end offered the most obvious exit. 'Come on,' he said, taking her arm and pulling her forward. If she held him up, he'd leave her behind. He promised himself that much, at least.

'Why are you helping me?' she asked.

'You've got pilot modifications. That means you can plug into the main computer. It'll be a lot easier to get a message to my crew if I don't have to try and manually hack a comm. station.'

'If I can plug in to a comm. station, why do I need you?'

'Really?' Dax asked. He loosened his grip. She just about remained standing, but he could see it was a struggle.

'I can take care of myself.'

'I can see that,' he said.

All he got in response was her middle finger. 'I thought you Dome women were supposed to have good manners.'

'I'm not exactly your average Dome woman,' she snapped back.

'You look like one to me.'

'Well, I'm not.' She gestured to the implant at her temple. 'Does this look like something an average Dome woman would have?'

'I guess not,' he said. 'What's your name? I assume you have an average Dome woman one of those.'

'Jinnifer.'

That was it. Jinnifer Blue. He remembered it now.

'Can you really get us away from here?' she asked.

'If I can find a working comm. station and get a message to my crew.'

'The control deck is the most likely place,' she said. 'This was used to haul kaelite before it became a prison. The central computer would have been left in place to run the air recyclers and the docking doors. I should be able to plug in.' She lifted a hand, showing him the Tellurium that banded her wrist. 'I guess pilot tech has its advantages.'

Dax gestured to the far end of the medical bay. 'Can you get those elevators to work?'

'I can try,' she said.

She half staggered, half walked across the bay. When she stumbled, Dax made a grab for her, but she shook him off. Leaning a shoulder against the wall, she reached for the control panel.

But Dax stopped her. 'Listen.'

'What is it?'

He yanked her away from the door. There it was again. The all-too-familiar sound of an elevator in motion. 'Elevator is on the move. We're about to have company.'

'More droids?' she asked. She paled.

'Do you want to wait long enough to find out?' There had to be another way out of here. *Think, Dax. Think.* Life-support vents crisscrossed the ceiling. He moved underneath one, stretched up.

The mesh was rigid, easily within reach. Curving his hand into a fist, Dax punched it, knocking it clean out of sight. The opening was narrow, but it was their only option.

He redirected his gaze, found Jinnifer Blue on the other side of the bay, crouched down in front of the wall, fumbling with something. A panel came loose and she shoved it aside. 'Come on!' she shouted, as she disappeared into the space behind it.

Dax didn't need to be told twice. She scrambled to the side as he shouldered his way in, then reached past him and made a grab for the panel, tugging it back into position.

'This place,' she whispered. 'Something isn't right. This is supposed to be a prison ship, not a medical facility. What in the galaxy is going on here?'

'I don't know,' Dax said, thinking of the bodies strapped to the beds. Through the narrow gap between the panels, he could see the elevator door spiralling open, and more droids spilling out into the medical bay. He watched them for a moment, then turned his attention to his surroundings. They were inside what looked like a service tunnel for the ventilation system. Tunnels like these ran the length and breadth of ships like this, forming a network of hidden spaces normally only used by maintenance droids. He'd never expected to find himself hiding out in one.

'Will this lead us to the control deck?'

'Eventually,' she said.

'Good,' Dax replied. 'Come on. Let's move.'


For the next few hours, Dax took the lead, and Jinn let him. She felt a lot safer having him in front of her than behind, even though she doubted they would see any droids. The tunnel was narrow and barely high enough for Dax to stand up in, and it was clear that it hadn't been cleaned out in a long time. It was everything she expected from a freighter. Metal, rivets, rust, filth. And, to the left, a broken panel and a stairwell. 'That way,' she said.

Without hesitation, Dax ducked through the opening and disappeared. The few steps she could see were old, brittle, leading down into darkness so complete that Jinn felt like she was being swallowed when she followed him into it. It terrified her and yet it was familiar, and there was comfort in that. She knew where she was.

And that meant she knew where the control deck was. She reached out, fumbling in the dark until her hand met the hard wall of his back. If she couldn't trust him this much, she was dead anyway. 'Get behind me,' she told him. 'I know the layout better than you.'

His silent acquiescence surprised her, as did the large hand that locked on to her shoulder, keeping him in constant contact as she thundered to the bottom of the staircase, took a right. Forward a short distance, then left, hand outstretched to find the wall. 'We need to get to the central stairwell,' she said. 'It will take us up to the top level.'

The tunnel widened, and she didn't know whether to be terrified or grateful when he moved alongside her. 'You seem to know a lot about the layout of a freighter,' he said.

'Of course I do,' Jinn replied, the words hard as she fought to get air. 'I used to work on them.'

'As a pilot,' he said. 'How does a pilot get to know their way around the service tunnels of a freighter?'

'You'd be surprised what you pick up.' Instinctively, Jinn moved to the side and pushed her shoulder hard against the wall. It was difficult to see in the dim light, but years of experience told her they'd just moved through into one of the freighter's vast cargo chambers. 'Keep left. We're on a narrow walkway about fifty metres up. There's no barrier on the other side. It's an awful long way to fall.'

'I'll take your word for it.' He kept his hand on her shoulder, although she sensed he didn't need to. The sound of her boots thudding against the metal grid of the walkway was so loud that it would be impossible for him to lose her.

The whole place stank of decay, as she'd imagined a prison ship would, only to her mind the smell seemed stale, and the silence was disturbing. There were supposed to be fifty thousand men on the *Alcatraz 2*. Fifty thousand desperate, starving men. They should have seen some sign of them by now. The few they'd seen back in the medical bay could barely have accounted for a tiny percentage of that.

Jinn took another step, and another. 'Where in the void is everyone?'

'I don't know,' Dax replied grimly.

'I don't like this,' she said. She slowed down. 'And the smell in here. It smells like . . . '

'Like what?'

'Like death.' She'd stopped completely now. 'We transported a prisoner here a couple of months ago. He opted to stay in the hold.'

'The Diborane?'

'I've never seen anything like it,' she said, her stomach twisting as the memory came flooding back. 'And the smell . . . '

'Diborane was used in here,' he said. It wasn't a question. It was a realisation. An acceptance. 'But you couldn't fit fifty thousand men in this chamber.'

'Not in one go.' She paused, thinking about it. 'Probably ten thousand though, if you crammed them in.'

'Lock them in here, pump in enough Diborane, and you could kill ten thousand men easy.'

Silence dropped around them as they both digested that bit of information. 'Even with clean-outs,' she said, her voice raw, 'it would only take a couple of days to gas everyone on board. But why would someone do this? Why? I mean, I know there are those who don't agree with keeping prisoners alive, who think that execution should be mandatory. But the government would never agree to it.'

'Whatever the reason,' he said, 'we can't stay in here.'

'No, I think you're right,' she said. Diborane was supposed to be inert after thirty minutes, but she wasn't prepared to take any chances. And if the place was rigged to work as a gas chamber, that meant the two of them were a sitting target.

'Move,' he said, tightening his grip on her shoulder and shoving her forwards. 'Move!'

They hit the end of the walkway in silence. Ahead of them, a narrow door blocked their route to the next chamber. Jinn sprinted towards it, set her hands to the wheel that would open the lock and heaved. Nothing happened. She heaved again, pulled until her boots lost purchase on the floor and the skin on her palms burned. 'I should be able to open it.'

'Corrosion?' Dax asked.

'Maybe,' she said.

He set a hand to her shoulder, moved her aside, and then put his own strength to the wheel. It sheared off in his hand, pulling away from the door with the whine of metal that didn't want to give. 'Bloody supernova,' Dax swore, dropping it at his feet. It hit the grating with a bang and rolled away, spinning off the edge of the walkway. It was several seconds before she heard it hit the floor below.

Dax moved in, examined the door. He glanced across at her. 'It's been sealed to make it impossible to open from in here. What's on the other side of this?'

'Another chamber,' she said quietly. 'Maybe twice the size of this one.'

'With a walkway?'

'Yes.'

'Stand clear,' Dax ordered her. He took another look at the door. 'And get those blades of yours out from wherever you've hidden them.'

'What are you going to do?'

'Kick the damn door in,' he said. 'And hope that there's nothing waiting for us on the other side.'

Placing a hand either side of the door, he pressed the sole of his boot against it. He gritted his teeth and swore out a curse, one that befitted a pirate, then gave the door a testing kick. The metal buckled under the impact, but it held.

Dax kicked it again, harder this time. The seal began to split at one side, cracking under the force of the blow, but still the door didn't open. 'I hope you're ready,' he said to Jinn. 'Because when this door gives way, every droid on this damn ship is going to hear it.'

With one final pistoning of his boot, the door flew back, landing with an ear-splitting bang against the narrow strip of walkway that ran along the side of the next chamber. Light flooded through the open doorway. Dax ducked through the space.

'What the fuck?' he whispered as she slipped through the doorway and stood next to him, blinking as her eyes took a moment to adjust. If what she had witnessed in the first chamber had shocked her, it was nothing compared to this.

The chamber was noisy, brightly lit, teeming with movement. She could see the scuttle of droids on the floor below, not just the upright humanoid forms of medidroids, but the small, fast-moving discs of cleaning bots, food delivery bots. And then there was the smell. It wasn't the poisoned air of the chamber they'd just passed through, but the hot, nasty stink of too many humans crammed in too close together.

'It smells worse than the *Mutant* does when the crew need some downtime,' Dax muttered.

Jinn didn't say anything. She couldn't seem to form words.

On either side of the chamber ran lengths of electrostatic wire, creating a crackling yellow field that ran in straight lines between the charging posts that speared up out of the floor. There had to be two thousand people in here. Each of them was penned in an electric cage like some sort of animal. Not all of them were too happy about it, if the constant screaming and smell of scorched flesh were anything to go by.

The walkway stretched out ahead of them, but as Jinn turned her attention to it, an arc of electrostatic discharge burned along its length. If they took that route, they ran the risk of being fried before they reached the other end, and if they stayed up here much longer, that would happen sooner rather than later.

Their only option was to head down to the floor of the chamber.

# CHAPTER

# 7

**22nd August 2207**

Vessel: The *Santina Hawk*. Class 2 transporter
Destination: Neutral Space
Cargo: None
Crew: One
Droids: Two

Bryant put enough distance between the A2 and the *Hawk* for the tension in his shoulders to ease before he let himself relax. It was always a relief to leave the prison ship behind, to feel the satisfaction of a job well done, to know that he'd put another flawed human where they belonged.

If you signed up for work on the Colonies, you worked on the Colonies until your debt was paid. That was the deal. It didn't matter if you hated the work, if the prosthetics made you sick, if you changed your mind. Underworlders knew that when they signed up for the genetic modifications and prosthetics that they couldn't afford. But too many of them seemed to think that the rules didn't apply to them. Too many of them tried to skip out on their contracts before they'd got even close to paying off their debts, and as far as he was concerned, they deserved their place on the A2.

Caspian Dax had earned his place ten times over, and as for Jinnifer Blue – Bryant didn't know what she'd done, and he didn't care. Flexing his hand inside his Smartware glove, he felt nothing but hatred for his former crewmate. He couldn't understand why a Dome-born woman would ruin her body with Tellurium when she had a perfectly good alternative. There were those who said that Smartware wasn't as fast as Tellurium, wasn't as sensitive, and maybe they were right. But it didn't disfigure. It didn't turn the user into something less than human.

Settling himself into the pilot's chair, Bryant checked the programming of the autopilot, satisfied himself that it was functioning correctly, then moved back over to his usual position at the comm. station. Soon he'd have another warrant to chase, but before that, he had time to kill. Maybe he'd dock at one of the quieter space stations and buy himself a few hours with a pleasure droid. Maybe he'd dock at one of the louder stations, get ragingly drunk, and buy himself a few hours with two pleasure droids. He'd been locked up with Jinn for too bloody long.

It had given him a thrilling sense of pleasure to shoot her with that stunner, to see her eyes widen, her mouth fall open in shock before she collapsed at his feet in a helpless, twitching heap. He'd seen the way she looked at him. She thought she was better than him. Thought she was better than everyone.

Stupid bitch.

Bryant wondered if she was dead yet. The A2 was a vicious place, a stinking cesspool filled with the sort of scum who weren't fit to mix with civilised society. He might have had some qualms about leaving a woman on board the A2, had that woman not been Jinn. She was a freak, a misfit, a fucking colony leech in a Dome-perfected body. What a waste. She could have been so much more.

As for Caspian Dax ... Personally, he thought Bugs should all be gassed rather than waste precious resources keeping them alive, and he wasn't the only one. Plenty of supplies destined for the A2 didn't make it there, and it was an unwritten rule that the

Security Service looked the other way. Why should the decent, hard-working people from the Domes pay tax just to feed lazy trash like that?

Turning to the console, Bryant logged in to the system and opened a secure channel. The screen flickered to life, bringing up the familiar pointy features of his direct superior back at base. It was a relief to see Dome-raised features that weren't marred by prosthetics. 'I've completed the contract,' Bryant informed him.

'Can you confirm that both prisoners are now on the A2?'

'Yes.'

'And both were unharmed and in good physical health?'

'Yes.' Bryant felt a streak of impatience, but procedure had to be followed, particularly with these classified warrants. There was no room for error, which suited Bryant just fine.

Because he didn't make mistakes.

'Excellent.' His commander smiled. 'I must congratulate you on a job well done, Bryant. I'm pleased to say that I have been authorised to promote you, effective immediately.'

Bryant felt a swell of satisfaction. A promotion meant a captaincy. That meant a bigger team, a bigger ship, more time in space, more credits. It meant more hunting, and fuck he loved the hunt. Most of all, he loved the moment when whoever he'd been chasing, sometimes for weeks, realised that the game was over. The look in their eyes when they saw the uniform, when they saw him, when they saw the end of their freedom standing in front of them. That was what he lived for. Bryant nodded his understanding. He didn't even try to keep the smile from his face.

'Return to base,' his commander said. 'I'll have your new ship and crew ready when you arrive.'

And then the screen went blank.

# CHAPTER
# 8

**22nd August 2207**

> Vessel: The *Alcatraz 2*. Prison ship
> Destination: N/A
> Cargo: N/A
> Crew: N/A
> Droids: Unknown

Jinn kept her gaze fixed firmly on the floor, on the stained panels that formed the base of the chamber. At some point this had all been shiny and pristine, but not any more. Now it was thick with years of human dirt, and the soles of her boots stuck to it as she kept walking, kept moving. It made her gag. All around her, the bars of the electric cages crackled and spat, throwing arcs of uncontained charge up to the ceiling. Sweat trickled down the side of her face. It soaked into her collar, making the fabric damp and uncomfortable.

She'd been bringing prisoners here for a long time. Six hundred warrants. Six hundred people. She wondered how many of them were in this chamber, trapped like animals inside these electrified cages. She slowed to a halt and risked a glance sideways. The cell closest to her held a young male, probably in his early twenties. He was tall and heavily built, his arms and legs thick with muscle though his face was lean. His dark hair was cropped close to his skull. The eyes were big and blue. There was no mistaking his Underworld heritage. Apart from the muscle, he looked relatively normal.

'Here,' he whispered, beckoning her over.

He moved closer to the bars, and she did too. 'Who are you?' she asked him. 'What happened to you?'

She saw his mouth move, saw him form words, but she couldn't hear him. She edged nearer, feeling the hot spark of the bars dangerously close to her face. 'What? What are you trying to tell me?'

A powerful arm swung out from between the buzzing yellow bars and grabbed her by the throat. The world swam before her eyes, yellow fading to swirling black as her oxygen supply was cut off. She slashed out with her blades, her legs starting to buckle, then, just as quickly, the hand was gone.

She sank to her knees. Her chest heaved as she fought down panic and fought to get air. Moving with a speed she could barely comprehend, Dax dug a fist into the front of her uniform and hauled her back onto her feet. 'Keep away from the cages. You don't know who is inside them, and we cannot get off this black hole if you get yourself killed. Understand?'

Jinn blinked. 'Yes,' she said, her voice thin and faint. Through the sparking bars of the cage, she could see the man huddled on the floor, nursing the slashed flesh of his arm. This time, when Dax motioned for her to move, Jinn didn't hesitate. She scrambled forward, breaking into a run, leaping over the cleaning bots that darted in front of her, refusing to look in any more of the cages. She didn't want to know. She didn't want to *see*. All she wanted to do was get out of this chamber.

Another spiralling staircase rose up at the far end, and she flung herself at it and started to climb. Her mind was a mess, fighting and failing to process everything that had happened and everything she had seen. She was almost at the top when Dax caught up with her. Her hands came up instinctively. Her blades were still out, and she saw his gaze lock on to them.

'What *are* those?' he asked.

She didn't answer. Instead, she lifted them a little higher, daring him to try something.

'Didn't you already try that?' he asked. 'As I recall, it didn't work.' His body moved close to hers, close enough to force her up against the central spine of the staircase. The metal was cold against her back. He angled her wrists up so that he could examine her blades, turning them this way and that. 'What is it? Something experimental? How does it work?'

'None of your damn business.'

He didn't argue. Instead he caged her wrists, holding her blades at waist height. The other hand came up to her jaw. He tipped her head from side to side. 'You're already healing.'

'Of course I am,' she snarled at him. 'Standard pilot modifications include accelerated healing so we can cope with the Tellurium.'

'But you don't have standard Tellurium,' he pointed out. 'Do you?'

'What is this, a personal evaluation?'

He raised an eyebrow, stared down at her. 'Not even close,' he said. 'I just wanted to make sure that you weren't injured. You're no use to me if you are.'

'You're no use to me either way,' she snapped back. 'So get off me.' She twisted free from his grasp, wanting to get out of this chamber, away from the heat and the noise and the stink and the creatures trapped within it. She could barely bring herself to think of them as human.

She scrambled onto the walkway, pressing herself tightly against the wall as she moved to the door that separated this chamber from the next. It only took her a moment to see that it had been sealed, just like the one at the other end. She had no choice but to step back and let Dax kick it out of the way.

Jinn pushed past him and clambered through into the

darkness of the next chamber, almost beyond caring what it contained. All she knew was that she had to keep moving. The A2 was crowding her, overwhelming her, making it almost impossible for her to think. She moved quickly, not waiting to see if Dax was following, knowing instinctively that he was. The air smelled different in here, fresher somehow, and she dragged in great lungfuls of it, wanting to clean out the filth she'd inhaled.

Dax came up behind her. 'How far are we from the control deck?'

'Not far,' Jinn told him. She studied him for a moment, as both of them worked to catch their breath. She was shaking with shock, with adrenalin. But she saw something else in him. 'You know something.'

'I know we're screwed if we can't get off this ship.'

'No.' Jinn shook her head. 'It's more than that. What do you know that I don't?'

'I could ask you the same thing,' he said. 'One minute I was in my chemicleanse, the next I was in the cargo hold of a transporter with you, and now I'm here.'

'The Security Service has been chasing outstanding warrants for months,' Jinn pointed out. 'It's hardly a secret. Everyone knows the government is trying to clean up, trying to persuade the Intergalactic Senate we're a race worth saving. You must have known we would come for you eventually.'

'So what did you do that was bad enough to have you left here?'

That was the question, wasn't it? And it was one she couldn't answer. 'Nothing,' she said. 'It was a mistake, that's all. Bryant, the agent I was working with, he must have had a breakdown. It happens sometimes, when people spend too much time in space.'

Although Bryant was the last person she'd expect it to happen to. In order to have a breakdown, one first had to be human.

'By my reckoning, we're in the central section of the ship,' she continued, changing the subject. The adrenalin surge was beginning to subside, something else taking its place. Her hands burned. She felt faintly dizzy. 'We should be able to access the ventilation tunnels from here. They'll lead us directly to the control deck.' She looked him up and down. 'It'll be a damn tight fit.'

'You worry about finding a way in,' Dax said. 'And let me worry about the fit.'

It didn't take her long to find what she was looking for. Jinn dropped into a crouch next to the ventilation duct. Her blades made short work of the mesh that covered it. Gripping the edge of the opening, she stared down into the darkness and forced herself to take a breath. She could handle this. It was simply mind over matter.

'I'll go first,' Dax said, setting a hand to her shoulder, stopping her from moving.

'Absolutely not.' Jinn shook her head, shrugging away the weight of his hand. 'If you get stuck, I'll have to use plan B.'

'What's plan B?'

'I have no idea.'

He made a sound that was almost a laugh, but didn't stop her as she scooted her way forward, sliding her hands down the tunnel, feeling the smooth lines of pipes and wiring. And then, with a single push of her feet, she tipped herself into it. She dropped vertically down, eyes tightly closed, the force of the fall making it impossible to breathe. The rush was incredible, and didn't lessen even when the tunnel began to level out. She jammed her feet into the sides, trying to slow herself down before she hit the solid wall at the end.

It still hurt like a bitch when she slammed into it. She lay there panting, listening to the sound of Dax swearing as he started his own descent. She rolled onto her stomach, started edging her way forward. The wiring would lead her to the control deck. Red and yellow tracked back to the phase drives at the rear of the ship. Green linked the comm. systems. Follow that, and she'd eventually find one that she could plug in to.

She didn't want to think about what would happen if she didn't.

She hadn't been kidding when she said it would be a tight fit. The edges of the shaft tore at his clothing and bit into his skin, and the hot smell of blood filled his nostrils. When he crashed to a halt at the bottom, the metal buckling under his weight, Dax decided that the next time Jinn had a bright idea, he would tell her where she could stick it. He lifted his head a little, saw her disappear out of sight, dropping headfirst into what he could only assume was another shaft. He closed his eyes and silently cursed. There was barely enough room for him to squeeze his shoulders through this one, and the last thing he wanted to do was tip himself headfirst down another vertical drop. But judging by the odd little scratching sounds echoing through the tunnel, his blood was attracting unwelcome visitors. Like it or not, he had to keep moving. He forced himself on, pulling with his fingertips, pushing against the side of the shaft. Every centimetre of movement caused another agonising rip in his flesh.

When he opened his eyes, he could see faint illumination coming from the hole she'd dropped through, and he felt a sudden touch of hope. The light was pale blue. That meant a comm. station. Nothing else on board would give off that particular glow. With another snarl and the closest thing he'd said to a prayer in years, Dax stretched out, grabbed the edge of the opening, and dragged himself through.

He crashed to the floor in a heavy, bleeding, clumsy mess, and it took him far longer than he would have liked to right himself. Jinn lay on the floor close to where he'd landed, curled into a small, shivering ball. Forcing himself up onto his knees, Dax shuffled over to where she lay. She better not be injured. He needed her in one piece if she was going to interface with the comm. and contact the *Mutant*.

He lifted a hand to her shoulder, shook her. 'Get up,' he said.

Her eyes flew open, those dark, fathomless eyes. And then she shot out a hand. He saw the flash of her blade, the lethal spike glinting in the pale blue light, as it shot towards his face in an explosion of movement that even he couldn't track. He knew what she was going to do, and he braced himself for the pain. But it didn't come. Instead, she collapsed back down, a wriggling, shrieking, spitting creature stuck on the end of her blade. 'It was going to bite you,' she said faintly.

His belly churned as he stared at the crax. Her blade had pierced its shell and the soft underbelly was exposed. Fluid dripped from it, creating an acid-yellow puddle on the floor. It stared at him with a dozen angry eyes, its wide jaw opening to reveal row after row of hooked black teeth, and it chattered. It was hungry. Dax got slowly to his feet, never taking his eyes off the creature. Then he put the heel of his boot against it, easing it off the end of her blade. He put his weight on it and kept it there until he was certain the damn thing was dead.

'Thanks,' he said. She looked pale, faint. 'Did one of them bite you?'

'No,' she said.

'Are you sure? You look like death warmed up.'

'I . . . I haven't eaten.'

The Tellurium. Pilots were notorious for getting sick if they didn't eat enough to fuel their tech, and she had far more of it than she should. He should have predicted this. If he hadn't been so caught up with trying to figure out what in the void was going on here, he would have. 'Can you stand?'

She set her hands to the floor, started to push upright. The skin under her eyes was dark, and she was so pale that he could see the blue tracery of veins under her skin. 'Of course,' she said, as she got unsteadily to her feet, but he could see that it took more effort than she was letting on.

'Steady,' he said, as she swayed on her feet. He caught her right before she fell, lowering her into the swivel chair mounted in front of what he immediately identified as the ship's main comm. station. The link was active, albeit suspended, the port gleaming.

Shit. They'd found their ticket out of here, and she was too weak to use it. He swept his gaze over the room, on the off chance that there might be an Autochef, or a supply of silver rice stashed in a corner. But no. The control deck was smaller than he expected, much smaller than the one on the *Mutant*. Enough room for a comm. operator and a pilot, and that was about it. He glanced across at Jinn, saw her slowly lift her hands to the console. With lightning-quick reflexes, Dax moved over to the comm. station. 'No,' he said. 'We need to find you something to eat first.' They were feeding the prisoners, which meant there had to be a supply room somewhere.

She slowly shook her head. 'No time,' she said. One wobbly hand lifted, pointed to the opening of the shaft they'd dropped through. 'There'll be more of them,' she said. 'We need to get out of here before they arrive.'

Dax glanced up. The opening to the shaft was a good four metres above their heads, a height which even he couldn't reach. From somewhere inside it, he heard the sickening scuttle of more crax. One or two he could deal with. But there could be hundreds living in those tunnels, and the blood trail he'd left would soon draw them in. Add to that the stink from the dead one, and he and Jinn were a sitting lunch.

They wouldn't be able to come back here once the crax started dropping through. It would simply be too dangerous. If they were going to make contact with his crew on board the *Mutant*, it had to be now. He dropped to his knees on the floor next to Jinn, put a hand on her shoulder to hold her steady. 'Can you open a channel?'

'I ... I think so.' She flexed her fingers and then placed her hands carefully over the ports. Dax held his breath as he waited for her to plug in. If she couldn't connect ...

A moment later he saw her tense, heard the quiet snap as the nanotech emerged from her hands and burrowed its way down into the console, providing the perfect interface between wetware and hardware. It was a technology that still astounded him. The screen flickered to life, code rushing across the screen as the computer recognised that it had been accessed.

'Damn it.'

'Problem?'

'It's got an intrusion-prevention system,' she said. 'It doesn't want to talk to me.'

'Can you bypass it?'

'I think so,' she said. Her body was stiff, her concentration absolute. She closed her eyes, her mouth twisting hard as she fought to control the system with nothing more than the flow of neurotransmitters across her synapses.

'Unplug,' he said, suddenly very aware of how white she was, the grey tinge to her lips, the glassy sheen coating her eyes.

'No,' she said. 'I can get in. I just need another minute.'

But they didn't have another minute. A sickening noise filled the control deck, the sound of dozens of pairs of legs marching in their direction. Dax glanced up, saw a black claw hook over the edge of the opening. 'No,' he said. 'We'll find another comm. station you can plug into.'

'What if we can't?'

Shit. 'We'll think of something,' he said, rising to his feet. 'Come on. We're getting out of here.'

A sharp thunk sounded behind him. Dax didn't turn around. He didn't need to see the creature that had just hit the floor. 'Now!' he said, his voice sharp as his chest tightened. When his time to die came, he'd deal with it. But he bloody well wasn't going to die from a crax bite. They were out of here, comm. station or no comm. station.

Then the screen flickered, the code disappearing, replaced by glowing white. 'I'm in,' she said.

'Channel seventeen.' Dax spat the words out, gripped the back of her chair. 'Stream six, data link one-four-seven. Code C.'

Another thunk came from behind him, and this time he did look. The crax that had hit the floor was a big bastard. Four claws rose a metre in the air, the end of each one rimmed with vicious teeth. It stared at him with flat, creepy eyes. A small dark tongue pushed out of its mouth, dripping foaming brown saliva onto the floor.

'Dax!' The voice, so familiar, came from the vid screen.

He didn't take his eyes off the creature, didn't look at the screen. The second he stopped watching, it would make its move. '*Alcatraz 2*,' he said. 'Rear docking bay.'

'We're six jumps out,' came the reply. 'Two days. Think you can hold on that long?'

Dax wasn't sure he could hold on for the next two minutes. 'Just fucking get here,' he snarled. And then he grabbed Jinn under one arm. 'Unplug,' he ordered her. Her head tipped back, her eyes unfocussed, her mouth slack. He shook her, not knowing what else to do. 'Unplug!' he said again, more urgently this time. He heard the crax scuttle behind him, felt the seeking pressure of a claw feeling its way up his leg. He turned to see a rush of them tumbling down into the room as that big one slid its open claw towards his groin. With a curse, Dax kicked it right in the face. Its flat, leathery body flew backwards, crashing into the others. They leapt on it, screaming with hunger.

'Come on!' he shouted, turning his attention back to the woman who might just have saved his life for the second time. The dead crax would buy them a few seconds, nothing more, and by the time the others finished with it they'd be angry. If she didn't unplug, she was as good as dead. And he wasn't going to let that happen. He dropped to a crouch, gripped her chin and turned her head, forcing her to meet his gaze. She was still conscious – just. 'Jinn,' he said. 'You've got to unplug. Now.'

She blinked, slowly. 'No-one calls me Jinnifer,' she said. Then she closed her eyes, her face screwing tight. The screen flashed as she disconnected. It was the only signal Dax needed. In one swift movement he had her over his shoulder and was sprinting for the control room exit.

The doors were closed. Thick moulded steel, he could kick his way through them, but that would take time, and let the crax follow them. Getting a tight hold on her limp body, Dax smashed the control panel at the side of the door. Sparks flew as he ripped away the wires, deactivating the electromagnets that held the doors closed. Then he stiffened his fingers, dug them into the gap between the doors. Slowly, painfully, he forced his hand between them, then his arm, his shoulder. With an almighty roar, he forced the doors fully apart and shoved his way through them.

They slammed shut behind him, trapping the stretching claw of a hungry crax. It twitched for a moment, then fell to the floor with the claw still clicking. Dax made a mental note to have the *Mutant* docked and deep-cleaned the moment he got back on board.

The corridor was long, narrow and smelled of rust and oil. It was also empty. Dax didn't wait around to find out if they were truly alone. He needed to find the supply room, and he needed to find it now.

# CHAPTER

# 9

## 22nd August 2207

Vessel: The *Alcatraz 2*. Prison ship
Destination: N/A
Cargo: N/A
Crew: N/A
Droids: Unknown

Someone was pushing something into her mouth, something foul and familiar. Silver rice. Jinn swallowed, forcing the sticky mush down her throat. More was shoved onto her tongue and she swallowed that too, the effort a little easier this time, though when the third mouthful came, she turned her head, resulting in a cold smear across her cheek.

She wiped at it with her fingers and struggled into a sitting position, forcing her eyes to open. Her vision swam before Caspian Dax crowded it. Dirt and what looked like dried blood streaked his skin, his hair a matted mess. His eyes, those bright green eyes, were fixed on her.

'What do they call you?' he asked.

'What?'

'If no-one calls you Jinnifer, what do they call you?'

'Bryant called me Blue,' she said, blinking. 'Or bitch, some-times freak bitch.'

'So what should I call you?'

'Jinn,' she said. Her voice sounded very far away, and darkness touched the edge of her vision again. A strong hand squeezed her shoulder, shook her back to consciousness.

'People call me Dax,' he said. The corners of his mouth creased into an almost-smile. 'Well, some people.'

'Not pirate?'

'You can call me pirate if you want,' he said, getting to his feet. 'But I wouldn't recommend it.' He took a couple of steps away, picked up another foil packet from a pile on what looked like a bunk minus padding and covers. He ripped it open and then took a bite, grimacing as it hit his tongue.

'Don't tell me you don't like it,' Jinn said.

'I grew up eating this shit,' he said. 'It's not an experience I like to repeat too often. I'm guessing it's still a novel experience for you, though.'

The food was hitting her system fast. It was designed to need minimal digestion, and her body was already starting to respond to it. The pain in her muscles was decreasing, and her head no longer felt too heavy for her neck to hold up.

'I've eaten my fair share of it over the years,' she told him. 'Just because I was Dome-raised doesn't mean my entire life has been comfort and luxury.'

'It's not exactly been bed bugs and malnutrition either, has it?'

'That's hardly my fault,' she said, then shook her head. 'Did we contact your crew?'

'Yes,' he said grimly.

'And?'

'They were six jumps out,' he replied. 'We need to be in the docking bay thirty-six hours from now.'

That many jumps … Jinn did a quick mental calculation. 'I've been out for twelve hours?' Half a day, lost to darkness. Anything could have been done to her in that time. Instinctively, she fumbled her hands over her uniform, checking to see if it was still fastened.

'I didn't touch you,' he said, 'if that's what you're worried about. I prefer my women awake and participating.'

'Good to know,' she said, switching her gaze to the floor, feeling heat sear her cheeks. It wasn't good. She didn't want to know. Silence drifted over them, broken only by the hum of the ship. She tried to think of something, anything to say, but her brain refused to cooperate.

'Who touched you?' His words made her jump, made her stiffen. 'Was it Bryant?'

Her hands burned, the tips of her blades scratching into the floor. It felt strange, no longer having to hide them. 'It doesn't matter.'

'Who?' he asked again.

'It was a long time ago,' she told him. 'Like I said, it doesn't matter.'

'Who?' he asked for a third time, and she knew he wasn't going to let it go until she gave him the answer he wanted.

'A couple of my old crewmates,' she said, scratching a swirling pattern into the floor. Under the grime, the metal was shiny.

'Did you report them?'

'No.'

'Why not?'

Jinn closed her eyes. 'Because I had prosthetics to pay for,' she said. 'And because I didn't want to make my life any worse than it already was.' She opened her eyes then, and looked at him, looked right at him. Twenty years might have passed, but in some ways it felt like only a few minutes. His hair might be shorter, and there might be a shrewdness in his gaze that hadn't been there before, but he was still the same man who had boarded the *Finex*. 'Turns out that some people were a little pissed that you let me go.'

He didn't say anything. He just tossed aside the empty wrapper, folded his arms, and watched her.

'Not only was I a Dome bitch,' she told him, 'I was a Dome bitch who they thought had done a deal with a pirate to save my own skin. Somehow, word got round that I was the one with the grenade, not Zane, and that I'd threatened to kill everyone unless you let me take that escape pod. First day of my next contract, some of my crewmates decided that I needed to be taught a lesson, and that they were the ones to give it to me. One of the men tried to rape me in front of the two women I was bunking with.'

'Didn't they stop him?'

'They held me down,' she said. Her throat burned at the memory of it, at the fear, the humiliation she'd felt when they had stripped off her trousers and one of them had put a knee to her throat. 'They only let me go because one of the grav generators went into meltdown and it was all hands on deck. When we got shore leave, I had the extra Tellurium injected. The next time someone tried to teach me a lesson, I stabbed him in the balls.'

Dax didn't move. His expression gave nothing away. If he was disgusted by what she'd just told him, he didn't let it show. 'Then I suppose I should be grateful that you only stabbed me in the thigh.'

Jinn curled her hands into fists at her sides, feeling the heavy weight of the Tellurium. 'How long did you say it would be until your crew got here?'

'Thirty-six hours.'

'Then let's hope you've still got reason to be grateful by then.'

He smiled. 'Oh,' he said. 'I'm sure I will.'

But he moved a little further away.

By the next time they stopped to rest, Jinn had completely lost track of time. They ate more of the silver rice that Dax had taken from the supply room and stopped in what appeared to be a makeshift camp with rough furniture hand-hewn from scrap metal. There was no sign of either prisoners or droids, and she was grateful for that.

Neither of them mentioned what they had seen in the hold.

That didn't mean that they didn't talk, however. Dax asked questions. Lots of them. 'So why did you leave the Dome?' he asked, as he chewed down another bar of silver rice.

'Didn't like it,' Jinn told him.

'Why not?'

Jinn sighed. 'Have you ever been in the Dome?'

'A few times,' he said. 'My mother used to work as a cleaner on the hovercarts and sometimes she'd take me with her. Dome people are messy sods.'

'*Dome people?*'

'What do you want me to call them? You live in a completely different world to the rest of us.'

'I hardly think . . . '

'Have you even been in one of the Underworld cities?'

'No,' Jinn said. '*Dome people* don't go to Underworld cities.'

'It's a bit like this,' Dax said, gesturing to their surroundings. 'Only busier. And smellier.'

'It can't possibly be as bad as this. There aren't crax down there, for starters.'

'True,' he said. 'We've got cockroaches and slugs the size of your hand instead. You must miss home.'

'Nope.'

'Liar.' He leaned his head back against the wall and closed his eyes. 'All that purified air and decent food. Hard to believe you aren't wishing you were back there, tucked up all safe and warm in your nice Dome apartment.'

Jinn ignored him. He didn't have a clue. Luxury didn't mean anything when you had a mother like hers.

'You must go back sometimes,' he continued. 'I thought you agent types got plenty of home leave.'

'First, I'm not an agent, I'm a pilot and, second, I haven't taken home leave in years. I always work through it.' Her legs were sore, her whole body aching from the endless walking and the lack of food, but her brain was suddenly wide awake. 'How about you? Do you go back?'

'First, I'm a Bug and, second, I've got nothing to go back for.'

'You must have family and friends. Cockroaches and slugs you were particularly fond of.'

'Nope,' Dax said. He folded his arms, settling himself a little more comfortably against the wall. 'I've got my ship. Don't need anything else.'

He didn't ask her anything else, and eventually she fell asleep. She woke some time later, stiff and cold, to find him already awake. 'Time to get moving,' he said.

They didn't have much further to go, not really, though progress was slowed by blocked passageways and worse. Without humans to keep it clear, parasites had taken over the A2. Much of their time was spent avoiding them. By the time they reached the docking bay, Jinn had seen more bilehores, crax and tetrapedes than anyone should see in a lifetime, and really wanted a wash.

'We've made it,' she whispered, her legs suddenly weak. Gently humming in the centre of the docking bay was a small transporter ship. Not the *Hawk*, but similar. It had to be a Security Service ship.

If she could get to it, get on board, she could tell the crew Bryant had lost it, talk them into taking her with them. She darted forwards, the desire to get off the prison ship driving her onwards as all thoughts of the past few days were drowned out by the need for escape.

Dax locked an arm around her waist, stopping her before she could even get to the end of the tunnel.

'Get off me!' she yelled, pulling against his grip. She kicked back, fighting him with everything she had. 'What are you playing at? There's a ship!'

But he didn't let go.

'Wait,' he said, pinning her against the wall and holding her in place. Jinn kicked out at him again, but if he felt the fierce impact of her thick-soled boots, he didn't let it show. Screaming was her only option until a large hand clamped firmly over her mouth, cutting off even that method of protest. His other hand grabbed her wrists before she could put her blades to use. And then Dax lowered his head and whispered softly in her ear. 'Look.'

Jinn slowly lifted her head, watching as the loading ramp of the transporter began to lower. It made contact with the floor of the docking bay, hydraulic arms hissing as they came to a halt. The smell of Diborane touched her senses a few seconds later. She instinctively held her breath.

But no-one appeared on the ramp. 'They're not coming out,' she said, after her heart had been pounding for what felt like forever. 'They're not coming out, Dax.'

And if she'd gone in, as she had intended, she'd be inhaling that gas right now, feeling her lungs start to burn as it ate through all the moist tissues inside her body. Jinn turned her head, pressed her face against the hard plane of his chest, disgusted with herself. She'd lost her head and he had kept his. Left to her own devices, she'd be dead.

Then Dax stiffened. 'Bloody supernova,' he said.

Jinn turned her head, blinking in shock as someone finally emerged from the transporter and made their way down the ramp. The man was at least as tall as Dax, and when he stepped into the light of the bay, she saw that he was stripped to the waist, displaying the well-developed muscles of his upper arms and abdomen. His jet-black hair was pulled back from his face and his skin was patterned with the angular ink of someone who had spent time on Sittan, a planet in the outer rim occupied by a violent race of humanoid creatures who had a penchant for fighting and – it was rumoured – an even greater thirst for human blood. She'd heard the stories of the Bugs who made their living in the Sittan arena, but she'd never seen one in the flesh before. She hadn't been entirely convinced that they existed.

'Who is he?' she whispered to Dax. 'Why didn't the gas kill him?'

'Jozeph Li,' Dax replied. 'He's a mercenary. A thief. A pain in the arse.'

'You know him?'

'We've had a few encounters.' His tone told her that those encounters had not been pleasant. 'The last one cost me a ship.'

Li swaggered to the end of the ramp. He looked loose and relaxed, but Jinn could see the subtle tension in him, the way his muscles were deceptively tight, his gaze sliding rapidly around the bay. It settled on the shadows they were hiding in, and for the briefest of moments, she thought he saw them. Then his gaze slid away, and she knew he'd seen the tunnel on the other side of the docking bay, the same one she'd sprinted down. 'We have to stop him,' she said to Dax.

'Agreed.' He rose to his feet, pushing her behind him. 'Li,' he called, as he stepped to the edge of the shadows, moving towards the other man with impressive stealth.

Li turned his head. 'Caspian Dax,' he said. There was no surprise in his tone. 'I heard you'd been arrested.'

Dax angled his head in confirmation. 'My crew are on their way. I'm willing to offer you transport.'

The edges of Li's mouth quirked up. 'You have nothing to offer me, pirate,' he said. He looked up, sweeping his gaze over the roof of the docking bay. 'This place can't hold me,' he said. 'Not unless I choose to let it.'

Jinn stepped forward, putting herself beside Dax. Li's eyes widened in surprise when he saw her. 'This place isn't a prison ship any more,' she told him. 'All the prisoners are gone. We think they've been gassed, their remains dumped out in space. We saw . . . ' But the rest of what she had wanted to say was lost in the roar of the transporter, its engines firing up as the loading ramp moved swiftly upwards. Li made a sudden movement, darting towards it and hooking his fingers over the edge of the ramp as it rose.

The cargo bay doors began to open. Beyond them, space stretched out to infinity, blue-black and dotted with the white light of all the visible stars. Then, seemingly from nowhere, another transporter filled the opening. It shot forwards, growing larger by the second as it moved towards them. This was not a

Security Service ship. It was battered and old, without Earth markings streaking the sides. As for the way it was moving … no-one could fly like that. Not even her. She watched in disbelief as it danced through the air, its trajectory anything but straight and yet surprisingly direct.

'That's our ride,' Dax said. 'Get ready to move.'

But the Security Service transporter was still moving, and there was no way that both ships were going to be able to fit through the open cargo-bay doors. There simply wasn't room. A collision was inevitable. Unless …

The battered transporter turned on its side, skimming the roof of the cargo bay as it shot towards them. Dax grabbed her hand and pulled her forwards and together they raced along the length of the bay. They couldn't risk getting too close to the open doors, though, not without being sucked out into the vacuum of space. The bay was designed to keep constant air circulation and gravity at the landing end, but the open end was exposed to the outside universe. The yellow line that marked the end of the safety zone was fast approaching. Jinn slowed. 'We can't cross the line,' she yelled at Dax.

'Hold on tight,' was all he said.

So she dug her fingers into his hand, hard enough to hurt, held her breath and trusted him. Ahead of them, she could see the dark figure of Jozeph Li, still hanging from the ramp of the Security Service transporter. The muscles in his arms bunched as he hauled himself up. He got his elbows onto the edge of the ramp.

A laser rifle mounted on the hull of the transporter swivelled and shot him.

His fall seemed to happen in slow motion, his arms circling as he plummeted to the floor of the bay. He landed with elegance, tucking his body into a roll as he hit the deck.

'Li!' Dax yelled. The word seemed to thunder around the bay, and Jinn saw the other man's head jerk up as he saw them. The Security Service transporter was almost at the cargo-bay doors. She could already feel the pull of space touching her skin, her hair flying to cover her face and her speed increasing as it dragged her forwards. The ramp on the new ship was down, revealing its dark insides.

And then it changed direction. Suddenly it wasn't moving towards them any more but away, back towards the cargo-bay doors. They were slowly closing, the black of space being replaced by the rusted brown of the doors, and Jinn felt her insides start to squeeze. She glanced back again, saw Li running at incredible speed, and stretched out her hand. 'Come on!' she yelled, but the words were snatched away by the air. He had to catch up with them. He had to.

She felt Dax's hand close over her arm. She was no longer in control. The pull had her now, dragging her out into the emptiness of space. Dax held on to her tightly, pinning her arms against her sides as they shot through the air like a bullet from a blaster.

And then they were in the belly of the little ship. Gravity dragged them down. The impact knocked the air out of her lungs, leaving her gasping and unable to breathe, unable to do anything but lie sprawled on the floor with the heavy weight of Caspian Dax on top of her as the hydraulics whined and the belly of the ship closed up, enveloping them in darkness and air that smelled of an engine pushed well beyond its limits. Then she felt the jolt that signalled that they had left the cargo bay and were out in the expanse of space, followed by the sharp pull of a phase drive working at full capacity.

'We have to go back for him,' she whispered.

'We can't,' Dax said, lifting his weight off hers. Without his warmth she felt cold, and without his weight to hold her down, she felt lost. But Jinn wasn't someone who felt lost, and when she felt cold, she dealt with it. She did so now, forcing herself to her feet. Her uniform was stiff in some places, slimy in others. She probably stank. No, she *did* stink. She felt sore and filthy and disgusting. Exhaustion weighed her down like a steel jacket.

But at least she was alive. She couldn't think about Jozeph Li, or all the others she'd seen trapped in that second chamber, because she knew that if she thought about them she might cease to function and she couldn't let that happen. Not when she was on board a strange vessel, she didn't know where she was going, and she was with a man she trusted far more than was wise.

Jinn hoped her legs would hold as a door opened on the other side of the small hold. Brightness scorched her retinas, and she whipped up a hand to shade her eyes. The days spent in the relative darkness of the A2 had left her unprepared for the sudden sensory onslaught.

In the full beam of the light, Dax looked even bigger, even darker. His jaw was rough with stubble, his thin top shredded almost to nothing, showing flashes of grimy skin. Dried blood covered his upper arms, his hands. Jinn tried not to stare. And then she got her first look at the woman in the doorway, and it became impossible.

'Dax,' the woman said, as she moved into the tiny loading bay. 'If you'd wanted to spend a few days living it rough, all you had to do was ask.'

'Eve,' he said. 'Good to see you.'

'You too,' the woman replied. 'I take it prison didn't suit you?'

He shrugged. 'I didn't like the food.'

The woman still hadn't spared Jinn as much as a glance, and if she'd noticed that Jinn was openly staring at her, she didn't let it show. But Jinn couldn't help herself. The woman, Eve, was small, with big eyes and full lips and obvious, feminine curves that would have been frowned upon in the Domes. Her dark hair was knotted back in a twist at the base of her neck. She wore a soft dress that covered her from neck to wrist, fitting to the hip and then dropping to the floor in jagged folds. It was a beautiful deep bronze, matched by tall boots and ornate metal cuffs at the wrist. Life as a pirate was obviously bloody good because it couldn't have been cheap.

But all of that was insignificant. Because Eve was green. Undeniably, inexplicably green. Every centimetre of visible skin was the colour of grass.

'Looks like you didn't like the cleansing facilities, either,' Eve said. 'What in the galaxy happened, Dax? When we came back from Zeta 3, you'd gone. Vanished into thin air. And the security feed had been tampered with.'

'Someone sold me out,' he said. 'Someone told a bastard agent where to find me. One minute I'm in my cabin, minding my own business, the next I'm in the hold of a Security Service transporter feeling like I've taken enough blockers to kill an arctic wolverine.'

'Someone in the crew?'

'Has to be,' Dax replied.

Eve swore softly, and then, quick as a spark, switched her attention to Jinn. 'And her?'

'She was dumped on board with me,' he said. His hands moved to the front of his shredded shirt, and in one swift move, he pulled it off, dropping it into the recycling chute concealed in the floor by his feet. Jinn averted her gaze, but not before she'd had more than a glimpse of acres of golden skin laid over heavy muscle, and dark body hair. Her throat felt strange, but she put that down to thirst, exhaustion, stress.

'That didn't mean you had to bring her with you,' Eve said. 'The last thing we need is security agents chasing after us because we kidnapped some Dome woman. Who is she, anyway?'

'My name is Jinnifer Blue,' Jinn said. 'I was the pilot on the Security Service transporter that took Dax to the A2. My partner stunned me and put me in the hold with Dax.'

The other woman stiffened, her mouth tightening. 'You're Jinnifer Blue? Daughter of that government minister?'

'Yes.'

The woman, Eve, moved closer, close enough for Jinn to see that her skin wasn't uniformly green. A swirling pattern edged up the side of her neck, almost to her ear. Eve's yellow eyes tracked over the prosthetic that curved around Jinn's temple. Then, without uttering another word, she turned on her heel and marched out of the small cargo hold. The doors slid shut behind her.

Jinn watched her go. She subtly curled and uncurled her fingers, feeling the heat from her Tellurium. When they'd found the caged people on the A2 and Dax had refused to tell her what he knew, she'd let it go. But not this time. This time she wanted answers, and he was going to give them to her.

'I want to know what you know,' she told him. 'I want to know why that man on the A2 was almost able to kill me. And I want to know why you've got a green woman on your crew!'

Dax stared down at her. His expression was grim. 'Because thirty years ago Medipro decided to experiment with splicing animal DNA into human cells, and we were the result. And going by what we saw on the A2, it looks like they've decided to have another try.'

# CHAPTER
# 10

News of Senator Rizzola's illness had spread fast. What had started as seemingly nothing more than a low-level virus had failed to respond to treatment, and the media had eagerly pounced on the story. Ferona had already made the necessary travel arrangements by the time Rizzola was admitted to a medical facility, though no-one other than her personal assistants were aware of it. Leaving Swain in charge of her office in the London Dome, she made the three-hour journey to Mexico City on board her personal hoverjet, accompanied by Lucinda and a beauty droid.

The jet set down on the Dome landing port, inside this time, instead of outside, as it had been in Paris. They ignored the train in favour of a private cab, paying extra to expedite the journey. It took thirty minutes to reach the medical facility. Press cameras were already hovering outside, filming the coming and going of patients and visitors, and Ferona was grateful for the attention of the beauty droid.

She used her personal comm. to check her appearance. It transmitted a small 3D hologram of her head and shoulders. Her hair was tidy, though not overly styled. But her makeup was a masterpiece. She looked exactly as she needed to – like a woman who was deeply concerned about the well-being of a colleague and friend. Her skin had the perfect hint of paleness, her eyes showed the perfect degree of strain.

With Lucinda at her side, she exited the private cab, ordering the driver to wait. She drew to her full height, giving the cameras the view they wanted for the newsfeed, and walked quickly towards the entrance, though not so quickly that the interviewers, identified by the flashing identification passes they wore on long silver lanyards, couldn't ask their questions.

'Minister Blue! What is the news on Senator Rizzola?'

'Is it true that she's been poisoned?'

'Many suspect our alien neighbours of foul play. What do you have to say about this?'

Ferona slowed and turned to them. Her voice held the perfect amount of distress. 'I am here to visit a respected colleague and loyal friend,' she said. 'Please do not bother me at this difficult time.'

Head bowed, she made her way through the doors and inside the hospital, Lucinda at her side. Within moments, those few seconds would be playing out on the streaming newsfeeds, exactly as she wanted them to be.

'The president arrived an hour ago,' Lucinda informed her discreetly as a greeter droid drew up alongside. They both submitted to identification checks and stood in the sterilisation booth for the necessary two minutes before the droid led them to the third level, and the isolation room where Rizzola was being treated. Despite everything, the senator's appearance was a shock.

The isolation room was small, containing little more than a medibed and a single medidroid. The lights had been dimmed. They cast a soft glow through the clear Plastex wall that separated Rizzola from the outside world. President Vexler sat on a single chair, staring into the room. Vice President Dubnik stood next to him, his back stiff, hands clasped tightly at his front. He wasn't wearing his usual dark suit. Instead, his clothes were crumpled and untidy, looking very much as if he had stumbled out of bed and come straight here, though Vexler was as perfectly turned out as always.

The place smelled of the expected cleaning fluids. Ferona wrinkled her nose in distaste. 'President,' she said, moving forward to place a comforting hand on his shoulder. 'Such a terrible thing to have happened. Is there any news?'

'We're waiting for the medic,' Dubnik informed her.

'Of course,' Ferona said.

She placed her hand against the cool surface and looked at the woman in the bed. Rizzola was almost skeletal. The bones of her face were deeply pronounced, and half of her hair was missing. She leaned forward, racked by a spasm of coughs that went on and on and on, then collapsed back on the bed.

Ferona had rarely seen illness. Few Dome dwellers had. There was little that modern medicine couldn't cure, provided you could afford treatment. She stared at Rizzola with curiosity. She hadn't known it would be so cruel, so ugly. Or so slow. In the Domes, when the Rejuvinix treatments no longer worked, when organs could no longer be repaired, an easy death at an End of Life centre was arranged. It was quick, tidy, painless. She couldn't help but wonder why Rizzola was refusing to take that route.

'Ferona.' The voice was weak, thin. It came from the woman in the bed, carried through the internal speaker system.

'Ana. How are you?'

'They can't find what's wrong with me,' Rizzola said. 'They think I might have picked something up on my last trip to Kepler. Are you showing any signs . . . ' She broke off for another coughing fit.

Ferona hesitated, but only for a moment. 'No,' she said finally. 'I am quite well.' She felt the faintest prickle of guilt, but it was slight, and it quickly disappeared. After all, it was Rizzola's choice to drag this out, to reject an easy death in favour of slowly rotting in a medibed with the world watching as every shred of dignity was torn away.

'You should have a medical assessment anyway,' Rizzola told her. 'Better to be safe than sorry.' She coughed again, splattering her hand and the bed sheets with black slime. The medidroid shot forward and started to clean as Ferona turned away.

Rizzola was right. It was better to be safe than sorry, which was why Ferona had scrapped the beauty droid that had sprayed the attenuated Shi-Fai toxin onto the lining of Rizzola's senatorial robes. It would be almost impossible for the medics here on Earth to figure out that it was the cause of Rizzola's illness, and even if they did, the Shi-Fai would be blamed. It would be written off as an accident, a hazard of the job.

The door at the end of the corridor quietly slid open and a medic entered. His identification badge indicated that his name was Christo, and that he was a toxicology specialist. He was young, blond, and looked outrageously healthy in his pristine white scrubs. His skin almost seemed to glitter. Ferona made a mental note to find out what rejuvenation procedure he used. It would look wonderful on screen.

'Minister Blue,' he said. His dark eyes shone as he looked her over, then let his gaze stray to Lucinda for a moment before sliding it across to Vexler. 'President,' he said. 'I have the test results you wanted.'

'Good,' Vexler replied. He got slowly to his feet, smoothed down the front of his jacket, and turned to the viewing window. 'Goodbye, Ana.'

Rizzola said nothing. Her eyes were closed, her breathing loud and laboured as the droid continued to clean around her.

'Please, follow me,' the medic said. He started to walk to the end of the corridor, away from the isolation room. Vexler followed, back straight, head held high. Dubnik looked at Rizzola. Then he followed the others. Not wanting to be left behind, Ferona went with them.

Dubnik stopped her. 'This doesn't concern you.'

'Of course it does,' Ferona said crisply. 'Ana is my friend. And if she picked something up on Kepler, I need to know. I've been there four times in the last six months alone.'

When the medic opened a door and ushered Vexler through it, Ferona followed, daring Dubnik to make a fuss. She could tell by the look on Dubnik's face that he didn't like it. His jaw was set hard, and his dark eyes remained sharp. But he said nothing.

The office was comfortable and spacious, the furniture informal. Ferona took a seat on one of the padded couches. Vexler did the same. The medic remained standing long enough to move to the Autochef and offer koffee.

Ferona accepted graciously. As she sipped the dark liquid, she took a moment to enjoy the landscape window. The outside world was hidden, replaced with green rolling hills and blue sky. Every detail was perfect, from the fluffy clouds to the individual blades of grass that swayed in the breeze. It was beautiful.

One day, humans would have this again.

'Her heart is failing,' Christo said, taking his own seat. 'The disease also appears to be attacking her brain stem. We've tried everything we can to reverse the process, of course.'

'Of course,' Vexler agreed.

Ferona waited for him to add something further, but he did not. So she leaned forward. 'There must be something you can do,' she said. She could feel the wet heat of tears in her eyes. She blinked and let one fall.

Vexler reached out and took her hand. His fingers were cool, firm, and Ferona knew the gesture hadn't escaped Dubnik's notice. She didn't want it to.

The medic rested one ankle against his knee and tapped his fingers on his calf. He looked at each one of them, and she could tell he was trying to decide what to say. He was facing three of the most powerful people on the planet. But none of them were blood relatives, and he had his own rules to abide by.

'We've run a full battery of tests,' he said finally. 'Until we can identify the cause of the illness, there is little we can do.'

'But you will be able to identify it,' Dubnik said. His voice was strained.

'Eventually,' Christo replied, though his tone betrayed his lack of confidence.

Ferona took another sip of her koffee, let it linger on her tongue. 'When will that be?'

'We don't know,' Christo admitted.

'You must have some idea what it is!' Dubnik exploded. 'A virus? Something in her DNA? What?'

'It's impossible to rule anything out at this stage. But we're doing everything we can. We think it might be connected to the flu outbreak in New York, so we've put Ms Rizzola on a combination of anti-virals but we don't know yet if they're going to work.'

'That's not good enough!' The vice president shot to his feet, his body vibrating with anger.

'Unfortunately, it's the best we can do,' Christo replied. He remained where he was, but Ferona could see that the outburst of temper had rattled him.

'Mikhal,' Vexler said. His tone was calm, controlled. Everything that Dubnik was not.

Slowly, Dubnik turned back to the window, but his shoulders were rigid with fury.

'Dr Christo,' Vexler said. 'As I'm sure you can appreciate, I'm a very busy man, and I've taken time away from my schedule to visit Senator Rizzola. Now, I understand that this is a difficult case. But I've got a planet to run, and I need some answers. Be honest with me, if you will. How long before Senator Rizzola is fit to return to work?'

Christo went still. He flicked an anxious glance at Dubnik, so quickly that Ferona would have missed it if she hadn't been looking for it. Then his gaze settled on Vexler. He cleared his throat and clasped his hands tightly together. 'I'm afraid Senator

Rizzola will not be returning to work,' he said, the words delivered in a practised, steady monotone. 'I'm sorry to tell you this, President Vexler, but Senator Rizzola is dying. And at the moment there's nothing we can do to stop it.'

Everyone in the room went still. There was a moment of perfect silence. On the view window, a perfect cloud tripped across the perfect sky. Ferona could almost smell the flowers, the grass, could almost feel the heat.

'I see,' Vexler said.

And that was it. With those two little words, the situation was understood and accepted. He rose to his feet, held out his hand to Christo. They shook hands, and Vexler thanked him for his time.

Dubnik asked him to keep trying.

Ferona lingered a moment longer. The next few minutes would be crucial, but her timing would have to be right.

'President,' she said. 'Can we talk?'

'Of course, Ferona,' he said. He stood up and followed her from the room, leaving Dubnik behind.

They walked together through the medical centre, led by an assistant droid that had zoomed in alongside them the moment they left Christo's office. Vexler was tall, his strides long, but Ferona was more than able to keep pace. The droid led them through into a garden. A waterfall rushed from the ceiling, plunging into a circular pool surrounded by a low wall built from shimmering rocks mined on Colony Two. It was a pretty, calming place.

'I did not expect Ana to be so ill,' Ferona said. It was not entirely a lie. 'It is ... this has come as something of a shock.'

She expected Vexler to agree, to mourn with her. But he didn't.

'Dubnik does not trust you,' he said.

Ferona opened her mouth, then closed it again. She sensed that now was not the time to defend herself. Instead, she concentrated on slowly putting one foot in front of the other, listening to the hum of the waterfall, feeling the tight hold of her dress.

Vexler stopped. 'Can I trust you, Ferona?'

She was forced to turn, slowly, so that she could face him. Spine straight, she linked her hands together. Her fingers were decorated with antique opals, her personal comm. unit tucked away inside the wide fall of her sleeve. She knew he would appreciate the jewellery. Vexler was big on appearances. 'Yes,' she said. 'Let us be honest with each other, William. Ana's ... illness has left you with a vacancy,' she said. 'Under normal circumstances, there would be time for nominations. For a ministerial vote. But these are not normal circumstances. You need someone who can represent Earth's interests in the senate, someone who understands our alien neighbours, someone who can walk into that role and get straight to work.'

'I don't have time to play political games, Ferona.'

'I know,' Ferona said. She understood what Vexler was not saying. He was afraid of his next in command. 'That's why I wanted to talk to you in private. I am willing to take Ana's place. I am already known in the Intergalactic Senate. It would be a simple transition.'

'It would not be an easy transition. And you would be required to continue your work as Minister for Off World Affairs, for the time being at least.'

'That will not be a problem. I have excellent assistants. They are more than capable of dealing with things when I am at Kepler.'

'Good,' Vexler said. 'Good.' He offered Ferona his arm and she took it as they walked together around the waterfall. A violet-winged butterfly settled on Vexler's shoulder for a moment before fluttering away.

'Your appointment will still be subject to a vote by the senior ministers,' he said. 'But I do not foresee any problems with a majority voting in your favour. Do you?'

'Not at all,' Ferona told him. She could barely breathe. But she could not let her excitement show. It was vital that she remain calm. She had hoped, when she had decided to remove Rizzola, that Vexler would make this move. But it was never possible to be sure how others would react. Not even Lucinda could always predict people correctly.

Vexler patted her hand. 'The timing of this could not be worse,' he admitted. 'I received another update from Environmental Research this morning.'

'Bad news?'

'The temperature is dropping far faster than we had predicted. Some of the Domes are already beginning to degrade.'

'Already?'

This was not Ferona's area of expertise, but if Vexler said the Domes were starting to wear out, she believed him, and it made it all the more vital that she take up her place on the senate. From there, she would no longer have to keep her meetings with the Sittan and the Shi-Fai a secret. No-one would question what she was doing. If anything, it would be expected.

'Nothing lasts forever,' Vexler said.

'No,' Ferona agreed. 'It doesn't.'

And with that, Ferona took her leave. Satisfaction bubbled inside her, though it did not show on her face as she swept through the throng of press outside. Lucinda was waiting, standing next to the private cab they had used earlier.

They settled themselves into the back. Lucinda ordered the privacy screen to turn on. 'Well?' she asked.

Ferona allowed herself a small, restrained smile. 'It is done,' she said.

By the time they reached London, the ministerial votes had been cast, and she had been appointed Earth's representative on the Intergalactic Senate by eighty-three votes to seventy-four.

# CHAPTER

# 11

**24th August 2207**

> Vessel: The *Deviant*. Short-haul Corvette
> Destination: Neutral space
> Cargo: None
> Crew: Three
> Droids: One

'You should have left her there.' Eve flung herself into the seat at the comm. station. 'I know you always had a thing for Dome girls, but this is stupid, even for you.'

'Anything else you want to add?'

'Her mother is Minister for Off World Affairs! Earth space is going to be crawling with security ships, all looking for her. If we're caught with her on board ...'

'Then what?' Dax asked. 'They'll send us to one of the prisons? They'll do that anyway, if they catch us.'

'She doesn't belong here,' Eve continued. 'She's not one of us. I don't trust her, Dax, and neither should you.'

'*She* has a name.' The voice came from the rear of the control deck, and Dax glanced back to see Jinn stood by the door that led through from the hold. Her pale hair hung over her shoulders in a knotted mess, and her uniform was filthy. Dammit, he should have at least offered her something clean to put on, but he'd been distracted. He'd wanted to connect with his crew.

'We know your name,' Eve spat.

'Then use it,' Jinn replied. But she didn't move any further forwards. She stayed at the rear of the control deck, arms folded, back pressed against the closed door, as if she was completely cool, as if she was completely in control. 'I don't want to be here any more than you want me to be here,' she said. 'But it looks like we're stuck with each other for the time being. So the least we can do is be civil to each other.'

He could tell by the way she kept looking at him, then at Eve, that she was thinking about what he had told her about the experimental modifications that had transformed them both. 'Are you going to tell her?'

'Tell me what?' Eve snapped.

Dax drummed his fingers on the arm of his chair. There was no point trying to pretty things up. 'There's something ... weird happening on board the A2.'

'What do you mean?'

'It's been turned into a medical facility.'

'How in the void can it be a medical facility? It's a prison!'

'Not any more,' Jinn told her. 'We saw medidroids, beds, Plastex walls, drug tubes, the works. And the people ...' She pushed away from the door, moved forwards. 'I can't explain it. But I've never seen modifications like those before, and I thought I'd seen pretty much every kind there is.'

Eve shot Dax a glance. 'What is she saying?'

There was no point withholding the information. 'The programme is running again,' he said.

And with that, he saw Eve's anger disappear, to be replaced by something else. Fear. 'It can't be,' she said faintly.

'It is,' Dax told her. 'There were maybe two thousand people on board. All Type One.'

Eve sank slowly back into her chair. 'Two thousand,' she said quietly. 'You're sure about this?'

Before he could answer her, an alarm sounded. Dax turned away from Jinn and Eve. A quick glance at the screens told him they had company. 'Theon?'

'There is a lane warden approaching,' Theon replied.

'Who is that?' Jinn asked.

'The pilot,' Dax told her, without glancing back. 'Now sit down, shut up, and strap in.'

'They are gaining on us,' Theon said calmly. 'At current speed, they will be within firing range in eight minutes.'

'Are they tracking us?'

'Of course they are,' Eve said grimly. She swung into the comm. seat, slotted on a Smartware headset and tucked the earpiece in place. 'This is an unmarked, unregistered vessel and we're in Earth-controlled space.'

'We are approaching Jump Gate Two,' Theon said, his tone flat. 'Do you wish me to make the jump, captain?'

'No-one can make that jump!' Jinn told him. 'It's impossible. Do you know how many pilots have died trying?'

'Four thousand, two hundred and seventeen,' Theon replied. 'We will be entering the jump zone in five seconds. Do you want me to make the jump?'

Dax turned and pushed Jinn into an empty seat. He held her there until the auto-restraints buckled her in. Then he flung himself back into his own seat. With a sharp click, the restraints bound him to it. 'Yes,' he told Theon.

Before Jinn could protest further, they were in it. The jump bit at her, the G-force digging in to her skin, squeezing her organs. She gripped the edge of the seat and gritted her teeth. Was this the way she was supposed to die? Really? Surviving the A2 only to crash out in the Daktarian wormhole seemed a cruel irony. She didn't want to live forever, but she didn't want to be just another name on the list of reckless individuals claimed by this notoriously difficult jump either.

And she didn't want to die before she had answers to more than a few questions, like why she'd been left on the A2. Why the A2 had been converted to a medical centre carrying out experimental modifications. What were those people for? Maybe it was a research programme. But she'd have an easier time believing that if it hadn't looked more like . . . a factory.

She also wanted to know how on earth their so-called pilot was flying this ship, given that he wasn't connected to it. Jinn focussed her attention on him. His clothes were very odd. Nothing matched. Everything appeared to be a size too big, from the wide shiny trousers that ended just below the knee, to the sleeveless shirt held together with straps that appeared to made from vat-grown leather. His skin was very pink, his hair a silvery grey. At first glance he seemed human, but on closer inspection there was something about him that wasn't quite right. And there was no way the ship was on autopilot, not given the way it was moving. She couldn't see any sign of prosthetics. He didn't have a retinal implant, or Tellurium bracelets fused to his wrists. But he wasn't wearing Smartware gloves either.

'He's a droid,' Dax said, as if he could read her thoughts.

'Droids don't have skin. They don't wear clothes.' Especially not flamboyant red ones. 'And they can't fly.'

'This one does.'

'You let your droid pilot?'

'It's OK. He's AI. He can handle the ship.'

Ownership of AI devices was tightly controlled. It required special licences which were almost impossible to obtain, as well as regular psychological testing of both owner and droid. In the main, they were used as nannies and personal secretaries by people in the Domes. They were not allowed to pilot transporters. 'How on earth did you get your hands on an A.I droid?'

Dax regarded her for a long moment. Then he rubbed a hand over his face, and sighed. 'Thirty years ago, I applied to Medipro for mods. Usual deal. I was young, I was poor, I wanted to work on the Colonies. They told me the assessments showed that I wasn't quite right for any of the available programmes, but they were starting a new experimental modification programme and I did qualify for that.' He dropped his hand to his knee. 'I went home, packed up my stuff, told my parents I was leaving and signed up.'

Just like hundreds of other eighteen-year-olds, desperate to get off planet and away from a life of endless acid snowstorms and silver rice. 'What does that have to do with your having an AI droid who, for reasons I don't want to know, is pretending to be human?'

'Six weeks into the programme, I started to wonder what sort of modifications I was getting. I'd grown twenty centimetres in height and I'd gained thirty kilos of muscle. There were . . . other changes. The other kids in the programme were experiencing similar things. None of us knew what was going on. We couldn't ask the staff, because we didn't see any after the first week. Only AI droids, and they were too smart to answer our questions.'

'AI droids were running the programme?'

Dax nodded. 'When the other kids started dying, I decided it was time to check out.'

She began to see where this was going. 'I can't imagine that went down too well.'

'It didn't. I was drugged and locked in solitary confinement.'

'And then?'

'Theon,' he said.

Jinn switched her gaze to the man sat in the pilot's chair. He looked back at her, his expression blank. 'The law states that a medical patient has the right to leave a treatment facility whenever they wish,' he said. 'That right was violated, and I would not be part of it.'

Jinn pulled in air. He was definitely a droid. There was something about the eyes, something she wouldn't have noticed if she hadn't been looking for it. 'How many escaped?'

'Four,' Theon said.

'You.' Jinn pointed at Dax. He nodded. She slid her gaze to Eve. 'And you.' Eve confirmed it with a scowl. 'Who else?'

'You met another one on board the A2.'

'Jozeph Li. And the fourth? He's a member of your crew?'

Out of the corner of her eye, she saw Eve's hand curl into a fist. 'He was, for a while,' Dax said. 'Then he decided he wanted something else.'

'So basically, I escaped from prison and now I'm on a pirate ship with a runaway AI droid and two people with a price on their heads.'

'Don't forget you've also got illegal prosthetics,' Dax pointed out.

Jinn buried her head in her hands. 'I'm screwed. How did this happen to my life? I've been good. I worked hard. I kept my head down, did my job.'

Before anyone could answer her, the ship shuddered, filling her ears with a sickening groan. On the screen in front of Theon, Jinn could see the swirling colours of the wormhole, twisting round and rushing past the tiny ship as it clawed its way forwards. This was uncharted territory, which meant that Theon was flying totally on instinct, if a droid had such a thing. He was reading the flow of colour on the screen, anticipating when the next loop, the next drop would be and directing the ship into it. The pilot in her burned with jealous excitement as she watched the screen and tried to memorise the path. The human in her cried out with fear. No-one had made this jump and survived.

Until now.

The wormhole spat them out with a shuddering jolt as they lost speed and space opened up around them. Even though the air pressure and gravity had remained stable inside the ship the whole time, Jinn still found herself gasping for oxygen, as if she'd spent too long underwater.

'Status and location.' Dax's voice rumbled towards her, the sound giving her something to hold on to as her head swam.

'We are clear of the Daktarian wormhole,' Theon said. 'We will be exiting the jump zone shortly. No other vessels in detectable range. We are two hours straight haul from Colony Seven. Eight hours straight haul from the Europa.'

'Eve?'

'They couldn't identify us. They know we jumped,' Eve said, turning back to the comm. station, still holding the earpiece in place. 'They probably assume we burned out along the way. I'm not picking up anything now.'

Jinn put her hand on the buckle of her restraints and released them. She needed to get on her feet, needed to move. There was so much adrenalin flooding her system that she could practically taste it, and it didn't surprise her when her blades shot out, the metal gleaming in the well-lit cockpit.

'Bloody supernova,' she heard Eve say. 'What in the galaxy is that?'

Jinn stared down at her hands, turning them over. Blood circled the base of the blades, red and warm, and she curled her fingers in to try and hide it. She wasn't supposed to bleed like this. Her genetic modifications boosted her healing rate, allowing her body to cope with the Tellurium. Unfortunately, it looked like they weren't boosting it enough.

She willed the blades back in and wiped her hands on her trousers. Whatever was going on with her body, she'd deal with it later.

'That,' Dax said, 'is one of the reasons I didn't leave her on the A2.'

'When you said she had illegal prosthetics I thought you meant claws or a tail,' Eve said. 'You forgot to mention that she could kill us.'

'I could kill you,' Dax pointed out. 'I wouldn't even need a blade.'

'Not without killing yourself in the process.' Eve pressed herself further back into her chair. She was watching Jinn closely. 'What is it? How does it work?'

'I've got additional Tellurium implanted in my system,' Jinn said. 'Normally, pilots only have enough to form a thin wire that can connect them to their ship. I've got enough to make a blade.'

'Galactinex did this to you? You're experimental?'

'No,' Jinn told her. 'I did it to myself.'

'But . . .'

Jinn turned her attention to Dax, ignoring whatever else Eve had to say, wanting the conversation to end. 'How likely is it that the lane wardens will be able to link this ship back to you?'

'Not very,' Dax said. He pulled off his restraints, stretching his big body out in his seat. 'Theon, how far did you say we were from the Europa?'

'Eight hours straight haul,' the droid replied.

'The Europa?' Jinn asked. 'Are you insane?' The space station was a stopping point in sector three of neutral space, frequented by Dome travellers as well as various of their alien neighbours. 'Shouldn't we be trying to figure out what's going on in the A2?'

'No,' Dax replied. 'I think a little downtime is a much better idea.' He looked her up and down. 'Why don't you make use of the sleeping quarters, get cleaned up, get some rest.'

'I don't need downtime!' she replied hotly.

'Well, I do,' Dax said. In one swift move, he was out of his seat, and Jinn found herself being hauled up from hers and pushed off the control deck into the rear of the vessel. Dax moved her along a short corridor, stopping by a closed door. 'Get some rest,' he told her. 'Eat.' And then he turned and walked away.

'What's on the Europa?' she called after him.

He paused for a moment, then glanced back at her over his shoulder. 'There's an Autochef in there,' he said. 'Use it.' And then he was gone.

Jinn wanted to follow him, but exhaustion was pulling at her. Damn Tellurium. He was right. She needed to rest, and she needed to eat. The last thing she wanted was to crash again, the way she'd done on the A2.

The time passed quickly. Almost too quickly. She cleaned up, ate, then lay on the narrow bunk with her eyes on the door and her blades ready. She didn't sleep.

She'd never been this far away from Earth. It was oddly disconcerting. Not just because of the people she was with, or where she was, but because her life seemed to be travelling down a path she did not understand and could not predict. There were so many questions, and not nearly enough answers. When Dax entered the sleeping quarters, she jerked upright, blades at the ready.

'We'll be docking in thirty minutes,' he said.

'OK,' Jinn replied, slowly lowering her hands. A moment of uncomfortable silence followed as they looked at each other. The closeness they'd found on the A2 didn't exist here. She didn't know him or the others. She didn't know this ship. She was once again the outsider, and that frightened her.

'You said that the people we saw on the A2 were Type One,' she said.

'That's right.'

'You've got more strength than is natural,' she said slowly, letting her gaze travel over him, over powerful arms and a broad chest, trying to imagine him as a skinny, underfed Underworld kid. 'And your healing rate is astonishing. Far better than mine.' He was watching her cautiously, his green eyes hard and wary. Not a topic he normally liked to discuss, she realised. 'Jozeph Li,' she continued. 'His mods are similar to yours?'

For a moment she thought he wasn't going to answer. 'He has a few unique modifications, but they're basically the same as mine.'

'And the man in the cage? Back on the A2?'

'He was at an early stage of the change, but yes.'

'Eve is different, though. What about her?'

His jaw went rigid. 'Her skin secretes a toxin.'

'What sort of toxin?'

'The lethal sort,' he said. 'It's completely out of her control. She can't have physical contact with humans.'

'Not even you?'

'That's not something we've opted to test.'

No contact. None at all. Jinn swallowed, trying to imagine it. Touch wasn't something she welcomed or invited, but she couldn't imagine knowing that if you did touch someone, you could kill them. And she didn't understand why anyone would experiment with that type of modification. 'Why?' she asked. 'What was the point of these modifications? What were they for?'

'The original programme was purely experimental,' he said. 'According to Theon, Medipro was a relatively small company at the time, and it wasn't doing particularly well. We don't have inherited disorders any more. Cancer is a thing of the past. The market was shrinking. The shareholders wanted something new, something lucrative, so the company started to explore more ... questionable avenues. They were convinced that if they discovered anything useful, someone would buy the technology even if the research was illegal.'

He opened a storage unit, pulled out a bundle of clothing and tossed it down on the bunk next to her. 'We'll be gone for a couple of hours. I want you to stay here.' And then he walked out, leaving Jinn alone with the bundle of clothes and her thoughts. His words played over and over inside her head. *Someone would buy the technology even if the research was illegal.*

Yes, she thought. They bloody would.

But what would they buy it for?

# CHAPTER

# 12

**25th August 2207**
Space Station Europa, Sector Three, Neutral Space

Jinn remained in the sleeping quarters until they'd docked with the Europa and Dax and the others had gone. She used the chemicleanse to wash away the stink of the A2 and got dressed in the clothes Dax had given her, plain trousers and jacket made from serviceable beige Texcryl that stretched to a snug but comfortable fit. She knew she was just going through the motions, that there were probably more important things she should be doing, but she couldn't seem to make herself do them. It felt safe, alone in the confines of the little ship. She helped herself to more Soylate and a meat sub from the Autochef, and settled down to watch Entertainment World.

But twenty minutes in, she felt a profound sense of annoyance with the spoilt, irrelevant people featured. After what she'd seen on board the A2, they had lost their gloss.

'Computer, switch to ADN.' All Day News was exactly that. News, all the time, without a break. She'd always found it heavy and stifling, but as the first item came on, she watched with new interest.

Ana Rizzola, Earth's representative on the Intergalactic

Senate, was dead. Few details were given, other than that her illness had been short and she had died in isolation in a medical clinic in the New Mexico Dome. The screen showed a young, serious woman in flowing senatorial robes. Her death was described as sudden and tragic. Jinn felt a strange tightness in her chest.

President Vexler appeared and gave a short speech. Vice President Dubnik stood next to him, head bowed, hands clasped together. It was all very proper, very dignified, despite the fact that nothing of real value was said until a journalist stepped forward and asked Vexler what would happen now that Earth was without representation in the Intergalactic Senate.

'A replacement for Senator Rizzola has already been chosen,' Vexler said.

'Who?'

'Minister Blue has been elected as senator,' Vexler said. 'We are very grateful to her for agreeing to take on this extra burden, and I am sure, with her experience, that she will prove to be an excellent representative.'

An image of Ferona flashed up on the screen. Jinn stared at it for a moment as her heart started to race and her hands to shake, just as they always did whenever her mother barged into her life, even virtually. 'Screen off,' she said. 'Screen off!'

The system obeyed her immediately. She stared down at her trembling hands and swallowed down the lump in her throat. Then she blushed, even though there wasn't anyone to see. It was pathetic. She was pathetic. It wasn't as though Ferona could see her through the screen.

'Screen on,' she forced herself to say. It came back to life. Vexler was still on screen, the interview still ongoing.

'Isn't that a lot of work for one individual?' asked the reporter.

'It is,' President Vexler agreed. 'This is why Minister Blue deserves the full support of not only the government, but the people she represents. This is a critical time for us. It is vital that we continue to foster positive relationships with our alien neighbours and Minister Blue is the ideal person to ensure that happens. As Minister for Off World Affairs, her recent efforts to reduce criminal activity in the neutral zone have been invaluable.'

'Didn't get her hands dirty, though, did she?' Jinn muttered. 'Left that to the rest of us. She wasn't picking up serial killers in bars.'

That made her feel a little better.

Ferona had never been one to do something herself if she could get someone else to do it for her, and that had included parenting. Jinn had been raised by an ever-changing series of nanny droids. She'd seen her mother maybe once a week if she was lucky, when Ferona would question her on her progress at school and her relationships with the other children. Every poor decision, every mistake was scrutinised. Ferona decided what courses she should study at school, what she should wear, who she could be friends with, where she could go.

Jinn had been twelve when she'd received her first course of behavioural modification drugs. Ferona had told her the pills were to help fix some of the defects in her personality that less-invasive therapies had failed to address. For six months, Jinn had felt nothing. It was as if all emotions had been turned off. And so it had gone for the next few years. There had even been one particularly hideous attempt at a memory purge that had left Jinn sick and disoriented for weeks. When she turned eighteen, Jinn had done the only thing she could. She had run away and taken what remained of her real self with her. And now she wanted to run again. She could feel the itch of it, deep inside.

But she couldn't, not this time.

If it had just been Bryant and his obvious breakdown, she could maybe have talked herself into forgetting about it. She had almost enough credits saved to retire, anyway, and she didn't have much loyalty to the service. It wouldn't be that difficult to have the Tellurium removed and set herself up with a place somewhere in neutral space.

But what she had seen on board the A2 was too big, too frightening to forget. Too much of her early education had stuck for that to happen. No-one understood better than she did how important it was for humans to be viewed in a positive light by the other members of the Senate. And she hadn't spent several years of her life transporting prisoners in order for everything to be screwed up by the greed of a medical corporation.

But more than that, she knew what it was like to be given medical treatments that you didn't really understand, and somehow she doubted that the prisoners on the A2 had consented to what was being done to them.

She got to her feet and dumped the remains of her meal in the recycling unit, then she took the ladder that led down from the hatch with shaking legs and nervous hands. By the time she reached the deck of the space station, three metres down, she had herself under control. The *Deviant* had an onboard comm. system, but using it would risk drawing attention to Dax and the others and she didn't want to do that. He had helped her. She owed him this much.

The ladder folded away automatically, the hatch quietly closing. A faint hum met her ears – the onboard computer sending an electric charge through the hull – and she had a momentary wobble when she realised that while getting off the ship might have been easy, getting back on it would be anything but. It seemed like overkill, given the way it looked. But she'd worry about that later, when she came back. If she came back.

The landing bay stretched out in front of her. Ships moved in and out of docking bays as she walked past them, some exquisitely curved, some fierce and angular. Metal gleamed and coloured paintwork sparkled as landing ramps lowered and passengers disembarked. Droids scuttled everywhere, cleaning up, loading and unloading cargo, selling food and drink and trinkets. So many people. So many aliens.

Jinn felt her skin prickle, turned to see a lean, cloaked figure watching her from two ships over. His hands were hidden, his face in shadow, but she saw the strange glow of his eyes, a pale amber, and knew that she'd just got her first glimpse of one of the Sittan. She'd seen images of them, learned about them during the endless hours of tutoring she'd had as a child. But she'd never seen one in the flesh before. They were notoriously violent. Fighting was a way of life for them.

Jozeph Li had spent time in the fight cages on their planet. The tattoos on his shoulders had told her that. The eldest son of each Sittan family was required by law to fight in the arena in the capital city. Winners earned respect, land for themselves, the right to marry. Losers usually didn't survive. Families were allowed to put forward a representative rather than lose a beloved son, and a human willing to enter the cages could earn himself a small fortune, if he survived.

She wondered how Jozeph Li had managed it, then thought about Dax, about what he had told her, and she knew. Because of his modifications. Experimental changes to his DNA that had rendered him something more than human.

The Sittan male moved. Jinn felt a snap of fear. Her palms turned clammy, her pulse kicking up. Turning away, she started to walk towards the exit of the docking bay, moving as fast as she could without breaking into a sprint. She had her blades, but she didn't want to get into a fight with a Sittan, not here, not now, not ever.

At least she wasn't still wearing her uniform. But her hair, so pale that it was almost white, always drew attention. It screamed of embryonic selection, and that screamed of money. Colourant refused to take to it, though she'd tried. Pulling up the hood on her borrowed jacket, Jinn moved faster.

The loading bay spat her out into what appeared to be some sort of market. The Europa was arranged in tiers, walkways ringing the edge of the space, climbing at least a dozen storeys up. There were moving platforms carrying people from side to side, buzzing through the space above her head. At least on this level, people walked.

And there were so many of them.

All of the outer rim planets were represented. She saw more Sittan males, and a female too. Everyone seemed to be giving them a wide berth as they moved slowly through the crowd, eyes blazing, faces concealed under heavily hooded cloaks. There were Qui, small fat creatures with eyeless faces, their prehensile tongues sniffing at the air, and Lodons, with their grotesquely humped backs showing where they carried the symbiotic creatures that fed from their bodies.

None of the simulations she'd watched had prepared her for the sight of these alien races in the flesh. They hadn't prepared her for the smell, or the sound, or the overwhelming feeling of being ordinary in comparison. And there was energy to the place, a buzz, as if everyone was on edge, watching, waiting to see who would make the first move. To do so would mean carnage, she could sense it, which was why no-one did. It was what made this place safe despite the mix of creatures.

She breathed in some of the tangy air and took a minute to think. If the Europa was laid out like the other space stations she'd been on, credit stations should be somewhere on this level. She wanted one away from the main thoroughfare, where it would be quieter, more discreet.

Jinn took a left, darting down one of the walkways that led off the main square. There were more stalls here, pushed up against one side. Vendors haggled over the price of brightly coloured bottles of drink, pulsating fungi the size of her head, huge vats of steaming liquid that they ladled into cones.

A rich, smoky smell filled the air. Some sort of meat, she decided, as she glanced across at it, seeing a couple of Qui reach out their tongues and lift dripping yellow pieces that twisted and wriggled.

Swallowing down her disgust, Jinn carried on down the street, moving quickly, not wanting to loiter. At the end she took a right. It swung her round into another street, and in the middle of it, stretching from floor to ceiling, was a bank of credit machines.

The machines buzzed with activity and she lost her nerve. Too crowded.

Tucking her hands inside her jacket, she hunched her shoulders, kept her gaze low and kept moving. There had to be another credit station around here, one that would offer more privacy, more protection from the various races that wandered the walkways. She was too well versed in politics to think that all the other species took kindly to humans.

The far end of the street was quieter, the mood edgier. Everyone here moved quickly, as if they were somewhere they didn't want to be seen. The buildings that edged the walkway were dirtier, less well maintained, the ground littered with detritus. She would have to be careful where she put her feet. But at the end of it, she found what she was looking for. The machine was old and crusted with something dark brown and gunky, but the glowing emblem in the corner of the screen indicated that it was working.

'Activate,' Jinn said, glancing behind her to make sure no-one was watching.

The tiny camera mounted just above the screen zoomed in on her. 'Welcome,' the machine replied, flashing into life, bombarding her with a sequence of advertisements. Sleep booths, pleasure droids, space sickness medication. 'How may I help you?'

It had identified her as human. It was a start. 'Credit withdrawal,' she said.

'Security code please,' said the holographic head that had popped up in front of her. It was designed to look female and friendly, with bouffant hair and a very white smile.

'44269,' she told it. 'I'd like to check my balance, please.'

'No information can be retrieved for that account,' the head informed her, smiling away.

'What?'

'Would you like to try an alternative security code?'

There was no alternative. 'Re-input,' Jinn said. '44269. Last-known transaction.'

'I'm afraid that information is unavailable,' the head said, before the screen flashed back to more advertisements. 'Have a nice day.'

Jinn kicked the machine.

It responded by sparking a little electric shock into her leg. 'Ow!'

Glaring at it, she rubbed away the pain.

'What do you mean, it's unavailable?'

The head reappeared. 'There is no information available for that account. Please exit the booth.'

Jinn did as it said before it could shock her again. She stood in the street, staring at it, feeling a deep sense of annoyance. It probably served her right for picking this filthy, malfunctioning machine instead of using one of the other ones. Damn it! As she stood there, someone else slipped into the booth. A couple of minutes later, they emerged, tucking a credit chip into their pocket.

The machine was working?

Jinn moved back into the booth. She went through the motions again, giving her security code.

'Account unavailable,' the head told her. 'Have a nice day.'

That was weird. She knew the machine was working. So the fault had to lie elsewhere.

How could her account no longer exist? Where in the void were her credits? She stared at the screen, which was showing an advertisement for a droid store, as fear washed through her.

*Stop it*, she told herself sharply. *You're being paranoid. Bryant is ill. He didn't leave you there on purpose. And there's clearly a problem with your accounts. This is all just a mistake.*

Jinn stepped away from the machine.

She rubbed her hands together and thought about what to do next. She wouldn't be able to stay on the station long without credits. These places didn't charge for air, but she was already getting hungry and her bladder was complaining. And she didn't know if she'd be able to return to Dax's ship. That electrical charge that had hummed over the hull hadn't struck her as friendly.

And she still needed to contact her commander. She'd have to use one of the secure channels. It was frowned upon, but it was free. She had no other choice.

At the far end of the alley was a public comm. station and she ran to it. 'Open channel nineteen, stream one, security level twelve. Access code 237441.'

'Access granted,' the machine said. 'Connecting in three, two ...'

'Ma'am,' Jinn said quickly, as the connection was made and the screen flashed bright.

'Pilot Blue?' The voice was filled with stunned disbelief.

Where should she begin? In the end, it all tumbled out in a rush. 'Ma'am, we've got a problem. Bryant, he went crazy. He left me on board the A2. And the A2, it's not a prison any more. It's some sort of medical facility. They're carrying out experimental modifications.'

There was a moment of silence, a pause. Jinn could see the familiar outline of her commander's features, the hawk-like eyes, the firm jaw, the hair that was nearly as pale as her own. If the woman had any issue with Jinn, she'd never let it show. But there was something in her expression now, something cold that made Jinn suddenly afraid. 'Don't worry about that now,' her commander said. 'A crew will be dispatched to your location. They'll give you whatever assistance you need.'

'Ma'am, you need to listen to me,' Jinn said.

'Remain close to this comm. station,' the commander ordered her. 'Agents will be with you shortly.'

A trickle of cold unease slid down Jinn's spine. 'No. No, this isn't right. End transmission.'

The system didn't obey. They had to be controlling it from the other end. A sudden sick fear swamped Jinn. First she'd been left on the A2, then her accounts had vanished, and now her commander was acting weird. She lifted her hand, plunged her blade deep into the machine and severed the connection. Sparks and smoke rose from the wreckage and with a crackle the screen burst. The smell of burning wires and destruction filled Jinn's nostrils as she took a step back from the machine.

She'd learned one thing, at least.

Her commander hadn't seemed the least bit concerned about the A2. She hadn't been concerned about Bryant either, which could only mean that he'd been acting on orders.

And she had no intention of waiting around for the retrieval crew to act on theirs.

# CHAPTER

# 13

**25th August 2207**

Vessel: The *Nero Hunter*. Stealth Cruiser
Destination: Jump Gate Fourteen
Cargo: None
Crew: Thirteen
Droids: Four

His new pilot had turned out to be a woman of many talents. Many useful talents, Bryant thought to himself as he tipped his head back, closed his eyes and savoured the hot pull of her mouth on his cock. He usually preferred to use the services of a pleasure droid. They were cleaner, more efficient, but he hadn't taken any downtime since his last trip to the A2 and he needed this.

His promotion ceremony had been quick, too quick for his liking. He'd wanted to savour the moment and bask in his new status, but a contract had been transmitted to his personal comm. less than an hour after his promotion to captain. A stealth cruiser had been assigned to him, complete with a crew of twelve agents. He'd assumed the responsibility easily, comfortably. It hadn't taken him long to ascertain that his new crew hated Bugs just as much as he did, and were just as eager to work.

Opening his eyes, Bryant stared down at the woman who was currently on her knees in front of him. Her pale hair was cut short around her ears, the front left to hang loose across one side of her face. It emphasised eyes that were a pretty shade of brown. She had good cheekbones, as well as a neat little nose that Bryant doubted was entirely original. She'd tugged her uniform down to her waist, exposing a nice pair of tits, and she was working him with skill, if not enthusiasm. She'd walked into his quarters shortly after they boarded and told him exactly what she wanted and exactly what she was prepared to trade to get it. He'd debated the possible consequences of giving her private quarters for as long as it had taken her to unfasten his trousers.

They were currently on their way to Omega Station to arrest a female who worked as a dancer in one of the clubs in the entertainment centre there. She had slaughtered her husband and two of his friends in a junkie rage, then tried to claim self-defence. Stupid Underworld whore, he thought to himself, as the pilot sucked him deep, held him there. What did she expect? Even if what she said was true, she'd been off her head on Euphoria when she stabbed the three men. Did she really think she wouldn't be held responsible for her actions?

That was the problem with Underworlders, Bryant thought. Pleasure rushed down his spine as the pilot wrapped a hand around his erection. They never wanted to accept responsibility for their actions. They thought they could do as they pleased, and screw the consequences. He closed his eyes and pushed that thought aside, focussing his attention on more immediate matters. He felt his skin heat, felt his balls tighten, and prepared to unload down her throat.

The comm. console mounted on the wall of his quarters started to beep right as he was about to climax. 'Fuck off,' Bryant muttered and closed his eyes. He put a hand on the back of the pilot's head, keeping her in place. He was almost there. Almost there.

'Security level twelve,' the system informed him. 'Are you free to take this call?'

He hadn't received a level-twelve call since he'd left Jinnifer Blue and Caspian Dax on board the A2. His skin prickled. He considered ignoring it, letting the pilot finish him off, but his concentration had been broken and he'd lost his hold on his orgasm. Shoving Sayrah aside, he pulled up his trousers and strode over to the comm. station, positioned himself for the iris scan.

'Level twelve,' she said. He glanced back over his shoulder. She was shoving her arms into the sleeves of her flight suit and watching him closely. 'My, my.'

Bryant narrowed his eyes at her, then gestured at the door. 'Dismissed,' he said.

She didn't move. 'I'd rather stay here.'

'Out,' he said again, as the comm. station continued to beep. 'Go find someone else to play with. You're done here.'

She pouted and he thought she was going to argue, but she got to her feet and strolled out of his quarters. The door slid closed behind her, leaving him alone.

Bryant didn't waste any more time. 'Open the channel,' he instructed the computer. The screen flickered to life immediately. Bryant squared his shoulders, put his hands behind his back.

'We have a problem.' There was no greeting, no niceties.

'Commander,' Bryant replied calmly, refusing to be equally rude.

'It seems you didn't complete your last contract,' his commander said. His tone was cold, hard, furious.

'Excuse me?'

'Prisoner X747F just made contact,' his commander said. 'She's on the Europa.'

Bryant stared at the screen. His heart started to pound. 'That's not possible.'

'Shut the fuck up and listen to me,' his commander snarled. 'I don't know what happened, or how it happened, but she's on the Europa. She just made a call to Bettison.'

This couldn't be happening. He had left Jinnifer Blue on the prison ship. He had watched her through the video feed as she stared up at the transporter and mouthed desperate words that he couldn't hear.

And somehow, the cunning bitch had managed to escape.

'I'm only an hour out,' Bryant said, thinking quickly. 'I'll find her.'

'A team has already been dispatched.'

'Cancel it.'

The man stared back at him, unblinking, mouth pinched tight in an unfortunately round face. The platinum stripes indicating his rank were pinned in a line across the front of his jacket. He had thirty years on Bryant, but Bryant knew he'd only managed five in the field before he'd pulled a desk job and he didn't want to lose it.

'We can do this off the book,' Bryant told him. 'I locate her, take her back to the A2, it's like none of this ever happened.'

'If you fuck this up, I am not taking the fall for it,' his commander said. 'Is that clear?'

Oh yes. That was pretty clear. 'Perfectly,' Bryant said. He held himself rigidly still. 'I assume I am authorised to use whatever means are necessary?'

'Yes,' his commander replied, dismissing the question with a wave of his hand. 'Though she must be delivered to the A2 alive.'

'Consider it done,' Bryant informed him. The screen went blank. Bryant stared at it for a moment. He could feel anger growing inside him. He didn't know how in the void Jinnifer Blue had got herself to the Europa, but he knew one thing for certain. She was going back to the A2. Straightening his uniform, he pulled on his jacket and fastened it before leaving his quarters and heading for the control deck.

Bryant took up position in the captain's chair and summoned the rest of his crew. Within a few minutes all of them were assembled on the control deck. 'Change of plan,' he told them. 'We're going to the Europa.'

'Thought we weren't due any downtime for the next month,' said one of the agents, Kryll, a sulky tone to his words.

'New orders,' Bryant told him. 'We've got a warrant to execute.'

'Who?'

'Computer, show image of Prisoner X747F.'

Silence fell as the image flashed up on the view screen and Bryant felt an instant kick of hate. Jinnifer Blue had embarrassed him. She'd made him look stupid in front of his superiors and he didn't like that. He didn't like it at all, and he was going to make her hurt. Deliver her alive, that had been his instruction. He was going to follow it to the letter. Alive didn't mean unharmed. It only meant . . . still breathing.

'She is currently on board the Europa,' he informed the rest of the agents. 'We are to apprehend her and deliver her to the A2. We have permission to use whatever force we deem necessary.' Bryant glanced around at his crew. 'I want everyone suited up and properly armed. Be prepared for close-range combat. This is going to be messy.'

'We're arresting *her*?' Kryll asked.

'Yes.' Bryant replied, daring him to say more.

'Didn't you used to work with her?'

Bryant turned his gaze on the man. 'We have our orders. If you've got a problem with them, feel free to contact base and request reassignment.'

Kryll smiled, a chilling curve to his mouth that even Bryant found distasteful. 'No problem. In fact, I'm quite looking forward to it.'

# CHAPTER
# 14

Although his crew often came here for shore leave, Dax usually preferred to spend his time onboard the *Mutant*. When the crew were on it he had to be there and when they weren't, he enjoyed the solitude. But the *Deviant* was too small for that, plus he had another reason for coming to the Europa. If he was going to find out which member of his crew had betrayed him to that agent, he was going to need help. There was an old friend of his here on the Europa who would be able to identify the culprit, and he could do it without breaking any bones. But Dax needed to talk to him alone before he suggested it to the others.

Pushing his way through the crowds, Dax took a right, then he turned to Theon. 'We need supplies,' he said. 'The Autochef needs restocking.'

'Of course,' Theon replied. 'I will take care of it.'

'Eve,' Dax said.

'What?'

He gestured to Theon. 'You're with him.'

'But I . . .'

Dax raised an eyebrow. She scowled at him from under her

loose curtain of dark hair, but he knew she'd follow orders, and she did. The two of them turned, slipped back into the crowd and quickly disappeared, leaving Dax alone.

He moved forward, weaving his way towards the street that ran off to the left. A couple of Sittan males were leaning against the wall at the edge of the street. He ignored them. They would see his size as a challenge, but if they were looking to start a fight, they'd have to find someone else to start it with.

Luxurious stores ran the length of the busy street, displaying all manner of high-end gadgets. He saw a case of throwing blades that looked interesting and some advanced comm. screens and sent Eve a message asking her to pick some up. For the most part though, his focus was elsewhere.

It would be better if that elsewhere wasn't Jinnifer Blue. No matter what had happened on board the A2, there was no changing who she was. A Dome brat. The daughter of a well-known government official. A Security Service pilot.

But she stuck in his mind as he strolled casually to one side of the street, ducking into the Spaceair showroom at the last possible minute. He knew why she stuck. He liked the way she looked, with all that pale hair and that lean, strong body.

A high-tech ground skimmer filled the front window, suspended at a ninety-degree angle. Dax had no need for such things, but he still took a moment to admire it. He liked knowing that if he wanted to buy it, he could.

His personal comm. pinged. He turned it off, not bothering to check. It was most likely Eve wanting to know how much she could spend, and Theon could deal with that.

Inside, the store was all polished steel and expensive ambience. A small fountain played in the centre of the space, the fall of the water creating a soft background noise. The walls were dotted with screens, showing beautiful people enjoying themselves on beautiful ships. Dax moved in front of a vid screen that was streaming clips of the latest in long-haul luxury travel and waited.

He didn't have to wait long.

'Caspian.' The man who drew up alongside was shorter than Dax, leaner in build. His dark hair was neatly cut and he was wearing a close-fitting suit of pale grey that gave him a polished veneer. He was so smooth that even Dome customers would buy from him. 'It's been a long time.'

'Alistair.' Dax greeted him with a slight tilt of his head. 'How are things with you?'

'As they always are,' Alistair replied. 'Looking for anything in particular?' He studied Dax for a moment, then lifted his hand, subtly stroking the skin behind his ear. To anyone else, it would look like he was smoothing his hair, but Dax knew better. He was turning off the tiny cochlea implant that filtered out the extraneous noise from his surroundings.

'I'm not sure.' Dax gestured to the screen. 'This model looks interesting.'

'It's one of our best sellers,' Alistair replied. 'An excellent choice, sir. Might I suggest that you accompany me to our refreshments area and we discuss your requirements further?'

*I don't have much time.*

Alistair glanced across at him as they walked together to the rear of the store. Dax didn't need enhanced hearing to know that look meant *in trouble?*

*I am. Government security picked me up, dumped me on the A2.*

'How unfortunate,' Alistair said smoothly, as he programmed the refreshment machine. A steaming cup of dark liquid was quickly produced and prepared fruit was dispensed into a bowl. Strawberries, melon, grapes. Foods Dax hadn't eaten until he was well into adulthood. He took one of the grapes, popped it into his mouth. The juice burst out, fresh and sweet on his tongue.

*I need your help, Alistair. I need to find out which member of my crew told the Security Service where to find me.*

'You don't need me for that,' Alistair muttered as he flipped a tablet over in his hand and thumbed the screen to bring up a catalogue of skimmers. 'I've got a life here, Caspian. A good job. Some days I even like it. I don't belong on the *Mutant*. Not any more.'

An image of a little four-seater rotated in front of him and Dax pretended to admire it.

*There's more. The A2 has been turned into a medical facility. Two thousand patients. Minimum. The programme is running again, Alistair. They're using that damn prison to make Type One.*

Alistair responded with raised eyebrows and a noise that he managed to turn into a cough at the last minute. A few heads turned in their direction. Dax glared until they looked away.

'Are you sure?' Alistair asked him.

'I know what I saw,' Dax said. 'This is big, Alistair. If they're working on that scale, then maybe . . . '

But Alistair wasn't listening. He was looking behind him, beyond the fountain and the browsing customers to the street beyond. Dax followed the line of his gaze. Eve stood in the street. A hand rose to her throat, lingered there for a moment, before falling back to her side. Theon stood next to her.

With a soft curse, Dax vaulted over the seat, his boots thumping as they hit the floor. He strode over to where Eve stood. 'I told you to go get supplies.'

'You didn't tell me you were coming to see him,' Eve said. 'You devious bastard.'

'Eve,' Dax warned her. He didn't have time to deal with this right now. 'You're attracting attention.'

On the other side of the street, a small group was gathering. Their pale, shiny skin was threaded with deep purple veins, their central eyes fixed firmly on Eve. He saw one of them open its mouth, push out a stubby set of pulsing tentacles. At the end of each one was a sucker which flexed and tasted the air. Shi-Fai, on board the Europa. And if there were three, there were more. They always travelled in large numbers and they were a long way from home. A very long way.

His personal comm. pinged again and this time he checked it.

It was the main computer of the *Deviant*, informing him that Jinn had left the ship.

Shit.

He barely had to think Alistair's name and the other man was beside him.

'I need you to keep Eve safe,' Dax told him, ignoring Eve's snort of disgust. 'I've got to go and find someone.' Eve kicked at the ground, but she shoved her way past him and stormed into the store. 'Bay 1214,' Dax told Alistair. 'Can you make sure she gets there safely?'

Alistair nodded. 'She's not going to like it.'

'She doesn't have to like it,' Dax said.

Alistair sighed. Then he turned to Dax. 'I can give you an hour,' he said. 'We'll talk. But I can't promise anything.' He went back inside, heading straight for Eve.

Dax turned on his heel and headed out into the street, Theon close behind. He deliberately kept his gaze away from the Shi-Fai. They would see eye contact as an indication that he was willing to trade Eve and that would bring others. He needed to find Jinn, and he needed to find her quickly. Lengthening his stride, he headed towards the Alpha Quarter, a busy, bustling place filled with food vendors and holographic performers. In different circumstances, he'd have taken his time and enjoyed the spectacle of alien theatre, but not today.

As he searched the crowd for a flash of white-blonde hair, Dax couldn't help feeling that his life would have been a lot simpler if he'd left her on board that freighter twenty years ago.

He couldn't see her. And he was drawing far, far too much attention. There was another reason Dax preferred to stay on the *Mutant* while his crew took leave, and this was it. He'd pissed too many people off. Too many gazes were following him now, too many people looking at him. The Europa was a strange, violent place, existing on a constant knife-edge of tension. Earth's government had no authority here. In theory, existing in neutral space, it was under the control of the Intergalactic Senate, but that didn't mean much.

'Where is she?'

'I will sync with some of the droids,' Theon said. 'They may have seen her.'

Shrugging off the gazes of several interested parties, Dax wandered over to a stall selling trinkets, little metal rings that could be pushed through ears, noses, nipples, anywhere else the purchaser desired. He fingered a thick silver ring, big enough to fit through the head of his cock, then glanced across at the stall-owner as Theon stood a couple of metres behind.

'Special price for you,' the female droid purred. She flicked back her silver hair. 'Nineteen credits.'

'Not interested,' Dax said.

'Something else, then? She ran her hands over her curves, down between her legs. 'A big man like you wants it rough, no?'

'Maybe.' He looked her up and down. 'Got a friend?'

'I have many friends.'

'I bet you do.'

Theon glided up to him. 'Much as I'm enjoying listening to the two of you chit-chat, Jinnifer Blue passed through here twenty-three minutes ago,' he said.

Dax acknowledged this with a nod. He tossed the droid a five-credit chip. She gazed back at him with dead eyes.

He shouldered his way back into the crowd, Theon close behind. He couldn't risk having his pilot sync with too many of the droids, in case one of them detected the intrusion. There would be plenty of merchants willing to cut their own throats to get their hands on an unregistered AI droid.

Dax scanned the crowd. 'Where would she go?'

Then something at the entrance to one of the streets caught his attention. A group of Shi-Fai, making those high-pitched sounds that he knew meant they were talking. Even if he couldn't inter-pret the language, some things were universal. Fury and pain were both in there. In the centre of the group, he saw one of them clutching at what was left of its arm. The end of it had been cleanly severed. Dark brown slime was oozing from the wound, spattering the floor. Another held a familiar-looking beige jacket with a large rip in the front. 'Jinn,' Dax said, tracking the trail of Shi-Fai blood on the ground before the cleaning droids could remove it all.

'They will be looking for her,' Theon said.

'So are we,' Dax pointed out. The trail led back into a narrow alley behind the group of Shi-Fai and Dax headed towards it, giving the aliens a wide berth. He could hear Theon's light footfalls, knew the droid was close behind. The alleyway meandered, the bright light of the Alpha Quarter giving way to pale, dirty walkway lighting. It was narrow here, filthy store windows illuminated to showcase their wares.

'You only had to inform me that you wished to visit a pleasure parlour,' Theon said. 'I would have remained behind with the others.'

Dax cast him a scathing look. 'Remind me to turn off your humour chip when we get back to the *Mutant*.'

'Unfortunately, I do not have a humour chip,' Theon said. 'Only the intelligence chip. Remove that and I'll be just the same as every other droid.'

'You'd do well to remember that,' Dax told him. The narrow alley was empty, save for the fresh splatter of brown and the Shi-Fai's hand, which lay in the gutter, still twitching.

'She is quite remarkable,' Theon said.

'Yes,' Dax said. 'She is.' He wished that she weren't. He had a feeling that Jinnifer Blue was going to cause him no end of trouble before this was done. When he'd put her in that escape pod all those years ago, he'd never expected to see her again and he hadn't given her a second thought. Not often, anyway. Not beyond doing a little private research and that had only been because a Dome brat on a Galactinex vessel was an anomaly.

None of the files had mentioned that she was such a pain in the arse. Jinnifer Blue didn't know how to follow orders. She didn't know how to accept authority, not even his authority. He was beginning to understand why her crewmates had acted the way they had.

Unfortunately, the blood trail ended with the hand. Where would she go? She would have Shi-Fai blood on her blade and she'd need to clean it up as quickly as possible if she was going to avoid being poisoned. Dax looked along the alleyway. A flashing sign at the end caught his attention. A public restroom. He walked towards it, Theon close by his side.

One of the cubicles was empty. The other was occupied.

Folding his arms, Dax leaned back against the wall and waited. If Jinnifer Blue had any sense, she was in that cubicle. The light flashed and the door slid open.

And Jinnifer Blue looked out.

Her dark eyes locked on his. He saw them widen. He walked over and grabbed the front of her shirt and hauled her out. 'I told you to stay on the *Deviant*!'

'Let go of me!'

'Why? So you can go deprive another Shi-Fai of its hand?'

'I didn't attack it on purpose! It was self-defence!'

'Do you know what Shi-Fai do to human women?'

'I'm not stupid,' she snapped back at him. 'Of course I do.'

'The Shi-Fai,' he said, as if she hadn't spoken, 'rape human women for entertainment. Their bodily fluids are toxic to our physiology. They rape you repeatedly and then they leave you to die.'

'Don't be ridiculous! They're poisonous to us, yes. But that's all.'

'Then how did you end up slicing one into pieces? It tried to grab you, didn't it?' She didn't meet his gaze and that made his anger flare. 'Do you have some sort of death wish, Jinn? Is that it?'

'If I did,' she yelled back, 'I've had plenty of opportunities to satisfy it, don't you think?'

As quickly as it had risen, his anger cooled. She was pale and shaking and he could see she was frightened. He let go of her shirt. 'If you start to feel ill, I need to know immediately. Understand? There are things that can be done, but only if we act quickly.'

'I cleaned my blades. I'm fine.'

Dax risked a glance inside the booth. 'If you cleaned them in there, Shi-Fai toxin may well be the least of your problems.'

'There's something you should know,' she said. And this time she did meet his gaze. 'Agents are on their way.'

Dax gritted his teeth and fought the urge to strangle her. 'Do I want to know?'

'I . . . Probably not.'

He could tell from the look on her face that she was going to tell him anyway, and that he wasn't going to like it.

'There's no way the Senate would agree to a vote if they found out that a prison was being used as a medical facility for experimental modifications,' she began. 'The Sittan hate us. They'd jump at the excuse to leave us on Earth. I couldn't live with myself if that happened and I had a chance to stop it and I did nothing. So I made a call to my commander. It was a mistake.'

'No,' he said. 'Leaving the *Deviant* was a mistake. There isn't even a word for what that was.' He turned to Theon. 'Find the others,' he said. 'We need to get out of here. Now.'

Theon nodded and spun away from them, his red coat whipping out behind him as he started down the alley. Dax turned his attention back to Jinn. Whatever tension had been between them before was gone now, drowned by the reality of the trouble they were in.

'Shouldn't we go with him?'

'No,' Dax said. 'They're looking for you. The others will be safer heading back to the ship without you.'

It was then he realised his hands were on her arms, that he was standing far closer to her than he had intended. But she didn't step back. Instead, she looked up at him, those dark eyes hot and determined.

'What about you?'

'What about me?'

'Won't you be better going back without me too?'

'Probably,' he said. 'But spending the next month watching the newsfeed for your obituary would piss me off. I didn't let you go just so you could get yourself killed now.'

'The bastards closed my accounts,' she said. 'All my credits, everything, it's all gone. I've got nothing.' Her mouth stiffened like she was trying not to cry. 'Get me out of this,' she said, 'and I swear I'll follow every single order you give me from now on. To the letter.'

'I'll hold you to that,' Dax told her. 'Don't think I won't. How long ago did you make the call?'

She rubbed a hand over her wrist, presumably where her comm. unit would have been. 'An hour, maybe?'

'If we're lucky, we might be able to get back to the *Deviant* before they find us.'

But it would be difficult. They were both so distinctive in appearance and they didn't have access to a change of clothing or anything that might alter the way they looked enough for them to slip past a security team undetected. Best-case scenario, they made it to the *Deviant* and away before the agents even made it to the Europa. It was time to stop loitering down dirty alleyways and start moving.

A noise at the end of the alley caught his attention. He lifted his head, held his breath, and there it was. The whine of a blaster. *Shit.* Jinn ducked her head and looked past him. She closed her eyes and that told him all he needed to know.

'How many?' he asked.

'Seven,' she said.

Dax considered this. 'Could be worse.'

'How could it be worse?'

'At least they don't want to eat us.'

She rolled her eyes at him. 'How do you want to play this?' she asked. He knew she was afraid. He also knew that she was every bit as tough as she seemed. The A2 would have destroyed her otherwise. And she'd never have left the *Deviant*. Doing so had been stupid, but it had also been bold.

'The easy way,' he said. 'Run as fast as you can and try not to get shot.'

She lifted her hands, flexed her fingers, and he watched as her blades lengthened into vicious points. 'I'll do my best.'

Jinn knew he could move fast. But she hadn't really known how fast. She didn't know it was possible for a man to move like that, especially not one built like Caspian Dax. But move he did, with a speed and grace that left her standing still as he charged towards the agents.

A stunner shot grazed by the side of her face, the spark of white flashing in her peripheral vision. The heat of it scorched her skin and shocked her into action. All the agents were wearing the same distinctive grey uniform, gold stripes crossing their upper arms to indicate rank, and not one had less than four stripes, which meant both experience and skills. Dax had already taken out three, leaving them in unconscious heaps at the end of the alleyway.

Another stunner shot missed her by less than nothing, singeing the edge of her hair, and Jinn knew she had to do something before one of those little flashes of nerve-paralysing charge found its target. She sprinted straight at the agent who was firing at her, hitting him with the full weight of her body. They crashed to the floor but before she could use her blades, he had her on her back, knocking her head so hard against the floor that she saw stars. He leapt to his feet and put a boot to her chest. 'Jinnifer Blue,' he said. 'You are under arrest. Do not move.'

When the sun freezes over, Jinn thought, as he levelled his weapon and trained it on her face. She slashed at him with her blades, scrambled to her feet as he staggered back. Blood gushed from a wound on his arm.

'Bitch.' He spat the word out and lunged at her. Jinn saw the move coming. She dodged left and kicked him in the balls. He sank to one knee, chest heaving, giving Jinn a clear route past. She didn't hesitate to take it. Planting one boot on his shoulder, she vaulted over him. Dax had told her to run, and that was exactly what she was going to do.

She didn't get far. Another agent appeared and blocked her path, this one carrying a wicked-looking length of sparking chain. A small smile twisted the corners of his mouth as he began to swing it. She could dodge agents. She couldn't dodge this.

Hands at her sides, she slowly backed up, her heart pounding a sickening beat in her chest. A flash of pain worked through her as something hit her in the back. She quickly identified it as a stunner blast. Not powerful enough to make her muscles lock up, but powerful enough to make her scream with pain. Through the haze of tears that filled her eyes, she saw the agent with the electro-chain flash white teeth as he laughed. The chain swung towards her and she dodged it, but only just.

The end of the alley opened out onto a walkway. It was a twenty-metre drop over the side. She'd probably survive it, but walking away from it would be out of the question. She risked a glance up, saw nothing but the smooth curve of the roof. There was no way out.

The tip of the electro-chain caught her on the front of her thigh, cutting a searing gash into her flesh. It burned with an agony she couldn't ignore, and that made her mad. These people were supposed to be on her side. With a scream of rage, she charged towards the agent, towards the burning lash of the electro-chain.

She never reached him. Strong arms locked around her and Jinn found herself being lifted clear off the floor. 'Hold on tight,' whispered a voice in her ear. A low, rough, familiar voice.

'Dax,' she said, the word forced out without air. His forearm was a vice around her waist, making it impossible to breathe. And then she was flying, the electro-chain slashing towards them in a bright yellow arc of promised pain. Dax took them over the side of the walkway, Jinn's stomach lurching as they dropped, as the air rushed past in a second that seemed to last forever.

Jinn closed her eyes, not sure if she could handle the pain of the impact, not knowing if he could either, only knowing that, in that moment, she was safe. He smelled of blood and sweat, his body was hot and hard against her back. She clenched her fists as she braced herself for the impact.

And then it came, with a hard, bone-shaking thump that she barely had time to process before they were moving again. Dax twisted her in his arms so that she was facing him, jerking her up so that her legs locked around his waist and her arms automatically caught around his neck. 'Don't let go,' he warned.

Then he started to run.

She could feel his muscles work, hear the fierce pull as he took in air. Around her, the world started to blur. She was tipped to the side and he put one strong arm around her again, holding her in place as he left the floor and used the wall instead. They climbed higher, higher, his pace never relenting for a moment, leaving the walkway and the security agents far behind. Stunner shots rushed past them, burning out as they hit the wall, the ceiling. Still he didn't slow, didn't show any sign of tiring. Everything around her was lost, Caspian Dax the only real thing in her world and she clung to him with everything she had, her heart racing.

He climbed higher, higher up the vertical wall before arcing across the curved roof. Then they were rushing down the wall on the other side, down, down to the crowded walkway of the lower floor. Dax charged his way through amid shouts and roars of complaint. As they pushed through, others pushed back, and behind him Jinn saw the first of several fights break out. Limbs, tongues and tentacles were involved, blades appearing from nowhere. The flash of metal was rapidly followed by shrieks of fury and spurts of bodily fluid in shades of blue and green and white.

Dax moved away from the open square, which was rapidly turning into a bloodbath, and into a narrow passageway. He pressed his back against the wall as several Sittan rushed past, hoods down, their facial spikes on full display.

Slowly, Jinn lowered her feet to the floor. His arm was still locked around her waist, her arms still around his neck. They clung together like lovers, pressed tight, sharing space, heat, air. He stared down at her, a muscle twitching in his jaw, then he slowly lowered his hands.

'Let's go,' she said. Without waiting for him to agree, she was off and running. Away from the fighting and the carnage, away from the agents, and away from whatever it was that she had felt when he had touched her.

# CHAPTER
# 15

**25th August 2207**

Space Station Europa, Sector Three, Neutral Space

They quickly found the ring of elevators that would take them down to the lowest part of the Europa, where the docking bays and workshops were housed. Dax followed Jinn into an empty elevator car. She put herself in the rear corner, hands tucked behind her back, one foot resting on the wall. She looked like she would gut someone simply because she didn't like the way they looked at her. It echoed the way he felt.

The lights on the control panel started to flash, warning them that the elevator was about to start moving. And then it dropped. His stomach was still somewhere on the second level when the car slowed to a halt and the gates opened. Jinn moved first, shoving past him. The slight contact put his body even more on edge. She moved through the packed concourse with determined speed, her white-blonde hair making it impossible to lose sight of her.

There was movement in all directions as passengers moved to and from the docking bays. Most would have tickets for the public transports. Those who had enough credits to own their own ships were heading through the wide walkway on the left, the entrance to which was blocked by a droid-operated barrier. Jinn kept charging forwards, dodging cleaning droids and aliens. Dax cut his own path alongside.

All they had to do was pass through that barrier and they were as good as gone. It went without saying that it wasn't going to be that easy.

Jinn grabbed his arm. 'Dax.' Instinct made him follow as she tugged him over to the side of the concourse, pressing herself against the wall. 'Agents,' she muttered, her attention focussed somewhere behind him.

Quickly, Dax moved beside her. A swift sweep of the crowd and he saw them. Six uniformed agents, four men and two women. Already the other occupants of the concourse were starting to scatter, the crowd starting to thin. He couldn't blame them. Fighting amongst themselves was one thing. Getting tangled with agents was another, especially here.

'Your blades ready?' He glanced down at her. She was pressed tight against the wall, but she moved her hands enough to show him that they were. 'Good,' he said. 'Get ready to use them.'

She nodded. A stray strand of hair fell across her cheek, obscuring her eyes. She tried to push it back, but her blade got in the way. Dax reached out, tucked it back behind her ear. Her skin was warm against his fingertips, her hair soft. There was a dark smudge under her nose. Without thinking, he touched it. When he brought his hand away, his finger was red. 'You're bleeding,' he said.

'What?' She jerked the back of her hand up to her face, scrubbing at the underside of her nose, then she angled herself away from him. 'It's nothing,' she said. Biting into her sleeve, she pulled the fabric down over her hand and then held it under her nose. 'I'm fine.'

Dax was about to disagree when a riot of blaster fire exploded around them. Shouts ripped through the air, interrupted by the staccato pop of sharp-tipped spitzer darts cutting holes in the walls, in the floor. These were no stunner shots, designed to disable. They were designed to maim, to hurt. Through the rushing, panicking, screaming crowd, he saw a sight that filled him with sick fury. Alistair, Eve and Theon, back to back, with agents moving to surround them. They were outgunned and outnumbered and in trouble.

'We've got to help them,' Jinn said, and for once Dax was in total agreement. She darted left as he broke right, pushing his way through the panicking crowd. With a swift kick to the head, he took out one of the agents. The man dropped to the floor, but he was already trying to get up even as his companion swung his blaster in Dax's direction. 'Don't be fucking stupid,' Dax yelled at him. With lightning-fast reflexes, he grabbed the shooter by the neck, lifting him clear off the floor. In his peripheral vision he saw a blaster clatter to the floor as Jinn disarmed one of the women, blades flashing. The attack scattered the agents, giving his crew all the advantage they needed.

The sickening sound of bones snapping pushed through the air as Theon delivered a crippling punch to the face of an agent. His victim dropped like a stone in a high-gravity chamber, his nose broken. Then Theon moved, shielding Alistair and Eve. In a swift move Alistair dropped to one knee, snatched up the weapon that the agent had dropped, and took aim.

Dax didn't wait to see if he hit his target. He tossed his agent aside, the man flying across the concourse and hitting the wall on the other side, then spun on his heel, prepared to take out whoever was left. Three more agents were down, thanks to Theon and Alistair, and as he watched, Jinn disabled another. The man staggered back, clutching his stomach, blood everywhere. Dax bent down to pick up another blaster that one of the agents had dropped. It was time to end this.

'I wouldn't do that if I were you.'

Dax jerked upright. The words had been spoken by a tall, blond man with a regulation crew-cut and dark, furious eyes. Where in the void had he come from? The agent had Theon in a stranglehold, a blaster pressed tight against the side of the droid's head. Dax stayed where he was, letting the agent think he was in control, watching the careful flick of Theon's fingers out of the corner of his eye.

Dax replied to Theon's suggestion that they leave him with a rapid twist of his thumb that indicated a definite no. He turned his palm out, touched his thumb to his little finger, making sure Eve could see his hand. He could only hope that Jinn would realise what he intended once it kicked off. 'Let him go,' he said to the agent. 'I'll come quietly.'

'You'll shut up and do as you're told,' the agent said. His chest was rising and falling rapidly, his nostrils flaring with every exhale. 'You should be on the A2, where you belong.'

Dax took a step forward.

The agent didn't move. 'Keep your hands where I can see them.'

'I'm unarmed,' Dax pointed out.

The agent ignored him. 'Blue,' he said, shifting his gaze to her. 'I would ask you how you got here, but the answer is obvious.'

'Bryant,' she said. 'Can't say I'm happy to see you.'

So this was the bastard who had shot him full of K and dumped them both onboard the A2. Dax looked him over. He was tall, though not as tall as Dax, and leanly muscled under his uniform. He looked like a vain bastard, from his neatly trimmed hair to his manicured hands and shiny boots, but Dax wasn't stupid. He knew danger when he saw it.

'I don't want to hurt you,' Bryant said to her. 'So don't make me.'

'As I recall,' Jinn replied, 'I could never make you do anything you didn't want to do.'

Bryant smiled. 'How right you are.'

Dax felt an instant rush of protective fury but he controlled it, right up to the point when Bryant shifted his blaster away from Theon and pointed it straight at Jinn. There was no hesitation, not this time. Dax flung himself at Bryant, hitting him full force. Theon rolled away and Dax found himself with his hands around the agent's neck. The killer instinct that normally lay dormant in him roared into life. He wanted to end this man, wanted to put him down for threatening Jinn. For threatening all of them.

Sweat trickled down his back, his adrenalin spiking as the agent stared back at him with those dark, flat eyes. Dax showed his annoyance with a fist to the face that had the agent's head snapping back.

Bryant fixed those flat eyes on him again, blood dripping from a deep cut below his eye. It fell onto Dax's hand, hot and unpleasant. 'I hoped you'd fight,' he snarled. 'It means I can justify doing this.' Dax stilled as he felt the cold, hard barrel of the blaster press against his groin. 'Look at you, you smug bastard, thinking it's acceptable for you to live outside the law. You're nothing more than Underworld scum. You deserve everything that's coming to you, Caspian Dax. I only wish it was more.'

A cold chill pooled in the pit of his stomach. Then Bryant went rigid. His mouth opened, a string of saliva trickling out of one corner. His dark eyes turned glassy and he exhaled with a slow, agonised groan. Then he collapsed to the floor, motionless.

Eve stood close to him, her eyes huge, her face pale. She lowered a shaking hand to her side. 'He was going to kill you,' she said. 'I had to do it.' She blinked fast. 'I had to.'

Dax nudged the unconscious agent with the toe of his boot. 'He got what he deserved.' Then he turned to Alistair. 'You're with us?'

'Doesn't look like I have much choice,' Alistair replied.

Dax risked a glance at Jinn. Her chin was held high, but she was shaking. Blood spattered her clothes, her face. 'Are you alright?'

She wiped her blades on the sides of her trousers and nodded.

No-one said a word as they made their way towards the barrier. The concourse was empty and oddly silent, the air thick with the smell of burnt-out darts and blood. It wouldn't stay empty for long. News of the incident would already be all over the station.

Dax shoved Jinn through into the tunnel when the barrier opened, taking her arm before she could stop him. He pulled her close and inspected her, wanting to see if any of the blood was hers. But there was too much to tell either way.

'I told you I was alright,' she said, tugging free from his grip. 'I can take care of myself.'

'I am more than aware of that,' Dax replied, as the others surged forward onto the walkway, which was wide and brightly lit. She staggered a little as the floor began to move beneath her feet, propelling her forward. 'But you don't seem to be doing a very good job of it.'

Ahead, he could see the sprawl of the private docking bays, some empty, some occupied, and the ugly shape of the *Deviant*.

'So I guess the question now is, are you going to keep trying to take care of yourself, or are you with us too?'

Jinn hesitated, but only for a moment. If her life had changed the moment she'd left the A2 with Dax, it had been completely smashed apart when she'd attacked those agents. She hadn't wanted to hurt any of them. But she'd done what she had to do.

*Better them than me.*

She focussed all her attention on the *Deviant*. It sat in its allotted bay, the battered, curving shell softly humming. The door at the side slid back and the steps unfolded. Eve and the strange man boarded the ship first, disappearing into the belly of the transporter a moment before something exploded on the ground next to Jinn's feet. Her heart stopped for a moment as she jumped away from the smoking spot.

Dax swore. Jinn glanced back and saw several agents running towards them. Their uniforms were spattered with blood, their expressions grim, and there was no mistaking their intent. A red tracker light shimmered on her sleeve. Keeping her focus on the entry ramp, Jinn blocked out everything else. All she thought about was putting one foot in front of the other. She could feel Dax's warm bulk close behind her, feel the floor shudder beneath her feet as he too broke into a run. He didn't overtake her, though she knew he was more than capable of it. Her head filled with a strange, pulsing buzz, everything happening too fast and yet too slow. The transporter seemed so very far away, and as another shot screamed past her head, she stumbled.

A strong hand caught her, steadied her. She looked up to see Theon. 'Hurry,' he said. He released his grip and Jinn kept moving. This time, when the fire came, she was ready for it. Shots whizzed past her head, one ripping through the skin of her upper arm, burning the flesh beneath. Her foot hit the bottom step and she scrambled upwards, grateful when the man who had jumped on board with Eve grabbed her upper arm. He pulled her deep into the *Deviant*, out of the line of fire.

Through the open entrance of the transporter, she could see Dax. She saw him grimace as a stunner shot struck him though he didn't stop, didn't falter. His gaze met hers, fierce and determined. 'Come on!' she screamed, not understanding why he wasn't moving faster, why he hadn't been right behind her. And then she saw Theon. He lay on the floor in a crumpled, twitching heap, his flamboyant red outfit riddled with holes. Smoke poured out of them. Dax swerved over to him, picking up the droid's bulk and hefting his weight onto his shoulder. Another shot met its target and Jinn winced as she saw Dax's thigh start to bleed. Behind Dax, she could see the agents moving closer, their weapons trained on him. 'Come on!' she screamed. 'Come on!'

Eve moved to the control panel next to the door. Her fingers flew over the touchpad. The steps started to fold inwards.

Jinn had her blades out in an instant. 'What are you doing?' she yelled. Dax was close, but not close enough. Blaster darts were still screaming towards them, exploding with flashes of orange light as they hit the outside of the transporter. The smell of hot metal was overwhelming, the smell of blood even more so. The steps were rapidly folding away with a smooth, quiet motion.

'Saving our necks,' Eve said grimly.

'What about Dax?'

Someone grabbed her arm, pulled her away from the door.

Jinn whirled, stopped with her blades a millimetre from the face of the man she didn't know. He had light blue eyes, neat dark hair. He looked like an Underworld version of Bryant. She controlled herself, just, and staggered back.

Through the open doorway, she could see Dax. He was running, legs pumping, but in a few more seconds the door would be closed. 'If he doesn't make it,' she said, her throat tight, 'I'll kill both of you.'

If either of them replied, she didn't hear it. Dax launched himself towards the open doorway. He soared towards her, flying through the air, one arm clinging tightly to Theon, the other circling as if he could pull himself forward. 'He's not going to make it!'

But he did. One foot caught the top step and then he collapsed onto the floor of the transporter, Theon's mangled frame sprawling out next to him. He lifted his head, caught Jinn with his gaze. 'Get us out of here,' he said.

She wanted to stay, to swear and rant and touch him. But his tone brooked no argument. Jinn sprinted out of the small loading bay, heading for the upper level of the transporter and the control deck. She flung herself into the pilot's chair, took a deep breath and pulled in her blades. Then she positioned her hands over the ports. Her brain tingled as the tech plugged itself into the hardware of the onboard computer system and then she was in.

She fired up the phase drive. The ship vibrated beneath her, her retinal screen switching on as she backed out of the docking bay. She would have liked a few moments to orient herself with the exact dimensions of the *Deviant*, but there wasn't time.

The doors at the far end of the bay were opening, slowly revealing the inside of the airlock that separated the Europa from the vacuum of space. She could see the fat bulk of a long-distance passenger barge moving slowly towards it, towards freedom.

'I need the departure code,' she called, hoping one of the others could hear her.

'Theon has it,' came the reply. Eve.

Without a valid code, she wouldn't be able to leave the Europa. *No.* She wouldn't accept it. She wouldn't. Her mind made up, Jinn flew the ship directly at the airlock. The phase drive was both powerful and responsive, giving her an instant burst of speed. She wouldn't need a code if she could time this right. If she could hitch a ride with the other vessel, slide in alongside it as it entered the docking bay and get them away from the Europa before they got caught in the tail stream of the barge, just as Theon had done when he'd flown them away from the A2.

It would take every bit of skill she possessed to achieve it. There was no margin for error. Focussing only on her link with the ship and the view from the screens, Jinn blocked out everything else and headed straight for the barge. Within seconds she was flying alongside it, close enough to see the rivets that held the steel plates of its hull together. The control room filled with the wailing sound of the onboard alarms, indicating that collision was imminent.

She didn't see the others come into the control room, not until someone moved to stand alongside her. Instinct told her it was Dax. The desire to look at him, to see the full extent of his injuries was fierce, but she didn't. Matching the speed of the *Deviant* to the barge was agonisingly difficult. She had to keep all her energy focussed on restraining the eager phase drive. The doors were fully open now, revealing the dark hole of the airlock and the stretch of space that lay beyond.

Her fingers curled on the control panel as she mentally fought for control of the vessel, fought to control her fear. It was all happening so fast. A hand curved over her shoulder. Dax. 'Breathe,' he said.

Jinn gritted her teeth. 'Everyone strap in. This is going to get bumpy.' She gave them a few seconds to get to their seats. And then she flipped the *Deviant* to the underside of the barge just as they flew into the airlock. Beyond the open exterior doors, escape beckoned and she took that breath, took it in deep.

Then she let the phase drive go and flew them out into the darkness. She didn't know where she was heading, only that she needed to fly and she needed to put as much distance as possible between the *Deviant* and the Europa. But the *Deviant* was small, the phase drive powerful, which meant that they would quickly burn off what had to be a limited supply of fuel. She couldn't keep going like this indefinitely.

She needed a destination. 'Where to?'

'Eve,' Dax said. At his command, the other woman hooked on the Smartware headset, her hands working the touch controls effortlessly. Then she turned to Dax. 'They're orbiting Zeta Three,' she said.

'No further communications,' Dax said to Eve. 'I don't want them to know we're coming.' Then he turned to Jinn. 'Know where that is?'

She nodded. 'Close to Jump Gate 89.'

'Can you get us there?'

Jinn smiled. With a single mental command, she powered up the phase drive. The *Deviant* hummed with a thrilling rush of power. 'Yes,' she said. 'Get ready to jump.'

# CHAPTER

# 16

**25th August 2207**

Santa Paula Plaza, New Mexico Dome, Earth

Ana Rizzola's funeral was a fussy, emotional affair, and that took Ferona by surprise. She had expected the pomp and ceremony, but not the tears. More than that, she had not expected them to be genuine.

She should have known better. Vice President Dubnik was not one to hide his feelings. At first she had thought that his outpouring of grief was a play for the media, but it continued as they sat through the holographic tribute detailing the important moments of Rizzola's life. Ferona kept her gaze fixed on the screen, dabbing at her eyes with a delicate lace handkerchief that matched the printed silk of her antique dress.

Cameras hovered overhead, broadcasting the entire spectacle on one of the news channels. The plaza itself was beautiful, decorated with white flowers and candles. Rizzola's body had already been recycled, so there was no coffin on display. There had been no post-mortem.

Ferona had seen to that.

As the tribute ended, Dubnik got to his feet and walked to the front of the crowd. He began to speak. His voice broke on the words.

Ferona was still waiting for him to pull himself together when her personal comm. flashed.

At first she ignored it, but it continued to flash, the little red light winking through the flimsy fabric of her bell sleeve. She glanced around. No-one was looking at her. They were all too busy pretending to be interested in whatever Dubnik was saying.

She discreetly pulled back her cuff and checked her comm. unit. Eight messages from Swain. Ferona pursed her lips. It was not like her assistant to bother her at a time like this. Whatever the problem, it was urgent.

Letting her sleeve fall back into place, she considered her options. She couldn't answer the call here, but if she walked out, it would look bad.

Her only option was to make it look good.

She slowly rose to her feet, her handkerchief pressed to her mouth. Dubnik turned his head and fixed red-rimmed, hate-filled eyes on her. Ferona ignored him. She was, after all, the newly elected Earth representative for the Intergalactic Senate, and she had managed to achieve this without losing her place in government, and despite Dubnik's opposition. She was now the most powerful woman in government.

It felt wonderful.

But she did have an image to maintain. So she stumbled as she made her way into the women's rest room, gripping the back of the nearest seat and accepting the offer of help from a nearby security droid. Once inside the rest room, she locked herself into one of the cubicles and called Swain. He appeared on screen almost instantly. His hair was untidy, and there was a look of flushed panic on his face.

'Whatever the reason for this intrusion, it had better be exceptional,' she told him. 'Or I will end your career before this call is over.'

'I've had a message from my contact in the Security Service,'

Swain told her. His voice was breathless, as if he'd been running. 'We have a problem.'

'What sort of problem?'

Swain hesitated. It was only slight, but Ferona felt her stomach tighten. 'Your ... your daughter has somehow managed to escape from the A2.'

For a moment, Ferona thought she had misheard. 'No-one escapes from the A2. It's impossible.'

'Apparently not,' Swain said. He reached into his pocket and pulled out a patterned handkerchief and wiped his forehead with it.

'Explain.'

'Your ... Pilot Blue made a call from a public comm. station to her direct superior approximately four hours ago.'

A chill settled over Ferona, a sense of deep, terrifying calm. She inhaled and then exhaled just as slowly. 'Forgive me, Swain, but I thought I heard you say that she made the call four hours ago.'

'She did,' Swain said. He was trembling now, his eyes darting nervously around the screen. 'A team of experienced agents was dispatched to her location.'

'Please tell me there was a tidy, bloodless extraction and that she is already back in custody.'

When he didn't respond, she had her answer.

'Would you care to explain to me what happened?'

'Perhaps you should turn on the newsfeed,' Swain said quietly. There was a tone of resignation in his voice.

Ferona stared at him, wondering how she could have missed a personality defect so profound. 'Computer, turn on the newsfeed.'

Swain shrank to a tiny corner of the screen, the rest filled with the newsfeed. Ferona had long considered the media to be a friend. She had connections in the press offices of all the main channels. She kept them onside with long lunches and snippets of gossip that were occasionally more than gossip.

And this was how they paid her back.

On the screen was an image of Jinn, pale hair flying wild, curving blades extending from her hands, slashing out at an agent. Her face was twisted in an angry snarl as blood splattered across her jacket and across the floor.

There was no mistaking her. Even though she hadn't seen Jinn in years, Ferona knew her own flesh and blood. She also knew the huge dark-haired man who crashed into the picture and punched another of the agents in the face. She shifted her gaze to Swain. 'You didn't tell me Caspian Dax had also escaped!'

'I . . . it didn't seem as important,' Swain mumbled.

'You're a bloody fool.' Ferona touched the corner of her comm. unit. The image changed again. 'Lucinda? I need you at the office. Yes, now.'

She ended the call and pressed her fingers to her temples as Swain came back on screen. 'I don't want to know how this happened,' she said. 'I only want to know how you're going to fix it. If you don't, I will destroy not only your career, but your entire life. Do I make myself clear?'

'Yes,' Swain nodded, his head moving too fast. His throat moved as he swallowed.

At the moment, the threat was only that. A threat. Swain was too useful to get rid of. And he knew too much. She needed him if things were to continue to progress. With her move to the senate imminent, it was vital that she was seen to be not only managing her ministerial and senatorial workloads, but doing so with professional ease.

Ignoring Swain, who now appeared to be in the middle of having a breakdown, Ferona turned her attention back to the newsfeed. She wanted to see exactly what had been reported. It might not be the truth, but she needed to know what story had been pieced together.

She watched the segment from start to finish. Twice. The A2 wasn't mentioned. But she was.

'The woman has been identified as Jinnifer Blue, daughter of

146

Minister for Off World Affairs and newly elected member of the Intergalactic Senate, Ferona Blue. It is not known how Ms Blue came to be in the company of Caspian Dax, a known pirate who has a substantial bounty on his head. However the official body count currently stands at seven, all members of the Security Service.'

Ferona stared at the image of Dax. Huge, dark-haired, fists flying. He was formidable. She couldn't help but admire the way he moved, with such power and grace that she found herself leaning forward, almost forgetting everything else.

Then the image changed.

'As yet, two questions remain unanswered,' said the reporter. The image zoomed in on Jinn's hands. 'What sort of prosthetics are these? Are they in fact prosthetics or are they something else? And where did Ms Blue get them?'

It was a damn good question and one that Ferona didn't have the answer to.

The reporter's face loomed large on the screen. 'And the most puzzling question of all,' he said. His dark eyes twinkled with what could only be described as excitement. 'This woman was also present during the altercation.'

At the side of the screen, next to the reporter's ice-white smile, was an image of a petite, apparently human, woman. She was wearing a beautiful dark coat that matched her dark hair. And she was green.

Ferona felt something that she hadn't felt in a very, very long time. She almost didn't recognise it at first, but as it grew stronger, sinking claws of ice into her limbs, she was forced to see it for what it was.

Fear.

Her mouth went dry, her nails digging into the palms of her hands as she stared at the image. This was bad. This was very, very bad. 'Who is she?' she snapped at Swain. 'Is this another escape?'

'I don't know,' he said.

'Then find out!'

He half nodded, half bowed as the call ended.

Leaning back in her seat, Ferona took a moment to find her calm. She needed to think, to calculate, to plan. Jinn would have to be found, and quickly. She had attacked agents and that made Ferona look weak. And those strange blades ... It wouldn't matter that off world crime rates were the lowest they'd been in several decades. That one incident would over-shadow it all.

Still, if she could get Jinn back to the A2 and have her modi-fied as she had originally planned, something could be salvaged from this. Regardless of what happened in the future, Ferona had no intention of remaining on Earth. Her daughter was still an astonishingly capable pilot. Add to that strength, speed and superb healing ability and she would make a bodyguard that no-one would challenge. Particularly with those blades.

If only she'd been able to correct Jinn's defects during child-hood, this could all have been avoided. But she had been busy, Ferona admitted to herself, sometimes too busy to ensure that Jinn was developing as she intended. She had only herself to blame. Now was the time to fix that mistake.

Then there was the issue of the green woman. Medipro had admitted some time ago that their original modification pro-gramme had been problematic. Most of the subjects had died. Several, including Caspian Dax, had escaped, but Medipro had assured her that the Type Two and Type Three subjects who had escaped with him would all have died within a matter of weeks.

Either they were wrong, or there was also an issue with secu-rity at the women's prison on the Moon as well as at the A2.

But that wasn't Ferona's biggest problem.

Caspian Dax was.

He had to be found. Promises had been made which had to be kept. Swivelling her chair from side to side, Ferona steepled her fingers together and considered her options. There weren't many.

In fact, there was only one. She had hoped to delay this, for a little while anyway, but circumstances had changed. It was time.

'Computer, contact Weston.'

Phase Three was Ferona's backup plan, her personal insurance against disasters such as this.

And it would not fail her now.

# CHAPTER

# 17

Vessel: The *Deviant*. Short-haul Corvette
Destination: Zeta trading post
Cargo: None
Crew: Four
Droids: One

It took a little over fifteen hours for them to reach the *Mutant*. Jinn bounced them through three separate jumps, each one skilfully controlled and taken at a speed that made Dax's eyeballs hurt. The only other person he'd met who could fly like this was Theon.

His friend lay in a pitiful broken heap in the small cargo hold. Dax had been in to see him several times, but there was nothing he could do to help. It would take engineering skill far beyond the basic knowledge that he possessed to put the droid back together.

And his wounds were taking their toll. He was healing, and with every passing minute he felt better, stronger, but such rapid recovery was exhausting and he needed to eat. So did Jinn. She was already starting to look pale. Dax left the control room and made his way to the upper level of the corvette, which housed a four-bunk dorm, a sanitation unit and chemicleanse and a small communal rec area.

He found Eve stretched out on a narrow bunk and Alistair pacing the floor, chewing on his index finger, his skin a shade best described as grey. 'I'd forgotten how much I hate space travel.'

'You'll get used to it,' Dax replied, slapping him on the back. Alistair groaned.

Eve twisted herself into a sitting position, gripping the edges of the bunk so tightly her knuckles whitened. 'How's Theon?'

'About as well as can be expected.'

Eve blinked, looked away. He could tell she was trying not to cry. What had happened on the Europa had been hard on her. It had been hard on all of them, but they would get over it. Eve might not.

'I've never seen agents on the Europa before,' Alistair put in. 'This is bad, Caspian. This is very bad.' He stopped pacing for a moment, folded his arms. 'Any idea what you might have done to piss the government off?'

'He's been pissing them off for years,' Eve pointed out. 'They've just never been able to catch him.'

'Or they've never wanted to,' Dax said. It was a thought that had been scratching at the inside of his brain for the past few hours. 'Why now? What's changed?'

'Is it something we stole?' Eve wondered.

'Most likely everything we stole,' Dax said. 'But they didn't come to the Europa for me. They came for Jinn.'

'How . . . '

There was no point trying to hide the truth. 'She contacted her boss. They tracked her location and sent in the agents.'

'What on Earth did she do that for?'

'Because apparently, she has morals. She worked for the Security Service, remember? She wanted to do something about what we saw on the A2. She thought it was the right thing to do, Eve. You can hardly blame her for that.'

151

Eve jumped down from the bunk. 'I'm going to see if we're in comm. range yet.'

'Eve,' Dax said.

'What?'

'We need a pilot,' Dax said. 'She's good and she's available. Whatever she's done, we're going to have to put it aside. She didn't do it to put us in danger. And we need her.'

'Do we?' Eve asked. She walked away before he could answer.

Alistair shot a swift glance at her retreating back, then turned to Dax. 'I hope you're prepared for trouble,' he said.

'Theon is in pieces. I've got security agents on my arse, a traitor on my crew and Jinnifer Blue is flying this bird. I've already got trouble.'

'Yes,' Alistair said. 'That's what I'm afraid of.' He moved to the bunk Eve had been sitting on, ran his hand over the top. 'How many do you have on the crew these days?'

'Twenty,' Dax informed him. He'd been hoping to recruit a few more on Zeta Three, but Bryant had screwed up that plan.

'How many Bugs?'

'Nineteen.'

'And the other one?'

'Space brat. Father was a smuggler. She was born onboard his ship.'

'How many like us?'

'We are the only ones like us,' Dax said, though his mind rushed to the things he'd seen on board the A2. 'No,' he said slowly. 'Scratch that.'

He knew the moment Alistair heard what he was thinking.

'You said the programme has been restarted.'

Dax turned away, fixing his attention back on the sophisticated Autochef mounted on the opposite wall. He thumbed the touch screen, ordered the first option that came up on the menu, then turned back to Alistair. 'The A2 has been turned into a mass medical facility. The kind that needs electrified holding cages.'

Alistair sat back on the bunk. 'I guess we should be grateful they weren't using those when we were modified.'

The Autochef beeped and Dax opened the hatch. It had prepared him a steaming platter of Argarian stew. He lifted it out, hungrily chewed it down before ordering another. 'The prisons are privately owned, right?'

'As far as I know,' Alistair replied. 'The government provides the funds, but they don't get their hands dirty.'

Dax thought about this for a moment. 'I wonder how hard it would be to persuade the owner of a prison to let you use it as a medical facility.'

'Probably not that difficult,' Alistair said. 'People will do just about anything if the price is right. And if you pay them enough, they won't ask too many questions about what you're doing.'

'So you could gas ten thousand criminals and no-one would care.'

'Medipro were crooks when we signed up for their programme. No reason to think they'd be any different now.'

'But why?' Dax asked. 'Why carry on with those modifications? And why on such a large scale?'

'Maybe they've changed the serum,' Alistair said. 'Maybe it's different now.'

'Whatever they're doing,' Dax told him, 'it's not good. And fuck only knows why Jinn was left on board.'

Alistair shrugged. 'Her partner could have gone rogue. It happens.'

Dax shook his head. 'He was on the Europa. He's a violent, unpleasant bastard. But he was totally sane. I'd bet my life on it.'

'So he was following orders.'

'Exactly. As far as I can tell, she's spent the past twenty years keeping her head down and generally trying to stay out of trouble. Why is she suddenly at the top of the most-wanted list? She's hardly a threat. And the A2 is a male prison. Either Jinnifer Blue is the most feminine man I ever saw ... '

'Or the government deliberately sent a woman to the A2.'

Dax nodded.

'It could have been a mistake,' Alistair said. 'Or it could have something to do with her prosthetics. The female prison is on the Moon. Maybe they thought she'd escape.'

'She escaped from the A2,' Dax pointed out.

'With your help.' Alistair shoved his hands back through his hair and leaned back against the bunk. 'And escaping from a vessel in orbit is an entirely different scenario to escaping on the surface. Let's be realistic. We know the government has decided they need to clamp down on any off world activity that makes it look like they can't control their people. They're trying to show the Intergalactic Senate that we're a race worth saving. She's got highly illegal prosthetics. Break the law, go to prison. It's as simple as that.'

Dax shoved his empty plate back into the Autochef, which instantly switched into cleanse mode. 'It's never as simple as that.'

Alistair rubbed a hand over his face. 'Only because you hate to see things as black and white, my friend. Do you really think one of the crew turned you in?'

'The take was too clean.' Dax turned back to the Autochef, ordered himself another plate of food. 'They knew exactly where I'd be. Shot me full of K in the bloody chemicleanse. I didn't even have my trousers on.'

Alistair laughed. 'It wouldn't be the first time you were caught with your pants down.'

'First time in a long time,' Dax said grimly. 'And the other times, at least a pleasure droid was involved. It was too tidy. One agent, Alistair. One.'

'Someone let him board.'

'Can you think of any other way it could have happened?'

Before Alistair could answer that question, the intercom buzzed. Eve's voice came through. 'Time to return to the control deck, boys,' she said. 'We're home.'

\*

This time, when the *Mutant* opened its huge jaws and swallowed them, Jinn was prepared for it. But when the phase drive powered down and she disconnected from the controls, she couldn't stop her hands from shaking. What had happened on board the Europa had changed everything. She had to face reality.

After years of a quiet, peaceful existence, she'd attacked a group of agents without hesitation. She didn't want to go to prison, but that was where she was headed if agents caught up with her again. She had no credits and the only place she had to go was this ship. A pirate ship, filled with Bugs, one of whom was probably passing information on to the Security Service.

Jinn didn't say anything when Eve strolled onto the control deck and took her seat at the comm. station. Eve ignored her right back, and that suited Jinn just fine. Now they had actually made it, now they were inside the belly of the massive pirate ship, she felt cold with nerves. The *Mutant* was full of strangers. They were hardly going to welcome a Dome pilot with smiles and open arms.

Holding the earpiece up to her ear, Eve thumbed a few buttons on the control panel. 'Hey,' she said. 'Yeah. We've got him. Get word round, will you?' The light of the control deck emphasised her unusual skin colour, making the pattern that extended down her cheek and neck look darker, highlighting the delicate swirls. Jinn dropped her gaze away, not wanting to be caught staring. She straightened her fingers and carefully willed the Tellurium back inside her body. The wires quickly pulled back inside her hands. The bracelets that circled her wrists blinked amber, indicating that the Tellurium had dissociated into microdroplets. It would remain inactive until she needed it again.

Jinn folded her hands in her lap, her palms burning as her body slowly healed the wounds. She was hungry. Her stomach ached with it. She needed food, but she didn't know when she'd be able to get any, or what would be available.

She risked a glance at Eve. Maybe she should at least try to connect with these people. 'Who is he?' she asked.

'Who?'

'The man who came onboard with us.'

Eve stared at her controls. 'His name is Alistair,' she said. 'He's . . . he used to . . .'

'Did he escape from the programme with you?'

'Yes,' Eve said.

'He doesn't look unusual.'

'That's because his modifications are hidden.' Eve unhooked her Smartware headset, let it dangle in her hands. 'They altered his hearing.'

'Altered it how?'

'He can hear the nerves firing in your brain.'

'You mean he can hear people's thoughts?'

'Yes.'

Jinn slumped back in her seat. 'That's scary.'

'Scarier than superhuman strength and toxic skin?'

'You can hide from strength and you can hide from poison,' Jinn said. 'You can't hide from someone who can hear every private thought going on inside your head.' She flexed her fingers, trying to alleviate the sting in her palms. They were still bleeding. She could feel the warm, sticky slide of it over her skin. But there wasn't time to deal with it now, as Dax and Alistair walked onto the control deck.

Alistair walked over to Jinn. He held out a bowl and a cup. 'I'm Alistair,' he said.

'I know,' Jinn said, watching him warily. 'Jinn.' She held his gaze as she tried desperately to empty her mind, to think of something meaningless. Snow. Yes, that would work. Snow snow snow. She took the cup, knocked the contents back in one. It was some sort of creamy soup. She wedged the cup between her knees and took the bowl.

'Eve told me who you are,' he said, giving her a brief smile. He moved away, settled himself in one of the empty seats. Then he gestured to his right ear. 'Aural implant,' he said. 'I can't hear you unless I deactivate it.'

'Oh,' Jinn said. 'And did you?'

'No,' he said. 'Space travel is bad enough without the noise from the phase drive making me bleed out of my ears.'

'Now that we all know each other,' Eve said, 'do you think we could talk about what we're going to do now? The crew is going to want to know what happened, Dax.' She set her heels on the edge of her seat and hugged her knees.

'Our first priority is to figure out who talked to the Security Service,' Dax said. 'We're on communications lockdown until I know who let that agent on board. I want all the comm. stations out of action ASAP. Eve, you're on that. If anyone asks, it's a technical issue. Alistair is going to assess all members of the crew. If there's a traitor on board, he'll find them.'

'What are you going to do when you find out who it is?' asked Eve.

Dax's face hardened and all at once, he was the pirate, the rogue, the remorseless criminal Jinn had believed him to be when she'd delivered him to the A2. 'Deal with it.'

'What about Theon?'

'For now, he's going to have to stay where he is. I'll tell the crew he was injured.'

'They won't like it,' Eve said. 'Any of it.'

'They're not paid to like it,' Dax said. 'They're paid to shut up and do as I say.'

A heavy silence fell. The sound of the outer door to the transporter opening broke through it. 'You know what you need to do,' Dax said to Alistair and Eve.

'I'll take care of it,' Eve said. With a nod, Alistair followed her out of the control deck.

Jinn watched them leave. It felt like days since she'd been alone with Dax, even though it had only been a few hours. She was sweaty and hungry and scared, and more than anything, she needed him to tell her that everything was going to be alright. But he didn't. 'What about me?'

'You're going to have to pilot the *Mutant*.'

'I can't fly your ship!'

'Yes you can. You're the best damn human pilot I've ever met, and you know it.'

Jinn shook her head. 'You don't understand.'

'Then explain it to me.'

'I'd need time to study the schematics, to get to know the phase drives. All engines have quirks. I can't just sit in the pilot's chair and fly. It's not as simple as that.' And more importantly, she had to keep out of the pilot's chair, at least until she'd figured out what was going on with her body.

'I'll tell you one thing I do know,' he said. 'I am not walking onto the control deck of my ship and telling my crew we don't have a pilot.'

'So what are you going to tell them?'

'That Theon was injured on board the Europa, they've got a new pilot and they damn well better show her some respect.'

'Who's flying the *Mutant* now?'

'The autopilot,' he said. 'And it's not smart enough to save our necks when the next lot of agents find us.'

'Do you think agents are going to find us?'

'Don't you?'

'I've no idea what's going to happen,' she said. 'My life is a mess. I've got no credits, there's an arrest warrant with my name on it, I attacked agents, and now I'm on a pirate ship. Not only that, but I'm a *Dome brat* on a pirate ship.' Her gaze locked on his. She found herself breathing too fast, talking too fast. Everything was too fast. She couldn't fly the *Mutant*. But it didn't look like she had any choice. She shouldn't feel the way she did when she looked at him, but she didn't seem to have any choice there either. 'My life wasn't like this until I met you.'

In a move that shocked her, he dug his hands into the front of her shirt and hauled her up onto her toes, crowding her in. 'Since I met you, I've been dumped on the A2, stabbed and shot at,' he yelled. 'My life wasn't like this until I met you, either.'

'Let. Me. Go.' She was far too close to losing control. Her

palms were burning and the bracelets around her wrists were flashing rapidly, indicating that activation of her tech was imminent.

But Dax didn't release her. He stared her down with those green, glowing eyes. His mouth was so close to hers and she could feel the heat pumping out of his body, smell traces of the Europa on him. 'Do you know what's really pissing me off, Jinn?'

Her chest heaved, her hands burning. She had to hold the Tellurium in. She had to. 'What?'

'This,' he said. And then he hauled her up higher, so that only the very tips of her boots were in contact with the floor, angled his head, and took her mouth in a move so swift and possessive that she forgot how to breathe.

Her entire body went rigid with the first thrust of his tongue, and limp with the second. He worked her mouth with hot, fierce desperation, almost as if he had hungered for her, for this. He tasted her deep, and the shock of it started something inside her. What had started out with fury quickly twisted into something else, something equally as potent.

She didn't know she meant to do it until she did. Until she met the slide of his tongue over hers with a ravenous, insatiable hunger. Until she tasted him back, just as he was tasting her, and knew the same desire, the same hunger, dark and overwhelming.

When he slid his hands down her sides to her arse and then pulled her into firm contact with his cock, she bit down on his mouth, bit down hard. Her teeth sank into the soft curve of his lower lip. She tasted blood and her hands slammed against the broad width of his chest. It was a reflex reaction that she couldn't control.

His snarl had her jerking back, heart pounding, eyes wide as she realised what she'd done. The front of his shirt was wet with blood, two neatly sliced holes revealing the puncture wounds she'd made when she'd stuck her blades into his flesh. His chest was heaving, his eyes dark as he stared at her with something she couldn't help believe was rage.

Jinn staggered back, away from him. 'I'm sorry. I'm sorry.' She dropped her hands to her sides, curving her fingers round the metal protruding hideously from her palms. She pressed herself harder against the wall, appalled to find that she was shaking.

'Why?' he asked. 'I forced myself on you, not the other way around.' He closed his eyes. When he opened them again, the glow had gone, but the fire was still there. She could feel it. He straightened up then, though his hands were still clenched in tight fists by his sides and twin roses of blood bloomed on the front of his shirt where she had stabbed him. He moved to the exit.

'Dax . . .' Jinn said.

He stopped.

She wanted to move closer. But she didn't. 'What now?'

He glanced back at her over his shoulder. 'We find you some quarters and introduce you to the crew.' He laughed, but there was no humour in it. 'Welcome to life as a pirate.'

# CHAPTER
# 18

27th August 2207

> Vessel: The *Mutant*. Battleship/carrier hybrid
> Location: Zeta Three trading post
> Cargo: None
> Crew: Twenty-four
> Droids: Eight

It wasn't the first time Dax had thought that his crew were a strange mix. It was, however, the first time he'd viewed them with mistrust. Somewhere on the control deck was the person who had betrayed him to the Security Service, who had directed the *Mutant* to swallow up the unidentified transporter, a ship that would normally never have been of any interest, and had given Bryant entrance to his cabin.

Dax slouched back in the captain's chair and drummed his fingers on the arm. He would have to be careful. He didn't want to spook the crew. They were already unsettled enough, which was understandable given that they'd gone on shore leave and he had disappeared.

He was feeling pretty unsettled himself. Somewhere on the ship was the person who had betrayed him to the Security

Service. Somewhere else on the ship was a pale-haired Dome woman that he couldn't stop thinking about.

But he had to keep focussed. The *Mutant* was a big bastard, and it needed constant maintenance. He settled his gaze on Alistair, who was stood quietly at the back of the room. Alistair met his gaze, answered with a subtle nod. He was listening.

Dax waited for a moment, making sure he had their full attention. 'I assume you all know that a security agent boarded this ship while you were all on downtime on Zeta Three, and that I was taken to the A2.'

A restless silence followed. Dax took that as a yes. 'The government has been cleaning house for months,' he said. 'It's no surprise that I'm on their list. We need to not only assume that they're going to try again, we need to be ready for it. From now on, we're on total lockdown,' he said. 'That means no comms and no shore leave until I say.'

'Might as well be on the A2 if that's how things are going to be,' grumbled a voice from the back.

Dax zeroed in on the speaker immediately. 'I'm the captain,' he said. 'I'm running this operation. You don't like it, feel free to leave.' He waited to see if anyone would move. No-one did. Too afraid, or too loyal? Either way, it didn't matter.

'We can't work without comms,' said someone else. Tyra, a young female modified to work in the shipyards on Colony One. Implanted bionic eyes gleamed at him as she flexed tiny robotic fingers.

'We're not taking any more cargo for the foreseeable future,' Dax told her.

'If we're not taking cargo, how are we supposed to make any credits?'

'You'll get paid,' Dax said. 'A thousand credits a day until we're operational again.' It was more than generous.

'Where's Theon?' asked someone else, one of the fuelling team. 'And what about him?' The man jerked his thumb back at Alistair.

'Some of you will remember Alistair. He used to be a member

of this crew. Those of you who don't will no doubt get to know him over the next few days, as he's decided he wants to be part of the crew again.'

'Doing what?' asked one of the others. 'He doesn't have prosthetics.'

'Maintaining the hydroponic suite that we're going to build in hold two,' Dax said. 'Theon was shot by an agent on the Europa.' There was no point pretending otherwise. The altercation on the space station was all over the newsfeed. But until the traitor had been found, he wasn't prepared to give them any more information than that. 'I brought a replacement pilot with me.'

A rumble of voices started up. His crew were naturally suspicious, even more so now. He couldn't blame them for it. Hydroponics. What was he thinking?

'Who?' Tyra asked.

'Me,' came a voice from the back. Everyone turned. Silence fell. And then the crowd parted and Jinn walked forward. She'd clearly made the most of the chemicleanse and Autochef in the cabin he'd assigned her. She was still pale, but she looked steady. Determined. And her gaze met his without hesitation. When he'd told her she would have to pilot the *Mutant*, she'd argued against it. He wondered what had made her change her mind, or whether it was simply that she had no choice.

'Getting back to the topic of payment, I want four thousand,' Jinn said. She folded her arms, her expression hard. The rest of his crew eyed her with cold suspicion, but she didn't seem to notice.

'You'll get one thousand,' he said. 'The same as everyone else on board.'

'Five,' she said. 'I won't pilot unless you pay me what I'm worth.'

'Five hundred,' Dax replied. He wished he hadn't kissed her. He wished he could kiss her again. 'Keep arguing with me and you'll be scrubbing out the sanitation units.'

'Six thousand,' she said. She walked forwards, coming to a

standstill in front of the pilot's chair. Her fingers stroked the back of it, before she spun it round and dropped into it. 'Or I can just let the autopilot carry on orbiting you round this rock.'

There was amused swearing, nervous laughter from the crew. 'You're the woman from the newsfeed,' someone muttered. 'Jinnifer Blue.'

'In the flesh,' Jinn replied. 'Got a problem with that? Because last I heard, you were down a pilot, and I am a damn good one.' She emphasised every one of those words. 'You need me,' she said. 'And I want six thousand a day.'

One of the Ordnance men stepped forward. 'You're really going to let that Dome bitch do this?'

Dax glanced at the man, saw the angry heat in his eyes. 'Flynn, unless you want to be confined to your quarters until the next time we dock, you'll shut up.' Flynn stared at him, fists clenched, but he kept quiet. 'Anyone else have a problem?' Dax scanned the deck. The rest of the crew wisely chose to stay silent. 'Good. Get back to work.'

The crew shuffled out. Eve dropped into the comm. chair and rubbed a hand over her face. 'Well, Blue,' she said. 'You sure know how to make a scene.'

'There was going to be a scene anyway,' Dax replied. He didn't feel angry. He felt ... turned on. 'So, six thousand?'

'It seems reasonable,' Jinn told him.

'You do know that I'm a pirate.'

'Yes,' she said. 'Which means that you can afford it.' She spun away from him and turned her attention to the controls.

Dax gritted his teeth for a moment. He wanted to shake her. He wanted to take her to his cabin and lock the door and not come out for a week. But there was work to be done. 'Alistair? You pick anything up?'

'There was a lot of noise.' Alistair pushed away from the wall, strolled across the deck, his hands tucked into his pockets. 'They're angry, and scared. I'd say you'll be lucky to keep any of them when this is over.'

If that was the price he had to pay, then so be it. Everyone was tense. He could feel it in himself, amongst his crew. He had felt it on board the Europa, too. Change was coming, for everyone, not just humans. Shoving that thought aside, he turned to Jinn. 'What made you change your mind?'

'You did,' she said. 'You told me I can't hide here, and you're right. So I decided to do the opposite. Plus now that my accounts have gone, I need the credits.' Her hands moved to the controls and the viewscreen switched on. In the distance, Dax could see the pale crater-pocked surface of Zeta Three. This was a little-used area of space, being some distance from the popular space lanes. The small cluster of asteroids had no useful natural resources. It had been mapped, then pretty much ignored, although there had been some attempt at terraforming and it was home to a small colony of traders. 'So, now that we've agreed, where do you want to go?'

'I didn't say that I'd agreed.'

'But you will,' she said, looking back at him over her shoulder. 'Unless, of course, you want me to dump you at the edge of a black hole.'

'You do that,' he said, 'and we're all dead.'

Jinn shrugged.

Alistair dropped into the just-vacated captain's chair. 'I see some things haven't changed,' he said. His tone was light, but the subtle movement of his fingers told Dax that he had something to tell him. Something he didn't want to share with the others.

'Fine,' Dax said. He turned to Jinn. 'You get your six thousand. I want to be in sector four neutral space in an hour.'

'What about me?' Eve said, her tone hopeful. 'What do I get?'

'You get to sit there and shut up,' Dax told her. Her laughter was still echoing in his ears as he strode away from the control deck, Alistair at his side. They walked in silence until they reached the elevator that would take them down into the storage bay. Dax motioned for Alistair to follow him. The ship was rougher down here, hot and dark, the walls unadorned, and he had to stoop to avoid hitting his head. The low rumble of the phase drive made the floor vibrate beneath their feet, and Dax felt the familiar pull in his gut when the drive powered up, indicating that the ship was moving out of orbit.

'I bet you five hundred credits she gets us there in thirty minutes,' Alistair said.

'Twenty,' Dax said, moving to the control panel set into the wall. He thumbed in the code, waited for the door that led through to the bay to slide open. He hadn't been down here in a few days and he made a habit of regularly checking on the vital parts of the ship. He waited for Alistair to move into the storage room and for the door to close behind him. Boxes of kaelite ore were stacked ceiling high in neatly ordered rows, leaving limited standing room. 'You heard something.'

Alistair acknowledged this with a nod. 'Yes,' he said. 'But not from the crew. From your very expensive pilot.'

Dax instinctively knew that he wasn't going to like whatever Alistair had to say.

'She pushed you for six thousand because she wants to have her Tellurium removed,' Alistair said. He picked up an electro-spanner that someone had left behind and tested the weight before setting it back down. 'She's worried that her body has started to reject it.'

'Bloody supernova,' Dax said. He should have seen this. The nosebleed on the Europa. How pale and ill she'd looked after the flight to the *Mutant*. Now he knew why she'd argued when he'd told her she would have to pilot it. He hated himself even more for forcing that kiss on her. If every time she used her Tellurium it made her sick, he had every reason to keep his distance. Getting Theon repaired had to be his number one priority now. If Jinn burned out before he did, they'd have no pilot and then they really would be in trouble.

He had to get to the control deck and make sure she wasn't in a bleeding heap on the floor. He made for the doorway, ducking his head again to avoid hitting it on the way out.

'Did you really kiss her?' Alistair called after him.

Dax groaned.

'Oh,' Alistair said. 'That bad?'

Dax shook his head. 'No,' he said. 'It was that good.'

A short while later, Dax stood in the medical bay and surveyed the remains of his pilot. Theon was a mess. He had brought the droid to the medical bay himself, after ensuring that none of the crew would witness the move. It would probably have been safer to leave him on the *Deviant*, but Theon deserved better than that.

The polyskin that covered his body had burned away in places, exposing platinum bones and plastic muscle. It was hard for Dax to look at him, at the brutal reminder that his friend was less than human no matter how hard he tried to be otherwise.

'Who is flying the ship?' Theon asked.

'Jinn.'

'She has considerable skill,' Theon said. 'A valuable asset, I believe.'

Dax couldn't disagree. 'She's costing me six thousand credits a day.'

Theon laughed. 'So she is both intelligent and beautiful,' he said. 'I believe I may have been permanently replaced.'

'No,' Dax said. 'We're going to get you repaired, Theon. This is just temporary.'

Theon's electric-blue eyes flashed. 'We do not have the necessary parts.'

'I'll get them.'

'That will not be easy. I am not a standard unit.'

'I know what you are,' Dax said. 'And if I say I'm going to get you repaired, I mean it. I don't make promises I can't keep.' There had been significant damage to the circuits that controlled the movement of Theon's legs, rendering him unable to walk, and a tangle of melted wires hung out of the shoulder joint where his right arm should be. But the key part of Theon, his memory circuit, was miraculously intact. The body might be ruined but

Theon was still in there. And a body could be repaired. 'I might not be able to stretch to a full polyskin suit though.'

Even damaged as he was, Theon still managed to look indignant. 'Polyskin would cost considerably less than keeping our new pilot employed.'

Dax raised a brow. 'Are you saying you won't pilot the *Mutant* unless I pay for new skin?'

'Not at all,' Theon replied. 'I am simply pointing out that you have expensive taste in crew members.'

'She'll earn it,' Dax said. 'I need her to fly us to the Articus.'

'It's not that far.'

'It is when you've got so much Tellurium in your bloodstream that your body is failing.'

'Ah,' Theon said. 'Did she tell you that?'

'Jinn? No.' Dax laughed to himself. 'It was Alistair.'

'Our resident spy,' Theon said. His face twisted into an ugly smile. 'It's good to have him back on board.'

Yes, it was. Dax hadn't realised how much he'd missed his old friend until now. Theon was loyal and intelligent, but he was still a droid and there were some aspects of the human experience that he'd never truly comprehend. Eve . . . he loved Eve. But she was still so angry. Dax didn't blame her for it. If he'd been in her position, he'd have blasted himself out of an airlock a long time ago. But they could never talk about what had been done to them.

Alistair understood all the things that Dax couldn't say, and he understood them in a way that Eve and Theon just couldn't. He knew why Dax had kissed Jinn even though it had been the wrong thing to do.

'She is very beautiful,' Theon said.

'Yes,' Dax replied, his mind lingering on soft, pale hair and a soft, eager mouth. 'She is.'

'You have noticed, then.'

Dax snapped out of his daydream and glanced at Theon. The droid's electric-blue eyes gleamed. 'I was concerned that perhaps you had not. It is a long time for a human male to be without companionship, Caspian.'

'I have a pleasure droid in my quarters,' Dax pointed out.

'You and I both know that a pleasure droid is not sufficient. Humans need more than that. She interests you, does she not?'

'My interest in her is irrelevant.'

'On the contrary,' Theon said. 'It is very relevant.'

Dax turned away, busied himself with a quick check of the medical supplies in the storage compartments lining the wall. He didn't know what he was looking at, or what he was looking for. Only that he didn't want to have this conversation with Theon. 'I don't see how.'

'You brought her with you when you escaped from the A2,' Theon said. 'Surely you must be wondering why.'

'I'm wondering a lot of things.' Dax moved on to the next cupboard, which was filled with Readi-Shots of various things, mostly designed to combat space fatigue and hangovers caused by too much shore-leave ale. 'Right now I'm wondering why I didn't leave you on the Europa.'

'Perhaps you should have done.'

A moment of silence fell. Dax closed the cupboard and turned back to Theon, to the wrecked, ugly mess that remained. He knew this would be emotionally painful for the droid, being so exposed. He had risked bringing him to the medical bay to try and protect Theon's feelings. Now he wondered if he had made the right choice. 'What are you trying to say?'

Those robot eyes flashed. 'Look at me. Look at how broken I am. If I was human, I would have died.'

Dax clenched his teeth so hard he thought his jaw might crack. Without Theon, he would never have been able to escape the Medipro facility back on Earth. A droid had cared more for the lives of the teenagers locked in the facility than the humans running it. 'But you didn't,' he said. 'And we're going to get you fixed.'

'I know,' Theon said. 'But I'm tired, Caspian. And I don't want to live forever. It isn't natural.'

'None of this is natural,' Dax said. 'Not you, not me, not Eve, not Alistair, not Jinn. We're all freaks. Life is precious, Theon, especially for people like us, and I for one will not let it go.' He was shocked to find that his hands were curled into fists, his chest heaving. 'I will have you repaired and then you'll be back where you belong, piloting this ship. Got that?'

'I will require fifteen thousand credits a day.'

'Then I'll have you demoted to the position of cleaning droid and keep Jinn instead.'

Before Theon could respond to that, the door to the medical bay hissed open and Alistair walked in. He didn't even try to hide his look of distaste as he saw Theon. 'You look dreadful,' he said.

Dax glared at him.

'I was talking about you, Caspian.' Alistair yawned.

Dax folded his arms. 'Have you got anything useful to say, or did you just come here to insult me?'

Alistair shook his head, then pushed a hand back through his hair. 'That's what I came to talk to you about. I've been in the rec room, getting myself more closely acquainted with your crew.'

'What did you find out?'

'Plenty of things I'd rather not know,' he said. 'For instance, did you know that a couple of your deck hands are attempting to brew Batlakian vodka in one of the storage compartments? One of your engineers is keeping a Rubian lizard in his quarters and I would strongly recommend a deep cleanse of entertainment suite four.'

Dax simply stared at him. 'Did you find out anything important?'

'Our new pilot spends an awful lot of time trying not to think about how you would compare to a pleasure droid. By the way, do you really think it's wise to keep one in your quarters?' For a moment, Dax thought that he might let his temper go after all. Then Alistair moved over to the storage units, opened one. 'I don't suppose you've got any pain-blocker shots in here?'

Dax moved aside, gestured to the cupboard he was currently

leaning against. He watched as Alistair bent down and found what he was looking for. Alistair tugged his shirt aside, pressed the shot to his upper arm and squeezed the trigger. He winced, then tossed the spent shot into the disposal unit, picked up another shot and dosed himself with that one too. It would take the drugs a couple of minutes to work, which was more than long enough for Dax to take in Alistair's ravaged appearance. His skin was grey, his eyes sunken, and Dax thought it was a pretty safe bet that it was more than just space sickness. Alistair's abilities were both a blessing and a curse.

'I didn't find out anything useful,' Alistair said. He moved over to the empty medibed, stretched out on it. 'Not one damn thing. I've been inside everyone's head. You've got some seriously sick people on your payroll, my friend.' His mouth twisted in distaste. 'But none of them know anything about how that agent got on board.'

'He didn't do it without help,' Dax said. 'Someone programmed the onboard computer system to pick up that transporter. And someone told him where to find me.'

Alistair closed his eyes. 'Yes,' he said. 'But whoever it was, they're not a member of your crew. Have you considered the possibility that your system might have been hacked?'

Dax hadn't, because Theon had built the onboard systems from scratch. They were stunningly advanced. Totally unhackable. Only Theon understood the system well enough to know how to get in.

Which could only mean that . . .

Every muscle in Dax's body went tense, his pulse kicking up. Leaning back against the wall of the medical bay, he let his gaze drift slowly back to where Theon lay unmoving on the medibed, his bright blue eyes flashing in their sunken steel sockets, casting dancing lights across the shiny metal planes of his face.

If the rest of his crew had nothing to do with the agent getting on board the *Mutant*, that left only one possible culprit. And he was looking at him.

# CHAPTER

# 19

**27th August 2207**

> Vessel: The *Nero Hunter*. Stealth Cruiser
> Location: Arunda Station
> Cargo: None
> Crew: Three
> Droids: Four

Only two other agents had returned to the transporter. Two battered, wounded agents, one of whom had been minutes away from bleeding out. Bryant had dumped Kryll in the cargo hold of the cruiser and instructed the onboard computer to activate a medidroid as Sayrah staggered off to the control deck. He hadn't looked at Kryll's crumpled, battered body. Instead, he'd stumbled into the sanitation unit at the side of the hold and puked his guts up. Then he'd ordered Sayrah to fly them to the nearest Earth space port with a medical facility.

Somehow he'd managed to get himself from the *Hunter* to the aforementioned facility. The medic had taken one look at him and started an immediate infusion of pain meds. It had been strong enough to take the edge off, to let him think as the medic ran a full battery of tests. He was sure that he'd been poisoned, and that the green woman had done it, though he didn't know how. He didn't remember the sting of a drug gun. But he remembered the warm brush of her fingers against his neck.

'I have your test results,' the medic said when he walked back into the room a short while later.

'And?'

'Physical examination reveals increased heart rate and sweating, which together with the muscle pain you've described, indicates poisoning. But the database didn't identify a known toxin. The closest match is Shi-Fai biofluid.'

'Then maybe it's not a known toxin,' Bryant managed through gritted teeth as another wave of pain hit him.

'It's possible,' the technician admitted. He took a step away. 'Or it could be psychosomatic. You've been in space a long time.'

'I am not having a breakdown!' Bryant could feel his temper rising. And if he didn't feel so damned awful, he'd prove it. But he barely had the strength to walk, let alone teach this fucking moron a lesson.

'We have a registered therapist available.' The technician didn't look at him as he said it. He kept his gaze on the floor and one hand on the alarm button attached to his belt. If he pressed it, a team of security droids would flood the room and Bryant knew there was no way he'd be able to fight them off. He'd be in Psych. Holding before he could blink.

'Look,' Bryant said, pulling together the remnants of his ability to be civilised. 'Assuming I have been poisoned, given that you don't have an antidote, is there anything you can do?'

'Blockers for the pain, and soothers for the other symptoms. But you can't keep taking those forever. Your immune system is attacking your body. I can inject you with unistem, and that should repair the damage, but it's a temporary solution. Until we know why your body is destroying itself, it's going to keep on doing it, and there's no guarantee the unistem will be able to regenerate your tissues fast enough to keep you alive.'

'Give it to me anyway,' Bryant told him. 'And I want the

173

blockers and the soothers as well. Whatever you've got.' He got to his feet. His vision began to swim and he blinked to clear it. He reached out, trying to find something to hold on to as another wave of agonising nausea took hold.

By the time it cleared, the technician was at his side, pressing a drug gun against the side of his neck. 'This should help with the sickness,' he said. He dropped the spent gun into a steri-bucket, picked up another. 'This is for the muscle spasm.' A third and final shot pumped unistem, the universal stem cells, into his bloodstream. They would seek out the damaged areas and replace the dying cells.

The drugs worked quickly. The absence of pain was blissful. Bryant rubbed a hand over his face and straightened up.

'If you can find out what you've been poisoned with,' the medic told him, 'we might be able to manufacture an antidote. But you don't have much time. The drugs only mask the symptoms. They're not a cure.'

He turned to a drug locker mounted in the wall, pulled down a small case, loaded it with more shots. He held it out.

Bryant took it.

'The blockers are addictive,' the technician said. 'Don't use them unless you have to, and not for longer than three days. There's a payment station on the way out.'

Bryant responded with a nod. He needed to get back to his ship. It didn't surprise him when he got to the payment station, to find that his Security Service health insurance wouldn't cover the blockers. As he paid with his own credits, it also didn't surprise him that he'd been charged at least twice what the shots were worth. But he didn't have time to argue.

He left the clinic quickly, heading out onto the walkway. The Arunda station was small, not much more than a stop-off, a place for refuelling. It offered little in the way of entertainment. At least he wouldn't have to haul Kryll and Sayrah out of a bar or a pleasure parlour. If he was going to have any chance of finding out what he'd been poisoned with, they needed to find the *Mutant* and fast.

Fuelled by the combination of blockers and soothers, Bryant felt oddly light as he strode in the direction of the docking bays. Everything seemed more brightly coloured and the world seemed to be moving in slow motion. If someone fired a blaster bullet at him, he was pretty sure he could catch it with his bare hand.

Taking a left, he strode past the food stations. He wasn't hungry, but at least the smell didn't make him nauseous. Perhaps he would manage something to eat, later, and if not, there were IV regen fluids in the medical bay on the *Hunter*. It would be enough to keep him going until the unistem started to work. The docking bay was a long, narrow stretch, his transporter at the far end. As he headed towards it, Bryant considered his next move.

The tracking tech he'd implanted on the droid that had helped him not only locate Dax but given him access to the *Mutant* could be the key to finding him now, if it was still working. The droid had taken multiple hits during the carnage on the Europa, but he'd seen Dax carry the broken carcass back on board before they'd escaped, which meant that there was a chance that he could use the tracker to locate them. It wasn't a certainty, but it was the best hope he had.

If he hadn't been so distracted, he might have noticed Sayrah and Kryll waiting outside the transporter as he marched up to it. He might have noticed that they were both holding stunners, and he might have noticed that those stunners were armed.

As it was, he noticed neither of those things until he was stood within touching distance of the pair of them. 'What the fuck is this?'

'We don't want to hurt you,' Sayrah said. 'So don't make this difficult.'

Bryant looked at her. He looked at Kryll. He looked at the stunners, and somewhere inside his drug-soaked brain, he knew what they were trying to do. 'Don't be fucking stupid,' he told them. 'I am your commanding officer.'

'Actually,' Kryll said, 'you're not. I'm in charge of this vessel. And I've got orders to bring you in for immediate psych.

assessment.' His posture was stiff, and he was holding the weapon awkwardly, hardly surprising given that he was barely recovered from the injuries inflicted on him earlier.

'Over my fucking dead body,' Bryant said. His hand went to the small of his back, to the blaster he always kept concealed under his uniform jacket. 'I will hurt you,' he said. 'Get out of my way.'

Sayrah took a step towards him and slid her finger over the trigger of her weapon. It was all the excuse Bryant needed. In one swift move, he pulled out his own weapon and ruthlessly used it. The two agents crumpled to the ground, their eyes wide open with shock, both of them bleeding from scorched holes in their foreheads.

Bryant barely gave them a second glance. He simply stepped over their bodies, walked up the ramp onto his transporter, and left before anyone could stop him. If the Security Service wanted to take him in, they would have to kill him first. If he couldn't find Caspian Dax and that weird green woman, he was dead anyway.

# CHAPTER

# 20

**31st August 2207**

Vessel: The *Mutant*. Battleship/carrier hybrid
Destination: The Articus
Cargo: None
Crew: Twenty-four
Droids: Eight

It had been four days since Jinn had arrived on the *Mutant*. She'd managed two jumps, then Dax had ordered her to programme the autopilot for the next few hours. The route was simple, the onboard system user-friendly, and it had taken her only a few minutes. She had argued with him for show more than anything. It had been a relief not to have to plug in and deal with the consequences.

Jinn had gone to her quarters, partly to rest and partly so she could keep out of the way. She needed some time to herself. So much had happened in the past few days.

Turning her hands over, she looked at her palms. The wounds weren't quite as fresh as they had been four days ago, but they hadn't healed either, despite her best efforts. An empty first-aid kit lay open on the bunk next to her. She'd used all the salves, the shots, and the bleeding had stopped, but that was about it. Every time she moved her fingers, it hurt.

In a few more hours they would have to jump again, and that would bring them almost to their destination, a repair station called the Articus. Apparently Dax knew someone there who could repair Theon.

She was not looking forward to it.

But that wasn't her biggest problem.

Dax was.

He had kissed her. All she could think about was the way he had pulled her close, the way his mouth had crashed down on hers, the way it had made her feel. It played over and over in her mind, making her feel hot and frustrated and scared. Scared that it would happen again. Scared that it wouldn't. Scared of what she might do either way.

She wasn't used to these feelings and she didn't know what to do with them. She had always been alone. Physical contact was something to fear, not something to want, but she wanted it anyway, and there seemed to be nothing she could do to persuade herself otherwise.

And she was scared of his crew.

A chime sounded and the panel next to the door started to flash, pulsing in time with the lights at her wrists.

'Jinn,' came a voice over the intercom. 'Are you in there?'

It was Dax. Of course it was. She tried to sound normal, despite her suddenly racing pulse. 'What do you want?'

'I'd rather not talk to you through the door.'

'I'm tired.' She bit her lip, waiting to see if he would buy it.

'Just let me in. Otherwise I'll have to let myself in, and then I'll feel like shit because I overrode privacy protocol.'

There was a pause.

'Please,' he said. 'I just want to talk to you.'

Dammit. Jinn drew in some air, let it out slowly. Anxiety settled like a brick in her stomach. She gripped the edge of the bunk. 'Computer, open the door.'

The door lock blinked, a slow flash of red. Then it flashed green. She stared at the floor. The door hissed open. She knew he was there. The light from the corridor outside cast his shadow into her cabin, broad and heavy.

'This cabin is too bloody small,' he said.

'It's alright.' And it was. It had an exercise station in one corner, a chemicleanse in the other, and the bunk was wide and comfortable.

'How are you?' he asked, not moving from the doorway.

'Fine,' she said, but she said it too quickly. 'Really. I'm fine.'

'Lights up,' he said. The cabin brightened. He moved into the cabin, the door closing behind him.

*Now* it was too small.

'Show me your hands,' he said.

Not that. Anything but that. 'I'm fairly sure you can only give me orders outside of this cabin.'

'Jinn, I know about the Tellurium. I know that it's making you ill. You demanded six thousand credits a day so you can afford to have it removed.'

'How did you . . . ' And then it came to her. 'Alistair.'

'If it makes you feel any better, none of us have any secrets any more.'

He reached out, took her wrists, turned her hands over so he could examine her palms. She hated the way her body reacted to even that modest contact. She didn't want to feel the hot, sexual pull. But she felt it anyway.

'This is a mess,' he said.

She yanked her hands free, scrambled back on the bunk. 'It's fine.'

'It is not fine. You're not healing, Jinn.'

'I'm aware of that.'

'Have you eaten?'

'Yes.'

'Something other than Soylate,' he said, looking around the perfectly tidy cabin, then down at the empty cup on the floor.

'I like Soylate,' she replied, refusing to meet his gaze.

'You need protein,' Dax told her. 'And lots of it.' He moved to her Autochef and programmed it. The control panel flashed and then the machine started to quietly hum as it prepared whatever he'd requested.

'I'm fully aware of what I need.' Jinn put her forehead on her knees.

'And what's that?'

She lifted her head, though she still didn't meet his gaze. She could feel the sharp prickling of tears. 'Well, given that I can't reverse time and stop Bryant before he dumped me on the A2, my options are somewhat limited. But I need to get rid of this damn Tellurium before it takes over completely. I'm not healing properly. Before, a jump would knock me out for an hour, maybe two. But now I feel like I never seem to really recover.'

'How long has this been going on for?'

'A few months,' she admitted. 'I can see that now. I thought I was coping. But . . . '

'You're afraid,' he said.

'Damn right I'm afraid! Everything was fine. I had a job, I had some credits saved. I had it all worked out. Now look at me.'

Dax said nothing. The Autochef buzzed and he turned to it, lifted out the plate. Whatever he'd chosen was black and it didn't smell exactly pleasant. He stared at the plate, at the rubbery black lumps resting on it, then he dumped the whole thing into the automatic recycling unit and programmed the Autochef to make Soylate.

He held the cup out. Jinn took it. She was careful not to let her fingers touch his.

'There are medical facilities on the Articus,' he said. 'You'll be able to have your Tellurium removed. I'll give you enough credits to buy yourself a ship, a new identity. If you keep smart, keep moving, you'll be able to outrun the agents.'

It was the right thing, she knew it was, and he was offering her a way out of the mess she was in that she knew she should take. And yet he said it so calmly, so easily, as if it didn't bother him at all.

It bothered her. After everything they'd been through in the past few days, everything they'd experienced, it hurt that he could put her out of his life so easily.

'That's it?'

His brow creased. 'Yes, that's it. What more do you want?'

'You kissed me!' Jinn told him. The words burst from her and she could feel her face, her hands start to heat.

'So?'

Jinn looked at him. She didn't want to, but she had to see his face. She had to know. His eyes were hard. His mouth, the mouth that had touched hers, was a thin, guarded line. Gone was the man she'd thought she understood. All that remained was the cold, calculating pirate.

'You're a bastard,' she whispered.

'I never claimed otherwise.'

She stared at him, unable to believe that he could be so cruel. 'What is wrong with you?'

The beep of the internal comm. interrupted before he could answer that question. 'Dax.' Eve's voice came over the system, sharp with panic. 'We need you on the control deck. We've got a major problem. Jinn, you better come too.'

They left Dax's quarters at a sprint, heading straight to the control deck. They had barely made it to the end of the first corridor when the onboard alarms started to scream.

They were under attack.

Swallowing down her fear, Jinn headed straight for the pilot's chair, slamming her hands down over the ports. There was no time to prepare. Her Tellurium was out almost immediately, linking her with the ship, turning on her retinal screen. She felt the rush of warmth and then she was in. 'That's a Security Service ship!' A stealth cruiser, designed to make multiple jumps with a full security team on board.

'They're hailing us!' Eve said, her tone frantic, her fingers flying over the comm. controls.

'Accept transmission,' Dax ordered her. 'Put the bastards on the screen. I want to see them.'

A split second later, an image flashed up on the large comm. screen directly in front of the captain's chair.

'Caspian Dax,' the man said.

Jinn knew that voice. 'Bryant,' she whispered. She switched off her retinal screen. The implant folded itself away. There on the main viewscreen that ran across the front of the control deck was her former crewmate. He looked bad. No, scratch that. He looked worse than bad. His skin was sallow, his pale hair a lank, greasy mess, and his dark eyes were sunken and ringed with black. He wasn't dead, but he didn't look far off it. And where was the rest of his crew? There didn't appear to be anyone else onboard the control deck of the cruiser.

'What do you want?' Dax asked him.

'I want to know what you poisoned me with,' Bryant snarled back.

Jinn slid her gaze to Eve. The other woman sat frozen in her seat, yellow eyes fixed on the screen, hands hovering unsteadily over the comm. controls.

'I didn't poison you,' Dax told him. His voice was calm, completely in control, even as Bryant raged.

'That green bitch, then,' Bryant said. 'She knows. And I want to know what the fuck it was!'

'If you've been poisoned, you should be able to pick up an antidote at any medical facility.'

'Do you think I haven't tried that? They can't help with an unknown toxin.' Bryant retched. It wasn't a pleasant sound.

'If it's unknown, then you weren't poisoned,' Dax said.

'Don't lie to me!' Bryant roared. 'I'm not a fucking idiot!'

'How did you find us?'

The change of direction seemed to take Bryant by surprise. He slumped back in his seat, almost smiled. 'Tracking you was easy. You're not as clever as you think, Caspian Dax.'

He was rambling now, and something about his tone made Jinn wary. If he was as high on blockers as he seemed, he'd make crazy, irrational decisions. 'Eve,' Jinn muttered. 'Can you hack into the Security Service comm. channel?'

'Yes,' Eve said.

'Check recent transmissions. Anything relating to Bryant, A. Employee number 442937.'

'Okay,' Eve whispered back. 'Why?'

'Because he's on his own at the controls of a cruiser and he's off his head on blockers.'

Eve turned back to the comm. station. Trembling hands lowered to the controls, and the little holoscreen in front of her flickered.

'What do you mean, tracking us was easy?' Dax asked Bryant.

'You still don't know, do you?' Bryant smiled. 'You still haven't found it. It was worth the price I paid, then.'

A muscle ticked in Dax's jaw. It was the first sign that he wasn't as relaxed as he appeared. 'What was?'

Bryant shrugged. 'Ask your droid,' he said.

Dax gripped the edges of his seat. Then he turned to Jinn. 'Get us out of here,' he said. 'Computer, end communication.'

The comm. screen went blank.

'He was declared unfit for service three days ago,' Eve said. 'Two of his crewmates tried to take him in. He killed them both, stole the cruiser. System-wide warrant has been issued. Kill on sight.'

'Bloody supernova,' Jinn said.

And then Bryant opened fire.

The *Mutant* was well shielded and the first couple of torpedoes were deflected, but they drained enough power to ensure that the next one would leave a gaping hole in the side of the hull. 'Where in the void is the navigator?' Jinn yelled as she spun the *Mutant* into desperate evasive manoeuvres. 'I need jump coordinates now!'

'I'm here.' The navigator, Selina, came running onto the control deck. She sat in the nav. chair, fighting for breath.

'How far are we from the nearest Jump Gate?' Jinn asked, urgency in every word she spoke. She wasn't sure how much longer she could keep plugged into the system. Her hands were already bleeding.

Bryant had Security Service training and she knew his flying patterns, his moves. But those laser torpedoes were lethal. A single hit could kill the electrics on board the *Mutant* and then they'd be a sitting target, with nothing to do but wait until they were boarded or the air supply ran out. She needed to put distance between them, and fast. 'Give me the bloody coordinates!' she yelled.

'Inputting them now,' Selina called. 'Jump Gate 39 is ten minutes from here.'

'Input coordinates to take us to the Articus from the other end,' Jinn told her as she swung the *Mutant* around and upped their speed to maximum. Selina had said ten minutes. She'd have them there in six. The *Mutant* groaned as she pushed the speed, draining the phase drives of everything they had.

They couldn't outrun the cruiser, and they couldn't outfly it. All she could do was force the phase drive to give her everything it had, as the onboard alarm screamed a warning and Dax gripped the edge of his seat and swore. She'd have laughed, if they weren't in such trouble. If her heart wasn't racing and her entire body wasn't on fire.

They hit the jump a minute later and she flew them into it at speed, a risky move that she had no choice but to make. If they could get into the next jump before the cruiser came through, they might have a chance to buy themselves some time. 'I could use those coordinates right about now, Selina.'

'Inputting,' the younger woman said.

In seconds Jinn had them and they were into the second jump, twisting and turning their way through. Jinn stared at the line of blinking lights and the small central touchpad for the flight controls. The simplicity of it hid the complexity of the machine underneath, the powerful computer that could interface with her neural networks and allow her to control a ship as large and powerful as the *Mutant*. She could feel the temptation, the pull of it. She hadn't even known that she loved flying until she'd been sent to the pilot programme. She'd completed it in under a month, been sent on her first contract a week after that. Flying had always been her escape, the place she felt safest, most at home. The place she belonged.

She'd never sat before the control panel and felt fear before. Not just a fear of the inevitable pain, although that was a part of it. A huge part, if she was honest. But the fear that this was about to be over. These two jumps were the last jumps she was ever going to make. After that, she'd have her Tellurium removed and she'd say goodbye to the *Mutant*, to Dax, to all of this. The thought didn't sit as comfortably with her as it should.

# CHAPTER

# 21

1st September 2207

The Articus. Repair Station, Sector Four, Neutral Space

The hangar owned by the man Dax referred to only as Grudge was a treasure trove of broken ship components, broken droids, broken just about anything, stretching to the height of the roof and further back than it was possible to see. A huge 3-D printing tank sat to one side, the edges patterned with drips of dried white polymer. Grudge himself was short and stocky with shoulder-length hair shot through with silver and matching silver eyes. He wore grease-smeared trousers that might once have been white, and a sleeveless jacket that buckled across the front. A brutal prosthetic took the place of his right arm. Connectors dug into the exposed skin of his shoulder. From them projected a thick cylinder, jointed where his elbow and wrist would have been. Coloured wires wrapped round it in a thick rope. At the end, in place of a hand, was a cutting diamond the size of a fist.

Jinn lingered at the rear of the workshop, trying to take it all in, trying to get a fix on the man they'd come to see. Dax had told her little. They'd barely spoken as they made their way through the busy walkways and open areas of the Articus, and she hadn't tried to force conversation. She'd been too busy focussing on breathing, on putting one foot in front of the other and not passing out. Her arms were on fire. The medidroid on the *Mutant* had sealed her palms with skingel, but she'd refused any pain meds. After seeing Bryant, she doubted she'd ever take them again.

'Caspian Dax,' Grudge said. 'Didn't I tell you that if you ever came near my workshop again, I would kill you?'

'You did,' Dax acknowledged. 'I was hoping you'd forgotten. It's been a long time.'

'Twenty-nine years,' Grudge replied. 'But I never forget anyone who steals from me. How is my ship?'

'You mean *my* ship?'

Grudge laughed. 'Call it what you want, you thieving pirate.' His gaze shifted to Jinn. He stared at her in silence for far longer than she was comfortable with. She couldn't hold back a shiver. 'Come here,' he ordered her.

She approached him slowly, warily, stopping when they were a couple of metres apart. He looked her over, his gaze lingering on the implant at her temple. 'Jinnifer Blue,' he said softly, lethally. 'That is who you are, isn't it? I recognise you from the newsfeed.'

'I'm Jinnifer Blue,' she said. 'What of it?'

Grudge stared at her for a moment, those silver eyes giving nothing away. 'Show me your blades.'

Her pulse sped up a little. 'Why?'

'Because I'd like to see them.'

'Don't,' Dax told her, moving closer.

Jinn ignored him. 'Will you promise to help us if I do?' she asked Grudge.

'I'll promise to consider it,' he said.

Jinn pulled in a breath and then she lifted her right hand. She was already in pain, already exhausted. She had no idea what this would do to her. She turned her hand palm up, focussed on the creases in the skin, the scar tissue on the heel of her hand. The sharp silver spike emerged slowly, pushing through the layer

187

of skingel. The sting made her eyes water. Her mouth tasted of blood and the inside of her nose prickled. She sniffed, felt more blood hit the back of her throat.

Grudge stared at her blade for a long time. 'Exquisite,' he said, rubbing his own clumsy prosthetic. Then he turned his attention back to Dax. 'You took a big risk coming here, Caspian. The incident onboard the Europa was all over the news streams. You've got a price on your head that is far too tempting for comfort.'

Jinn willed the blade back in. There was an upturned barrel close to where she stood and she slowly sat down on it. Her head felt strange and there was an unpleasant crackling noise in her ears. She forced herself to focus, refusing to faint, even though it felt like a good idea.

'Are you going to turn me in?' Dax asked Grudge.

'No,' he said. 'But bring trouble my way, and I will send it in yours. Steal from me again and I will send the Security Service your head. Literally.'

'I'd expect nothing less,' Dax said in return. 'Fortunately, this time I can afford to pay for your services.'

'What do you require?'

Dax gestured to Theon's mangled body, which was slung over one broad shoulder.

'A pleasure droid?' Grudge raised an eyebrow. 'You don't need me to repair this. You can get whatever perverted alterations you require at any walk-in repair shop.'

'I am not a pleasure droid.' It was Theon who spoke.

Jinn found herself holding her breath. She knew how important it was to Dax that Theon was repaired, how important it was to all of them.

'It speaks,' Grudge said. 'Tell me, droid, what else can you do?'

'My name is Theon.'

Grudge looked at Dax. 'You gave it a name?'

'Not it,' Theon answered the question in his flat, robotic monotone. 'He.'

Grudge motioned for Dax to set Theon down and he did,

laying him carefully on an empty workbench close to where they all stood. Grudge said nothing. He merely walked around Theon's mangled frame. Dax grabbed an empty barrel, turned it upside down, and sat next to Jinn. He stuck his hand in his pocket, pulled out a packet of fruit candies and handed it to her. She opened it up and shoved a couple in her mouth. It helped.

'Who is this man?' Jinn whispered to him. 'That looks like a mining prosthetic, but I've never seen one so primitive.'

'Grudge was part of the first team to be sent out to Colony Three,' Dax replied, his voice soft and low.

'A first-generation mod? I didn't know any of them were still alive. Weren't they all killed by an explosion on the colony?'

'Officially, yes.'

Jinn took a moment to process this. 'And unofficially?'

'Let's just say their modifications hadn't been tested as fully as was claimed. Three hundred of them died from complications due to their alterations before they even made it to the colony. The explosion you spoke of took care of the rest.'

'And Grudge?'

'Didn't wait around for anyone to realise he'd been working in a tunnel on the other side of the dig site.'

There was more she wanted to ask him, more she wanted to know, but Grudge had finished his examination of Theon. He stepped back, surveyed the droid. 'You're AI,' he said.

'Yes,' Theon replied.

'Registered?'

'No.'

'I thought not. Inhibitor chip?'

'It malfunctioned.'

'When?'

'18th February 2187.'

Grudge flicked his attention to Dax. 'Forgive me if I'm wrong, but wouldn't that be around the time you escaped from a certain medical facility on Earth?'

'It would,' Dax said.

'Was he with you when you came here?'

'He was.' Dax smiled a little. 'Who do you think was flying the *Mutant* when we took it?'

'I have assessed my systems,' Theon said. 'My personality chip is intact. Several of my other systems have been destroyed, however.'

'Mind if I ask how?'

'I was shot eight times with an ion-blaster armed with spitzer darts. Four times in the torso, three times in the leg and once in the arm.'

'That's a lot of hits. You're lucky to be alive.'

'I am aware of that, sir. Although my current capabilities suggest that I am something less than alive.'

'Can you fix him?' Dax asked.

Grudge lifted his head. He slipped his gaze to Jinn for the briefest of moments before shifting it to Dax. 'It will be expensive,' he said.

'I'll pay,' Dax told him.

'How much?'

Grudge narrowed those silver eyes, then clicked his fingers. From nowhere, a dozen droids appeared. They looked like pleasure droids, except that pleasure droids weren't armed with stunners and electro-chains. 'Three million. Universal credits, not dollars. And I want full payment up front.'

'That's outrageous!' Jinn exclaimed.

'Done,' Dax said.

The droids lowered their weapons, but they didn't step back. Grudge held up a personal palm comm. Dax took it, transferred the credits in silence.

'Come back in two days,' Grudge told him.

'Twelve hours,' Dax replied.

'In that case, she'll have to stay.'

Dax stepped forward, putting himself in front of Jinn, blocking her view entirely. 'No,' he said. 'You've got your credits, more than enough of them.'

Jinn moved round him. 'What do you want me for?' she asked Grudge.

'Repairing an AI droid is a tricky business,' Grudge said. 'It's not simply a case of attaching replacement parts. I need you to interface with his neural circuitry. Each connection I make needs to be correct. You'll be able to tell me if it is.'

That would mean using her Tellurium. That would mean more pain. More blood. 'And if I say no?'

'I'll still be able to repair him,' Grudge said. 'But it will be a slow, difficult business, and there's no guarantee that he'll be functional at the end of it.'

Dax pulled her aside, one big hand locked around her upper arm. 'You don't have to do this,' he said, his voice low.

If she hadn't heard the desperation in his voice, if her skin hadn't throbbed at the contact, she might have been able to agree. 'Theon needs to be fixed,' she told him. 'You need a pilot.'

'It's not worth your life.'

'I won't be risking my life. It's one last job, Dax. Only a few more hours. You said I could have the Tellurium removed here, and that's what I'll be doing. But I have to do this first.'

'Promise me that you'll stop the second it gets too much.'

'I . . .'

'Promise me, Jinn!'

'I . . . I promise.'

His head lowered further, until they were standing so close that his mouth was almost on hers. They stood like that for a moment, neither of them moving, sharing heat, sharing air.

'Dax,' Grudge said. 'There's a pile of scrap steel over in section three that needs to be sorted.'

'So get a droid to do it,' Dax said, his gaze not leaving Jinn.

'Dax,' Grudge said again, and this time there was something in his voice that even Jinn could feel.

Dax let go of her arm. She watched as he disappeared deeper into the workshop. A moment later, there was a loud bang, followed by a couple of quieter ones.

'Why doesn't he want you to help?' Grudge asked her.

'Using the Tellurium is hard on my body,' Jinn told him. 'I don't really heal fast enough to handle it.'

'But you are willing to do this?'

'Yes.'

'Then we'd better get to work.' Grudge had already opened up the back of Theon's head. 'Come on.'

He held out a pair of magnifying goggles. Jinn took them, slipped them on. Without ports to guide her tech, she'd have to rely on what she could see to make the first connection. She leaned in, the lights mounted on either side of the goggles shining onto a complex array of thumbnail-sized circuit boards and endless platinum wires. Theon had to be worth a fortune for scrap value alone. Jinn breathed deeply and then she extended her tech, seeking out the connections that would link her into his personality chip, his consciousness. It took her three attempts to find something more than darkness and white noise, but when she did, Theon's world exploded inside her mind, a riot of colour and flawless memory. 'I'm in.'

Grudge slipped on his own pair of goggles. A droid moved alongside him and he held out his arm. The droid detached the cutting diamond and fitted a delicate laser scalpel in its place. In silence, he cut away mangled limbs, burnt wires and splintered circuit boards with surgical precision. He worked fast, but that didn't mean he was clumsy or careless.

'How did you land yourself in the company of a rogue like Caspian Dax?' he asked. 'The truth, if you please.'

The question caught Jinn off guard. 'I was left with him on the *Alcatraz 2*,' she said, as Grudge detached the remains of Theon's mangled arm and tossed it aside. A droid scuttled over, picked up the discarded arm and immediately began to take it apart, throwing the components into various different bins.

'In my experience, people are not simply left on the A2. They're dumped. Incarcerated. Removed from society.'

'Then I was dumped,' Jinn said. 'And so was Dax.'

'How did he take it?'

'Badly.'

Grudge smiled. 'That I can believe.'

'You have known him a long time.'

'Yes,' Grudge said, lifting the replacement arm from the motorised trolley parked next to him. He laid it on the workbench next to Theon, began to connect up the wires. Some of them were barely thicker than a hair. Her Tellurium seemed remarkably basic in comparison. 'I caught him trying to break into the workshop.'

'How old was he?'

'Nineteen,' Grudge told her. 'Had he been any older, I'd have killed him for it.'

Jinn tried to imagine Dax at nineteen. 'What was he like?'

'Frightened,' Grudge recalled. 'Angry. It wasn't long after he'd escaped the mod programme. The four of them had stolen a vessel back on Earth. They ended up here in need of repairs, but they couldn't afford to pay for them. Dax decided to steal the parts they needed. He wasn't quite the size he is now, but he wasn't far off. I told him he could either spend six months hauling wreckage for me or I'd report him to the local authorities.'

'He chose to work for you,' she said.

'Yes,' said Grudge. 'And at the end of the six months he took the *Mutant* from right under my nose and disappeared.' He sounded more proud than angry.

'You wanted him to take it.'

'I wanted him to live his life on his own terms.'

'Like you have?'

Grudge's hands stilled. He lifted his head, met her gaze. 'Yes,' he said. 'The corporations think they can make slaves of us by modifying our DNA. Turn us into nothing more than biological machines that they can use to do their bidding and discard when we're no longer useful. Did you know that most prosthetics cost less than a cleaning droid?'

No, she hadn't known that. 'That's sick.'

'The truth usually is,' Grudge said. 'That's why people work so hard to avoid hearing it. Even with the population restrictions, the Underworld cities still supply more workers than the corporations need. Why bother paying for droids when life is so cheap?'

He lapsed into silence again as he wired up a particularly complex sequence of connections. Jinn's role was simple. Interface with Theon's personality chip, access his memories, all the things that made him who he was, make sure that no damage occurred. Her constant monitoring allowed Grudge to work more quickly. If he got too close to any crucial components, Jinn would know immediately.

She already knew the entire history of Theon's relationship with Dax, from their first meeting back at the medical centre on Earth right through to today. Theon's emotions, his memories, his hopes for the future were all burned into her brain, as clear as if they were her own emotions, her own memories, her own hopes. She knew, too, about the information Theon had transmitted to Bryant. The memories were buried deep in Theon's unconscious, stored as hidden files. They hadn't been hidden from her.

She knew all this even before Grudge located the small, dark mass fused to Theon's spinal column, its wires stretching up to interface with the circuits that formed his brain. He poked at it with the end of his laser scalpel, slicing a cut into the mass. For a moment, nothing happened and then the cut simply healed over.

'What is that?' Jinn asked.

'I don't know,' Grudge said slowly. 'It appears to be some kind of nanotech, but it's not human made. We don't possess the kind of technology that is self-healing.'

'Can you remove it?'

'Possibly,' he said. 'But it could potentially destroy the AI chip. It's fused to the behavioural control centre.'

'You mean it can control him?'

'When it's activated, yes. I believe so.'

Jinn exhaled. She felt sick. So that was how Bryant had done it. He had somehow managed to implant this tech, whatever it was, on Theon, and it had given him access to everything. It had given him control.

'I did not know,' Theon said.

'Do you remember being injected with something?' Grudge asked him as he flipped down the magnifying lens on his headset and examined the tech more closely.

'Perhaps on Omega Station,' Theon said slowly. 'I took shore leave there six weeks ago. My memory system indicates that I have lost a small section of time from that visit.'

'We went to Omega Station,' Jinn said, almost dazed with horror. 'Bryant went off alone. I thought he was going to visit one of the pleasure parlours, so I stayed on the transporter, caught up with my admin work. I had no idea he was going to do something like this.' And they had tracked the *Mutant* from Omega Station. There was no doubt in her mind that she was looking at the reason why.

Theon's blue eyes flashed. 'It is not your fault, Jinnifer Blue,' he said. 'You are not responsible for this.'

Maybe not, but she was responsible for enough. 'Dax needs to know about this,' she said to Grudge.

He nodded. 'Yes,' he said. 'I think he does.'

Dax had known that the news wouldn't be good. He had known that even before Jinn came clambering through the piles of metal he was sorting.

'I take it you found something,' he said, sitting back on his haunches and watching her climb.

'You knew, didn't you?' she asked, coming to a halt a couple of metres below him, balancing on top of a pile of skimmer propellers. 'That's why Bryant said "ask your droid".'

'It wasn't anyone else,' Dax told her. 'Theon was the only remaining possibility.'

'Why didn't you say anything?'

'I wanted to be sure.' He snapped the propeller he was holding in half and tossed the pieces into a half-empty crate, then jumped down from the pile. Jinn started to climb down after him but the pile was unstable and she hesitated.

'Come on,' Dax said, holding out his arms. 'Jump.'

'I don't . . .'

'Jump,' he said again, and this time it was an order. She looked tired, the pile was unstable, and going up was a lot easier than coming down. He told himself that was why he did it. He caught her easily, hands sliding round her body. She was warm and soft. He held tight for longer than he should have before she pushed him away.

She raked her hair back from her face and didn't meet his eyes, but he could still feel the kick of her pulse. And he could feel his own thumping in response. It was the situation, he told himself. She was female and she was close, and something about the combination of white-blonde hair and dark eyes had always made him weak. He needed a couple of hours with a pleasure droid, that was all.

They walked back to the other end of the workshop in silence, Jinn leading. Theon was sat on the end of a workbench, sparks flying as Grudge welded his new arm in place.

'Tell me what you found,' Dax said.

It was Theon who spoke. 'It's fused to the circuits of my spinal column. We believe I was injected with it, possibly whilst I was on shore leave on Omega Station. It appears to have the capacity to access my memory banks and temporarily disable my AI function when activated.'

In other words, it could make him into an ordinary droid. 'Is the tech still functional?'

'It is inactive,' Theon said. 'But I think we should assume that this is temporary.'

'This is serious, Caspian,' Grudge said. 'It won't have been cheap. Someone paid an awful lot to find you.'

Dax closed his eyes. Angry frustration roared through him.

He had no-one to blame but himself. He should have gone onto the Omega Station with the others, not stayed behind on the *Mutant*. If he'd done his job as captain and protected his crew, this would never have happened.

'The tech itself is fascinating. The Sittan use similar technology on their ships,' Grudge said, his expression thoughtful. 'They're self-repairing. A highly interesting technology, though not one they've been inclined to share with us.'

'They're hardly alone in that,' Jinn pointed out. 'We've refused to share our genetic technology with them.'

'Agreed,' Grudge said. 'Which makes the presence of this tech in our friend here all the more interesting. You said an agent implanted this?'

'So we've been told,' Jinn answered. 'But where would an agent like Bryant get Sittan technology?'

'It doesn't matter where he got it,' Dax cut in. 'All that matters is whether or not you can remove it.'

'Possibly,' Grudge replied. 'But it has connected itself to his personality chip.'

'Leaving it in could allow the agent to continue tracking us,' Theon pointed out. 'I will not allow that. It must be removed.'

'No,' Dax said firmly. He'd failed as captain once. He wouldn't fail as captain again. 'I won't see you destroyed, Theon. We'll find a way round this. There has to be something we can do, some way to render the tech permanently inactive.'

'I do not believe that it is your decision to make,' Theon told him. He turned to Grudge. 'Remove it,' he said. 'I am prepared for the consequences.'

Dax started to move forward, but Grudge signalled to his droids. They moved into place, holding him back. 'Get off me,' Dax snarled at them. They didn't obey.

'This isn't your decision to make, Caspian,' Grudge said. 'He's AI. That means he gets to make his own choices.'

There was nothing Dax could do but watch as Theon lay face down on the work trolley.

'I need you to power down,' Grudge told him. 'Jinn, you know what you need to do.'

Jinn moved forward. She didn't look at Dax. She turned her back to him, blocking his view as Grudge gave orders in a low, soft voice.

Dax clenched his fists at the sound of a laser cutter slicing through metal. He didn't know how long he sat there, but it seemed like hours as the two of them worked in almost silence. Never had Dax felt more useless, more frustrated, and never had he hated himself more. He was to blame for this. He was to blame for all of this. He had failed to protect Theon. He had made a complete mess of things with Jinn, and worse than that, he didn't know how to fix any of it. He didn't even know if it could be fixed.

Grudge moved away, dropping a strangely shaped lump of dark metal into a tray obediently held by one of his droids. 'It's finished.'

The droids stepped back and Dax moved forward, reaching Theon in only a few quick strides. Jinn remained bent over Theon's body, her hands buried inside his torso as she used her Tellurium to interface with him.

'Well?' Dax asked.

'I don't know,' she said, her voice quiet. 'I just don't know. It's almost as if he's . . . asleep.'

'According to these readings, he's still functioning,' Grudge said, looking at the screen of a hand monitor. 'All we can do now is wait.'

But Dax was tired of waiting. He felt like the world was closing in on him. Everything was too close, too loud, and if he didn't get relief from it soon, he was going to hurt someone.

He turned to leave.

'Where are you going?' Jinn asked him.

'To the nearest pleasure parlour,' he told her. 'Want to join me?' He held out his hand. He didn't even know why he'd asked. What in the void was wrong with him? From the look on her face, she was wondering the exact same thing. He could feel the others staring at him and he told himself he didn't care. 'Thought not,' he said, and left the workshop.

It didn't take him long to find a pleasure parlour. He walked in, slid a credit chip across the grimy counter.

'Male, female, or other?' asked the man behind the counter, not even bothering to look up from his game cube.

'Female,' Dax said.

The man pressed a button on the counter and the screens mounted on the wall behind him lit up, showing an assortment of female droids.

'Second from the left,' Dax decided.

'Room 4,' the man said. 'End of the corridor, turn right.' He slapped down a keycard. Dax palmed it. It was cold and heavy in his hand and he didn't like the feel of it, but he didn't seem to be in control of his actions any more. He strode down the corridor with his pulse a heavy thud under his skin. He was hard before he even opened the door. It slammed behind him, shutting him in a sparsely decorated room that smelled of bleach. A large bed was pushed up against one wall, covered in a creased hygiene sheet. No pillows, no blankets, no comfort. Steel rings were set into the wall, two at head height, two more by the floor. A cracked vidscreen hung at an angle on the wall opposite, with a credit slot next to it.

The droid strolled out, sat on the edge of the bunk. She leaned back, hands resting on the bed behind her, all the better to display her enormous breasts.

'Turn over,' Dax said, his hand reaching to the fastening of his trousers.

'As you wish,' the droid said. Obediently, she turned on to her belly, spread her legs. Dax lowered his hand to his cock. He forced himself to look at the exposed cunt of the droid, perfectly formed, lubricated and plump. He moved closer.

He wanted this to be Jinn, and that was why he was here. He wanted soft skin, dark eyes, pale hair. He wanted the feel of her hands on his body, of her mouth under his, of heat and flesh. But he couldn't have Jinn. Sinking to his knees, Dax pushed his cock into the ready cunt of the droid and began to fuck. He quickly found his rhythm, hard and deep, over and over, his hands digging into the bunk.

All he wanted was release. All he wanted was to deal with this part of himself, with the rush of aggressive testosterone that overtook him when he was aroused. He didn't want to think about Theon. He didn't want to think about Jinn. He didn't want to think about the world outside these four walls. He fucked the droid harder, deeper, gripping the curve of its hips tightly as he pounded it into the bed.

His first orgasm rode him hard, but not hard enough. It barely even took the edge off. He grabbed the pleasure droid by the waist, flipped it over. Automatically, it lifted its legs, exposing itself to him. Dax didn't hesitate. Digging his hands into the sheets, he settled himself between its thighs and got to work. He needed this, needed it to be over, needed to get rid of the raging ache that burned like a fire inside him. He hated this part of himself, this uncontrollable animal. It made him feel dirty and uncivilised. He fucked the droid harder, harder, letting out his second climax with a roar and jets of hot semen. The droid writhed, groaned, all of it fake, so fake. A real woman, a human woman, would be begging him to stop.

But Dax didn't stop. He couldn't. Sweat covered his skin, his pulse sky-rocketing as he only got more aroused. He closed his eyes, trying to shut out his surroundings, the sight of the droid and the bunk. With a snarl, he pulled the droid up. It purred at him as he settled himself on the edge on the bunk and spread his thighs. The robot wiggled its backside lasciviously, and Dax took everything that was offered. He took and took and took, until his third climax obliterated the others. Chest heaving, heart racing, muscles hard and burning, he finally emptied himself completely.

When he opened his eyes, he saw the price of that calm. The droid was propped between his thighs, no longer moving. A leg was twisted at an awkward angle, the metal plate that covered its back was crumpled, and he could smell burning Plastex mingled with the scent of his sweat and his climax.

'Shit,' Dax said, staring at the broken remains of the droid. He rubbed a hand over his chest and then over his face, disgusted with himself. It wasn't the first droid that he'd broken, and it probably wouldn't be the last. He'd accepted a long time ago that he couldn't change what he was, that all he could do was live with it, handle the more brutal of his urges as best he could, and hope that it would be enough.

And until now, it had been enough.

He shoved his hands through his hair, then pulled on his clothes, dragging them over sticky, sweat-drenched skin. He barely saw the droid any more, the broken machine already forgotten as he strode out of the building and onto the street.

He had come to the Articus to have Theon repaired, and that job was done. He knew how the agent had tracked him. He was safe, for now. It was time to focus his attention elsewhere.

First step would be to get medical help for Jinn, then buy her a ship and a new identity to go with it. Then he was going to find out exactly what Medipro were doing. He had made himself a promise a long time ago, one which he had forgotten as the years had passed.

Now it was time to find out if he could keep it.

# CHAPTER

# 22

Ferona ran her fingers over the touch screen of the personal comm. she wore on her wrist. The video link expanded in front of her, a tiny circle spinning in the centre of the screen as the connection was made. When Darlan Riche had first approached her on behalf of Medipro, he had made promises of a perfect soldier, a perfect assassin, a perfect spy. His vision had been limited. Ferona had seen beyond it. She had seen the true potential of the new modifications that Medipro had devised.

Although the Type One and Type Two were all Underworlders, the Type Three modifications had been given to a carefully selected network of Dome-raised men and women. She enjoyed the advantage they gave her, with their unique ability to listen in to the thoughts of those around them, to hear all the secrets they worked so hard to keep. It was one of the things that made Lucinda so good at her job.

What she wasn't enjoying was the current lack of communication from the man she'd put in charge of the Type Threes. This was the fifth time she had tried to contact him in the past hour alone, and she was starting to get more than a little angry.

Suddenly the screen flickered to life and a familiar face appeared on it. Weston was a thin, sharp-nosed man who wore his pale hair cropped so close to his head that he appeared almost bald. He didn't bother with the skin enhancements used by most Dome dwellers, designed to give them some colour in their complexion and disguise the fact that they rarely, if ever, ventured outside.

In the background, Ferona could see his workshop. It was surprisingly small, housed in a bunker somewhere close to the New York Dome. Weston was obsessed with weaponry, and most of his creations were made in that small space. He was responsible for numerous devices that had been declared illegal, as well as the current lightweight stunner that was the standard weapon for an agent.

'Minister Blue,' he said. 'To what do I owe the honour?' He smiled, showing dark yellow teeth.

'Where in the void have you been?' she snapped at him. 'I've been trying to get hold of you for days. You better have a fucking good excuse this time, Weston.'

Weston's pale brown eyes darkened momentarily. The whites of his eyes were as yellow as his teeth. 'I've been busy,' he said.

'Doing what?'

When Ferona had decided to work with Medipro, she had known that she would need allies if she was going to make it work. She had chosen Weston to deal with the Type Threes because he had already proven himself open to things that skimmed the edge of what was considered legal. With his training, they had become exactly what Ferona had hoped for – a network of spies, hiding in plain sight.

'This and that,' he said.

Ferona could feel rage starting to bubble even hotter inside her. 'I take it you've seen the news,' she told him. 'Caspian Dax is at large somewhere. I need to know where he is, Weston, and I need to know now. If anything happens to him, I will hold you personally responsible.'

'There are agents on every major space station, every colony,' he said. 'The moment he sets foot on any of them, you'll be the first to know.'

'What about the smaller stations? The repair stations? I want ears everywhere, Weston. In twenty-four hours, I want Caspian Dax back on the A2.'

'What about the others?'

Ferona thought about this for a moment. 'Bring them in if you can. All of them. Kill them if you have to. But Dax must be alive.'

Weston blinked slowly. He lifted a tumbler that sat on his desk and took a deep swallow of the pale pink liquid within. 'Anything else?'

'Yes,' Ferona said. 'I don't care how much of that shit you drink, but get your fucking liver rejuvenated. You look awful.'

She ended the call to the sound of Weston's laughter.

But there was nothing to laugh about.

She had called Weston from her office in the government building of the London Dome. She was here because Vice President Dubnik had called an emergency meeting, but the start had been delayed and the calls to Weston had partly been a way to occupy her mind so that she didn't think about it too much. But as she sat in her chair, legs crossed at the knee and hands resting firmly on the sides, the virtual meeting room opened and she found herself staring right at Dubnik.

Ferona knew he was behind it, even if Vexler was the one sat at the head of the table, as was his right as the president. Such was the state of the emergency that there hadn't been time for the ministers to travel to the government building in Paris.

Their images were holographic, their voices playing out in stereo. They were so perfect that she would have thought they were real if it hadn't smelled like her office and the chair hadn't been her personal favourite. They were small comforts given the circumstances.

Ferona fixed Vexler with a polite, open smile, though inside she felt anything but calm. She didn't have time for this. Every day that Caspian Dax was free was a day closer to everything that she had worked for falling apart.

She had managed to limit media coverage of the incident on the Europa to the initial reports, though it had been difficult. But she had known it was only a matter of time before she was asked to explain exactly what was going on.

Swain and Lucinda sat behind her. None of the others would be able to see or hear the two of them. It might have felt devious if Ferona hadn't also known that every single person in the meeting had their own assistants working unseen in the background.

'As everyone is here,' Vexler said, 'I suggest we begin. I have called this special session in accordance with the laws of Earth's Global Government. As required, all current ministers were invited to attend, and all have done so.'

Ferona looked around the table. Yes, they were all here. Some met her gaze. Others did not. Dubnik met her stare head on, with a ghost of a smile at the edges of his mouth.

'We are here,' Vexler said, 'to discuss an incident which occurred on the Europa space station. I assume you are all aware of the incident, however I feel it would be appropriate if we viewed the footage again.'

Ferona felt her smile slowly fade. It was all she could do to keep her expression neutral as the air above the table flickered into coloured life and the scene from the Europa was replayed in all its bloody glory. She didn't need to look at it to know that she would see agents failing to apprehend a known pirate, despite the fact that they outnumbered him three to one. That her daughter would be in the middle of it, not as an agent, a position which might have garnered some respect, but fighting alongside the pirate, long silver blades extending from her hands, clear evidence that her prosthetics had been altered.

The image paused and Vexler got to his feet. He walked slowly around the table. His hands were clasped tightly behind his back. His hair, pure white, was brushed neatly back from a high forehead, and his suit was a pristine midnight blue. Clearly he had had some time to prepare. 'We have identified this man as Adam Bryant,' he said, highlighting one of the agents. 'New York Dome, educated at Columbia University. He has been an agent for a little over thirty years, and up to this point, his record was exemplary.'

He moved a little further round the table, pointed to the screen again. 'This man,' he said, 'is Caspian Dax. Prior to this incident, there were seventeen warrants out for his arrest. He is now a kill-on-sight target.'

No. No! She couldn't let that happen. 'With all due respect, president,' Ferona said, 'as Minister for Off World Affairs, it is my responsibility to ensure that Caspian Dax is apprehended. I have already . . . '

Dubnik exploded to his feet. 'Already what?' he said. 'We all know that's your daughter up there, Minister Blue. You are supposed to be in control of this situation.'

'I am in control of it,' Ferona replied, struggling to remain calm.

'No you're not!' Dubnik told her. 'But you bloody well should be. You're a senator now. You represent us in the senate. How are you going to convince them to consider our relocation to Spes when your own daughter has been caught running riot on a space station?'

'I have already taken steps to ensure that all those involved in this incident will shortly be apprehended.'

'What steps?'

'That's classified information.'

'Classified?' Dubnik said in disbelief. 'I am the vice president. How can it be classified?'

Vexler leaned across and said something to Dubnik. Ferona couldn't make out what it was, but she could tell that Dubnik didn't like it. His face flushed and he shot to his feet.

'Well, whatever you're doing, it isn't working!' Dubnik yelled. 'Because not one of these individuals is in custody!' He stormed to the head of the table. Vexler's image blurred, then disappeared, as Dubnik's signal took his place. 'I call for the immediate resignation of Minister Blue.'

The figures around the table went completely still. There was silence, nothing but silence, as Dubnik placed his hands on the table and leaned forward, his gaze fixed on Ferona. His eyes were so dark they were almost black, and for the first time she saw something in them that she'd never seen before. A wildness, a raging anger. Dubnik wasn't just ruthless, he was emotional, and that was a far more dangerous animal to deal with. How had she not seen this coming? She had known that he disliked her, and the feeling was mutual.

But she hadn't predicted that he would try to destroy her, not yet, not now, and not so openly, so blatantly. Behind her, she could feel the steady presence of Swain and Lucinda. And she could feel their shock. Swain leaned forward. 'He can call for your resignation, but he cannot force you to do it.'

Ferona looked at Dubnik, at the angry fire burning in his eyes, visible even in the holographic image. She looked at Vexler, standing now at the side of the table, so polished, so weak. She could not expect help from that department. Her heart was pounding sickeningly and her stomach felt like she had eaten something bad. It could not end like this. She would not allow it. She needed to breathe, to think. Dubnik might not be able to force her to resign, but he could make life very, very difficult for her.

She rose slowly to her feet and smoothed down the front of her gown. The draping sweep of red and ivory emphasised her gender, her wealth, the status that she had worked so hard to achieve. In contrast to the austere cut of Dubnik's dark suit, she knew it made her look soft. Defenceless.

Ferona fluttered her lashes, let her eyes brim with tears, but inside she was as hard as the ice that surrounded the Dome, and just as cold. 'I would like one hour to consider the request,' she said.

'Denied,' Dubnik snapped out.

'Just one hour,' Ferona repeated, letting her voice tremble. 'Surely that isn't too much to ask for.'

She didn't bother looking at Vexler. The man was utterly spineless. The past few minutes had swept away any remaining belief in his power. Instead, she kept her gaze fixed on Dubnik, willing him to cave. If he refused, the other ministers would see it as cruel and unreasonable, and they would remember it.

Ferona blinked. A solitary tear slowly crawled down her powdered cheek.

And Dubnik caved. 'One hour,' he said.

As the hologram switched off and the space instantly emptied, the walls switched to panelled grey and the table disappeared. Ferona shot to her feet. 'Fucking prick,' she screamed. 'Fucking self-righteous interfering prick! He has no idea who he's dealing with. No idea at all.'

She whirled around, her full skirts sweeping around with her. 'Get me a way out of this,' she shouted at Swain and Lucinda. 'He has to have a weakness. A mistress. An addiction to Euphoria. A sexual perversion that he wouldn't want others to know about.'

'I've sat next to him more than once,' Lucinda said. 'There is nothing. No mistress, no unauthorised children, nothing.'

'There has to be something. There's always something. Find it!'

Fingers flew to smart comms and started to work as Ferona began to pace the length of the meeting room. Finding a way to keep her position wasn't enough, not any more. If she wanted to keep moving forward, to keep the Second Species programme running, she would have to do more than just defeat Dubnik this time. She would have to destroy him.

She spun around, glared at her two assistants. 'Well?'

'He's clean,' Swain told her. 'He's never even dodged a tram ticket. He took Euphoria when he was at university, but turned himself in the next day. He was given a fine, which he paid, and two weeks' community service at a rehab clinic. He did three. If we tried to use that against him, we'd look like idiots.'

'Lucinda?'

Lucinda shook her head.

Frustration boiled up inside Ferona. If they said Dubnik was clean, then he was clean. 'The man is human,' she said. 'And humans make mistakes.'

'Not this one,' Lucinda replied.

Ferona folded her arms and resumed pacing. 'Then we will make one for him.' It would have to be something believable. Something irrefutable. Something that Dubnik could have easily kept private, unlike a mistress, or a sexual fetish. 'He thinks he is untouchable. But he is not.' And there was one thing that mattered to government ministers more than anything else.

Money.

She had skimmed her own budgets to pay for the Second Species programme. Thanks to Swain, the trail was almost impossible to follow, though if anyone was clever enough to unpick what he had woven, they would find that almost 500 million credits had vanished, seemingly without a trace.

'Swain,' she said, turning to him as inspiration struck. 'I am suddenly very worried that our esteemed vice president has some discrepancies in his accounts.'

Swain looked at her. His eyes narrowed and then he smiled, showing a lot of very expensive white teeth. 'I do believe that you are right, minister.'

'How long will it take you to find them?'

'How long do I have?'

'Thirty minutes,' Ferona told him.

Swain nodded as he got to his feet and slid his personal comm. unit into his trouser pocket. 'I'll be in the public library if you need me,' he said. He left the meeting room at a brisk pace, without looking back.

'Dubnik will deny it,' Lucinda pointed out. She crossed her legs at the knee and steepled her fingers, flexing them against each other.

'He can deny it all he likes,' Ferona said. 'But the evidence will speak for itself.'

'If you bring it up, it will look highly suspicious.'

Her assistant had a point. And Dubnik would seize it like a suffocating man given a breath of oxygen. There had to be another way. And there was. 'Are you still sleeping with De Couerts' assistant?'

'Of course,' Lucinda said.

'Anyone else?'

'Berry's security liaison, Ivanov's personal physician, and one of Vexler's drivers.' She counted each one off on her fingers as she spoke, as if she wanted to make sure she didn't forget any of them. 'Oh, and both of Robinson's sons.'

'Who is the most easily manipulated?'

Lucinda considered this. 'Jomy Robinson,' she said.

'Contact him,' Ferona ordered her. 'Tell him that you've discovered something irregular in Dubnik's accounts and you don't know what to do about it.'

A smile curved Lucinda's full mouth. 'Yes, minister.' She rose to her feet. 'May I use your office?'

Ferona dismissed her with a wave of her hand. While her assistants took care of the Dubnik problem, she had another issue to deal with. The kill-on-sight order that had been placed on Caspian Dax. She couldn't countermand it, not yet. She had seen the faces of some of the other ministers when Dubnik had called for her resignation.

They were afraid of her. They were afraid of her power, and what it meant.

She would have to allow the order to stand.

But she could not allow Dax to die. He was far too valuable for that. Dax had to be found and captured alive. It had been done before, and it could be done again. All she needed was a little more time. The Type Threes would find him. She had faith in that.

Two hours later, Ferona Blue walked away from the

reconvened emergency meeting with her position as Minister for Off World Affairs intact. Mikhal Dubnik had not been so lucky. Jace Robinson, Minister for Education, had voiced some concerns about a massive irregularity in Dubnik's financial records. It appeared that close to 500 million credits had gone missing from his departmental accounts. Dubnik had protested, denying all knowledge of wrongdoing, but the evidence was right there for everyone to see.

There was no call for his resignation. There didn't need to be. Dubnik had screamed in rage as two security droids dragged him away from the meeting seconds before his holoimage had been switched off.

Vexler had floundered, and Ferona had stepped in. She had been the calm voice of authority in the middle of the chaos.

And if anyone had remembered that they were meeting to discuss her resignation, they had kept it to themselves.

# CHAPTER
# 23

**2nd September 2207**

The Articus. Repair Station, Sector Four, Neutral Space

'I'd forgotten what a bad idea drinking with you is,' Alistair said. Covering his face with his hands, he groaned loudly.

'You've only had three ales,' Eve pointed out.

'Three is enough.'

At the other side of the table, Dax lifted his nineteenth jar to his lips and emptied it. 'You should learn when to stop,' he said. 'Like me.'

'Easy to say when you have no limit and therefore never have to stop.' Gripping the edge of the table tightly, Alistair pushed to his feet and staggered off in the direction of the sanitation unit, bumping into an empty table and almost falling over on the way.

They'd been in the bar most of the night, Eve, Alistair, Grudge, Jinn and himself. The rest of the crew had abandoned the *Mutant* as soon as they'd docked, and Dax couldn't blame them. He doubted he would ever see any of them again. It was a shame. There had been a couple that he almost liked.

Fortunately the Articus was big enough to avoid the others. The bar Grudge took them to was far enough away from the public walkways that it was unlikely any of the *Mutant*'s former crew would find it. It was, for want of a better word, a dive, and his crew preferred something brighter, louder, somewhere they could see and be seen.

This place wasn't bright or loud. Dax had wondered what Jinn would make of it, but she'd walked straight up to the bar and ordered a shot of Batlakian vodka, a viscous yellow liquid that could strip space grime from a ship's hull. The barman had looked at her hair, her face, her implant. Then he'd looked at Dax. His expression hadn't shifted a millimetre, though he turned just enough for Dax to see the crossbow hanging from his right hip. His hair was streaked red and purple, matching the stones that studded his upper lip and cheeks, and he wore only trousers, no shirt, showing off his prosthetic shoulder plates. They would fold out to form gliding panels, the sort that would let him fly over the fields of Colony Four so that he could inspect crop growth from the air. Definitely a Bug. He was too young and too wary to have worked out his contract. He'd served them all, then got back to the business of watching the Flyball match currently playing out on the vid wall.

'Do I want to offer him a place on the *Mutant*?' Dax asked Grudge, jerking his head in the direction of the barman.

'Nope,' Grudge said.

Dax didn't push further. He had other questions to ask. 'You said you thought the nanotech was Sittan in origin.'

'I did,' Grudge said.

'You've seen it before?'

'Not like that, no,' Grudge said. 'But I might have spent some time visiting stations on the edge of Sittan space, and had a look at their ships.'

'You've been on board?' Jinn asked.

'No,' Grudge said. 'A friend of mine did though. They were still finding bits of him six weeks later.'

Eve shuddered and knocked her drink down in one. 'At least they're not as disgusting as the Shi-Fai,' she said, setting the tumbler back on the table and spinning it round with gloved fingers. 'We don't have tentacles for hands, or ooze slime.'

'It's all a matter of opinion,' Grudge said. 'From where they're standing, we probably seem pretty foul.'

Eve pulled a face and Grudge smiled. Then he switched his attention to Dax. 'Why were the agents after you?'

Dax slowly set his drink down on the table. A hush seemed to have descended in the bar. Suddenly a lot of faces were turned their way and he could see a lot more weapons than he'd been able to a moment ago. Even the barman had stopped pretending to watch the Flyball match. He cracked his knuckles and kept his gaze on the room until they all looked away. 'Because I'm a thieving scumbag pirate who escaped from the A2.'

'I'm aware of that,' Grudge said. He sat back in his seat. He set his prosthetic on the table top. The cutting diamond at the end began to slowly spin, decorating their surroundings with an intricate pattern of dancing light. 'I strongly suggest that you tell me whatever it is that you aren't telling me.'

The door to the bar opened and several people filed out.

'Medipro has taken over the A2,' Dax said. 'At least, we assume it's Medipro. They're using it to carry out genetic modifications.'

'What sort of genetic modifications?' Grudge asked. The cutting diamond had stopped spinning, leaving the light as a static pattern that caught patches of skin, of clothing. Everywhere else seemed to have faded into deeper darkness.

'Modifications like mine,' Dax said. He picked up his ale and took a long swallow as Alistair returned to the table. 'Which has me wondering.'

'Wondering what?' Eve asked.

'The A2 is a big operation,' Dax said. 'It can't have been cheap, setting that up.'

'Medipro can afford it,' Jinn pointed out. 'They must have a dozen drug patents at least.'

'And they're probably hoping to get a patent for the serums

they used on us,' Dax said, looking at Alistair and Eve. 'Which means that they have most likely worked out how to reverse-engineer it. Where are their manufacturing plants?'

Alistair's gaze sharpened, and he sat up straighter in his seat. 'Colony Seven?' he asked, looking at Grudge.

'What about Colony Seven?' Jinn leaned forward in her seat. 'I thought you were drunk.'

'I was,' Alistair said. 'But that piss-hole they call a sanitation unit has a sober-up machine.'

'How many shots did you take?' Jinn asked him.

'Three,' Alistair said.

'You're insane,' Eve said.

'My son works on Colony Seven,' Grudge said.

Everyone stopped and stared at him.

'I didn't know you had a son.' Dax leaned back against the wall, folded his arms, curious.

'You do now,' Grudge said. 'He works for a construction company. He's got terraforming qualifications too. It's good money and he seems happy enough.'

'He's got prosthetics?' Jinn asked.

'Yes,' Grudge said. 'But I paid off his debt. He's free to leave whenever he wants to. About twelve months ago, Medipro had a new facility built on the south side of Colony Seven.'

'That's not unusual,' Jinn said. 'They've got facilities all over the place. People always need medical care.'

'This isn't a clinic,' Grudge said. 'It's a manufacturing plant.'

Dax felt suddenly cold. 'What sort of manufacturing plant?'

'No-one seems to know,' Grudge said. 'That part of the asteroid is prone to sandstorms, so people aren't too keen to take a closer look. They used local workers to drill out the foundations and put up the building, but they brought in their own staff to run it.'

'Do you think they could be making a reverse serum there?' Eve asked, her eyes wide with hope.

'I don't know,' Dax said. 'But I think we should find out.'

'That will have to wait,' Grudge said, glancing down at the small comm. unit strapped to his wrist. He got to his feet. 'Your droid is awake.'

Swathed in a length of bright purple cloth, Theon moved forward. His electric-blue eyes gleamed. His movements were awkward, but he was on his feet. 'Caspian,' he said. 'You look dreadful.'

Dax exhaled. For the first time in hours, he felt like he could breathe. 'Spending a night wondering if you're going to lose a friend will do that to you.'

'Especially if you spend that night poisoning your insides with Batlakian vodka and Rovian ale,' Alistair added. He moved past Dax, set his hand to Theon's shoulder. 'Glad to have you in one piece,' he said.

'I am most happy to be in this state,' Theon replied. 'Although my appearance is humiliating.'

'Well, it's better than being dead,' Eve said.

Theon almost smiled. 'Jinnifer Blue,' he said. 'I understand I have you to thank for my current condition.'

'Grudge did the work,' she said. 'He's the one you should be thanking.'

'Thank Caspian,' Grudge said. 'Or rather, thank all the people he's stolen from over the years. They're the ones paying the bill.'

Dax rubbed a hand over his face, realised he needed a cleanse. And a shave. And something to eat. Between the drinking, and the pleasure droid, and the rest, he was running on empty. 'What about the nanotech?' Dax asked Grudge.

'I disposed of it,' Grudge said.

'How?'

'I attached it to a vessel belonging to a customer of mine who had some difficulty remembering to pay his bill.'

That sounded like the Grudge he knew. 'So you're completely fixed?' Dax asked Theon.

'It would seem so,' Theon replied. 'There is perhaps a little more work to complete on my balance sensors – I am not yet entirely steady on my feet. But I would describe myself as fully functional.'

'Good,' said Dax. 'Because I need you to fly me to Colony Seven.'

'And me,' Jinn said.

'No,' Dax told her. 'You're staying here, and you're getting medical treatment.'

'I'm part of this just as much as you are,' she said. 'You want answers? Well, so do I.'

'You need to have your Tellurium removed.'

'If Theon is piloting, I won't need to use it. I've survived this long. A few more days won't kill me. I'm going to Colony Seven, Dax. I can go with you, or I can find my own way. It's up to you.'

She wasn't safe with him. The broken droid he'd left in the pleasure parlour was proof of that. But he also knew that she meant what she said. She was just foolish enough to try and get there on her own.

He could keep his distance. It wouldn't be easy, but he could do it. Colony Seven had a large Dome population, which meant it would have high-end medical centres, far better than they'd find here. 'Alright,' he said, telling himself it was for the best, that it had nothing to do with the fact that he wasn't ready to say goodbye to her just yet.

'I'm coming too,' Eve said.

'So am I,' Alistair added.

'I'll stay here,' Grudge said. 'And look after my ship.'

'You mean my ship,' Dax told him.

Grudge just smiled.

The journey to Colony Seven was short and uneventful. They left the *Mutant* under Grudge's care and took the *Deviant* instead. With Theon in the pilot's seat, the others stretched out in their seats and played a strange game that Jinn hadn't seen before, involving six dice, the real thing, not a hologram. They bet with whatever they had in their pockets, which in Dax's case turned out to be a handful of gleaming dark rubies. Eve had a couple of credit chips and Alistair had an angular twist of polished gold. 'Starter chip for a particularly nice skimmer,' he said. 'Top of the range.'

'A pity it's on the Europa,' Eve said.

Alistair shrugged. 'A minor detail.'

Dax took the pair of them for everything they had in the first couple of minutes.

'You cheated!' Eve said.

'I'm a pirate,' Dax replied. 'What did you expect?'

Eve glared at him and Jinn found it hard not to laugh. Then the onboard alarm sounded, indicating that they were coming out of the jump. She settled back into her seat as the restraints fastened her in. The *Deviant* was small, which meant that leaving the jump would be rough, and rough it was, even with Theon's undeniable skill.

Ahead of them, the space lane that led to Colony Seven was rammed with slow-moving traffic. Traffic police ships darted in and out, small one-man vessels designed simply to control speed and keep things moving.

Grudge's son, Ase, had supplied them with a landing permit. If anyone checked, they were visiting family, with a temporary thirty-eight-hour visa. But no-one did, and they soon landed at the public port, where Dax used one of those dark rubies to buy them a secure hangar for the *Deviant* with no thumbprint identity needed and no questions asked. Theon remained on board. Without polyskin, he was too conspicuous, and the last thing they wanted was to draw attention to themselves. Eve pulled on gloves and a long coat with a deep hood. Provided no-one got too close, she'd pass for an Underworld worker. Jinn tucked her hair under a soft cap and hoped no-one would look past her implants.

Ase met them at the exit. He was young and lean, his neck and forearms studded with the docking bolts that would allow him to connect to a huge construction suit. With the suit in place, he'd be able to lift huge steel girders, siding plates, concrete slabs the size of a skimmer. His hair was neatly cut, his clothing basic but clean, and his eyes a light grey that spoke of calm intelligence. He was Grudge as he would have been sixty years before, and Jinn liked him on sight.

Unfortunately, she didn't find Colony Seven quite so pleasant. Ase led them out of the port and took them over to a landroller, a battered eight-seater which was about as comfortable as it looked. A woman sat in the driver's seat. She had dirty brown hair, her eyes an odd sort of hazel.

'This is Mara,' Ase said. 'She's a friend of mine. The roller belongs to her.'

'Hey,' Mara said. Then she turned back to the controls.

'I'm not sure about this,' Jinn whispered to Dax. 'We don't know anything about her.'

Alistair deactivated his implant, then shook his head and activated it again. 'I need to get closer to her,' he said, but before he could move, Ase settled himself into the driver's seat, leaving the rest of them to climb into the back.

Food wrappers littered the floor, and the seats were split and peeling. Even with her boosted immune system, Jinn felt a wave of disgust. She noticed Dax grinning at her as she chose the cleanest-looking seat, and showed him her middle finger.

'So,' Ase said. 'You want to see the Medipro warehouse.'

'Yes,' Dax said. 'What can you tell us about it?'

'Not much,' Ase replied. 'They just turned up and hired workers. The whole thing was up in less than a fortnight.'

'Is that unusual?' Jinn asked.

'It is here,' Ase told her, as the roller jerked away from the kerb and bounced into the flow of traffic. 'We've got the Domes, and then we've got the refineries. We're the furthest colony from Earth. Why build a medical manufacturing plant here, especially if you're not going to use locals to run it, and everything is going to be exported? It doesn't make any sense.'

'Because you don't want anyone to know what you're doing,' Dax said. 'Didn't the unions complain?'

'The unions complain all the time,' Ase said. The roller shot forward and overtook the vehicle in front. 'No-one listens to them. Why would they? No-one cares about Underworld workers. We're too easily replaced.'

It was a story that Jinn had heard so many times now. Yes, the roller was tatty and old and needed a clean, but Mara had probably had to save long and hard to be able to afford it.

Jinn slumped back in her seat, feeling all at once ashamed. The feeling had shrunk in the time she'd spent with Dax and the others, because they treated her as one of them. The differences between them didn't matter. But they might matter to Ase and Mara. She tugged her cap a little lower on her head, turned her gaze and focussed on the view outside.

They were on a busy six-lane highway perched high up in the air. Smog clouds decorated the sky in twisting spirals. She couldn't see where they were coming from, until Mara swung the roller left and they started to descend. This wasn't the beautiful Colony Seven she'd heard of. This was rough and industrial, and so unlike Earth that she couldn't tear her gaze away. Freighters, repair stations and space stations were all different to that frozen landscape too, but there was no escaping the feeling of being closed in, of knowing that you were in a contained unit with space all around.

This was different. There were no edges, no walls. It stretched out around her, as far as the eye could see, and although she knew in theory that the Colony was far, far smaller than Earth, she couldn't feel the difference.

'Where is the facility?' Dax asked Ase. 'I want to get a look at it as soon as possible.'

'On the other side of the asteroid,' Ase told him. 'It's what we affectionately call the wasteland. There are no mineral deposits worth mining over there, and the landscape isn't exactly what you'd call pretty.'

The roller sped down the ramp and flew out into another lane of traffic. Music blasted from the speakers, something electronic with a thudding bass, and Mara tapped the steering wheel in time to the beat.

They were much lower now, beneath the clouds from the refinery. Terraforming had made the air breathable, though the people she could see walking around all wore anti-pollution masks that covered the lower halves of their faces.

Within a few minutes, they'd left the dirty industrial zone behind and were skirting the edge of a city laid out like a glistening jewel amongst the twists of the road. A river ran alongside it, red as blood. The buildings speared up towards the sky. They were so tall that Jinn had to tip her head back to see the top of them.

She recognised the skyline from the brochures she'd browsed back when she'd still been thinking about making this place her home. And she wondered how she could ever have believed that she could belong here, that it was somewhere she could settle and be happy.

It was as much a prison as the Domes had been.

They left the towering city behind, kept moving, as all around them the landscape became flat and barren, a seemingly never-ending sea of sand and dust. It was a couple of hours before Mara pulled the roller off the road. Ase reached under his seat and pulled out a bag. From it, he took anti-pollution masks and tossed one to each of them. Water bags followed suit, as did goggles.

'We need to walk the rest of the way,' he said, as his door slid open. He climbed out without waiting for a response. Mara followed suit.

Jinn looked at the others, then at Dax. 'Do we trust him?'

'Well?' Dax asked Alistair.

'If there's trouble, he'll deny having anything to do with us,' Alistair said. 'But he's telling the truth about the facility.' He brushed a hand behind his ear, then reached into his pocket and pulled out a strip of pain pills. He popped three, dropped them onto his tongue. 'I didn't get the chance to read Mara. Music was too loud. I suspect she's defective anyway.'

They all knew what that meant. Genetic modification wasn't perfect. Sometimes people were left with the hard wiring of their brain irreparably damaged. If it was low level, they could still work, still function, but they would always be a little different.

Eve poked a mouldy drink bag with the toe of her boot. 'That would explain a few things,' she said.

Jinn followed Dax as he climbed out of the roller. Alistair and Eve climbed out too. The air moved around them, warm against her skin, though it only took one breath for her to cough and pull on the anti-pollution mask. It had an odd, chemical smell, but at least it stopped the grit from coating her airways.

Ase had already put on his own mask. With a jerk of his head, he motioned them closer. 'Mara's going to wait here with the roller,' he said. 'She doesn't want to leave it unoccupied in case it gets stolen.'

Jinn thought that was unlikely, but she kept it to herself.

The wind had picked up, carrying more of the dust with it, and they tramped in single file through what started out as nothing and soon became a vicious, swirling storm.

Jinn tugged on her goggles, pulling the strap tight to keep them in place. She began to wonder if Ase was leading them to the Medipro facility, or leading them out into a wasteland to die. She reached for Dax, but the wind pushed her back, and he would never hear her over the howl of the storm.

And then she saw it. A light up ahead, bright, artificial, cutting through the haze. She blinked behind the thick lenses of her goggles. She could tell that the others had seen it too, because they had all picked up speed. Single file changed into side by side, as they all fought their way towards the light.

A building rose from the ground, a sprawling single-storey warehouse. It was huge and windowless, painted the same dull yellow as the sand that seemed to have crawled inside her clothing.

The light came from the roof. A huge, swivelling searchlight. Others joined it, scanning the ground, sweeping in random arcs that would make them impossible to avoid.

Ase beckoned them closer. He pulled down his mask, shouting over the roar of the wind. 'This is as far as I go.'

Dax turned to Alistair and Eve. 'Go with him.'

The two of them nodded.

'Don't trust me?' Ase shouted.

'I don't know you,' Dax shouted back. 'And I'd rather not walk all the way back to find our ride has gone.'

'I could get thrown off asteroid just for bringing you here,' Ase told him.

'Then consider them your protection.'

'Those two? They couldn't fight off a stoner in a skin bar.'

'Then you won't have a problem with them.'

The searchlight swept around again, skimming the ground close to where they stood.

'Time to move,' Dax said. 'Jinn, you're with me. We'll meet the rest of you back at the roller. It we're not back in twelve hours, get back to the *Deviant* and get away from here.'

He looked at Ase. 'Thanks,' he said.

'Don't thank me yet,' Ase told him. 'Thank me when you make it back.'

Those words played heavily on Jinn's mind as she and Dax started to move. The searchlight separated them, forcing them to dance around the glare of the light. It got close, too close, and Jinn dropped to a crouch, closing her eyes as it skimmed over her head. Dax was crouched low too, fingertips skimming the ground, muscles tensed. Reaching into his pocket, he pulled out the skimmer key he'd won from Alistair.

Then he threw it into the light.

It exploded.

They looked at each other and swore.

'Ready to find out what sort of a pirate you really are?' Dax asked.

'I don't think I'll ever be ready for that,' Jinn muttered.

'On the next sweep of the light, get ready to move,' he ordered her. 'Wait for it. Wait for it.'

Jinn risked a glance behind her. She saw nothing but dust, thick enough to get lost in. There was no turning back.

'Go!' Dax grabbed her jacket and pulled her forwards. They ran together, hand finding hand, following the narrow passage of darkness that the beams left behind. Somehow, they managed to reach the edge of the building, and dropped to the ground beside it. They huddled together, arm pressing against arm, thigh pressing against thigh, breathing fast.

They sat there until their breath had slowed, watching the sweep of the lights and the gentle swirl of the sand. Then Jinn reached out, took his hand, and laced her fingers through his. She stared at their linked hands.

'Whatever we find in there,' she said, 'I'm glad I got to know you, Caspian Dax.'

He lifted a hand, let it drop. Then he lifted it again and touched her face.

'When they altered me,' he said, 'when they did what they did, I . . .' He stopped, shook his head. 'Back on the Articus, when I asked you if you wanted to go to a pleasure parlour with me, it was . . . I acted like a creep. I'm sorry.'

'What for?'

'I don't want to be this way,' he said, staring out into the dust. 'But sometimes it seems like I can't stop myself. I shouldn't have kissed you. It was . . . I just shouldn't have done it.'

'So why did you?'

'Because I wanted to.'

'Did it ever occur to you that maybe I wanted it too?'

He turned his head sharply and looked at her.

'I've been alone for a long time too, Dax. And don't tell me you're not alone. I've seen how it is for you.'

He didn't say anything else. He didn't have to. She searched his face, the strong lines and bright eyes. It was time to be brave. It might be all the time she had. 'But it doesn't have to be that way,' she said. And then she touched her mouth to his.

'Jinn,' he whispered, his lips moving against hers.

It didn't have the hot, angry passion of the first kiss they'd shared. It didn't need it. Instead, it was soft and intimate, as if both of them were trying to put into this something they couldn't put into words.

When it ended, when they broke apart, they got to their feet in silence. The searchlights didn't come this close to the building, so they were safe. The first building ended and they found themselves moving alongside a second smaller one that budded out from the first. And then Jinn heard something, something that she recognised. 'Hear that?' she shouted back at Dax.

He nodded. 'Landing drives,' he said.

Right on cue, the sky above them lit up as twin rings of twinkling purple lights moved closer and closer. Jinn recognised the underneath of a frigate, a ship built to work both on land and in space. It was relatively small, highly manoeuvrable, and they were usually used to transport more delicate cargo, like electrical components and medical supplies, things that might not survive a trip in a land train and needed to be delivered right to the doorstep.

'We need to get a closer look,' she said.

'Agreed.' Dax reached under his coat, pulled out a blaster and charged it, then looked at her. 'Do you know how to use this?'

Jinn took it. It felt strange and heavy in her hand, and warm from where it had been close to his body. 'Point and shoot.'

He grinned. 'I'm so glad you're on my side.'

They moved forward cautiously as the frigate sank lower, coming to a rest in the centre of the landing plot. It was a good bit of flying. The phase drive powered down and hissed out multiple jets of chemical steam that clouded the air for a moment before dissipating. Then a door in the side of the ship folded down, creating a low-level loading ramp.

The crew were wearing deep purple uniforms with gold insignia, their faces distorted by close-fitting bubble helmets that would work far better than her mask and goggles. Jinn pulled her cap a little tighter down on her head. It would take forever to clean the sand out of her hair.

On the other side of the landing pad, the seemingly never-ending wall of the warehouse was broken up by a long line of loading doors. One was open. Three refrigerated storage crates were wheeled out. One of the crew gave a thumbprint ID to the warehouse worker who accompanied the crates. Then the crates were loaded onto the frigate and the crew disappeared back on board.

They needed to get inside. They weren't going to find anything out here.

The phase drive of the frigate started to roar. 'Come on,' Jinn yelled, tugging on Dax's sleeve. He moved in behind her and together they sprinted for the open loading door. The worker had already disappeared back inside.

There was little more than a narrow gap by the time they reached the door and rolled underneath it. A dozen rows of shelving ran from floor to ceiling, the painted lines on the floor indicating that droids were used to pick and pack the crates. The worker they had seen was in a small office at the other side of the space. He had his feet up on his desk and his eyes glued to a small portable viewscreen, a colourful pattern of light flashing over his face. Whatever he was watching, it was clearly more interesting than the warehouse.

Dax pointed ahead. Jinn gave him the thumbs-up, and they ran in between the first row of shelves. Brown boxes filled the shelves, each one sealed in a tough layer of Plastex. Dax pulled a blade from his boot and cut into one.

Plastic drug bags spilled out, falling to the floor as silently as snow. He cut into another, and another. More bags.

They left the warehouse behind and journeyed further into the building. Dax led this time, and Jinn let him. Beyond the storage area, they found a huge packaging plant. It was noisy and hot, drug bags snapping as they were plunged into steaming baths and then upturned, swinging by overhead. The machinery rattled and hummed, in a never-ending process. Dip, rinse, dry, fill.

Each bag was about the size of her hand, printed with a label that she couldn't decipher. The liquid flowing into them was pink, like watered-down blood, a thick, viscous fluid that swelled each bag before it was sealed and dropped onto a conveyor belt.

'This looks like the stuff they used on me,' Dax said.

So they were making the serum here. It was a start. At the side of the room was a door, the old-fashioned kind that had to be pushed open. It had a window in the top. Jinn walked over and looked through. Then she swung the door open.

It was a lab.

She recognised some of the equipment. Some of it was so high tech that she had no idea what it was for. A tall cooling unit with a flashing display held multiple shallow dishes, each one half filled with pale gold gel. Sitting on top of the gel, in every dish, was a piece of what looked like human skin. The skin samples on the middle shelf were flesh-toned, pale.

The ones on the bottom shelf were green.

'Dax, you've got to see this,' she said, as footsteps approached. 'Tell me if you think this is what I think it is.'

He leaned in. Their eyes met in the reflection on the door. 'Don't touch anything,' he said.

Jinn backed away from the cooling unit, keeping her hands firmly by her sides. She could feel sweat trickling down her back, even though the lab was cool. 'We've got packaging and we've got testing,' she said. 'So where's manufacturing?'

'Through here,' Dax said, his voice grim. He was on the other side of the lab. Carefully moving past the benches and the testing equipment stacked on them, Jinn moved alongside him.

A window ran the length of the lab. Through it, she could see three huge, stainless steel vats, each easily twice her height. Pipes ran from each one, up to the ceiling and along, leading to other, smaller vats. The room was white, sterile. 'It looks like a giant chemistry set,' she said.

'Thermocyclers for PCR, distillation, purification,' Dax said. 'Everything you need to make yourself a steady supply of serum that will turn an average human into a monster.'

'So where is it going?' she asked. 'Okay, we know some of it is going to the A2. But what about the rest? There are green flesh samples in that cooling unit. That means they must be making the serum that was used on Eve. Everyone we saw on the A2 was like you.'

'Type One,' Dax said.

'Yes. So where are they making the others?' She looked around, at the vats, at the lab, at the equipment. The answers were here, she knew it. 'The computer system,' she said, darting towards a desktop terminal.

Before Dax could stop her, she ripped out the wires from the side and sent her Tellurium plunging deep into the system. She connected in a heartbeat. The screen flickered to life, and she heard Dax inhale.

'Fucking supernova,' he said. 'There are test files on here.'

He touched the screen, opened one. There was a lot of data, and a lot of complicated scientific language. Jinn was still trying to decipher it when Dax scrolled the screen up. 'Shi-Fai,' he said. 'Of course.'

'What?'

'Eve's modifications,' he said. 'Poisonous to humans.' He looked at her. 'Immune to Shi-Fai. We've all been modified with alien DNA.'

# CHAPTER
# 24

3rd September 2207

> Vessel: The *Deviant,* short-haul Corvette
> Location: Colony Seven
> Cargo: None
> Crew: Four
> Droids: One

'We have to destroy it,' Eve said. 'I'll burn the place to the ground myself if I have to.' She paced the confined space of the cruiser, as she'd been doing for the past half an hour. She seemed unable to stop, unable to sit still, and they were all giving her space.

'How?' Ase asked.

Eve spun around, glared at him. 'Do you think that I can't?' she yelled. 'Do you think that just because I'm female and I look like this that I couldn't raze that place to the ground?'

'He's got a point,' Dax said. 'In fact, it's the question we should be asking ourselves. We all agree that place can't be left operating. So how are we going to deal with it?'

After leaving the Medipro facility, Dax and Jinn had trekked back to the roller, where the others had been waiting. They had intended to go to Ase's home near the refinery, but they had passed a local security skimmer and Mara had panicked due to the fact that she had a small amount of locally produced Meth in her jacket pocket and a larger amount in a box in the back of the roller. She'd turned the roller around and gone full speed straight back to the port.

She sat in a corner now, a haze of grey smoke circling her head as she sucked on a long pipe and muttered to herself. Apparently she'd decided to deal with the Meth problem by smoking it, and she'd put that plan in action as soon as she got on board the *Deviant*.

Dax had turned the air recycler up to max, and then Jinn had told the others what they had found, including the fact that Eve's modifications made her immune to Shi-Fai toxins, and that there was no reverse serum.

Eve had paled. She had locked herself in the sanitation unit, refusing to speak to anyone, until she had emerged twenty minutes later, red-eyed and in her current mood.

'The only reason they would modify women to be immune to Shi-Fai toxin is for the flesh trade,' Eve said now. 'Everyone knows what the Shi-Fai want with us, why they hang around the space stations in the neutral zones. Clearly Medipro have seen a gap in the market.'

'You're saying that a drug company has worked out a way to modify human women so they can be sold to the Shi-Fai?' Ase asked, as Alistair handed round the bowls of spicy noodles that the Autochef had prepared. Ase shook his head. 'They'd never get away with it.'

'Why not?' Eve asked. 'It's only a few Underworld women. Who cares what happens to them as long as the corporations are making credits?'

'Look,' Ase said. 'I'm not happy that place is here any more than you are. But alien modifications? Selling women to an alien race? I'm sorry, but I'm finding that a little hard to believe.' He gestured to Eve. 'For all I know, this is some sort of full-body tattoo.'

Eve moved in on him. 'Then let me touch you,' she said.

Ase dodged out of her way. 'No,' he said.

'Why not?'

'Eve,' Dax said. She glanced across at him. He'd never seen her like this before, so wired, so agitated. If she didn't calm down, she would hurt someone. 'Sit down,' he ordered her. 'Eat something.'

Her jaw tightened, but she did as she was told, sticking her spork into the noodles.

Then Dax turned to Alistair. 'Show him,' he said.

Alistair brushed the skin behind his ear. The others fell silent as he stared at Ase. 'Last Friday you left work twelve minutes early. Your chemicleanse unit is leaking, but you've been avoiding having it fixed because you hope that it will bring the wall down and then you'll be eligible for a transfer to one of the units higher up, where it's quieter. And you've been sleeping with your supervisor's wife for the past three months.'

Ase dropped the spoon he'd been holding, splattering the table top with food. 'How on Earth did you know that?'

'Because he's been modified with DNA that lets him hear people's thoughts,' Dax said. 'According to what we found, it originally came from the Lodon symbiont.'

Ase sank slowly back into his seat. 'So this is real?'

'It's real,' Dax said. 'There are three types. Eve, Alistair, and me. Thirty years ago, we signed up for a small-scale experimental modification programme with Medipro. They didn't really tell us what the modifications were, just that they were new.'

'So why did you agree to it?' Ase asked him.

'Because I was eighteen and stupid and it didn't even occur to me to question it. What was there to question, anyway? Everyone who wants to leave the Underworld cities gets mods, it's just what you do. And I was worried that if I made too much of a fuss they'd turn me down, and then I'd be stuck living in a two-room apartment with my parents for the rest of my life. But these mods . . . they were a death sentence. Twelve of us took part. Eight didn't survive. We escaped.' He gestured to himself, Alistair and Eve. 'Now it seems that they're having another go. Only this time, it's not a dozen people. It's thousands. With a one in three survival rate, that place is basically a death factory. They start using this serum, most of the people they use it on will die. And fuck only knows what awaits the ones who survive. When Medipro signed the code of ethics they did it with their fingers crossed behind their back. I won't let them get away with it. Not this time.'

Ase pushed his hair back from his face and glanced at Mara, but she was too busy sucking on her pipe and giggling to notice. 'My dad vouched for you. I trust him. If you say this place has to go, then it has to go, and I'll do whatever I can to help you. But if I do this, you owe me.'

'Owe you what?'

'The colonies are living on borrowed time,' Ase said. 'Once people start leaving Earth and heading to Spes, everything here is going to shut down. And I'm not stupid enough to think that anyone is going to be offering free passage to colony workers. Even if they do, we'll be stuffed in the cargo hold of some freighter. We'll be half starved and eating each other before we've even left neutral space.'

'What are you saying?'

'I want a life on Spes,' Ase said simply. 'If I help you with this, you're going to get me there. You pay for my transport, and I'll do whatever I can.'

'Sounds fair enough,' Dax said. 'What about her?' He gestured to Mara, who sat glassy-eyed and grinning in the corner.

'Her too,' Ase said. 'And anyone else who agrees to help.'

Dax considered this. He was already taking a risk. Every time the circle got bigger, so did the chance of being caught. He didn't know these people. But they didn't have much time. His visitation permit was due to expire in a matter of hours. Even if one of them did try to contact the local agents, Dax and the others would be long gone by then.

'Don't tell them anything they don't need to know,' Dax told

Ase. 'For their safety and yours. That includes telling them any-thing about me or my crew.'

'Then we have a deal?'

'We have a deal.'

Ase got up, pulling a personal comm. from his jacket pocket, and went outside to make the calls. Mara stayed where she was. Dax debated offering her a shot of Sober Up, but decided against it. She seemed happy enough. It could just as easily have been him, stuck on a colony in a dead-end job, forever held back by a brain that no longer worked quite as it should. If it was, he'd probably be off his head on Meth too.

Jinn pushed her bowl aside. 'When we've destroyed the plant, then what happens?'

'It's gone,' Eve said.

'What's to stop Medipro from rebuilding? From setting up another plant somewhere else? It's not enough to just destroy this plant.'

'What are you thinking?' Dax asked.

'We need to expose Medipro. Put a stop to this now. And we need to do it before the Intergalactic Senate realises that humans really are as bad as they think we are.'


Colony Seven was a twenty-four-hour asteroid. It was a place where nothing ever stopped, nothing ever shut down. Shifts simply changed and a new group of workers went in as the others came out and went home to rest.

They left at shift change. The roads were busy, the roller heavy. As well as Ase and Mara, two other colony workers sat in the back, their faces grim. Ase had introduced them as Riff and Olivier. Both worked as blast-setters at the mine that sup-plied the refinery. They hadn't asked any questions, and once again Mara had the music blasting too loud to allow for much conversation.

That was fine with Dax. The less they knew about each other, the better, as far as he was concerned. All he wanted to do was get in and get this done, and then get away from this rock and never come back to it. He didn't like the way it looked, the way it smelled, the way it made him feel. He let his gaze linger on Jinn. Her nerves were showing. She'd pulled her cap down low on her head, trying to hide her hair from the colony workers, and she was chewing her thumbnail. He remembered the feel of her mouth, and took her hand.

The roller bounced past the Dome city, out into the desert. The journey seemed far shorter than it had been first time round. Tension crackled through the inside of the roller, his heart pounding in time with the heavy beat of the music. When Mara swung the roller off the road and pulled to a halt, it settled on Dax like a heavy weight.

He tugged on his mask and goggles and climbed out of the roller. The sandstorm they had walked into the last time had dropped, the wind barely more than a light caress. They'd be easily visible to anyone watching the area around the factory. They would have to move quickly.

The others climbed out of the roller, including Mara. They moved as a group, Dax taking the lead. Alistair and Eve brought up the rear, both of them armed. He was taking no chances this time. Riff and Olivier had the charges, slung over their backs in armoured carryalls.

They reached the perimeter of the plant in under an hour.

'Ready?' Dax asked, as the searchlights swept the ground in their slow, looping circles.

'I've got it,' Ase said. He lifted his bow off his shoulder and pulled an arrow from the tube on his back. He thumbed a button next to the flight, and the pointed tip crackled with charge. Dax hadn't seen this sort of homemade weapon in years, though they were common in the Underworld cities. He'd had one himself that he'd used to shoot feral dogs on the surface. The meat had been tough, but it was better than starving on the all-too-frequent occasions when the silver rice didn't turn up.

Ase loaded the bow and took aim. Then he fired. The arrow hit one of the searchlights dead centre. It crackled then went out.

'Nice shot,' Eve said.

Ase pulled out another arrow and took out the other light. 'Thanks.'

'Which way?' Alistair asked.

'We followed the edge of the building,' Jinn said. 'That way.' She gestured left.

Dax turned to Riff and Olivier. 'Where is the best place to lay the charges?'

'Inside,' Riff said. 'As close to the power lines as we can get.'

'How long will it take you to set up?'

'Place this size, probably an hour,' Olivier said.

'You've got thirty minutes,' Dax replied. 'We've got one objective here. Get in, get it done, get out. The last thing we want is local security descending on the place. We're not here for a holiday. Don't stop to look at anything, don't stop to admire the view. Don't even stop to scratch your arse.'

There were murmurs of understanding. And then they were on the move again, keeping low, not wasting any time. Even Mara seemed to understand the danger they were in. The landing area loomed ahead and Dax motioned to the group to stop.

It was quiet. It was very, very quiet. Good timing or something else? There wasn't time for it to matter either way. They had a chance to get inside unseen and they took it. The warehouse was just as he remembered, the boxes lined up in their perfect, neat rows, the lights overhead softly humming. The little office was empty. Dax felt a twinge of unease, but he told himself he was imagining it. No-one knew they were here. Alistair would know if they did.

'Get to work,' he ordered Riff and Olivier. The two men nodded and headed off into the plant. Mara went with them. Ase busied himself reloading his crossbow. Alistair had already put in Smartware lenses and he activated them now. Dax wanted a recording of everything they found inside. Although he intended to leave nothing behind, he wanted evidence. There was no telling when it might prove useful.

They walked through the warehouse, falling into single file, Dax leading. From there they went through the packaging plant and on to the lab. Eve pressed her hands against the clear Plastex of the cooling unit. 'I didn't want to believe it,' she said, in a small voice. 'I hoped . . . I don't know what I hoped.'

'You hoped they were wrong,' Alistair said. He picked up a large glass flask then set it down as the others opened cupboards, storage drawers, everything they could get into as the tiny camera recorded everything. Jinn accessed the desktop unit and Alistair recorded the data as it streamed across the screen.

'There's just the production room,' Dax said. They'd been here long enough. It was time to get out. They didn't need hours of footage, just a few minutes' worth. He was almost at the viewing window when the lab door slid open and Mara walked in.

This Mara didn't look like the Mara that had gone with Riff and Olivier. This Mara was sharp-eyed and straight-backed. And this Mara was carrying a fully charged blaster.

The sort of blaster issued to agents.

'Mara?' Ase asked. 'Is everything OK? Where did you get that gun?'

Mara swung the blaster in his direction and squeezed the trigger. With a crack, the weapon fired and Ase crumpled to the floor, a smoking mess where his right shoulder used to be. 'Oh shut up,' she said, when he moaned in pain. 'Unless, of course, you want the next shot to hit you in the face. Bloody whining Underworld scum.'

Every muscle in Dax's body locked tight. He should have listened to his gut. He'd known something was off, but he'd chosen to ignore it.

Mara was . . . what the supernova *was* Mara?

'No,' Alistair said and Dax saw his friend go white. 'You can't be.'

'Unfortunately for you, I am,' she said. 'Put that down, if you don't mind.'

'She is what?' That was Eve, half hidden by a workbench, but still too close, too exposed. Dax knew he could get to Mara. The blaster shots would hurt like hell, but they wouldn't kill him. But he didn't know if he could get there fast enough.

'She's Type Three,' Alistair said, slowly closing the door of the storage unit he had been looking through. 'That's why she had the music on so loud, why she took Meth at Ase's. So I wouldn't be able to hear her.'

'But she's a colony worker,' Eve said. 'Ase said she works at the refinery with him. How can she be Type Three?'

Alistair didn't move. 'Because she's not a colony worker,' he said. 'She's a Dome-raised security agent modified to look like one.'

'This is all very fascinating,' Mara said, the blaster whining as she slipped a finger over the trigger and set it to recharge. 'But I'm afraid I don't have time for small talk.'

Dax had heard enough. Carefully, deliberately, he took in the room and assessed his target. The weapon was still the most immediate issue.

'There's no point trying anything,' Mara said, carelessly swinging the blaster in his direction. 'Whatever you think of, I'll know before you can do it.' She swung it away from him and pointed it at Jinn. 'And I'll know exactly how to hurt you the most.'

'Go ahead,' Jinn said. 'Shoot me. I don't care.'

'Maybe not,' Mara told her. 'But loverboy over there does. And anyway, you're terrified. Look at you. Poisoned with Tellurium, relying on an Underworld pirate to survive. It's pathetic.'

'No more pathetic than smoking Meth.'

That's it, Dax thought to himself. Keep her distracted. Keep her focussed. It's four against one. Five, if he counted Ase. Out of the corner of his eye, he could see that Ase was still breathing, his fingers flexing on the trigger of his homemade crossbow.

'I can handle a little Meth.' Mara rolled her eyes.

'Are you sure about that?'

'Of course I'm sure. I've caught you,' Mara said. 'And you didn't have the faintest idea.'

'Maybe not,' Jinn said. She held up a hand and a blade shot out of it. 'But if you think we're going to quietly hold up our hands and surrender, you're very, very wrong.'

Mara couldn't hide her look of surprise. 'You can't seriously think there's a way out of this.'

'Why not? There are five of us and only one of you.'

'Four,' Mara said. She gestured at Ase. 'He doesn't count.'

'So what's the plan, here?' Jinn asked. 'You've got a security team waiting outside, ready to arrest us as soon as we walk out of this place?'

'No,' Mara said. 'It's much simpler than that. Dax comes with me and I kill the rest of you, then I dump your bodies outside. I could take you all in, but it's just easier this way.'

The light flashing on the side of the blaster showed that it was fully charged. The slightest pressure of her finger on the trigger and she could take out any one of them. And Dax couldn't allow that. 'What makes you think I'll agree to that?'

Mara whistled. A large black animal prowled through the open door of the lab and sat obediently next to her. Another followed it. Panther sleek, they were both dense with muscle, huge through the shoulders, the top of their heads reaching her waist. One of them yawned, revealing white teeth the size of a finger.

Attack dogs. Dax hadn't seen them since he left Earth. Bred for speed and aggression, they had a behavioural modification chip implanted in their brains which allowed their owners to completely control their actions. Mara reached into the pocket of her oversized coat and pulled out a pair of magnetic restraints. 'If you wouldn't mind,' she said, tossing them to Dax.

'Actually, I would,' he said.

And then things got messy.

Dax caught the cuffs and hurled them at one of the dogs. In the same moment, Alistair picked up a half-full flask from the bench in front of him and threw it at Mara. She tried to move, but she wasn't fast enough. The liquid, whatever it was, clung to

238

her exposed skin. It began to blister. She screamed. Blaster shots rang out, hitting the ceiling, the wall.

Jinn went for the first dog as Dax pulled a blade from his boot and threw it at the second, spearing it through the gut. Blood sprayed everywhere, but the dog kept on coming. It sank its teeth into his forearm, ripping deep into flesh, grinding against bone. He roared with fury and pain.

And then the dog let him go. It released its hold and dropped to the floor, padding away to sit next to Mara. The agent stared at him with crazed, angry eyes, that strange hazel that he could now see was an attempt to change brown to green that hadn't quite worked.

She had one hand in Jinn's hair and the blaster pressed against her temple. Jinn's hands were at her sides, her blades scraping against the floor, blood dripping from her palms. The other dog lay stretched out beside them, reduced to little more than fur and meat.

'I'll only tell you once more,' Mara said. 'Put on the *fucking cuffs*.'

He moved towards the cuffs, taking his time about it.

'Hurry up!' Mara snapped. 'I don't have all day!'

Dax looked at Jinn. She looked back at him.

And then everything got even messier.

Maybe Mara did have an edge because she knew what they were going to do before they had done it. But she couldn't hold off four of them at once, especially not when all of them were genetically enhanced, not even with a blaster and an attack dog.

Dax went for Mara. So did Eve. The agent sank to her knees, howling in shock as Jinn went for the dog. Eve held on, held on, as Mara crumpled to the floor, her fingers curling as she clawed at the polished surface.

'Eve,' Dax said. 'Step back.'

Eve looked at him, fury burning in her alien eyes. 'She deserves it,' she said.

'Maybe she does,' Dax said. 'But that's not our call to make.'

'Maybe this time it is.'

239

There was a twang, and a hiss. Mara went stiff. Her back arched. And then she collapsed to the floor. A length of dark steel protruded from between her eyes, the end of it feathered with carbon quills.

All eyes fell on Ase. His skin was sickly pale, sheened with sweat, and there was a dark pool spreading on the floor underneath him. 'I'm afraid one of you will have to give me a hand. I don't think I can make it by myself. Not you, though,' he said, pointing the end of his empty bow at Eve.

Alistair helped him to his feet, slinging Ase's good arm across his shoulders so he could bear his weight.

'How much of that did you get?' Dax asked Alistair as together they staggered out of the lab and back to the warehouse.

'All of it,' Alistair said, checking the data pick-up attached to his lapel.

'Good,' Dax said.

Because he had a feeling they were going to need it.

Close to the warehouse entrance, they found Riff and Olivier. Both had smoking blaster holes where their faces should have been. Their bags lay on the floor next to them.

There was a moment of stillness, of silence.

That could have been any of them. All of them.

'Come on,' Dax said. 'Let's get this done.'

'Everything is here,' Eve said, rummaging through the bags. 'Charges, explosives, the works.'

'Lay them out,' Dax said.

All of them silently got to work, apart from Ase. He sat next to the bodies, staring off into the distance. There was nothing anyone could say, Dax knew. Nothing they could do that would make it right. Ase would have to figure his way through it on his own. Dax grabbed a couple of charges and headed into the warehouse, following Jinn.

They worked together silently, placing the charges, setting the detonators. 'Set it for ten minutes,' Dax told her.

'Is that long enough?'

240

'It'll have to be. I'm not risking leaving this place standing.'

With the explosives in place, they headed back to the exit and the others.

From somewhere deep in the warehouse, they heard the sound of the first of those charges going off. They felt the effects of it a moment later, as the floor underneath their feet vibrated. A couple of packing boxes fell from the shelf, bursting open when they hit the floor and spewing their foamy white innards all over the place.

And then the next charge went off, stronger, closer, shaking not just the floor but the walls. Huge metal shards plummeted down from the ceiling, stabbing into the floor. 'I think we should leave,' Eve said, already scrambling towards the exit.

'I second that,' Alistair said. He lifted Ase off the floor, pulled his good arm round his shoulder and half carried, half dragged the man towards the exit. There was another boom, another, another. 'Come on,' Dax said to Jinn. 'We need to get out of here.'

She was bent double, hands on her knees, hair hiding her face. 'I'll be right there,' she said. When she straightened up, Dax could see that her face was tight with pain. She was still holding on to her right thigh, fingers dark with blood.

He moved to grab her, but she waved him off. Then she broke into a run. He could see she was favouring her left leg, but there wasn't time to stop and do anything about it. He sprinted after her as the building collapsed around them, every piece that fell like a blade aimed straight at his head. The floor cracked, moved, tipping at unpredictable angles.

There was a crack in the wall of the warehouse too and Jinn changed direction, heading towards it. Dax followed her. He had cut the distance between them almost to nothing now, though the constantly shifting floor meant that he had to choose his own route. Surviving this would be ten percent physical skill, ninety percent pure bloody luck.

Luck had damn well better be on their side.

And it was.

He caught up with her just as she got to the split in the wall and jumped. They fell, fell, twisting their bodies together in mid-air. The landing was hard. Bloody supernova, it was hard. Something crunched and Dax knew it was bone, and it was his. The pain was instant and vicious, but he didn't care.

He rolled onto his back and watched as the warehouse collapsed. The dust cloud seemed to take forever to settle, and when it did, he realised that Jinn was draped across him, her head on his chest, her fingers gripping his shirt.

'It's done,' she said.

'Yes.'

But it wasn't. Not by a long shot.

# CHAPTER
# 25

**3rd September 2207**

> Vessel: The *Nero Hunter*, Stealth Cruiser
> Destination: Articus Repair Station
> Cargo: N/A
> Crew: One
> Droids: Four

The Articus. What a dump. As Bryant manoeuvred the cruiser into dock, he caught sight of the *Mutant*, the unusual shape of the vessel making it instantly recognisable. They were here. A ripple of satisfaction drifted through him, even through the haze of blockers. It was only thirty minutes since he'd last injected and the drugs were kicking in nicely. He felt no pain, no fear, just the warm, satisfying confidence that every decision he made was the right one. Soon Caspian Dax and Jinnifer Blue would be on the A2 where they belonged, and the green bitch would be in his custody. He'd take her back to the medical facility on the Arunda, and he'd get his antidote.

His comm. screen flashed, indicating that someone was trying to connect with the cruiser. A moment later it flashed on, revealing a hefty-looking woman with artfully styled gold hair, a penchant for facial jewellery and a bored expression. Dome-raised, but fallen on hard times – and it showed. 'State your identity and business.'

Bryant hesitated. Officially, he wasn't an agent any more. And officially, the cruiser was stolen. On the other hand, the Articus was a long way from Earth, and he doubted anyone here cared who he was or what he had done. Still, it didn't hurt to be cautious. 'Kryll, P,' he said. 'Identity code 335698. My phase drive needs an overhaul.'

'Do you wish to hire a maintenance crew?'

'Sure,' Bryant replied. Saying no would only draw attention, and the cruiser could probably do with a little work.

'Acknowledged,' she replied. 'Please proceed to docking bay seventy-four. A maintenance team will be sent to assess your vessel shortly. Do you require any further assistance?'

'No,' Bryant told her, killing the connection. In his peripheral vision he could see the *Mutant*. Rage burned happily in his gut as he docked the cruiser without too much care. It thumped against the docking arm, setting off the internal alarm.

Bryant shook his head. Stupid thing was clearly in the wrong place. The cruiser finally lined up with the docking arm, and then powered down. He unfastened his restraints and got to his feet. His head spun. A half-second later, his stomach heaved. The sensation was deeply unpleasant. Gripping the back of his seat, Bryant tried to breathe. It had come out of nowhere. One minute he'd been fine, the next …

Doing his best not to throw up, he staggered to the case the medical technician had given him, flipped it open. Only one blocker shot remained. With a shaking hand, he administered it, swallowing hard as the drugs kicked in. His body was burning through the medication too quickly. Sourcing more shouldn't be difficult, though he'd most likely have to buy them illegally. But even through the chemical haze, he knew this wasn't good. A full-blown addiction wasn't far away.

Closing the case, Bryant shoved it to the floor. He grabbed his personal comm. unit, his weapons, and the tiny tracking device that enabled him to locate the Sittan nanotech. Then he left the cruiser.

The Articus was just as rough, just as dirty on the inside as it looked from the outside. He'd barely made it off his ship before a pleasure droid approached him. It invited him to make use of a nearby parlour. Bryant felt the pickpocket rather than saw him, and broke the man's hand without hesitation.

The man snarled something unpleasant, then scurried away, clutching his fingers, and Bryant shoved the droid aside. Fortunately, the Articus was relatively small, so locating Dax and the others shouldn't take long. He flipped the small locator open and activated it. The small stick grew warm against his palm and then the end began to flash before a square screen unfolded, showing his location as a small red dot. The tracker appeared a second later, flashing blue.

Bryant started to move, his heart rate kicking up. According to the locator, Dax's droid couldn't be more than a couple of hundred metres away. And where the droid went, Dax went too. Bryant headed away from the docking bay, but quickly realised that he was going in the wrong direction. The droid was in the docking area somewhere, not in the main area of the Articus.

Checking the blaster at his hip, he turned and started back towards the docking bay, moving past the agency cruiser and heading further along the bay. Odd. He couldn't recall the *Mutant* being positioned so close by when he'd docked. The blockers must be messing with his memory.

He was going to make Caspian Dax and Jinnifer Blue pay for this. Over and over. The thought put power into his stride, and within minutes, Bryant found himself standing next to a luxurious space yacht, the sort used by wealthy businessmen travelling between Earth and the colonies. He wondered what Dax was doing with a vessel like this, then decided he didn't care. Whatever the pirate was selling or stealing, it made no difference.

Bryant shoved the locator in his pocket, pulled his blaster out of its holster and armed it. He was taking no chances this time. If he could take the pair of them alive, he would, but if he couldn't, it didn't matter. As long as he got to the green bitch. His jaw set hard, Bryant made a quick sweep of the area. The cameras didn't appear to be working. There was no giveaway blinking light. The bay was otherwise empty. He wouldn't get another chance like this and he didn't hesitate to take it.

His service-issue scrambler made quick work of the door lock and he slipped on board the yacht unchallenged. The interior was warm, dark, and smelled of cinnamon. Underneath it, though, was an underlying taint of something else, something Bryant couldn't quite put his finger on. It made him think of fear, of sickness, of blood, and for a moment his stomach rebelled.

But once an agent, always an agent. A yacht like this would have a cargo bay underneath, with a separate hatch, so that the wealthy owner and their guests would be able to bypass it, so instead he was in what amounted to an entry hall. A waste of space in any other vessel, but someone who could afford a travel yacht didn't have to worry about such things.

Bryant moved further into the yacht, his blaster raised, wondering who the owner was. Wondering if he would need to kill them, or if they would make it easy for him. The large entertainment suite, with its low-level couches and artificial ferns, was empty.

He stood in the middle of it, staring at the floating liquor stations that hovered in the corners, fully stocked with glass bubbles of various spirits, in green, pink, blue. At the padded table in the centre of the room, complete with auto-restraints.

And the sense of unease returned.

Where the fuck was the pirate? Where the fuck was the owner, come to that? Unless Dax was the owner, which he doubted. He'd tracked Dax for long enough to know that the man stole ore, droid parts, platinum. Hardware. He'd seen no evidence that his tastes ran to anything more primitive. But all his years of agent experience were telling him that whoever owned this yacht had very primitive taste. And indulged it.

Just outside the entertainment suite, Bryant found something that made even his blood run cold. Bolted to the walls on either side of the corridor were a series of cages, stacked two high, eight in total. The smell of fear and blood and sickness was almost overwhelming, and he had to work hard not to throw up.

Bryant knew instantly what he'd walked into. Pale eyes watched him from behind sharp mesh, the children shrinking back into their cages in terrified silence.

'Take me,' said a voice from the cage nearest to him. 'I won't try to fight you off. Or I will, if that's what you prefer.'

He turned, saw a boy of no more than about ten. Underworld brat, based on his colouring. He was naked, his pale skin littered with bruises and scars. Even hating Underworlders as he did, Bryant couldn't help but feel a stab of horror at the sight of the boy.

'Who owns this vessel?'

'Darkos,' the boy told him. 'He has a workshop on the upper level.'

'Where is Caspian Dax?'

'I don't know who that is,' the boy replied.

'Tall,' Bryant said. 'Dark-haired, like you.'

'Oh. We only see blond men,' the boy said. 'Like you.'

'Are any of those men on board this yacht?'

'On the control deck,' one of the boys told him, his voice quiet.

Bryant had heard enough. Blaster in hand, he walked onto the control deck and killed the three blond men he found there. He dumped the bodies in the cargo hold.

And then he went back down below. He unlocked the cages. Only the boy he had spoken to earlier dared to come out.

'What's your name?' Bryant asked him.

'Davyd,' he said.

A common Underworld name. 'How old are you?'

'Ten.'

The boy stood there, defiant in his nakedness, wearing only bruises. Bryant shrugged off his jacket, handed it to him. 'Put this on,' he said. 'And then take me to Darkos.'

247

'What are you going to do?'

Bryant smiled. For a moment, all the pain, all the sickness, was forgotten. 'Enjoy myself,' he said.

Less than an hour later, Darkos was dead. Bryant stood over what was left of him. He'd possibly gone a bit overboard, but he'd wanted answers and when Darkos had burst into tears and sworn that he had never even met Caspian Dax, it had pissed him off even more. The tracker had led him to that yacht, and that yacht had led him to Darkos, but none of it had led him to Dax or the green bitch who had poisoned him.

'What happens now?' Davyd asked him. He'd managed to find clothes somewhere, the too-big shirt hanging off his skinny frame. 'Are you going to sell us?'

'No,' Bryant said.

'Then what?'

Bryant didn't know. 'Are there any drugs around here?'

'Darkos sells Euphoria,' Davyd told him. 'There's bound to be some here somewhere.'

'Alright,' Bryant told him. 'I'll start with that.'

# CHAPTER
# 26

**3rd September 2207**

Southgate Medical Centre, Minco City, Colony Seven

The medical centre was a walk-in place, situated on the outskirts of the Dome city. It was the sort of place people went as a last resort, when their insurance had run out or when they wanted a procedure that they didn't want anyone to know they were having.

Dax walked straight up to the reception desk, Ase slung limply over his shoulder. Both of them were covered in blood. Eyes were on them, silence falling around the cramped waiting room. 'He needs a medic and a medibed,' he said to the receptionist, shoving aside the Dome woman who stood in his way. 'Now.'

The receptionist looked at him, then she looked at Ase. She slapped a payment machine down in front of him. 'Payment is upfront,' she said.

Dax reached into his pocket, pulled out a handful of dark rubies, and dropped them on the desk in front of her. 'A medic and a medibed,' he said.

The woman quickly scooped up the rubies. 'Room two,' she said, gesturing to the sign to his left. She pushed a button under the desk and the door that led from the reception area to the treatment rooms beyond slid open.

The medic was waiting when Dax got there, as was the bed. He dumped Ase's unconscious form onto it. He didn't wait around to answer any of the medic's questions, to explain the injuries. He left the clinic via the back entrance, grabbing a portable medical kit on the way out. No-one tried to stop him.

The others were waiting outside. There was no sign of the roller.

'Someone stole it,' Eve said. She shrugged. 'There was nothing we could do.'

'Good,' Dax said. The last thing they needed was to be caught with Mara's vehicle. He looked at the three of them, dirty, battered, exhausted. They were at least an hour's travel from the port, assuming they could find transport quickly and weren't stopped on the way.

They needed to get out of sight. Lingering in the sort of neighbourhood where someone would steal your vehicle when you were stood on the other side of the street was never a good idea. Looking around them, Dax saw a number of boarded-up shops, the kind that had cramped apartments built over them. There was a burnt-out skimmer in pieces in the gutter, and scabby, balding skunkrats were digging through a pile of rubbish.

On the side of the row of shops, a cracked video screen flashed, advertising sleep booths that could be rented by the hour. 'Over there,' he said to the others.

Eve wrinkled her nose, but she was the first to cross the road. She didn't even bother trying to hide her face. There was a laser blade in her hand, and a determined strength in her stride. Alistair followed her.

'Come on,' Dax said, turning to Jinn.

She hobbled to the edge of the walkway and almost stumbled into the gutter, righting herself at the last moment. They crossed the road together, Dax moving in just close enough that he could catch her if she fell. The medical kit that he'd pinched was a steady weight in his pocket. As they rounded the far side of the abandoned shops, he saw the sleep booths. The row was six wide, stacked three deep, and looked like it had been here since the place was colonised.

It also looked like it should have been knocked down a long time ago. Half of the doors were broken. The ones that weren't were split and peeling, the locks corroded. And yet there were plenty of signs of activity. Underworlders lounged naked in open doorways. A couple of dealers leaned against the wall. They'd be selling various chemicals designed to enhance the sexual experience.

An exquisitely dressed Dome couple rounded the corner, eyes darting left and right, shoulders hunched as if that could make them invisible. The man broke away to speak to one of the dealers. The woman hurried over to one of the booths. She slipped something to the young Underworld man waiting in the doorway, and slithered inside.

'Why can't they use droids like normal people?' Eve whispered.

'Where would be the fun in that?' Alistair asked. The two of them made their way to one of the booths on the lower level and disappeared inside. The door closed behind them, leaving Dax outside with Jinn.

The dealers were starting to take an interest in them, and that was something he didn't need. He took her arm, led her to the elevator platform that would transport them up to the higher-level booths. He slipped that arm around her shoulders as the platform hovered, then swooped upwards, coming to a rest outside an empty booth. Dax pulled a credit chip from his pocket and pushed it into the slot. The door slid open. They stepped inside.

There was a sanitation unit and chemicleanse at the far end, plus a bunk that had seen far too many sweaty bodies, and that was it. Exactly what he'd expect for a booth that charged an hourly rent.

It was the dirtiest, grottiest place Jinn had ever seen, but she was too exhausted to make a fuss. She hissed in air as she lowered herself slowly onto the bunk. Her leg was a mess. The bleeding had almost stopped, but the wound was savage and deep, and every time she moved, every time she breathed, it hurt.

'You need to clean that up,' Dax said. He stripped off his coat, tossed it down onto the bunk, then rolled up his sleeves, one of which was tattered and blood-stained, though there was no sign of the wound in his forearm. He tugged at her jacket, threw it on top of his coat, then started on her trousers.

'Dax,' she said softly. 'I can do it.'

He flicked a glance at her, then looked away, his cheeks flushed. He pulled a medical kit out of his pocket, opened it up, and started examining the contents.

As quickly as she could manage, which really wasn't very fast at all, Jinn pulled off her top, boots, trousers. She left her thin vest and shorts on. She limped the short distance to the chemi-cleanse, shut herself inside it, and turned on the spray. 'Ow,' she cried, as the spray hit the wound on her leg. 'Ow, ow, fucking ow.'

She touched the edges of it, trying to push the open sides back together, but it didn't help. The wound was too deep, far too much for her body to heal. On top of everything else, it tipped her over the edge. She sank to the floor of the unit, put her face in her hands, and wept.

She didn't hear Dax pull open the door of the unit. She didn't realise he was watching her. She didn't notice when he turned off the spray. It was only when he sat down next to her and she felt his hard warmth press against her side, that she knew he was there.

'She should have been on our side,' she said finally.

'Yes,' Dax said. 'But she wasn't. And there's nothing we can do about that.'

'She'd have killed us.'

'Yes, she would.'

'It wasn't even her fault,' Jinn said. 'Not really. She'd been changed into that.'

'Maybe,' Dax said. 'Or maybe she was always that way. Maybe the modifications only enhanced what was already there.

It doesn't really matter. What matters is that we know for certain something we didn't know before.'

'What's that?'

'The government knows about the Second Species programme. Not only do they know about it, they're already making use of it.'

'And if there are others like her . . .' Jinn pushed her still-wet hair away from her face. Every bone in her body ached. 'They could be anywhere. On the colonies, on space stations, even in the Domes, listening in. Nothing is private. Nothing is safe, not any more. Did Alistair get the recording?'

'Yes,' Dax said.

'Then we need to get back to the *Deviant*,' Jinn said. 'We need to get it to Theon as soon as possible.' She tried to get to her feet, but her wounded leg wouldn't take her weight and she crumpled.

Dax caught her on his way up. 'You're not going anywhere,' he said. 'Not in the state you're in.'

'Unfortunately we don't have a week to sit around in this flea-pit and wait for my body to heal.'

He helped her out of the chemicleanse and lowered her onto the bunk. 'Fleas were eradicated in 2098,' he said.

'Whoever said that clearly hadn't spent any time here.' Jinn shifted her position. Her vest and shorts had already started to dry, but they were clingy and thin and she felt a little exposed. She rubbed her arms and decided not to think about it. She didn't really have enough energy to worry about Dax seeing her half naked.

'You've had your leg almost chewed off by an attack dog and you're worried about fleas?' He knelt at the side of the bunk and leaned in to examine her leg.

She had to bite her lip to stop herself from crying out as he probed the wound. Then he opened the medical kit, rummaged around inside it. 'Shit,' he muttered. 'No skingel.'

Jinn said nothing. She was cold and he sounded suddenly very far away and hard to hear. All she needed was to sleep for just a few minutes. Just a few minutes. She laid her head on the bunk. It was hard and didn't smell particularly nice, but she couldn't bring herself to care.

'Jinn?' A hot hand touched her face. 'Jinn, look at me.'

'Don't want to. Tired.'

'Where is a fucking medic when you need one?'

She heard rattling sounds and tried to open her eyes, then gave up. Everything was blurred anyway. Not even the sharp dig of something against the inside of her arm seemed to matter. And then she was drifting into darkness, but it was a warm, comforting darkness, and she floated in it for what seemed like hours, until something yanked her out of it, dragging her back into the bright light of the grotty sleep booth. She jerked upright. Her heart was racing. She was hot. She was so hot. Her blades rushed out.

'I guess you've had enough, then,' came a voice from her side. A deep, rough, familiar voice.

'Dax?'

'What's left of me,' he said.

He was sat on the end of the bunk, forearms resting loosely on his knees. A tube ran from his arm, and she watched, wondering what in the galaxy it was as he tugged it loose, pulling a long metal needle out of his flesh. The end was coated red.

She felt a tug on her own arm and looked down to see that the other end of the tube ran into the vein in the crook of her elbow. 'You gave me blood?'

'Yes.'

'You gave me *your* blood.' She stared at the tube in disbelief, then yanked it out. 'Why?'

'You needed it,' he said, rubbing a hand over his face and leaning back against the wall. 'And I didn't want to risk taking you to a medical facility. Not after what happened with Mara. I took enough of a risk taking Ase to one.'

Her entire body felt hot, sensitive, tight. Her pulse pounded in her head. In her chest. Between her legs. 'What else did you give me?' She wiped a hand over her face, combed her fingers

254

through her hair, but the feeling didn't lessen. If anything, it grew stronger.

'Nothing,' he said.

'You must have given me something,' she said, and this time she could hear desperation in her voice. She could feel it, too, an odd sensation in the pit of her stomach, sinking lower, lower. She looked at Dax. 'There's something wrong with me.'

'It's the blood,' he told her.

'What do you mean, it's the blood?'

'Hot?' he asked her. She nodded. 'Feel like you're losing control of something, but you don't know what, or why?'

'How did you know?'

'Your heart rate is up,' he said. 'Your mouth is dry. And I can smell the arousal on you.'

'I am not aroused!'

'Aren't you?'

Yes. Yes, she was. And now that she had a word for it, knew what it was, she could feel it in every part of her body, running hot through her veins, crying out to be sated. 'Did you know it would do this to me?'

'I knew there was a possibility.'

'Then why did you do it?'

'Because I thought you were going to die.' His voice was low, rough, and when she looked at him, she saw that he was holding the edge of the bunk so tightly that it was collapsing under his grip. His eyes burned into her, alive with green fire. He was breathing slowly, his massive chest rising and falling with each breath, as if each one was a struggle.

'What do you want from me, Dax?'

'I don't know,' he said. 'I don't want to want anything.'

'But you do.'

'Yes,' he said. 'I think about you all the time. About what it would be like.' He half-smiled. 'I should tell you that I've always had a thing for Dome women.'

'Are you saying that's all it is? You want me because of that?'

'No,' he said. 'I want you because you're you. But I can't do it. I can't.'

'Why not?'

'The way I'm feeling right now,' he said, 'I could hurt you. I would hurt you.'

'I don't believe you.'

'You should. I'm not like you, Jinn. You were there, in the lab. You saw what was in those records. I've been modified with Sittan DNA. I'm not human any more. I don't know what in the void I am. And there's no way to fix it.'

'Do you think you're the only one who feels that way? I'm scared, Dax. I'm scared of what we've seen, of what it means. I'm scared of this stupid body. But I'm not scared of you.' She swallowed down the lump in her throat. 'Show me.' She gestured to his body. 'Show me what it is that I should be so afraid of.'

'Jinn,' he said. He closed his eyes. And then he opened them again, as if a decision had been made. His eyes never left her face as he tugged off his shirt. What had been pristine white was now filthy and shredded, stained with blood. The skin underneath was just as she remembered, flawless gold, his upper body heavy with muscle, patterned with dark hair that started a strange, hot throbbing between her legs. His body was so different to hers, so much bigger, stronger, unmarred by prosthetics, and yet at the same time, it was familiar.

He was familiar.

'Look at me,' he said. 'It's not normal. I'm not normal.'

Jinn pressed back against the cold, hard wall of the booth, not trusting her legs to keep her upright. He shoved his trousers down. One big hand went straight to his groin as he kicked them away.

And then there was nothing else to say, because he was walking towards her, and she had nowhere left to run. She pressed her hands flat against the wall as her blades came out. It didn't sting. It felt natural and right.

256

He moved in close, caging her against the wall. She tipped her head back and looked up to find him looking down at her. He slid a hand around the back of her neck, his thumb coming up to trace the line of her jaw. Her heart was pounding so hard that it felt like it might break through her ribs. It was nothing compared to what she felt when he leaned closer, resting his forehead against hers, and slid his free hand down over her slick skin. He caressed her shoulder, her arm, the side of her hip, fingers skating slowly over sensitive flesh.

'Did you really think I was going to die?'

'I didn't think it,' he said. 'I was watching it happen.'

'But you didn't let it.'

'No.'

She willed in her blades, found it easy. She lifted a hand to his face, touched his mouth. 'Dax,' she whispered. He was so close that she could feel the rush of his breath on her face and she realised that she wasn't the only one trembling.

'I want you,' he said. 'But I don't want to hurt you.'

'Then don't.'

'I broke the last droid I had sex with.'

'I'm not a droid.'

'No,' he said. He closed his eyes. 'No, you're not.'

She moved closer, pressing her body against his. His erection lay thick and hard against her belly and she pushed a hand between them, wanting to touch him. He grabbed her wrist and pulled her hand away. 'Let me do this my way,' he said.

Then he kissed her. Her hands scraped over his chest, down the hard ridges of his belly, up the wide lines of his back. His hands found her breasts and she found that she liked it, and she told him so, in tight, breathless words that she lost completely when he pushed her legs apart with one heavy, muscular thigh, pinning her to the wall with his weight.

One hand slid to her belly, and then it traced lower.

'And that?' he asked.

Jinn nodded, a tight jerk of her head. She couldn't manage

anything more. She forgot everything she thought she knew about herself, about sex, as his mouth followed the path of his hand and he sank to his knees in front of her. She dug her hands into his hair as the heat of his hand was replaced by the heat of his mouth.

It was unlike anything she'd experienced before, and broke open a bottomless well of longing that she hadn't known she was capable of feeling. This wasn't just about pleasure any more, though there was plenty of it. This was about needing to feel alive. About taking whatever she could have of him, any way she could have it. She'd used droids, everybody did, but she'd never wanted them the way she did Dax.

He held her up with a hand on her hip as he hooked her thigh over his shoulder. She squirmed against him, but he held her steady. She looked down at him, kneeling in front of her, at the broad expanse of his back and the powerful curve of his arms and the dark fall of his hair as he fit his mouth between her legs again.

One shoulder jerked and she shifted position just enough to see that he held himself in a tight fist. She watched as he stroked himself, shocked, aroused, scarcely able to breathe. He licked into her and she tipped her head back and closed her eyes, drowning in the sensation of this, of him. Droids gave pleasure, but they didn't give this. There wasn't intimacy. They took nothing from you, other than payment. It didn't . . . it didn't change you.

But this would.

When she tried to push him away, he resisted. 'Inside me,' she told him.

'No,' he replied, and then it was too late anyway.

She came long and hard as he groaned against her, his big body shuddering as he gave himself over to his own climax. When her legs finally gave way, he caught her as she fell, pulling her close against his body. They sat tangled together, an Underworld pirate and a Dome woman on the floor of a grubby chemicleanse unit in a rented sleep booth. It should have been sordid and wrong. But it wasn't.

His fingers traced the newly healed skin on her thigh. Only the faintest difference in the colouration of her skin indicated that the savage wounds the dog had inflicted on her had ever existed. She touched his face, brought his mouth to hers, and he let her kiss him the way she wanted to.

And then he got to his feet, pulling her with him. He picked up her clothes, still blood-stained and dirty. He handed them to her, and she pulled them on. Then he tugged on his own clothes. He looked at the bunk for a long moment. Then he turned back to her. His expression was grim. The sharp lines of his face were shadowed. 'We need to get moving,' he said. He gestured to the cracked vidscreen on the wall. On it, Jinn could see the newsfeed, showing the remains of the Medipro warehouse. Smoke was rising from the rubble, dirtying the already polluted sky.

'It is not yet known what caused the explosion at the Medipro warehouse on Colony Seven earlier today,' the reporter said. 'But early indications are that several workers were inside the building when it collapsed. Rescue workers are on the scene but it is not believed that anyone will be pulled out alive.'

'How long until they realise that we were in there?'

'Not long enough,' Dax said grimly, thumbing the button to open the door. 'Not nearly long enough.'

# CHAPTER
# 27

**3rd September 2207**

Twin Rock District, Minco City, Colony Seven

They bartered a skimmer from one of the dealers and flew their way back to the port. No-one spoke. All of them were too on edge, too lost in their own thoughts.

Jinn pressed herself back into her seat, leaned her head against the window and felt every second like it was an hour. Paranoia clawed at her. Mara had been an agent, with Bryant's attitude and Alistair's abilities. There could be others. She had no way of knowing.

Was it her imagination, or were there more local security vehicles on the road now than there had been earlier? When they passed the fifth one, she decided that no, it was not her imagination. When the traffic around them slowed to a crawl, she knew they were in trouble.

'Get us out of this,' Dax said to Alistair, who was at the controls.

'I would,' Alistair said. 'But I don't think this thing has the juice. It's running on fumes as it is.'

'Fucking supernova,' Dax said. Through the front screen, they could see the reason for the slowing traffic. A roadblock, cutting across all lanes, surface level and above. The skimmer engine choked and cut out for a moment before restarting.

'I'm going to have to drop to ground level,' Alistair said.

Through her window, Jinn could see the local security in their dark uniforms, standing out against the pale rock of the surface. All of them wore polished helmets, their faces concealed behind lowered visors. All of them were armed with spiked batons and stunners. 'This is serious,' she said suddenly, sitting upright as she saw several of them drag a man from his roller. They pinned him to the ground before one of them pulled a stunner from a holster at his side and shot the man in the chest. He twitched helplessly then lay still. 'Are they looking for us, do you think?'

'They're looking for someone,' Dax said. 'And given that we left a burning factory on the other side of this rock two hours ago, there's a pretty good chance that someone is us.'

They were almost at the front of the roadblock now. Jinn held her breath, watching as the skimmer in front was waved to a halt.

Alistair held the skimmer in a gentle hover. 'Dammit,' he said.

'What is it?' Eve asked.

'They're checking every vehicle. I don't have a registration for this thing, or a licence, never mind the fact that we bought it from a dealer and we're here on a visitor's permit.' The skimmer moved forward as he worked to keep pace with the flow of traffic. 'If any of you felt like having a moment of brilliance, now would be a good time.'

Jinn moved out of her seat. 'Switch places with me,' she said to Alistair.

'Why?'

'Because I'm Dome, and you're not,' she said. 'And I might be able to buy us enough time to find a way out of this.'

He started to move, then stopped. He reached for her. Jinn jerked back and jerked up a blade. 'I'm not going to hurt you,' Alistair said. 'But that implant at your temple is a dead giveaway.'

Jinn slowly lowered her hand as he pulled a lock of hair across her forehead and tucked it behind her ear. 'Sorry,' she muttered. 'I guess I'm not quite myself right now.'

'I don't think any of us are,' Alistair said, glancing back at Dax.

Jinn took a moment to acquaint herself with the controls, then she let the skimmer drift. 'We could just take off,' she said. 'I can outfly them.' The drive stuttered. She checked the fuel gauge. Alistair was right. It was almost empty.

Gripping the controls tightly, she eased back on the throttle. There was no way round it. They were going to have to go through the roadblock. When one of the local security waved her to the side, she slowed to a halt as he approached the side window. He gestured to her to remove the screen. Jinn reached slowly for the button. She didn't want to use her blades on him, but she would if she had to, and she was ready. 'Keep him talking,' Dax said in a low voice, as the door at the rear of the skimmer slid silently open.

'What are you going to do?'

'I don't know yet,' Dax said. 'Just keep him talking and hope he can't hear your thoughts. And get ready to run.'

Jinn found the button and pasted on a wide smile as the air shimmered and the screen disappeared. 'Hello, officer,' she said. 'Is there a problem?'

'Step out of the vehicle.'

'Why?'

'I said, step out of the vehicle.'

She could still hear movement behind her. 'Are you sure that's really necessary?'

Through the man's visor, she could see dark eyes creased with anxiety. He didn't want to offend a Dome woman, but he didn't want to risk not doing his job, either. She would have to try a little harder. 'I've got a clinic appointment. Don't want to be late.' She leaned forward, and whispered, 'Rejuvinex. You know how it is.'

For a moment, she thought he was going to argue.

Then he stepped away. 'This one is clear,' he said to one of the others. He waved her forward and Jinn started the skimmer. The open window had let in the stink of the air outside and she rubbed her face, trying to clear the grit.

'I . . .' he began, and then stopped. He whipped up his stunner and pointed it straight at her. 'Get out of the vehicle,' he ordered, and this time his tone was harsh. 'Now.' His gaze flicked to her temple. Her implant. Crap.

'You don't really want me to do that,' Jinn said.

'Get out of the fucking vehicle!'

'No,' she decided. 'I don't think I will.'

She powered up the skimmer, selected her target, and put it in motion. The man had barely a moment to leap out of the way before the front end of the skimmer smashed into the side of a police roller. The jolt bounced her back in her seat, but she shook it off. Then she rammed the roller again. And again. Dax had told her to keep the guard busy, and that was exactly what she intended to do.

More guards were running at the skimmer now, their dark uniforms standing out against the pale yellow of the ground, making them look like panicked ants. The skimmer smacked into the parked roller again, and it burst into flames.

And what had been an orderly line of traffic turned into utter chaos. Skimmers shot out of line. Rollers took off in whatever direction they could. She could see the guards scattering, not knowing whether to deal with the burning vehicle or stop the unsearched vehicles from leaving.

Her blades were out before the door to the skimmer had finished rolling back, and she jumped out and started to run. A police roller swerved towards her and she tried to dodge it, until the side opened and she saw Dax. 'Come on!' he yelled.

Jinn put on a burst of speed that she would never have managed before. Her legs pounded across the rocky ground, but her heart rate barely seemed to shift. She got closer, closer, judged the distance and jumped.

Dax caught her hand and pulled her into the roller. The door slammed shut, and Jinn collapsed onto her back. She closed her eyes and focussed on breathing as the floor of the roller vibrated underneath her.

'Well,' said a voice that she identified as Eve, 'that was fun.'

Jinn opened her eyes. 'I don't know if I'd call it fun, exactly.' She locked gazes with Dax. He held out a hand and she took it. He pulled her up, pushed her back into an empty seat. 'A police roller?' she asked, looking around. 'Do you think that's wise?'

Eve and Alistair were sat up front. Alistair was driving. On the screen in front of him, she could see the APS tracker flashing, indicating their position.

'It has snacks,' Eve said, holding up a box. 'And weapons.'

'And as soon as they realise it's been stolen, we'll be locked in,' Jinn pointed out.

'It's not stealing if you've got a starter chip,' Eve said.

'How did you . . . '

Eve pointed at Alistair.

'Look,' he said. 'I'm not the strongest, I'm not the fastest, I don't have blades in my hands. I have to make the most of what I have, and a universal starter chip happens to be one of those things.'

'Can they track us?'

'Yes,' Alistair said. 'But given the mess we left back there, I suspect they're too busy, and anyway, the roller thinks I'm a local security guard called Cameron.'

'How far to the port?'

'Another twenty minutes,' Alistair said.

It felt like an age.

A sign ahead indicated a left turn for the port and Alistair took it, winding the vehicle down a tight corkscrew that took them to a narrow tunnel that cut under the refinery. Orange lights flashed past as he sped through it. Another roadblock loomed ahead.

Jinn tensed. Beside her, she knew Dax had done the same.

The guard at the block waved them straight through.

The tunnel spat them out close to the port. She could see the storage hangars and waiting ships, most of them long-distance cruisers. Light glinted from custom-paint jobs that were utterly pointless up in space, but mattered down here. Cleaning droids scuttled up and down loading ramps.

Alistair directed the roller towards the hangars. He pulled to a stop around the corner from the one that housed the *Deviant*. Dax was the first to get out. He moved away from the roller with long, powerful strides. His clothes were ripped and dirty, and he looked like he'd walked out of a bar fight several hours before and was ready for another one.

The owner of the hangar took one look at him and ran back inside his office. Falling in with the others, Jinn heard the buzz of the lock. 'How are we going to get in?'

Dax dug his fingers into the edge of the hangar door and pulled. There was a sound of tearing metal, then it rolled back out of the way.

'Oh,' she said. 'I see.'

The *Deviant* was just as they had left it. The side door opened and the ladder unfolded, and they quickly made their way inside. Theon had the transporter in motion almost before any of them had made it to their seats. They shot out of the port and into the transport lane, and were gone before anyone could stop them.

When they were clear of the atmosphere, Theon set the autopilot.

Dax turned to Alistair. 'Got the video?'

Alistair slipped off the lenses. 'I hope so.'

Theon stepped forward, took the data chip that Alistair held out. He took a seat at the comm. station and pulled up the link. 'It's there.'

'Good,' Dax said. 'I think we should upload it to the universal net.'

'All of it?' Theon asked, the image speeding through on the screen in front of him.

Dax looked at the others. 'Yes,' he said. 'All of it.'

Eve nodded. 'Do it,' she said.

'Alistair?'

'I guess it's time we stopped hiding,' he said, though his voice was heavy with regret. There was no going back after this and they all knew it. Once the video was uploaded, once it started to spread, there would be no more denying who they were, or what they could do.

'Jinn?'

Jinn looked at Eve. She thought about what they had seen on the A2, about the man in the electrified cage, the one who had tried to grab her, about all the people she had taken to the A2, none of them knowing what awaited them. And she thought about Mara, the agent hiding in plain sight. What was happening was wrong. There was no denying that. And the public had a right to transparency, to know what the government were doing.

But this was bigger than just them.

'What happens if we do this?' she asked. 'What happens if we put this out there, and the senate decides to block Earth ships from going to Spes as a result?'

'They might do that anyway,' Alistair pointed out. 'Nothing has been agreed, remember.'

'I don't want to get in the way of that,' Jinn said.

'None of us do,' Dax said.

More than anything, Jinn wanted the senate to allow humans to travel to Spes. But at the same time, she couldn't help but think of those who would die from the serum, all those who would be irreversibly changed by it. And the thought that agents were hiding amongst them made her feel sick.

She rubbed a hand over her face. Politicians were hypocrites. She knew that better than most. They would smile at you right as they stabbed you in the back. For all the talk of relocation to Spes, she didn't know if it would ever really happen. But she did know that right at that moment, another human was being sent to the A2, thinking they faced a prison, not knowing that instead, they would be drugged and strapped to a bed before having alien DNA grafted into their cells, DNA that would most likely kill them.

And that was why she knew they had to do this.

'Upload it,' she said.

# CHAPTER
# 28

**4th September 2207**

**Apartment 77b, Mayfair District, London Dome, Earth**

Ferona Blue was awoken by the sound of her apartment bell. It was a soft, tinkling chime made by the antique French bells that hung in the entrance and echoed around her apartment.

She jerked up in bed, her heart racing. Her dreams had been vivid. In them, she'd been standing on the podium of the Intergalactic Senate, wearing a swirling gown the colour of a tropical sea. Pear-shaped diamonds had sparkled at her throat. One of the other senators had interrupted her and she had shot him through the head with a five-hundred-year-old duelling pistol.

It had been glorious.

The bells tinkled again, and Ferona tossed back the covers and climbed down from the bed. It folded away automatically, as it always did when her weight left it. 'Who is that?'

'President Vexler is outside,' her internal security system informed her. A screen popped up, and there, illuminated by the crystal lights that hung between her door and the exit from her private elevator, was the man himself.

'What in the galaxy is he doing here?'

'The reason for his visit is unknown,' the system replied. 'Do you wish to grant him entry?'

'Yes,' Ferona said. 'Have a hostess droid show him into the formal salon. Give him whatever he wants to eat and drink.'

'Understood,' the system replied.

Ferona tugged off her sleeping robes and hurried over to her dressing room. The dressing tube glowed as she stepped into it and lifted her arms over her head. The door closed, and in under a minute she was clothed in a casual truesilk tunic and trousers, both in a pale dove grey. Her hair was smooth and her makeup immaculate.

She made her way to the formal salon, her soft slippers sinking into the thick rose carpet that decorated her private space. She barely saw the antique French furniture, or the oil paintings, or the silver knick-knacks. She was too busy wondering what could have brought Vexler to her door in the middle of the night. She hoped it wasn't sex. That would be an unpleasant and uncomfortable conversation for both of them.

'President Vexler,' she said, gliding into the salon. 'This is something of a surprise.'

Vexler took a moment to sip from the cup that the hostess droid had placed on the delicately carved side table next to him. 'I take it you haven't seen the newsfeed,' he said.

Damn. Damn! She hadn't seen anything since lunchtime. The last few weeks had been exhausting. After her appointment with her Rejuvinix technician, she had taken a sleeping shot and gone to bed intending to shut out the rest of the galaxy for a few precious hours. Should she lie, and hope he would fill her in, or admit the truth – that she had no idea what he was talking about.

In the end she did neither, as Vexler got to his feet and started to pace. The formal salon was a substantial room, and it took him a while to make his way around.

'I want you to tell me what on earth is going on,' he said, when he finally strolled back over to where she sat.

It was the first time she had ever seen him act with any

semblance of authority, and she didn't quite know what to do with it. 'I'm sure I don't know . . .'

'There has been a video uploaded to the universal net,' he said, 'featuring your daughter, in which she makes some wild claims about humans being modified with alien DNA. She says they're already living amongst us, working for the Security Service. Spying on us. She says that the A2 isn't a prison ship, it's a medical facility where more of these creatures are being created. And she seems to think that the government is bank-rolling it.' Vexler did an abrupt about-turn, hands behind his back. 'Are we?'

'I . . .' Ferona began, and then stopped herself. Clearly a lot had happened in the past twelve hours. She had to think quickly. But it was difficult, with the Rejuvinix boiling just under her skin.

*Think, Ferona, think.*

She pressed a hand to her temple. There was nothing she hated more than being put on the spot like this, without time to plan, to prepare. She needed to buy herself that time. She certainly wasn't going to admit the truth.

'What makes you think I know anything about it?'

'I may be a lot of things,' Vexler said. 'But I am not stupid. I want to know what's going on.'

Ferona turned, facing the wall and the huge mirror that spanned the length of the room, doubling the space. She saw her own reflection, preened, controlled, tired, then she saw the reflection of the man who was supposed to be in charge of what remained of the human population and something snapped inside her. Maybe it was the Rejuvinix. Maybe it was being woken in the middle of the night to answer his questions. Maybe she was just sick and tired of having to answer to this spineless, useless excuse for a man.

'Your secret is out, Ferona,' Vexler continued. 'You've been working with Medipro to produce humans modified with alien DNA. And if the video currently spreading on the universal net is to be believed, this isn't some small-scale, experimental programme. It isn't testing. It's production.'

She turned slowly, using the time to school her features, to control her voice. 'You seem to know an awful lot about it.'

'People talk,' Vexler said, smoothing his fingertips along the arm of a polished rosewood chair. 'Particularly if they are properly motivated.'

'Who?'

'That's not really important,' Vexler told her. 'What is important is what happens now. You've been modifying male subjects on the A2. Three hundred have already been sent to Sittan. Several thousand more are awaiting collection. The A3 has also been converted to a medical facility which is dealing exclusively with female subjects. I assume those are for the Shi-Fai.'

'You didn't come here in the middle of the night to chat,' Ferona said. 'Please. Get to the point.'

'Why are you selling people to the Sittan and the Shi-Fai? What are you getting in return?'

'Shouldn't you know?' she snapped. 'You are the president, after all. A useless one, but the president nonetheless.'

'How dare you!'

'How dare I?' Ferona marched over to where Vexler stood. 'I dare because if it were left to people like you, the human race would stay and rot on this planet forever! Do you really think our alien neighbours will let us cross their space on the basis of a few compliments and a few consignments of platinum? Do you?'

His cheeks flushed.

'We're nothing to them,' Ferona informed him. 'They don't care what happens to us, and why should they? I am offering the Sittan and Shi-Fai something they want. I made sure that I *had* something they want. It takes more than hollow words and empty promises to make progress. It takes action. Something that neither you nor anyone else was prepared to accept. The senate will put the issue of our exodus to a vote, and the vote will pass. Because I will make sure of it.'

Vexler's anger was gone as quickly as it had arisen. 'I see,' he said, and he was utterly, disturbingly calm. He found a seat on a beautiful sofa upholstered in zinc-coloured velvet, settled himself down. 'You know, Mikhal Dubnik disliked you intensely. He repeatedly recommended that you be removed from government. He was not at all pleased by your recent promotion.'

'I fail to see why that matters.'

'He wanted to get rid of you,' Vexler said. 'He felt you lacked humanity. He said, and I quote, that you had the morals of an attack dog. He would have succeeded, if it weren't for those peculiar irregularities in his accounts.'

Something in the way he said the word peculiar made Ferona pause. This Vexler was not the Vexler she thought she knew. There was something calculating in his eyes, an intelligence that she had not seen before. She wondered how Lucinda had missed it, then remembered that her assistant had never spent any time alone with the president. Dubnik had always been in the way.

'What do you want?' Ferona asked him.

'With Mikhal no longer part of the government, I find myself in a rather difficult position,' Vexler said. 'You see, he and I had what you might call a mutually beneficial relationship. I ensured that he was able to pass his precious constitutional amendments, and in return, he protected me.'

Because Vexler was weak, Ferona realised. Because he was weak and incompetent and everyone knew it, including him, and there were those in the government who would use Dubnik's departure as an opportunity to force Vexler out.

'My sources have informed me that Alta, Rowan and Harriott have had three meetings in the past two days,' Vexler continued. 'It is a concern for any leader when his juniors start meeting in secret, don't you think?'

'I expect that it is,' Ferona replied. She moved to the side of the room and touched a concealed button in the wall. A console folded down, and she instructed her hostess droid to bring more refreshments. Her head was starting to pound and she doubted the Rejuvinex was entirely to blame.

'I like my job,' Vexler said. 'I have no intention of losing it. Unfortunately, now that Dubnik has gone, I fear that I am in something of a vulnerable position.'

That didn't surprise Ferona in the slightest. The hostess droid appeared, carrying a tray, and zipped over to where she stood. Ferona took the tumbler of whisky and knocked it back. 'What do you want from me, Vexler?'

'It's quite simple,' he said. 'Dubnik's termination has left a vacancy. You are going to fill it.' The hostess droid tiptoed over in his direction and offered him a fresh cup of steaming jasmine tea. He took it, but didn't drink.

'You're going to make me vice president?'

'I can see that interests you.'

'Of course it interests me.'

He made it all sound so easy, so straightforward. 'As vice president,' Vexler continued, 'you will be in a position to continue the work you have already begun. Expand it, even. It is already out in the public domain, and I see no point in trying to cover it up. This is not going to go away, Ferona.'

'And in return?'

'You will make a public announcement in which you will explain this situation in a way that the public will find acceptable. It's up to you to figure out what that way is. You will also make it clear that all of this is happening with my full support.' He leaned forward in his seat. 'When historians write about the human relocation to Spes, they're going to write about me,' he said, his dark eyes gleaming. 'I'm going to be remembered as the president who saved the human race.'

'You want to take credit for this?' For all her work. For all her years of planning, of sacrifice, of making the decisions that no-one else wanted to make and seeing what no-one else wanted to see.

'I *will* take credit for this,' Vexler said. 'When we settle on

Spes, they'll erect statues in my memory. Name streets after me. A city. A country.'

He was talking to himself now. He almost seemed to have forgotten that she was in the room, gripped by the madness of his ambition.

There were enough security droids concealed in the walls that he could be easily dealt with. She could make him disappear and no-one would ever be able to find evidence to prove that he had been here.

The disappearance of the president would provide the media with new fodder. The video of the Medipro facility on Colony Seven would be forgotten about. She would be able to continue her work unhindered as the other ministers scrambled to fill not only Dubnik's position, but Vexler's.

And everything she'd worked for could be lost. The deal she'd brokered with the Sittan balanced on a knife-edge, and that knife-edge was Caspian Dax. Ferona didn't know why the Sittan wanted him so badly, only that the empress had requested him personally. Without Dax, there was a possibility that the Sittan empress would change her mind. Add to that a government that was falling apart, and that possibility became a certainty.

But perhaps there was another way. After all, Vice President Blue had a nice ring to it.

She looked Vexler up and down. He could have his statues and his fountains. She would have something far more important. She would have control.

'I accept,' she said.

# CHAPTER
# 29

**5th September 2207**

Vessel: The *Mutant*. Battleship/carrier hybrid
Location: The Articus, Sector Four, Neutral Space
Cargo: None
Crew: Eighteen
Droids: Eight

'She organised the whole thing,' Jinn whispered. Her hand rose to the screen, then dropped away before she could touch it. 'All of it.'

And it went far beyond what they'd uncovered on the A2 and the facility on Colony Seven. The sheer scale of it was astounding. The women's prison on the moon had been converted into a medical facility. There was another one on Earth. A holding facility had been built on Colony Four. There were thousands of each type.

In the captain's chair of the *Mutant*, Dax sat in silence watching as Ferona Blue took everything that he had done and everything that he was and twisted it into something false, something wrong. It was made all the more devastating by the fact that just enough of it was true. People would watch this, and they would believe. They would want to believe.

'I'm sorry,' he said to Jinn, though that didn't even begin to scratch the surface of how he felt. He hadn't touched her since they'd walked out of the sleep booth on Colony Seven, but he wanted to. He needed to.

Alistair and Eve were at a medical clinic with Theon, who was having his polyskin replaced. Grudge was in his workshop. In some ways, it had been a relief. He didn't want to have to deal with their questions. He didn't want to deal with any of it. He wanted to forget all of it, the whole bloody mess, and lock himself in his cabin with Jinn and never come out.

The broadcast on the newsfeed had been playing on a loop for the past hour. Ferona glowed in a dress made from layer upon layer of lace tinted the colour of Soylate. Her skin showed signs of recent Rejuvinex treatment, hence the glow. Manicured hands folded neatly in her lap, she addressed the camera directly, and Dax felt the impact of every perfectly enunciated word as if it was being spoken to him personally, and maybe it was.

'Two days ago,' Ferona said, as the video began yet again, 'a video was uploaded to the universal net which claimed that a medical company has been modifying humans with alien DNA.' She paused for a moment, carefully considered, timed to perfection, and then she dropped the bombshell.

'I am here to tell you that this is true.'

Dax rubbed at his temples, trying to ease the pain in his head that had started when he first heard those words. It didn't help.

'The company in question, Medipro, has been working closely with the government for the past fifteen years, on a highly classified project called Second Species. There are, as the video said, three types of modification. Each one is unique, and uses DNA from a different alien species.'

Ferona got to her feet. The dress draped around her, displaying her lean Dome figure. His own mother hadn't looked like that. She'd had the unhealthy, pasty bloat you got from a constant diet of silver rice.

'However,' she said, 'the video didn't show you everything.

Which is why I have decided to share with you, today, the real story behind the Second Species programme. What it is, what it means, and most importantly, what you can do to help.'

'I guess at least now we have some answers,' Jinn said. She dropped into the pilot's chair, hugging her knees tightly to her chest, and glanced back at him. Her eyes were bright. 'She's buying the favour of our alien neighbours. And she's using modified humans to do it.'

'I know.'

It had been prettied up in political rhetoric, but the cold, hard truth of it couldn't be changed. Dax had been away from Earth long enough, and had crossed paths with enough of their alien neighbours to know that the Second Species humans currently being sent to Sittan and Shi-Fai weren't ambassadors, even though that word had been used. They wouldn't be making friends. They were slaves. Possessions to be used as their new masters saw fit. But most of the population weren't as cynical as he was. They would believe what they were being told.

'I always knew my mother was cold,' Jinn said. 'But this takes cold to a whole new level. This is evil.'

'Was she always like this?'

Jinn thought about that. 'When I was a child, she terrified me. Everything had to be done her way. There was no discussion, no compromise. I was just another project to her, something that needed to be fixed. But she worked a lot. I didn't see her that often. She was always out campaigning for something, constantly on the local newsfeed. People would come up to her in the street to tell her how wonderful she was. I used to think they were delusional. They had no idea what she was really like beneath the pretty clothes and the smile.'

'Where was your father?'

'He died when I was a couple of months old,' Jinn said. 'Skimmer accident.'

'I'm sorry,' Dax told her.

She shrugged. 'You don't miss what you never had. And by all accounts, he wouldn't have made a great parent. Anyway, I had nanny droids and school. I saw my mother maybe once a week. Less than that after she was elected to the local council in our Dome.'

'She's a long way from a local council now,' Dax said.

'Yes.' Jinn folded her arms. 'Vice president and Earth's representative in the senate. She's not making deals to cut water supply costs and fund personal hydroponic suites now. She's selling people.'

She turned away, but not before Dax had seen the single tear that moved down her cheek. 'Did you see her, Dax? Not a flicker of remorse. She actually looked pleased when she talked about it. But that's not the biggest problem, is it? The biggest problem is that this plan of hers just might work. Selling these people to our alien neighbours could be the thing that gets us to Spes.' She rubbed her hands over her face. 'But it's still wrong. Do you know why I left Earth? Why I ran away?'

'Tell me.'

'When I was twelve, she started me on behaviour-modification drugs. It started out with the mild stuff, a couple of pills a day with breakfast. She said I was too emotional and it would help me calm down. Then it was four pills a day, then injections. Three months on, three months off to see if I had improved enough to manage without them, but I never did. I wasn't even sure what was wrong with me. By the end I could only figure out that it was pretty much everything. When I was seventeen, I had personality reprogramming.'

'But that's mind-wiping,' Dax said, horrified. 'That's for psychopaths, not children who don't quite fit your idea of perfect.'

Jin shrugged. 'She thought she was helping me. But it made me so bloody ill. I knew then that I had to get away. Whatever it took. So when I turned eighteen, I walked out and never looked back. And she's doing the same thing here. It's another problem to be fixed. The people being modified don't need to know what's going to be done to them because she knows what's best and that's all that matters.'

At that point Dax forgot all the reasons why he shouldn't touch her. He moved close, invaded her space, turned her to face him. An hour ago, despite everything he'd seen on board the A2 and on Colony Seven, despite his own experience, he knew he could still have walked away. He could have gone back to the life he'd been living for the past thirty years, stealing what he needed, dodging the law, carving out an existence that was, if he was honest, centred on nothing more than surviving each day as it came.

But not any more.

'When was the government video first broadcast?'

Jinn checked her personal comm. 'Just over an hour ago.'

'Then we've still got time. We're a long way out, and people here don't particularly care about Earth politics. There's a chance most people won't have seen it yet.'

'Time for what?'

'Time to sort out some of this mess.' Dax walked off the control deck, sensing Jinn move behind him. He stopped off at his cabin, found himself a coat. He pulled twin blasters down from the secure storage unit concealed in the wall, and holstered one either side of his hips. He offered one to Jinn, but she shook her head. 'I'm good,' she said, giving him a flash of her blades.

'The blood is still working?'

'Seems to be.'

Within a few minutes, they were outside the *Mutant* and heading down the space tunnel that would take them to the Articus. They moved quickly, silently.

The docking port was busy, packed with bodies, droids circling.

'What in the void is going on?' Jinn asked, moving closer to him as they made their way towards the exit. 'Who are all these people? Where are they going?'

'I don't know,' Dax said. 'But I don't think we should hang around and find out.' He reached out, pulled the hood of her jacket up over her hair, tugged up the collar on his coat. He kept his walk casual, but every sense was on high alert, and he kept Jinn close.

He steered her closer to the edge of the port as the crowd

surged. Voices joined the push, loud and angry. A droid crashed to the ground. Another stepped forward, waving an electro-stick, and the smell of burning flesh made Dax grimace. He reached out and grabbed Jinn's hand, upping his speed, wanting to get away from the pushing and shoving and the desperate, panicky crowd.

More people were spilling into the port as they forced their way out. They barely gave Dax or Jinn a second glance. Some of them were Bugs, their prosthetics obvious. Some of them were older, retirees most likely, and a couple of them were Dome brats, the kind who had spiked bars through their lips and noses and swayed drunkenly as they walked. All of them were leaving.

And Dax suspected that he already knew where they were going.

He led Jinn through to a quiet walkway, where they pressed themselves into the shadows and watched the pushing crowd. A woman stumbled towards them. She was a Bug, young and skinny, with her hair shaved at the sides and implants at her shoulder and neck. She held up a blade. 'Give me your credits,' she snarled.

Dax looked at her. 'Put that away before I have to hurt you,' he said.

She jerked the blade a little higher. 'Shut up!'

'What do you want them for?' Jinn asked her.

The woman stared at her in disbelief. 'What do you think? Didn't you see the newsfeed? Everyone who signs up for the Second Species programme gets a guaranteed place on the ships going to Spes.'

'I saw the newsfeed,' Jinn said. 'The Second Species programme has a thirty percent death rate. And if you are unfortunate enough to survive, you'll be given to the Shi-Fai as a slave.'

'Not as a slave,' the woman said. 'As an ambassador. Six months on their planet, my debts are wiped out. My criminal record disappears. And I'm on that ship to Spes.' She angled the blade right at Jinn's throat. 'Now give me your *fucking credits*.'

Dax shoved the woman back. He pinned her against the wall of the alleyway, then he shoved a hand into his pocket and pulled out a credit chip. He held it up in front of her face. The woman's eyes gleamed, and she snatched at it, but he held it just out of reach. 'If you get on that ship, you'll die,' he said.

The woman never took her gaze off the chip. 'Maybe,' she said. 'Or maybe you're just full of self-serving anti-government shit.' She snatched the chip out of his hand, sprinted to the end of the alley and disappeared into the crowd.

Dax stared at the wall. Then he punched it. It crumpled inwards, the hole the size of his head. Smoke billowed out.

'Come on,' he said to Jinn.

'Wait.'

He turned back to her.

'It's started, hasn't it?'

'Yes,' he said. 'It's started.'


It was hard to believe that only a couple of days ago, she'd thought this was just about Medipro, about the greed of a corporation. Now she knew differently. Not only was this far bigger than she could possibly have imagined, it was government sanctioned. Jinn felt utterly sick when she thought about the fact that her mother, the woman with whom she shared DNA, was part of this solution.

But the worst thing was that she didn't feel surprise, not really. It was a long time since Jinn had seen Ferona in action but she knew, was probably one of the only people who *really* knew, how ruthless Ferona could be, and just how far she would go to get what she wanted. Something twisted painfully in Jinn's gut. She should have at least tried to warn people what Ferona was capable of. Instead she had put all her energy into saving herself. Just as Ferona had always said, Jinn had let emotion dictate her actions. She'd been too self-absorbed to see what was going on outside of her little bubble. But not any more.

Now this wasn't just about her. It was about Dax and Eve and Alistair, people who had become her friends. And it was about all of the people who would sign up for the Second Species programme, thinking they had a future.

As they walked deeper into the Articus, Jinn saw more people moving in the direction of the port. But she also saw plenty of others who were not, who remained on their seat in the bar, who lingered in the stores, on the walkways, despite the fact that Ferona's video message was playing in stereo on all public viewscreens.

Dax pushed back his coat, pulled out one of the blasters, and shot a particularly large screen dead centre. It exploded in a shower of sparks, smoke dissipating to show a black rectangle with a massive hole in the middle.

'Damn thing was annoying me,' he said, when Jinn looked across at him.

At the end of the walkway was a medical centre. High-end, or as high-end as it got here on the Articus, with holographic advertisements for facial refiguration and body alteration in the wide front window, and secure entry. *Walk-in appointments available* flashed a sign by the door.

'We should go in,' Dax said. 'They might be able to remove your Tellurium.'

So this was what he'd meant when he said *sort out some of this mess.* Her feet moved her to the window. She stood in front of it, staring at the scrolling list of treatments that were offered. 'There aren't any prices,' she said.

'It doesn't matter,' Dax told her.

He moved to stand alongside her and she watched his reflection in the window, the stark contrast between his build and hers, his darkness compared to her light. He lifted a hand, and for a moment she thought he was going to touch her, then he let that hand sink back to his side, where it curled into a fist. 'As long as you're with me, you're in danger,' he said. 'It'll be easier for you to hide on your own. Once the Tellurium has been removed, chances are no-one will recognise you. I'll give you credits for a ship and Smartware. You'll be able to fly yourself to Spes if that's what you want.'

His reflection disappeared as he moved to the door, but Jinn lingered for a moment longer, watching herself. Once this was done, she would be permanently changed. She would never have the Tellurium refitted. She would never be able to fly again, not the way she did now. She flexed her fingers, heard the reassuring hiss of her blades as they slid slowly out of her hands.

She willed them back in with a snap.

'What about you?' she asked him.

'I'll figure something out,' he said. He was stood sideways on, giving her a view of his profile, and all of a sudden she found herself transported back to the first time she had met him. It had been a moment that had changed her life.

And this could be another one of those moments, if she let it. If she was brave enough. He had saved her before. There was only one way to find out if he would save her again. She didn't let herself think beyond this moment, didn't let herself think about what life would be like if he said no. All she knew was that she didn't want to walk through that door.

'Wait,' she said, as the door slid open and Dax moved towards it. The smell of lavender and cleaning fluids wafted out onto the street, the floral scent unable to fully drown out the chemical tang. The cheaper medical centres didn't even bother trying to hide it, and the really cheap ones didn't have a cleaning-fluid smell to hide in the first place.

'What?'

Jinn hesitated. She tried to pull her courage together, but it was flimsy and weak. If he said no ...

'I don't have much time, Jinn,' he said. 'I've got to get the *Mutant* away from here before someone identifies it.'

'Where will you go?'

'Does it matter?'

She took a step towards the door. The smell got stronger,

burning her nasal cavity. She could taste the lavender. 'Can I ask you something?'

'As long as you're quick about it.'

'If you could go back, if you could change yourself back to how you were before, would you?'

Dax stepped away from the door. Sensing that he had moved, it slid silently closed. 'I don't know,' he said. 'The body I have now ... it's different, but it works. In a lot of ways, it more than works. I'm strong. I heal ridiculously fast. I'm better than human. But if you asked Eve or Alistair the same question, you might get a different answer.'

'I don't want to have my Tellurium removed.' Her breath came unsteadily, and her head spun dizzily with the lack of oxygen. And then the truth of it hit her, all at once. 'I know it's not better, but I still don't want to change it. I don't want Smartware. I don't want to disappear, to change my identity. I made myself into this. It was my choice. Mine. I like how I am now.'

And she wanted to be with Dax. For the first time in her life, she didn't want to be alone.

'You can't keep it, Jinn. It's killing you.'

'I can,' she said, her hands shaking as she looked up at him, 'if you give me your blood.'

# CHAPTER
# 30

She saw him react to her words, a sudden but subtle shift in his stance. 'You would have to stay on the *Mutant*,' he said.

'I know.'

'Is that what you want?'

'Yes.'

'And if it has the same effect on you as last time, do you want that too?' He didn't move from the doorway. He simply stood there, watching her, assessing.

Afraid.

It hit her like a stunner shot, that realisation.

'Yes,' she said. It was the truth. It felt as if everything that had happened had been moving her towards this moment, towards making this choice. 'I want that, Dax. I want to know what it's like. I want to know what it would be like with you. I've spent my whole life running. Hiding. I don't want to do that any more.'

He shook his head, dropped his gaze to the ground. 'I'm not like other men,' he said.

Jinn leaned in against him. Her body hurt too much not to.

His shirt was hot against her skin and she could hear the fierce pounding of his heart. 'I know,' she said. 'I wouldn't ask this of you if you were.'

His arms came around her, strong and hard, and they clung to each other. Closing her eyes, Jinn pushed her face against his neck, drinking in the warm scent of his skin and the way his powerful body felt against hers, his big hands holding her tightly against him. 'Will you show me what it's like?' she asked. 'What it's really like?'

They made their way back to the *Mutant* without speaking. All around them, other people gathered together, making their way to the port to fight for tickets on the next ferry that would take them to Earth, where they could be assessed for the Second Species programme. They took no notice of the tall, dark-haired man or the blonde woman pressed closely against his side.

Dax took her straight to his cabin. As the door closed behind them, he pressed her back against the wall. 'I don't know if I can go easy on you this time,' he said, his voice low, strained, urgent. 'It won't be like it was before.'

'I don't want it easy,' she said. 'I just want it to be you.'

With a snarl, he found her mouth. His fingers dug deep into her hair, tugging on the strands until her head jerked back and she opened up to him. She could feel the thick, hard press of his long cock against her belly. Without hesitation, she shoved a hand between them and got hold of him, squeezing him through the fabric of his trousers.

His hand came between them, pushing hers away. She heard the catch on his trousers give, then he found her hand and pressed it firmly back against his erect length. She could hear the fierce pattern of his breathing. 'You make me hard,' he said. 'Every time I look at you, I want you. It's always there, no matter where we are, what we're doing. When I close my eyes, I can still taste you in my mouth.'

'Is that so wrong?' she whispered, barely able to catch her own breath, his weight pinning her back to the wall of his cabin, just as he had on board the *Hawk*, moments before they had boarded the A2.

'You need to understand something,' he said. 'When they modified me with Sittan DNA, when they put that into my body, it changed me.'

'I know it did.'

He shook his head. 'Not just the size,' he said. 'Not just the strength, or the healing, or the ability to run up walls.' He was rocking against her as he spoke, rocking himself into her grip. She wasn't sure he even knew he was doing it, but she didn't move her hand, didn't loosen her grip. 'My orgasms are different,' he said. 'The first couple make me more aroused, not less. After that, if I don't come again,' he said, 'I start to hurt. And when I start to hurt, I'm going to do whatever it takes to make it stop.'

His voice was rough in her ear, his breath hot against the side of her neck. 'I want you,' he said. 'But I don't want to hurt you.'

She willed out her blades. They erupted smoothly, without pain, without bleeding, her control absolute. He had given her that. 'You won't,' she said. 'Because I won't let you.'

'Jinn,' he said, his voice harsh with longing. 'If you're not sure about this, you need to leave. Now.'

She refused to let herself be afraid, though that didn't stop her heart from pounding or her legs from turning to water. She turned to him, pressed her face against his neck and breathed him in. 'I can take care of myself,' she said. 'Now let me take care of you.'

She stopped his protest with the firm press of her mouth against his, willing him not to resist her. He ignored the first flick of her tongue against his mouth, and the second. But she didn't let him ignore the third. Not when her hands found his erection again and circled it, squeezed it, stroked it.

She kept up the pressure, working him with her hands as she kissed him. She didn't know what she was doing, not really, but it didn't seem to matter. His hands sank into her hair as he crowded her back against the wall. His face flushed. 'Jinn,' he said hoarsely against her mouth. 'Jinn, I . . .'

But whatever he had been going to say next was lost, as his hips bucked and he spilled himself all over her hands. She gentled her grip, was astonished to find him trembling, though when he looked down at her it wasn't fear she saw.

It was desire. Hot, all-consuming desire. His hands dug into her clothes, ripped them aside, exposing her body. Wordlessly, he lifted her, his hands digging in to her flesh, hard enough to bruise. He didn't speak now, didn't say anything as he pulled her with him over to his bunk. He pushed her down on it, straddling her as he stripped off his shirt and threw it aside. His hands dug into the waistband of his trousers, then paused. 'Turn over,' he ordered her.

'Why?'

'Turn over,' he said again.

Slowly, carefully, she did as he asked.

'Get on your hands and knees,' he said.

Her palms tingled as she did what he asked, granting him the total control he asked for, he needed. She felt the heat of his body as he moved closer, the weight of his hand as he laid it upon the small of her back and caressed the skin there for a long, precious moment. Then his thick fingers traced the curve of her buttocks, the sensitive place in between, before finding the slippery heat at her core. Air hissed out of her lungs as he touched her, teasing places that made her clench her teeth and cry out.

A hand slid back up to her shoulder and she felt the press of his body against her back. And then he thrust his thick length inside her. All the way inside her. Only the grip of his hand on her shoulder stopped her from pitching forwards onto the bunk, her arms unable to handle the force of that first thrust. He stayed inside her, not moving, until she was steady, until the shock had subsided.

And then he began to move. Steady, strong strokes that had her digging her fingers into the bed as he pinned her legs together between his own and set her hips at the angle he wanted. The sensation was blinding, each thrust making her moan, filling her further, pushing her closer to a state of pleasure she'd never experienced before. The tingle in her hands grew stronger, fiercer, and she gave up trying to hold her weight up on her arms, letting her body collapse forward so that her cheek rested against the softness of the covers. In the polished surface of the cabin wall, she could see their reflection, and the image took her breath away. Her backside was curved up, his hands resting possessively on her hips as he moved, and from this angle she could see the hard jut of his cock as he moved in her. It added a whole new dimension to what she could feel, what she could hear, as their slick bodies moved together. She couldn't tear her gaze away, not even when the sensation became too much, as the first tendrils of her climax began to wrap themselves around her, making her body clench around him. His fingers dug harder into the flesh of her hips as he swore. Jinn gritted her teeth. Her whole body was shaking now, her arms burning as the Tellurium that flooded her system started to fire up, but she wouldn't lose control now, she wouldn't. She had to stay strong, stay here. She could tell from his harsh roar and the sound of his breathing that Dax was in pain.

'You're hurting,' she whispered, as her whole body started to burn.

'So are you,' he said.

'It doesn't matter. Please, Dax, don't stop. Just ... don't stop.'

'I have to,' he snarled. With a roar, he pulled out of her, and an instant later, Jinn felt the heat of his mouth replace the hard thrust of his cock. For a moment, she felt her body soften, let herself submit to the pleasure of it, but only for a moment. It took all her strength to move away from him, to turn herself over on the bed, but she did it.

'Don't look at me,' he said.

But she did. He was knelt on the end of the bunk. His cock jutted up, impossibly huge, impossibly thick. She lifted a hand,

289

reached out to him, but he moved before she could touch him, moved with the speed that still had the power to shock her. His face twisted in agony and he made a rough, harsh sound with every breath he took. The sound of an animal in pain. This was what he had hidden from everyone, she realised. This was the truth of his modifications, of the tiny strands of DNA that existed inside each and every one of his cells. This was who he really was. 'Caspian,' she said softly. 'Caspian, we need to finish this.'

'Don't ... want ... to hurt you.'

'Then stop fighting it.'

'Mustn't.'

He was almost at the far side of the cabin and Jinn knew she was losing him. Her whole body was still thrumming with arousal, still burning from the effects of her tech and the climax she so desperately needed. There was only one thing she could think of to do, one possible way out of this. 'I won't let you,' she said, her hands trembling as she lay back down on the bunk, and opened herself to him. 'You have to trust me.'

For a moment she thought that she'd made a mistake, a horrible mistake. Then she found herself pinned back on the bed, his full weight upon her. He pushed her legs apart, set his hips into the cradle of her thighs, and then he was inside her. This time there was no hesitation, no apology. Just a relentless, fierce sequence of pounding thrusts that brought her to a screaming climax in a matter of seconds. She couldn't control it, couldn't control herself, but he didn't stop, wouldn't let her stop. He took her wrists and pinned them high above her head, taking the control from her.

And then he covered her mouth with his and possessed it, his tongue mimicking the movement of his cock, and she knew that something had to give. Something had to break. The question was whether it would be the bunk or it would be Dax.

He reared up above her, and with an almighty roar he answered that question. His climax went on and on and on, filling her with wave after wave of hot, spurting pleasure, until it gathered her up into a climax of her own and they rode the seemingly endless wave for what felt like forever.

When Jinn awoke, they were curled up together on the floor of his cabin, a sheet draped over them. She vaguely recalled Dax pulling it over the pair of them before she'd drifted off into a deep, dreamless sleep. They'd abandoned the bunk, which had collapsed under them only moments after Dax had collapsed on top of her, spent and exhausted from an orgasm that had astounded her. She could tell from the slow, steady sound of his breathing that he was asleep.

Jinn slowly lowered the sheet, tucking it down over his naked form, then rolled onto her back. His surrender had been so fierce, so perfect, and she wanted to savour every single reminder of it, every single aching muscle, to hold onto the feeling that he had given her something that could never be taken away.

He was right about one thing, she thought to herself, as she stared up at the ceiling. He was nothing like a droid. Droids were emotionless. Clinical. They gave nothing of themselves, because there was nothing to give. They provided a service, met a need, scratched an itch, and that was it.

A large hand settled heavily on her stomach. When she turned her head, she found him watching her, though his eyes were heavy-lidded. He didn't say anything. He just watched her, as she watched him. 'We broke your bunk,' she said.

'Looks like it,' he replied. 'Are you alright?'

She was sore, she was tired, she was more alive than she'd ever been before. 'You didn't break me,' she told him.

'No,' Dax said, but there was a gleam in his eyes, a look that she recognised, and a shiver of anticipation ran through her. 'But then I haven't really tried.'

He hadn't broken her, though fuck knows he should have. He'd ridden her hard, maybe too hard, but she'd taken it all. He'd tried to give her pleasure. He even thought he might have succeeded a time or two, in the moments where he'd been capable of coherent thought. And when she'd closed her arms around him, when her thighs had been locked tight around his hips, he had felt something that he hadn't felt in a long time, if ever.

He'd felt wanted.

And for those few precious minutes, he'd forgotten that he was different. There had been nothing but Jinn and the welcoming heat of her body. She had been right. He had been lonely. He had accepted it, had grown used to it, but that didn't mean he had enjoyed it.

He felt her gaze on him now and glanced across at her. She was sat at the other side of the table, slurping down a tall cup of soup. Eve sat next to her. Alistair was at the end of the table, dumping enough molasses in his koffee to make the spoon stand up straight. Theon sat next to Dax. Polyskin covered his right hand, and was rapidly making its way past his wrist. It was still bright pink and thick, but over the next couple of days it would expand and stretch until it covered his entire skeleton and then it would start to fade, turning to a more natural colour.

'I had forgotten how much it itches,' Theon said, flexing his fingers. 'It is very difficult not to scratch.'

'Try,' Dax said. 'I'm not paying for a third lot.'

'I shall do my best,' Theon responded, pressing his palm flat against the table as the polyskin crept a little further past his wrist. Each time it grew, it fused with more of his sensory receptors, causing almost unbearable itching. Humans were usually sedated until the process was finished, and they also didn't usually have their entire skin replaced. Theon could have shut down, but Dax knew he would rather feel the discomfort.

They had left the Articus several hours before, after Grudge had contacted Dax to inform him that several bounty-hunters had been spotted on the station, and they were showing far too much interest in the *Mutant,* and if someone wanted to make it disappear, now would be a good time. There hadn't been time for a proper goodbye. Dax wasn't sure what he would have said, anyway.

Jinn had flown them to an uninhabited minor planet four hours out from the Articus. It was on the way to precisely nowhere, so it was unlikely that anyone would come looking for them here. They were orbiting the planet now, floating dead in space, power on minimal in order to conserve fuel. They could probably fly around this planet for years and no-one would ever find them. It would keep them alive. But it would hardly be living.

'I want to go to Spes,' he said suddenly. 'I want to walk outside and breathe clean air with starheat burning the skin on my back.' The desire rose in him suddenly, unexpectedly. His life had been Underworld London, and then it had been this ship. He had never imagined that it could be something else.

He hadn't allowed himself to want it to be. But now, as he looked at Jinn, as he breathed in dry, recycled air, he wanted that more than anything. He had almost persuaded himself, before she had told him she wanted to stay, before she had shared her body with him, that he was going to join the Second Species programme. He didn't want to spend the rest of his life hiding. Agents would find him eventually anyway, and he'd had a good run. If he was honest, he'd had a good time. Might as well accept the inevitable.

He understood now that what he really wanted was a life on that planet. He wanted to breathe air that wasn't recycled and listen to something that wasn't the hum of an engine. A tiny part of him had wondered if maybe the government was telling the truth and the Second Species programme was the answer, and that told him just how desperate he'd become.

All his life, he'd believed that he was less because he was from an Underworld city, because he'd been turned into a monster and had killed and stolen to survive, and later because he'd enjoyed his life as a pirate. He'd assumed that he would always have to live his life on the fringes of society.

Jinn had changed that. Now he had to survive. He had to do it for her. And he wanted to give her more than this ship, more than life as a fugitive. They both deserved it.

'Spes?' Eve said. 'Good luck with that.' She got to her feet, picked up her empty bowl, and dumped it in the recycler.

'It would be something,' Alistair said. 'They say it has oceans, and rivers, and that plants grow outside.'

Eve slammed the recycler shut. 'How are we supposed to get there?' she yelled. 'Look at us! We're the test batch. The ones no-one was supposed to know about. We're nothing more than an experiment. We don't even know if how we are is the way Second Species are supposed to be. And we've got bounty-hunters and bloody security agents sniffing after us and I very much doubt it's because the president wants to give us a medal for all we've done.'

'Eve,' Dax said. 'Sit down.'

She opened her mouth to argue, then closed it again and did as she was told.

'The way I see it, we've got two options,' he said. 'We can either live out the rest of our lives hiding out on this ship, or we can start again. On Spes.'

'How?' Eve asked. 'We're pirates. We steal for a living. And I for one am not going to the Shi-Fai. I don't care what anyone says. Nothing is worth that.'

'We'll find a way,' Dax said. He didn't know how they would do that, but he generally lived life by the seat of his pants. There was no reason why this should be any different. 'We'll make a way.'

'And what about everyone else?' Eve asked. 'What about all the people who are going to sign up for modifications? What about them? You and I know what it's like to live with these modifications. I remember the clinic,' she said. 'And I'm sure you do too.'

Alistair moved towards her, but she moved away, her reaction automatic. She gripped her upper arms, rubbed them. 'I still have nightmares,' she admitted. 'We can't let them do this to people, Dax.'

'I agree,' Jinn said. 'People aren't ships. They're not a commodity to be bartered. Like Dax said, if they want to sign up for the programme, we can't stop them. But they deserve to know what they're signing up for.'

'So what do we do?' Eve asked. 'Take out an advert on Channel One? Hand out leaflets on the Europa? Hijack a transporter ship and refuse to let it go until everyone on board listens to what we have to say?'

'All excellent ideas,' Theon said. 'But we need to see the bigger picture. We are all agreed that the government hasn't been entirely honest about the Second Species programme,' Theon said. 'I dislike dishonesty. It is one of the few human traits that I have worked hard not to develop.'

He sat back in his seat, made as if he was going to scratch his arm, then stopped himself at the last moment. 'We discovered the programme was running again, and we exposed it,' he said. 'In so doing, we forced the government's hand. But they were able to use it to their advantage. Fear is a powerful tool, Caspian, and we underestimated that. We've been away from Earth for too long. And we aren't scratching out a living on a Colony. You're modified, but you don't have prosthetics. We were naive. We didn't really understand what people are living with, what they face. The government offered them the biggest prize of all – the chance to change their lives. We shouldn't be surprised that they want to take it.'

'So what do we do?' Alistair asked. 'Sit back and watch?'

'No,' Theon said. 'Trading with our alien neighbours in this way sets a dangerous precedent. If this programme goes ahead, selling people will become the norm. It will be expected. Say the vote passes, and the population reaches Spes. What then? What if the Sittan decide they want more people or they will invade and kill us?'

'No-one will see it that way,' Jinn said. 'They can't see beyond Spes.'

'Because they don't know what it's really like to be Second Species,' Theon said. 'Only people who have undergone the modifications know that.'

'So we have to show them,' Dax said.

'How do we do that?' Eve asked. 'No-one is going to listen to us, not now.'

'If we could show them what we saw on the A2,' Jinn said, turning to Dax, 'then they would at least know what was coming. I certainly wouldn't volunteer if I saw those electrified cages.'

Alistair rubbed a hand over his face. 'Getting on board would be tricky.'

'We did it before,' Eve pointed out. 'Theon flew us in. Could you do it again, Theon?'

'Certainly,' said Theon. 'But I think it would be wise to assume that changes will have been made since then to prevent a reoccurrence. It is unlikely to work a second time.'

'Anyone got any better ideas?' Dax asked, looking around at them.

Eve shook her head.

Alistair yawned. 'We could steal the A2.'

'We'd still need a way to get on board,' Eve pointed out. 'And that's the problem, isn't it? Our great plan all depends on us doing something that's basically impossible.'

'It's not impossible,' Theon said. 'Merely extremely difficult and highly dangerous. Perhaps our esteemed captain could get himself arrested and sent back there.'

'When the sun freezes over,' Dax told him. 'Let's take a break. Sleep on it. And hope that one of us is struck by genius by morning. Whatever we're going to do, we need to do it soon.'

He left the control deck and prowled the empty corridors of the *Mutant*, trying to think of a way to get the information they needed. Jinn was right – the A2 was the key to getting the message across. But getting on board would not be easy. At least it wouldn't involve being caught naked in his chemicleanse this time.

He went down into the lower levels of the ship, did a quick walk-through of engineering. Everything seemed to be working, though he spent some time cleaning out the pipes for the water recycler and programmed the repair droid to check the air filters.

The lives of the people on board the A2 were worth something, and it was an awful lot more than the government seemed to think. Everyone deserved a chance to start again on Spes. And Theon was right. If Spes was going to be a safe place for all of them, it couldn't be bought this way. People from the Domes had to stop using Underworld lives as a commodity, and Underworlders had to stop letting them.

Dax left the lower levels of the ship and kept walking until he found himself outside his cabin. He lingered a moment, and then he went in. He undressed, used the chemicleanse, stretched out on his bunk and watched the newsfeed. He hadn't intended to fall asleep. He didn't realise he *was* asleep until a warm female body crawled in alongside him.

'Jinn,' he whispered.

Bodies tangled together, they loved each other into a haze of warmth and comfort.

Eventually Jinn drifted into sleep, or so he thought, and he let himself drift there with her. He dreamt of the A2, of the endless passageways and the crax and silver rice.

He didn't feel her slip away. He didn't see the look she gave him as she stood in the doorway, watching him sleep. If he had, he might have stopped her before she climbed into the pilot seat of the *Deviant*, powered up the phase drive, and set a course for Earth.

# CHAPTER

# 31

## 6th September 2207

Vessel: The *Heritage York*. Class I transport yacht
Destination: Earth's Moon
Cargo: None
Crew: Seven
Droids: Four

The pleasure yacht still stank of things Bryant didn't want to imagine. He was lying on the floor of the control deck, shivering, his face pressed against the cold steel. The ship was flying on autopilot. It had been flying on autopilot for the past twenty hours, heading for the Moon.

Why did space have to be so fucking big?

Bryant scrubbed at his eyes. He opened them a crack, and even that was too much. He needed another hit of Euphoria, but he couldn't seem to make himself get off the floor to get one. His arms and legs were numb. His head was heavy. Breathing was hard.

A hand pushed against his shoulder. Another hand joined the first, pushing, pulling, until Bryant found himself in an upright position. The room span. He spat out a curse. 'Get your hands off me.'

'Do it,' said a child's voice.

Something pressed against his neck. There was a click, and a hiss, and then the warm flow of drugs into his system. He tried to sink back against the floor, but those hands wouldn't let him. 'Bryant,' the voice said sharply. Davyd. It was Davyd. The eldest of the boys he had found on board the pleasure yacht at the Articus.

'What is it?'

'We're nearly there,' Davyd said. 'You need to eat. Here.' He pressed something against Bryant's palm.

Bryant looked down at his hand. Squashed between his fingers was a packet of silver rice. He stared at it, vision blurring. His first attempt to rip open the packet failed, and it was gently prised from his hand and torn open. He snatched it back, and at least managed to get it to his mouth and swallow. Several pairs of hungry eyes focussed on him, or rather, they focussed on the food.

'The Autochef is out,' Davyd said. 'Silver rice is all we have left.'

Bryant said nothing. He got to his knees, and then he got to his feet, several pairs of small hands holding him steady. They guided him into the captain's chair. He gripped the arms, forced himself to focus. 'Screen on.'

It popped up in front of him, a small hologram of subtle colours that made space look small. It lied. But Davyd hadn't lied. They were almost there, almost at the Moon, where according to Vice President Ferona Blue, there was a medical facility modifying human women with the Type Two DNA. There was no doubt in his mind that somewhere in that facility, he would find a cure for whatever he'd been poisoned with.

He hadn't allowed himself to listen to any doubts. He was an agent. He was Dome-raised. He had been top of his class at the academy and had graduated twelve months early having fast-tracked through most of his courses. He had been the one to capture Caspian Dax and take him to the A2, even if the bastard had then escaped.

299

'What do you want us to do?' Davyd asked.

'Shut up and let me think,' Bryant said. He hadn't wanted to bring the boys with him. But after the initial wave of people leaving the Articus, there hadn't been anyone left he was prepared to leave them with. So he was stuck with them.

He needed a crew. All he had was half a dozen stray children. If they'd been dogs, he'd have shot them all in the head and put them out of their misery. And they were miserable. Dark-eyed, hollowed-cheeked. Half of them had a strangely vacant look in their eyes, as if the body was functioning but the soul was missing. Fuck, what had he been thinking, bringing them along?

'Do you know how to use a comm. unit?' he asked Davyd.

The boy shook his head vigorously.

'Then it's time you learned.' Bryant gestured to the seat to his right. Davyd hesitated for a moment, then slipped into it. The chair almost swallowed him up, designed as it was for a large Dome male, not a bony Underworld kid. The boy snatched up the Smartware headset that sat on the console, and slipped it on.

'See the screen?' Bryant told him. Davyd nodded. 'That shows all available transmissions that we can currently pick up. If they're green, they're being broadcast on a public channel. That means anyone can access them. We're not interested in those. We want the blue. They're encrypted. That means whoever is sending them doesn't want the rest of the galaxy to hear what they're saying.'

Davyd touched one of the blue channels. 'I can't hear anything,' he said.

'That's because you don't have the key,' Bryant told him. He shoved a hand in his pocket. It was empty.

One of the boys stepped forward, a chain of small gold discs dangling from his fingers. 'Sorry,' he whispered.

'Thieving little shit,' Bryant said. He made a grab for the boy, but the child dodged away. 'Who taught you?'

'Davyd.'

'Steal from me again and I'll rip your throat out.'

The boy didn't even flinch.

Bryant took the string of discs and tossed them to Davyd, who snatched them out of the air. 'The square disc,' Bryant told him. 'Codeword is sentinel.'

Davyd slotted the disc in place, entered the code, then stilled. His mouth fell open. 'I can hear it,' he said. 'It's a Security Service ship, I think.'

'Keep listening,' Bryant told him. 'The rest of you, find yourselves a seat and keep the fuck out of the way. I don't even want to hear you breathing. Understand?' He turned back to the controls and ended the autopilot, putting himself in control. Then he turned on the viewscreen that wrapped around the front of the control deck.

They were at the entrance to Space Lane Two. It was solid with transporters, all of them heading in the direction of Earth. It was as if the entire human population had decided to return home on the same day.

'Bloody supernova,' Davyd whispered. 'Look at all the ships.'

'I told you to shut up,' Bryant snapped. His muscles were locked tight, his spine so rigid that it felt like it might crack. He should have anticipated this. The traffic was moving slowly, too slowly, drifting in what could only be described as a crawl.

He drummed his fingers on the console, the sound echoing the pain in his head. There had to be another way, a quicker way. Damn it all to the void. His palms were drenched with sweat inside the Smartware gloves and he yanked them off, tossed them aside, rubbed his hands on his trousers. The inside of his mouth tasted foul. The drugs were was already starting to wear off.

He grabbed the controls with shaking hands. The yacht jerked to the right. It jerked harder when he swung the nose away from the space lane and fired up the phase drive, sending them shooting away from the flashing buoys that marked the edges of the lane. One of them burned out as the side of the yacht clipped it, exploding brightly, though it made no sound.

Bryant laughed. Even to his ears, it sounded strained, slightly hysterical. He knew he was starting to lose his grip on sanity. But it didn't seem to matter. None of it mattered.

'Someone is hailing us,' Davyd said. 'Bryant, what do I do?'

'Tell them to fuck off.'

'Bryant, it's the traffic police.'

Police. Fantastic. Bryant leaned across, thumbed the button on the comm. console. In the seconds it took for the transmission to connect, the traffic police ship slid into view. It was small, little more than a glorified cutter, designed to keep traffic flowing within the lane boundaries. When the screen came on, the officer was equally as pathetic as his ship. He was young, dark eyes darting nervously around the screen. His beige uniform looked uncomfortably new. 'You are in violation of traffic code seventeen,' he said. 'You must return to the space lane immediately.'

'No,' Bryant said. He sat back in his seat and propped his feet up on the console.

'No?'

'That is what I said. It's only a short word. I'm sure you can understand it.'

'You must return to the space lane!'

'No.'

'Then you will be boarded and your vessel and all contents seized.'

The screen went blank.

Bryant dropped his feet to the floor and lazily reached for the manual controls. The yacht started to speed up.

And then it slowed down.

It shuddered.

'What was that?' It was Davyd who spoke. He turned wide, pale, frightened eyes on Bryant.

'We're being boarded,' Bryant said.

He hadn't thought the traffic officer would actually go through with it. He hadn't thought at all. One of the boys at the rear of the deck burst into tears, his sobbing high-pitched and painfully loud. The others remained silent. Leaning back in his seat, Bryant closed his eyes.

He didn't open them, not even when the sound of the control deck doors opening filtered through the roar of drug hunger that filled his head. It would be fine, he told himself. These were traffic police, not agents, barely able to scratch their arses without help. They weren't going to seize the vessel. They weren't going to do anything. They would look around, give him a telling off and a ticket and then leave him to get on with his business.

One of the boys screamed. Bryant opened his eyes to see the young officer pointing a blaster at one of the boys. The child had a dark mark on his cheek and he was rubbing at it, tears spilling down over his dirty little hand. 'I said,' the officer leaned in closer, his voice filled with disgust, 'where are your travel documents?'

'I . . . I don't have any.'

'Then you are in violation of code CX128,' the officer told him. 'Underworlders are not permitted to travel without appropriate documentation, and must produce that documentation when asked.'

Bryant opened his mouth to say something, but nothing came out. He gripped the arms of his seat tightly. His entire body was trembling. He was the one in the wrong here, not the children. He was the one who had ignored a direct order, who was sitting in the pilot's seat desperate for a hit.

'We don't have documentation,' Davyd said, 'because it was all destroyed by a man called Darkos so that if he was caught transporting us, he wouldn't be held responsible for us.'

Because that was the way the law worked. It was an odd loophole, one which allowed flesh traffickers like Darkos to freely trade children without fear of reprisal. If children were found without paperwork, it was considered to be their responsibility, not that of any adults who might be with them.

'You wouldn't believe how many Underworld rats have told me that story,' the officer said.

'Then maybe you should believe it.' Davyd stared up at him, eyes determined, chin jutting out stubbornly.

The officer punched him in the face. Davyd crumpled to the floor and lay there, not moving.

And it was that, that moment of unadulterated cruelty, which finally broke something inside Bryant. He got to his feet and lunged at the officer. But he was sick and sore and coming down and the officer was none of those things. Bryant went for his throat. He would have made it, too, if the officer hadn't moved first.

Pain exploded in the side of Bryant's head and he found himself lying on the floor, something hot and wet trickling out of his ear. It made its way down his neck, across his cheek, dripping into his mouth. Blood. His blood. It tasted foul. He had just enough energy left to spit.

The officer crouched down next to him. His eyes narrowed. 'I know you,' he said. 'You're the agent from the Europa.' A smile spread over his face. His cheeks dimpled, completely at odds with the hard cruelty in his eyes. 'Well, well. Isn't this an unexpected surprise.'

He got to his feet, nudged the side of Bryant's face with the toe of his boot. 'There's a bounty on your head, you know. A very tidy sum. You're lucky I found you before anyone else.'

The blaster was charging. Bryant could hear it whine. He dug his fingertips into the floor, but he couldn't get purchase, and the rest of his body stubbornly refused to move.

'I could bring you in alive,' the officer said. 'But you resisted arrest, you see, and I can't take any chances.'

He pointed the blaster at Bryant's stomach. 'It'll be quick,' he promised. His finger slipped over the trigger. There was movement behind him, but the officer didn't seem to notice. He was too busy.

But Bryant noticed.

He saw all of it, even though it all happened impossibly fast. The blade that the boy who had stolen the discs slipped out from under his shirt. It was a blade that had been tucked into Bryant's left boot. He hadn't even noticed it was missing. The boy caught Bryant's eyes as he moved closer to the officer, softly, silently. He couldn't have been more than eight years old, an awkward, ugly little thing with teeth that stuck out at odd angles.

He raised the blade.

Bryant couldn't breathe.

The kid struck, but he didn't have the height, the strength. The blade sliced through the back of the officer's jacket, shredding fabric. The officer yelled, spun, back-handed the kid across the face. He flew across the space, crashing into the wall with a bone-breaking thud. The blade clattered to the floor. The officer went for it. Bryant went for it.

And so did Davyd, battered, bleeding Davyd. His fist closed around the hilt, and then he charged at the officer. He did it silently, quickly, without emotion. It was chilling.

The officer grabbed at Davyd, caught hold of him by the back of his shirt. He hauled Davyd up onto his toes and his fist went back, but it was too late. The blade stuck out at a right angle from his neck, clinging to the edge of a wide slash that poured blood. The man coughed, a wet splutter that sprayed blood everywhere. His eyes widened in surprise. 'You . . .' the officer spluttered. 'You . . .'

He lost his grip on Davyd. And then he sank to the floor, his body slowly folding down so that he landed almost softly, blood still gushing from the wound on his neck. It pebble-dashed the control room.

'You killed him,' Bryant said.

Davyd's gaze darted from the body to Bryant and back again. 'He was going to kill you.'

'Why didn't you let him?'

'Because you helped us.'

Bryant looked at him. Looked at all of them. He was on a stolen ship with a dead body and half a dozen trafficked boys. Reality was staring him in the face. It was time he stopped running from it. 'I'm going to die anyway,' he said.

And that was the cold, hard truth of it. There wasn't going to be an end to this. There wasn't a cure. He was chasing a ghost, something that didn't exist, something that was out of his reach even if it did. He had thought that being Dome-raised would always protect him. He'd thought wrong. Whatever protection it had afforded him had been nothing more than an illusion. He was alone.

Except . . . except that he wasn't.

Gritting his teeth, Bryant got unsteadily to his feet. He had to hold on to the back of the seat to keep himself upright, but he did it. 'Any of you ever used a spacewalk before?'

A couple of the boys nodded. 'Get to it,' Bryant told them. 'Start making your way across.'

'What are we going to do?' Davyd asked him.

'First off, we're going to get rid of this.' Bryant gestured to the dead officer. 'And I figure that traffic cruiser has a well-stocked Autochef and medical bay. Take anything that looks useful and bring it back here. You'll need to be quick, though. Then I'm going to get you somewhere safe.'

'Darkos has a condo on Colony Seven,' Davyd told him. 'He took me there once. It had a glass ceiling that let in the sky. I liked it.'

'Then that's where we'll go,' Bryant told him. After he had killed Darkos on the Articus, he had dumped the body into a recycling unit. Chances were that no-one on Colony Seven even knew he was missing, let alone dead. No-one would be looking for him.

For the first time in his adult life, Bryant wanted to cry. All he had ever wanted was to join the Security Service, to uphold order. Maybe he'd had a taste for violence, and for power, but he'd never crossed the line. And now he had become what he had always hated the most. He was a murderer, and a thief, and he was dying, and it was so fucking unfair that he wanted to howl.

The government had lied to him. The government had lied to all of them. All those months spent taking prisoners to the A2, thinking he was making things better, when in fact he had been giving those criminals a second chance. They would be modified and they would get a place on the ships going to Spes.

He should have been on one of those ships. Not as a Second Species, but as a decorated security agent. Jinnifer Blue was to blame. She had reduced him to this, to a snivelling, puking mess that had to rely on a group of Underworld children for help. It was all because of her.

He hauled himself up to his feet. Every step was agony, but eventually he dragged the body across the spacewalk and onto the control deck of the traffic cruiser. The boys had already made short work of taking everything that wasn't nailed down back to the yacht.

Bryant staggered back across the spacewalk, disconnected it, then made his way back to the control deck. 'I need a hit,' he said as he collapsed painfully into his seat.

'So what now?' Davyd asked him, as he loaded a drug gun and handed it to Bryant. He turned his chair so the boys wouldn't see before he used it. It only took a couple of seconds to start working. When he'd started on the Euphoria, he'd only meant for it to be a one-time thing. But it was stronger than blockers. And it felt so good.

'We're going to Colony Seven.' Bryant powered up the phase drive, felt the roar, and with it, a new and surprising sense of purpose. And once the boys were safe, he'd take care of himself.

The medical clinic hadn't been able to help him. But maybe, just maybe, whatever they were doing on board the A2 could. It had turned Caspian Dax into something more than human, a man who could heal blaster wounds and run up walls. Bryant had witnessed it first-hand. And the people who went there would be going to Spes.

Bryant wanted to be one of those people. He deserved to be.

He was a criminal, after all.

# CHAPTER
# 32

**6th September 2207**

> Vessel: The *Mutant*. Battleship/carrier hybrid
> Location: The Articus, Section Four, Neutral Space
> Cargo: None
> Crew: Five
> Droids: Eight

There was a way to get on board the A2. Theon had given her the idea, though she knew he hadn't intended to. The more Jinn thought about it, the more she'd been convinced that it would work, though she couldn't tell Dax. He would never agree to it. It was something she had to – should – do alone. But she'd wanted those few precious hours with him first.

Now it was time.

She gathered up her clothes and silently slipped out into the corridor, clutching the bundle to her chest. The door to his quarters sounded unfeasibly loud as it closed behind her and Jinn held her breath, hoping it hadn't woken him, wondering how she would explain herself if it had.

She stood there for precious seconds, too many precious seconds, before she accepted that the only sound she could hear was the thump of blood in her ears. She wasted precious more pulling on her clothes. Knowing she had to do this didn't make leaving him behind any easier and she could feel the steady pull of him from the other side of the door, feel temptation tugging at her limbs. It would be so easy to slip back inside, to stay with him.

But that wouldn't get her on board the A2.

With tight lungs and a painful heart, she forced herself to head for the lower decks of the *Mutant*. She hadn't spent much time down here, yet the corridors were still familiar, built with the same rough precision that characterised the rest of the ship.

*I will see him again*, she told herself as she slipped down to the hold where the two small transporters were located. *This is not the end.* She clung to that thought, clung to it desperately as she boarded the *Deviant*. It wasn't a long-haul vessel, but she could make it work for her needs. She had to.

Jinn worked through the pre-flight checks as quickly as she could, aware that at any moment someone could come down here and find her. As soon as she'd confirmed that the *Deviant* was fuelled and operational, she settled herself into the pilot's chair and fired up the phase drive. She released the long metal arms that held the transporter steady, floated it down to face the slowly opening jaws of the *Mutant*. Ahead of her, space opened up, the stunning darkness dotted with so many shining spots of light, so many places she had never been. The universe was a glorious expanse of space, bigger than she could comprehend, more than she could take in, and she was leaving behind the only part of it where she'd ever felt like she belonged. Jinn allowed herself one more moment inside the *Mutant*. One more second to feel the comfort of this place, the protection, to know that Dax was still within reach.

And then she fired up the phase drive, put the *Deviant* in motion, and left it all behind.

*

Dax knew he was alone before he opened his eyes. He could sense it in the cold air of his quarters, in the silence that was marred only by his breathing. Jerking upright, he ordered the lights to turn on, forced himself into the chemicleanse, closed his eyes as the spray removed the scent of sex and Jinn Blue from his body. He stepped out of the cubicle before the cycle had finished, letting the air evaporate the remnants of the spray from his skin, then pulled out clean clothes and dressed without particular care.

'Computer,' he said, as he tugged on his shirt. 'Locate Jinnifer Blue.'

'Jinnifer Blue is no longer onboard.'

'What do you mean, she's no longer onboard?'

'Jinnifer Blue left the *Mutant* exactly thirty-one minutes ago.'

Dax froze. 'What do you mean, she left?'

'Jinnifer Blue boarded the *Deviant* at 0630 hours. At 0642 hours she exited the *Mutant* via the transporter.'

What in the void was she doing? 'Open a channel to the *Deviant*. Now!'

The computer fell silent for a moment, the lights at the side of the screen flashing to show that it was busy. 'Unable to connect,' it said. 'The transporter is currently in jump mode.'

'Jumping to where?'

'A final flight destination was not given,' said the computer. 'But based on her inputted jump coordinates, it appears that Earth is the final destination.'

'Earth? You're sure about that?'

'Yes, Captain Dax.'

'Why would she go to Earth?'

'I am unable to answer that question.'

'Then what fucking use are you?'

'I do not know, captain.'

Dax paced the length of his quarters. The need to break something was strong. He ripped his exercise station apart. It didn't help.

'According to the log, a message was left for you at 0615 hours,' the computer informed him. 'Would you like to view it now?'

'Yes I'd like to bloody well view it!'

The screen on the wall flashed immediately to life. 'Jinn,' he said, staring at the image on the screen. Her pale hair was a mess, and if he wasn't mistaken, that was his shirt she was wearing. She spoke quickly, quietly. 'I'm taking the *Deviant* and going back to Earth,' she said. 'I'm going to turn myself in.' She rubbed a hand over her face and then stared directly at the screen. 'I'm going to get myself sent back to the A2. Theon was right. It's the best way to get one of us on board. It'll be alright. I'm Dome-raised and my mother is vice president. Agents won't touch me unless I provoke them, and I have no intention of doing that. I know the layout of the A2. And I've got Tellurium. We already know I can connect to the onboard computer.' She paused for a moment and then she went on. 'Once I'm onboard, I'll contact you. So you better stick close to your comm., because I'm going to need you to be ready.' He could see the shimmer of tears in her eyes and it physically hurt when her voice broke on her final words. 'I love you,' she said. 'Jump Gate Four. Be there.'

'Message ended,' the computer said as the screen went blank. 'Do you wish to view it again?'

'No.'

Pulling on his clothes, Dax left his quarters. He couldn't contact the *Deviant* until she was out of the jump and he willed her to get through it quickly and safely. But no way in the void was he going to let her go back to Earth on her own.

He found Theon sat at a workbench in Engineering, his newly polyskinned hands moving rapidly over what looked like a blaster. The skin had grown past his shoulders and across his chest. A few more hours and his face would be covered. His joints whirred and clicked as he moved, faster and more smoothly than any human.

'Caspian,' he said, as Dax approached him. 'I did not expect to see you until later.'

'We've got a problem.'

Theon turned his head, his blue eyes glowing. 'Explain.'

'It's Jinn,' Dax said, hating the fear in his voice. 'She's taken the *Deviant* and headed out to Earth.'

There was a pause, and Theon's eyes flashed. Dax knew he was interfacing with the onboard computer and verifying the information for himself. Needing something to keep his hands busy, he reached out and picked up the blaster Theon had been modifying. 'She has this insane idea that she can get herself sent back to the A2. She seems to think it's the best way to get one of us on board so we can record what's going on.'

'Ah,' Theon said.

'She got the idea from you!'

'That was not my intention.' Theon frowned. 'I did not consider how independent she is. She is used to doing things on her own, Dax. It is her way.'

'Will it work?'

'It's possible,' Theon concluded.

'It's also possible that she might get herself shot in the head,' Dax pointed out.

'This is true,' Theon acknowledged. 'I assume you wish to follow her, so that you too can risk the possibility of getting yourself shot in the head.'

'I love her,' Dax said.

'I'm aware of that,' Theon replied. 'Thank you for not making me point it out.'

They found Alistair and Eve in the rec station. Eve was asleep, her head resting on the table. Alistair sat opposite, watching her with the pale, exhausted pallor of someone who'd sunk far too many measures of Alterian gin. He glanced up as Dax strode towards their table. 'She challenged me to a drinking contest,' he said. 'I had forgotten what a bad idea that is.'

Dax reached out, poked Eve on the arm. She responded with a muttered *sod off*. Normally he would have laughed, told them to suffer, but he didn't have time for that now. 'Computer, get the medidroid down here with two shots of SoberNow.'

'Yes, Captain.'

Within a couple of minutes, Alistair and Eve were on their feet, dishevelled and stinking of stale alcohol, but fully alert and sober.

'Jinn's gone,' Dax told them.

'Gone where?' Alistair asked.

'Earth.'

'What does she want to go to Earth for?'

'She's going to try and get herself arrested and sent back to the A2.'

With a grimace, Eve unfastened her gin-spattered jacket and discarded it. The vest she wore underneath left her arms and shoulders bare, and she rubbed at them self-consciously. 'It might work.'

'I don't care. She's not doing it,' Dax said. 'She'll get herself killed.'

'You're going after her,' Alistair said.

Dax nodded. 'I'll take the *Curiosity*. It's too dangerous to take the *Mutant* into Earth-controlled space.'

'We're coming with you,' Eve replied.

'No,' Dax said. 'The *Mutant* can't manage without a crew, and it's too recognisable for us to take it anywhere near Earth-controlled space. Eve, you know the best places to hide. I'm taking Theon, he can handle the jumps, so you'll have to use the autopilot.'

Eve reached for him, then dropped her hand back to her side. 'Come back in one piece,' she said.

'I intend to.'

Within minutes he was settled on the control deck of the *Curiosity*. Theon connected with the onboard computer as Dax strapped himself in.

'Systems check complete,' Theon said. There was a jolt as the holding arm that kept the *Curiosity* steady inside the belly of the

*Mutant* disengaged, then the droid set the ship in motion, pivoting until they faced the slowly opening jaws of the *Mutant*. They would track Jinn down. They would stop her before she reached Earth.

They had to.


The *Deviant* bounced out of the third jump and Jinn gritted her teeth, trying desperately to hold it steady. Such a small vessel wasn't designed to handle jump after jump, and the damage was starting to show. 'Hull integrity sixty percent,' the onboard computer informed her. 'Fuel fifteen percent.'

Fortunately it was a short haul through straight space to Earth. She could see her home planet ahead, see the dense, swirling layer of white cloud that covered the surface, the small moon that orbited it. The last time she'd been this close to it had been when she'd been delivering Dax to the *Alcatraz 2*.

The comm. system crackled to life. 'You are in Earth-controlled space,' came the voice, crisp and sure. 'State your identity and destination.'

Jinn straightened her shoulders. She took a deep breath, forced herself to stay calm. 'I am Jinnifer Blue,' she said. 'I understand that there is a warrant out for my arrest. I am here to turn myself in.'

'Standby,' said the voice.

On her retinal screen Jinn saw a trio of small single-seater vessels moving towards her. Small fighters, designed to defend Earth space. She doubted any of these pilots had fired their weapons since they graduated from the training camps. She hoped they wouldn't fire them now. She wondered what they were doing, as sweat soaked through her clothes and each breath grew louder and harder to take. Her hands shook and her blades scraped the floor. Knowing why she was doing this didn't make her any less afraid.

'Prepare to be escorted to planet,' the voice said.

The journey to Earth was conducted in steady silence. As the planet grew closer, Jinn could see the details in the thick, swirling cloud that filled the atmosphere. She followed her escort through the layer of rubbish that circled the Earth, the result of years of garbage being dumped out here after room on planet had run out.

And then they were entering the atmosphere. Jinn pressed herself further into her seat as the *Deviant* bounced. It had been a long time since she'd landed on a planet rather than simply docking with a space station or another ship, and the skills needed were different. The external heat shield prevented the temperature on the control deck from rising as the nose of the *Deviant* met the thick collection of gases that enveloped the planet, but it didn't stop sweat from trickling down the side of her neck. It took everything she had to keep the transporter on course, as the entire vessel began to shake with the force of re-entry. The hull had sustained some damage during the jumps. She couldn't afford to be careless. If she didn't judge this perfectly, there was a chance the entire ship would come apart before she got even close to landing.

Tense minutes rushed by. Eventually the onboard gravity system switched off, power transferring to the landing systems. Ahead of her, Jinn could see the London Dome, the strange yet familiar shape of the curved glass making her heart pound in her chest.

At the side of the Dome was the landing area, a vast expanse of black in amongst all the white. Huge generators that ran on the kaelite crystal mined on Colony Two supplied the Dome with heat and light, and some of that heat was directed here, keeping the landing pad free of snow. There was little sign of activity.

Jinn remembered a bustling, active port, a place where goods were constantly being brought in from the colonies. The people who lived in the Domes were wealthy enough to own their own skimmers, so that they could visit the other Dome sites easily without having to use the rundown public transport system. Most could afford ships that would take them off planet, though many kept their homes here even though they spent most of their time on Colony Seven. They paid less tax that way.

The comm. system beeped. 'Prepare to land.'

Jinn lowered the landing gear, then settled the *Deviant* down gently on the landing area. The ship touched down with the lightest of jolts, and then it was steady. Silence followed. Then several armed security agents boarded the ship. They wore bulky uniforms to protect them from the cold that suddenly filled the inside of the transporter, their faces shielded by tinted masks designed to protect their eyes and their skin from the biting winds outside. All were heavily armed. All had stunners pointed directly at her, the glowing lights on the sides warning her that they were set to max.

Jinn didn't protest when they cuffed her. She followed them off the ship without question. The cold cut straight through her shirt. Hunching her shoulders, she dipped her head and let them lead her inside the Dome, inside the place that had been her home for the first eighteen years of her life.

There was only one reason they would have brought her here.

They were taking her to see Ferona.

She breathed in deep, aware of every centimetre of her body. She had known that this was a possibility when she had decided to come back to Earth and she had thought she was prepared, but being faced with it now, she knew that wasn't the case.

Everything came back to her in a rush of familiarity. The smell of the purified air. The bright colours and carved stonework that characterised the inside of the London Dome. Droids were everywhere. Everything looked more polished than she remembered it, more gaudy, more excessive. The lighting was too bright, the heat a couple of degrees too warm to be comfortable, the decor too ornate, the trees too green. It was all so artificial, so unnecessary. It was too easy, living here, to believe that the Underworld cities weren't real, that the majority of the population wasn't living in filthy poverty.

It shouldn't be so easy.

The guards surrounded her in a tight circle, not touching her, but not giving her room to slip away from them, either. They led her not to the lower level of the Dome, where the apartment she'd shared with her mother had been, but to the upper levels, where the more senior politicians kept their apartments. Further away from the generators and entrances, they were quieter, more private, more exclusive. When they reached the top level of the Dome, the luxury of the lower areas gave way to spaces that were nothing short of astonishing. They led her through a private courtyard, complete with orange trees and an extensive hydroponic garden. Pools of heated water housed schools of brightly coloured fish, and the droids here were shiny and new, a definite upgrade on the ones below. The curved glass of the Dome was concealed behind a vidscreen showing exquisite blue skies and rolling white clouds. Stay up here long enough, and you could convince yourself that the outside world didn't exist.

The guards halted outside a set of double doors made from thick one-way glass that was intricately carved. A camera winked overhead, the small silver sphere silent as it floated above them. The doors slid open. A woman stepped forward, clothed in swathes of silver-blue truesilk.

Ferona hadn't changed. Her pale hair curved to her chin, cut laser straight, and her eyes were the same mid brown they had always been. She didn't look a day older, her skin still flawless, her figure trim. 'Jinnifer,' she said. 'How wonderful to see you.'

Jinn couldn't speak. All the things she needed to say, wanted to say, were lost to her. She didn't know what she'd been expecting, but it wasn't this. It wasn't friendliness.

'Suspicious as always.' Ferona sighed. 'I suppose I should have expected that. Please. Come in.' She stepped aside, waiting for Jinn to come into her apartment.

And like she was no more in control of herself than one of the droids that was busy polishing the floor, Jinn obeyed.

*

By the time they bounced out of the third jump, Dax was about ready to take the *Curiosity* apart with his bare hands. Frustration gnawed at him. 'Try the comm. link again,' he said to Theon.

'She may already be on her way to the A2,' Theon said.

He didn't voice the other possibility. If the *Deviant* hadn't survived the jump, they wouldn't be able to contact her. She might be dead right now and he would have no way of knowing. And that was just about killing him. 'Keep trying,' Dax said.

'Of course.' Theon didn't bother to argue, and Dax was grateful for that.

Dax got to his feet, moved to the rear of the control deck. The *Curiosity* was too small to be fully equipped, but it had some onboard supplies and a limited number of weapons. He took a blaster, ran through basic weapons checks to keep himself busy. The closer they got to Earth, the more crowded the space lanes became. Freighters took up the centre of the lanes, with other smaller ships moving alongside them, occasionally attempting to overtake and being pulled aside by the traffic patrols that kept things moving.

Theon slowed their speed, bringing them in behind one of the huge freighters. The thing was so massive it made the *Mutant* look like a toy. The vast rear end filled the retinal screen, blocking out their view of everything else and forcing them to drop their speed.

'Fly past it,' Dax said through gritted teeth.

'I cannot,' Theon said. 'Not unless you wish to draw attention to our vessel.'

Dax kicked the wall in front of him, denting the metal. She was here somewhere. She had to be.

There was nothing he could do but keep looking.

Ferona's apartment was vast and modern, fitted out with every possible technology. A hostess droid discreetly brought drinks and then fitted itself back into the wall, concealing itself perfectly.

Ferona sipped at a tall glass of water. 'It has been a long time, Jinnifer.'

'Twenty years,' Jinn responded automatically. A drink had been set in front of her, but the electro-cuffs had not been removed so all she could do was look at it. Not that she would have drunk it anyway, she decided.

'You look different,' Ferona said.

'You don't.'

Ferona smiled. 'Life has been kind to me.'

So much time had passed, and yet her mother was acting as if none had. As if they sat together like this every other day. 'So you are vice president now,' Jinn said. The words seemed to stick in her throat. 'Congratulations.'

Ferona inclined her head. 'Thank you.'

Jinn looked down at the cuffs that bound her wrists, then at her surroundings; at the beautiful furniture, the antique crystal glass in front of her and at her mother, in her exquisitely tailored clothes. Maybe the reason Ferona was acting as if nothing had changed was because nothing had changed.

'So,' Ferona continued. 'Let's get down to business. Why are you here, Jinnifer? Why did you deliberately fly into Earth-controlled space?'

'I got tired of running,' Jinn said.

Ferona stared back at her, unblinking, her expression giving nothing away. 'I see.' She took a sip from her own drink, then set down her glass. 'The pirate.' She crossed her legs at the knee, set her hands in her lap. 'Where is he?'

Jinn felt her heart miss a beat. 'I don't know,' she said carefully.

'I find that highly unlikely,' Ferona replied. 'You were with him on the Europa. It was most embarrassing. And then there was the mess you created on Colony Seven. The two of you have caused me a considerable amount of trouble.'

'I don't know where he is,' Jinn said again.

'You always were a dreadful liar,' Ferona told her. 'But it doesn't matter. We'll find him.'

'What do you want with him, anyway?'

'He is a criminal,' Ferona said. 'All criminals are being rounded up and sent to prison.'

'I thought that wasn't such an issue now that you had volunteers for the Second Species programme.'

'You make it sound like simply a game of numbers. The reality is far more complicated than that, Jinnifer.'

So she must want Dax for a reason beyond the fact that he was a pirate. 'Why don't you explain it to me?'

'There's little point. You couldn't possibly understand it.'

'Try me.'

'No.' The word was snapped out, cold and vicious. Gone was the pleasant, polite woman of minutes before. This was the Ferona that Jinn recognised, the one she remembered, the woman who would stop at nothing to further her ambitions. 'Tell me where he is. Or I will be forced to make you tell me.'

Jinn didn't doubt for a moment that the threat was real, or that Ferona could make good on it. 'What makes you think that I have the faintest idea where he is?'

'You were with him on the Europa, and on Colony Seven.'

'And I left him on Colony Seven,' Jinn replied.

'Why?'

Jinn shrugged. 'We had a difference of opinion. When I saw your broadcast, I realised what the Second Species programme really meant, and decided I wanted to be part of it. You were right when you said that we cannot go back, we can only go forward, even when the path is difficult. We need to do what is best for our species as a whole, and if that means making some sacrifices, then so be it. Dax disagreed. But then he is a badly educated Underworld pirate. At this point, I wish you would catch him. But I don't know where he is.'

'You'll get your wish,' Ferona told her as her wrist comm. flashed. She glanced at it and a smile caught the edges of her mouth. 'Mark my words, Jinnifer, he will be going to the A2. And he will be going to Sittan.'

All around her, the walls moved as security droids uncurled themselves from their hidden positions. Red spots of light dotted Jinn's body, the mark of a dozen blasters aimed straight at her gut. She forced herself not to flinch. 'You're going to have me killed? Here? Isn't that a bit messy even for you, Mother?'

'Oh no. Not killed. You're far too valuable for that.'

'So you are going to send me to the A2?'

'Eventually,' Ferona replied. 'Once you give me Caspian Dax.'

'I told you, I don't know where he is.'

'Jinnifer,' Ferona said, 'stop lying.'

'I'm not lying!'

'Of course you are,' Ferona replied. 'Did you really think that I didn't know about the two of you? The Type Three agent that found you on Colony Seven sent back regular reports before you unfortunately killed her. We were watching you, Jinnifer, every step of the way.'

Jinn didn't know what to think. All she knew was that she had a dozen blasters aimed at her vital organs and that she'd made a terrible, terrible mistake. Hatred for her mother swelled inside her, together with the all-too-familiar fear. It was as if it had been merely dormant for the past twenty years and was suddenly fully awake.

'You don't need him,' she said desperately.

'But we do,' Ferona said. She looked faintly amused. 'Dax has been promised to the Sittan,' she continued. 'They're quite annoyed by how much he has stolen from them, and they're very keen to see him punished for it. He should do quite well in their arena, I imagine. But not too well. We wouldn't want that.'

'Even if you could catch him, he won't fight. I know he won't.'

'Oh I think you'll find that he will,' her mother said, leaning forward in her seat, watching her intently. 'You see, he won't be quite the same as he is now. Not once his modifications have been completed and his behaviour altered. Once his aggression genes have been switched on, he'll be more than willing to kill anything that comes within a metre of him.'

Jinn shook her head. 'You're wrong.'

'We'll see,' Ferona said, 'although as long as he ends up on Sittan, it doesn't really matter. Earth is dying, Jinnifer. If we are not evacuated from the planet within five years, we will all die with it. The Colonies aren't big enough to support all of us, and they have their own problems. But if we're going to get to Spes, we need the Sittan and the Shi-Fai to vote in our favour. The Sittan want men to fight in their arena. The Shi-Fai want females who won't die from skin-to-skin contact. We give them what they want, they give us what we want. It's as simple as that.'

It wasn't simple. Not when she was twelve, and not now. This wasn't how problems should be solved. 'But genetically modifying people, selling them as slaves to alien races we barely know, let alone understand! Barbaric, violent races. How can you do that? How can you live with yourself?' A horrible thought struck her. 'And to the Shi-Fai. Do you know what they're like? What they do to human women?' She thought of Eve, and wanted to scream. 'Everyone deserves to go to Spes. Not just a select few.'

But Ferona remained unmoved. 'You simply cannot see the bigger picture, Jinnifer. It was always your weakness.'

'There has to be another way.'

'Do you not think that if there was another way, I would take it? There are three million people living in the Domes, Jinnifer. Three million. Our best scientists estimate that the temperature will drop another ten degrees over the next fifteen years. At temperatures that low, Earth will be completely uninhabitable. Those three million will die without mass evacuation. There are another fifty million in the Underworld cities. Too many for all of them to be evacuated. With so many, we can only take the best. I am offering them a chance to be one of those people. And plenty of them are willing to take it.'

'Only because they don't know the truth,' Jinn said. 'Who are you to play God, anyway? Why do you get to decide who lives and who dies?'

'I'm not playing God,' Ferona replied. 'I'm simply being realistic. To give the human race the best possible chance of survival, we can only take the strongest. The most intelligent. We have to stop pretending that everyone can be saved, that everyone is worth saving.' Ferona glanced down at her wrist comm. again, then lifted her head and smiled at Jinn, a smile that made her stomach turn over. 'It appears that your pirate is on his way,' she said. 'He's been messaging the ship you flew in on for the past hour. Remind me, what was it you said about my not being able to capture him?'

*No, Dax. No.* 'You won't,' Jinn said boldly, as the chill of fear drenched her insides. 'You failed before, and you'll fail again.'

'Oh, I don't think so,' Ferona said. 'You see, he's coming here for you.'

'You don't know that.'

Ferona touched her wrist comm. again and a vidscreen slid down from the ceiling, angled itself in front of her, and switched on. Jinn recognised the other emergency transporter from the *Mutant* immediately. *Don't come here*, she silently willed him. *Turn around. Leave. Hide.* 'Dax!' she called out, unable to stop herself.

'Foolish child,' chided Ferona. 'He can't hear you. Computer, message that transporter. Channel fourteen. Force the connection.'

The vidscreen image changed as they were linked into the transporter.

'Caspian Dax,' Ferona said. 'I take it you know who I am?'

Dax didn't respond, not immediately. 'Vice President,' he said eventually. 'This is somewhat unexpected.'

Jinn dropped to her knees and tried to move out of sight. If he didn't see her, there was a chance he might not believe she was here. He might not come for her.

'I believe I have something that belongs to you,' Ferona informed him. With a flick of her wrist, she directed one of the security droids to seize Jinn. The robot took her upper arm in a punishing grip, hauling her to her feet. Jinn struggled, tried to lash out with her blades, but the droid was too strong.

'Dax,' she said desperately. 'Listen to me. She's going to send you to Sittan. They will kill you. You've got to get away.' She lifted her head and their gazes locked. 'Please,' she begged him. 'Don't come here. Whatever happens, get away from Earth. As far away as you can.'

'Shoot her,' Ferona said casually.

Jinn heard the sound of the security droid moving closer, the whine of the blaster, but the reality of what was about to happen didn't register, didn't fully hit her, not even when pain screamed its way through her body, not even when blood bloomed on the floor beneath her feet.

'Jinn!' Dax roared.

Only the grip of the droid on her upper body stopped her from crumpling to the floor. 'I'm sorry,' she said. 'I'm so sorry.'

And then the world went black.

On the other side of the view screen, Dax stood frozen, unable to believe what he was seeing. Ferona Blue had ordered a security droid to shoot her own daughter. A blaster shot, right in the guts. Even with her mods and his blood, Jinn wouldn't be able to survive that without immediate medical treatment.

'Captain Dax,' the vice president said to him. Her words filtered through the haze of his fury and disbelief and pain.

'What?'

'If you want my daughter to receive medical help, you will surrender yourself to the agents onboard the security ship that is currently drawing up alongside yours. Is that clear?'

'I just watched you order a droid to shoot your own daughter,' Dax said. 'How do I know you're telling the truth?'

'You will simply have to trust me,' Ferona said, as she stood there in her truesilk suit with her expensively cut hair, not a single flicker of emotion in her face. 'Hurry now. She doesn't have much time.'

On the viewscreen, Dax could see the approach of a security

cruiser that dwarfed the transporter. There was a jolt as a tractor beam was locked on. He could fight his way out of this. Easily.

But it wasn't an option. He shot a glance at Theon. Theon held his gaze, said nothing. He didn't need to. Dax knew he understood. 'Get back to the others,' he said. Theon nodded.

Then Dax turned back to the view screen. 'Jinn,' he said desperately. 'If you can hear me, I need you to know that I love you.'

And then he left the control deck, walked down into the small cargo bay of the transporter, and prepared to surrender.

# CHAPTER
# 33

**30th September 2207**

Intergalactic Senate, Kepler System, Sector Five, Neutral Space

The senate had agreed to vote. Until that moment, Ferona had not been sure that they would. No emotion showed in her face, she was sure of it, but her hands were shaking under the soft fall of her white robes as the discussion moved on to the next issue.

She kept her gaze fixed straight ahead as the Sittan empress folded herself into the seat next to hers. 'Empress,' she said, acknowledging her presence.

'Senator Blue.'

'I take it that he has arrived.'

'Yesterday,' the empress informed her. 'I must seek your reassurance, Senator Blue, that he will perform as required.'

'He'll do what you need him to do.'

'You are sure of this?'

'Absolutely,' Ferona said. 'You have my word on that. His death will be quick and honourable.'

'Not too quick, I hope,' the empress said. She got to her feet, her robes swirling around her ankles. 'May the future bring you everything you desire.'

'I'm sure it will,' Ferona replied, as the Sittan empress slowly slipped away. 'I'm sure it will.'

She watched as the empress walked away, long robe grazing the floor behind her, blue skin bright and other-worldly. She looked around at the other members of the senate, at the strange, sometimes beautiful, sometimes grotesque creatures that inhabited this galaxy, her galaxy. One month from now, these creatures would decide the future of the human race.

It was time for the real work to begin.

# ACKNOWLEDGEMENTS

I'd firstly like to thank my agent Ella Diamond Kahn of DKW Literary Agency, who took a chance on this book and worked with me to make it into something really special. I would also like to thank Anna Boatman and the team at Piatkus for taking it on, for the wonderful cover, for making a dream into a reality.

All writers have help, usually from other writers, and I am no exception. Jessica, Julia and Maggie – thank you for your support over the past few years. It has kept me going through times when all I really wanted to do was throw my laptop in the bin. Julie Cohen – you believed in this book from the start, and in space pirates, and in me. Thank you.

During the writing of this book, I became very unwell with endometriosis. For those who don't know, this is a condition in which tissue like that which lines the uterus grows inside the pelvic cavity and causes unbearable pain. It can't be cured, only managed, and managing it is hard. I would like to give a special thank you to Karen Smith, the nurse at my local GP's surgery, for her endless patience and kindness. There have been times when I have only coped because you made it possible, Karen, and I wish that all medical staff were like you.

I would like to thank my kids, Caroline and Matthew, for the bad jokes and the nerd obsessions and the love.

Finally, I would like to thank my husband Patrick for paying the bills so that I could write, for making sure that there is always chocolate in the cupboard, and for the nights in A&E. Love you always, manly.